NOBLE

EVERGREENS

Aubrey M. Horton

Book design and cover photo by Aubrey M. Horton

LIBRARY OF CONGRESS
CATLOGUING-IN-PUBLICATION DATA
on file

Title ID: 5491258
ISBN -13:   978-1512145861
ISBN-10:   1512145866

First Edition -- 2015

to purchase this book, go to:

www.createspace.com/5491258

to all of those who've suffered from
intolerance and hate

Chapter One

In the little alcove that was just big enough for his desk, Mooney stood up and stretched his legs. For the last couple of hours, he'd been mousing through his computer, attempting to uninstall an out-of-date encryption program. He wanted to delete all of its files, which wasn't as easy as he had hoped it would be. To break up the frustration, he'd also spent part of the afternoon weeding through the hundreds and hundreds of emails that he had saved in order to expunge all of the ones that were tagged with fake IP addresses so as to hide his identity from the cyber cops.

And the reason it was taking him so long to do the uninstall was because he wasn't a hacker, nor did he have an instruction manual that would help him make sure he'd completely cleaned his hard drive of the various cohabiting drivers and backup interfaces which might, for some unknown reason, retain a traceable digital fingerprint of the encrypted info that he didn't want anyone else to get their grubby hands on. Of course, Mooney also had to be careful what he deleted since he didn't want to corrupt any of the functional software applications that he needed to do his online work with.

And so . . .

Being as he was quite limited by his own technological inadequacies, Mooney was stuck using a less-than-foolproof and somewhat haphazard trial-and-error approach to searching through the silicon guts of his desktop computer . . .

Because this was about all he was capable of attempting vis-a-vis his narrow understanding of digital wizardry . . .

Whereas the social-media skills that he was at least halfway proficient with involved a fairly narrow segment of eco blogging . . .

Which meant that his keyboarding abilities were seriously weak when it came to the heavy-duty techy stuff since his competency at manipulating a hodgepodge of dated software was marginal at best.

Arching his back to take the kinks out of his spine, Mooney turned his head and looked across the living room. The sliding glass door was open, and Becky was standing outside on the wooden deck. She'd just gotten back from a class at the university, and her sleeves were rolled up so she could soak in the sun.

"Well, thank goodness the rain's stopped," she said. Becky was his younger sister; and they both lived in the rent house, which was a funky bungalow circa 1930's. The small two bedroom had been upgraded with a number of energy-efficient conveniences, such as the triple-paned sliding door that she'd left open when she'd stepped out onto the back deck. The high-tech glass in the door's panels brought a good bit of light into the living room without sacrificing much heat loss in the process. But since the door was now slightly ajar, its specialized design to keep the BTU from escaping wasn't working as well as it should.

"I checked the weather radar a few minutes ago. It doesn't look like we're going to have any more rain until sometime later tonight," Mooney said.

Gazing across Lake Whatcom, Becky watched the fading rays of the sunset extend out into the water. "I saw two otters today."

"Otters?"

"Uh-huh."

"Where?"

"In the pond over in the park."

"Are you sure they weren't beavers?"

"Well, at first I thought they might be beavers. But then I saw two furry heads sticking up in the water, playing around like little kids."

"Y'know, last spring a beaver gnawed a cotton-wood down on the other side of that pond."

"Yeah, I know. But I'm sure these were otters."

"Otters. I hope you're right. But I've never heard of any otters in that creek."

"Moon, they weren't beavers, okay? I got a look at

their tails when they flipped up on their rear sides and dived under the water."

"They weren't flat, huh?"

"No. They weren't flat. They didn't look like paddles. And, like, I'm pretty sure they weren't nutrias, either, because they didn't have white snouts with those long rat whiskers."

"Well, I hope you're right. Otters would be better for the habitat than nutrias."

"You know they're down in Olympia, right?"

"Yeah, I wrote about 'em in a blog. An invasive species. They were first brought up from South America years ago to eat the water hyacinth clogging the bayous in Louisiana. Now they've made it all the way up here."

Still standing on the back deck – Becky then pressed her flattened palm up to her forehead to shield her eyes from the reflective glare that was bouncing off the water. It appeared as though something out in the middle of the lake had caught her attention. "Oh, great. I think that guy's, like, staring at me."

Mooney was now sitting back down at his desk, scrolling through his application screen. "What guy?"

"Some guy with a pair of binoculars standing on a sailboat."

"Is he flying a Jolly Roger?"

"You mean, like, a flag?"

"Y'know, a skull and crossbones. A pirate's flag."

"Stop it, okay? I'm serious. He's staring at me with a pair of stupid binoculars."

"Maybe he's a peeping Tom. Why don't you come inside and close the curtains. If you keep that door open, we might have to turn on the heat."

"Oh, wait. Now I see a flag. It's Canadian."

"So . . . is he still looking at you?"

"Actually, I'm not exactly sure what he's doing. But he's obviously looking at something."

"Why don't you wave at him and see what he does."

"Yeah, right. Wave at him, uh-huh."

Sighing, Mooney then slowly began to ease up out of his chair, thinking he would walk out onto the deck to check the guy out . . . when he saw his sister suddenly lower her hand from her head, lean forward, and glance over at the next-door neighbor's boat dock.

"Oh, now I see what he's staring at. Never mind."

"What is it?" Mooney said as he stepped toward the sliding glass door to take a look for himself.

And just as he did this, three ducks took off from the shore and swooped out over the mast of the bobbing sailboat, making a beeline toward the other side of the lake. Swiveling his head, the guy with the binoculars tracked the birds' trajectory.

Becky shrugged and rolled down her sleeves. "I doubt he's, like, up to anything. I think he's a birdwatcher. Some ducks just flew out over his boat."

"Nancy Drew solves another whodunit. Glad the guy wasn't a terrorist or Homeland Security reading our lips."

"Me, too. I wouldn't want to have to turn you in

for breaking the law."

"Hey, c'mon. You know I don't break any laws."

"Yeah, right. You don't fool me. We both know you're harboring a radical environmentalist."

"Oh, right. You mean a certain graduate student who's enrolled in Environmental Studies? Is that the no-good criminal you're talking about?"

"Moon, you're not supposed to give away my secret identity when we're being watched, okay?"

"Sorry. I forgot about Big Brother's super-sensitive dish microphones that can eavesdrop from a mile away." And even though it might have sounded as though Mooney was poking fun at his sister, he really wasn't. But she didn't know that.

In other words, they both knew that she wasn't a gung-ho radical by any stretch of the imagination, yet her comment about Mooney's illegal activities had not been that far off the mark since there were quite a few things that Becky didn't know about her older brother. She didn't realize that her witty comeback had actually been much closer to the truth than she was aware of because Mooney had never told her about his underground activities. Indeed, there was a bunch of incriminating stuff that she didn't know about him. But keeping her clueless and completely in the dark as to what he had been up to for the last eight years was the best way for her name to stay off the FBI's watch list. The less she knew; the better off she would be.

Anyway, after the birding enthusiast had hoisted his jib and sailed away – Becky stepped inside, closed the door, and retreated down the hall to her bedroom, which meant that Mooney was now able to return to his task at hand and thus refocus his attention on cleaning up his hard drive. As best as he could tell, it looked as though he had successful deleted all of the encrypted files; so now he thought he was good to go in regards to any prosecutable evidence being found in his possession.

So with that burden lifted from his shoulders, Mooney then proceeded to surf through some of the comments that had been posted on a friend's blog about saving the old-growth forest . . .

Eat a quick sandwich . . .

Then scoot out the door for a nighttime bike ride down the hill into Bellingham proper. He had a limited time window for a rendezvous that he had to hit, and he didn't want to be late. If he couldn't make it to Happy Valley in time, it would mess up his plans for the rest of the week and cause a couple of dominos to fall out of place. He had already penciled in his to-do schedule, and postponing the info pickup at his subcommander's trailer would create an unneeded delay that he didn't want to have to deal with since the last thing he needed to happen was to have to reconfigure his time allocation. He was anxious to get started, ASAP, on his new L.E.A.F. assignment. If at all possible, he wanted to have his next task finished before the really cold weather moved in since a precipitous drop in the temperature, per an unseasonable low blowing in off the upper Pacific, might distort his operational timeline and screw up his shadowy interface. In other words, when a L.E.A.F. illegality went awry per stormy weather, that was when a small problem could easily become a much bigger problem and create an unforeseen vulnerability that might get a guy like him arrested.

Not cool.

Riding his mountain bike along the greenway's muddy trail, Mooney squeezed the handle of his rear brake lever. The tall trees were blocking out the moonlight, and there wasn't enough visibility for him to see very far in front of him. He wanted to slow his speed down so he could reach up and adjust the headlamp that was strapped around the top of his head underneath his helmet. He needed to nudge the lens up a bit so it would cast its light several yards ahead of him. He didn't want to plow smack-dab into a tree. And in this part of south Bellingham, there were plenty of hefty trees to be concerned about. Some of the old conifers were four-feet wide and over a hundred feet tall.

Satisfied with his headlamp adjustment, Mooney pumped his legs and continued up a sloping humpback. The trail was hilly. It felt sort of like riding on a roller coaster, bouncing along up and down . . .

Up and down . . .

As he wove in and out of the trees, pedaling as fast as he could pedal.

Soon, he noticed the blur of houselights off to his

left side, and the adrenaline rush faded as the land leveled out. This part of the woods ran along the edge of the Happy Valley neighborhood, and it didn't have as many tall trees since most of them had been cut down years ago. Mooney always felt a slight bit of sadness each time he biked through here, knowing how beautiful it must have been when those old trees were still alive.

Why were people so blind to what was happening to the planet? If only they would wake up and stop the corporate greed.

At least there wasn't anyone else on the trail, which was why he was making his bike trip so late at night. He didn't want anyone recognizing him, nor did he want anyone to know where he was going. It was extremely important for him to keep his destination a secret. He was fairly sure the FBI couldn't tail a fast-moving cyclist through Bellingham's vast spider web of interconnecting trails when it was so dark outside.

After another couple of minutes of vigorous effort, Mooney then made a quick turn out of the woods and was now speeding down the sidewalk in a low-rent area that was favored by the college students. The curbside parking along the street had the prerequisite fuel-efficient imports . . .

Jammed bumper-to-bumper with a few mini-vans. And except for a rare late model here and there, most of the vehicles were covered in road crud and appeared as though they hadn't been washed in several months.

Steering his handlebars up to the top of a small hill at the end of the street, Mooney skidded to a stop and waited to see if anyone was behind him. It never hurt to be extra careful, just in case he was wrong about the FBI being able to track him.

Satisfied he wasn't being followed, he then turned down a back alley and quickly sped into the nearby RV park, stopping at a green-colored travel trailer. This was a vintage 30-foot model, which had a good bit of wear on its exoskeleton, along with a small patch of clinging moss that was precipitously hanging down from its roof.

Luckily for him, the front porch light was still on and the three-foot-tall scarecrow (that was guarding the little vegetable garden outside) was wearing a green baseball cap. This meant that the coast was clear.

Dismounting from his bike, Mooney leaned the 21-speed up against the side of the trailer, snapped on his bike lock, and walked up the metal steps to the front door. Hanging above it was a hand-painted wooden sign which read: "Mother Nature is crying, and her tears are being sadly ignored."

Sucking in a deep breath, he pulled off his bike helmet, unstrapped his headlamp, and pressed the doorbell button. A mechanical chime reverberated through the thin metal wall.

"It's open."

Assuming this to be an invitation to go inside, Mooney turned the doorknob and entered the trailer.

Darwin Digbee, or so he called himself, was sitting in an old rocking chair over in the corner underneath a window. "Hey," Mooney said.

"What's up?"

"Nothin' much."

"Have a seat."

As instructed, Mooney plopped down on the couch. "I guess Karen's asleep, huh?"

"Yeah, she's doing the high school tomorrow and has to get up early."

Darwin's wife was a substitute teacher. She had a master's degree in education and probably could easily have gotten a regular gig teaching almost anywhere; but because the two of them shunned conformity and wanted to avoid putting down roots, Karen preferred to take odd teaching assignments here and there to pay the bills. Darwin worked part-time as a bike mechanic at the community bicycle shop, donating his time for free.

He was the real deal.

"Oh, before I forget, did you hear about what's going on with the salmon and the hydroelectric dams?" Mooney asked.

"Yeah, I saw that. It's about time. If they don't do something soon, all we'll have left in our rivers will be mutant-bred monster fish from the hatcheries. Goddamn idiots. The fishmongering breeders don't have a clue what they're doing. And the electric companies have already killed off most of the wild fish runs with their godawful dams. I think we need to blow up every single one of 'em and let the rivers run free, if you ask me."

"Well, I'm all for saving the fish, but what about the cheap electricity? We've gotta have electricity."

"Wind turbines and solar panels. We don't need no stinkin' dams," Darwin said.

Not one to argue, Mooney didn't say what he was actually thinking. Sure, he wanted to save the wild salmon, and he was also quite serious about doing away with most of the fish-killing concrete behemoths that were preventing the sockeye from swimming up stream to spawn, but he was pragmatic and practical, too. As best as he could understand it, the NW economy simply wouldn't be able to efficiently function, for the foreseeable future, without the low-cost power that was being generated by all of the region's hydroelectric dams. So, to him, hydro generation wasn't the problem. The true environmental issue was the decimation of the salmon runs. He thought it would be much more productive if both sides of the political spectrum got together and agreed that well-credentialed biologists should be given the task of picking and choosing what dams the citizenry should keep and what dams should be eliminated, in order to make sure that the wild salmon were given priority over the blocking manmade structures that were harming so much of the fishery habitat. Such a solution seemed to be a more realistic goal to shoot for than trying to sway the public to vote for an increase in their electric bills in order to bring back the big salmon runs.

Of course, Mooney also knew that his subcommander wouldn't change his mind about the dams, so there wasn't much point in getting into a heated debate. "Well, I don't know. Maybe so. I know a heck-of-a-lot more about trees than fish."

Darwin then leaned forwarded and adjusted his eyeglasses. "Hey, look at you. Growin' a beard, eh?"

"I thought I looked too clean-cut. I'm hoping more people will open up and talk to me when they see the long hair and beard."

"Never know. Some folks might keep their mouths shut 'cause you look like that."

"I can always shave it off."

"Yeah, you can always shave it off. I think I sheared my last one . . . maybe two years ago after the cops caught me on camera at a protest march." Darwin then got up, walked over to the kitchen table, and sat down in front of his laptop. Flipping open its lid, he proceeded to click onto the Net. "Moon, I read your last blog. I liked the part about getting people to lie down on the tracks to stop a coal train."

"A lot of people are really upset about that shipping terminal being built up at Cherry Point. Eighteen trains passing through here every day will screw things up."

"It's a goddamn horror story. All those big railcars and cargo ships coming and going and all that acid rain spewing up in the air in China when they burn the damn coal."

"That's a lot of mercury poisoning, that's for sure.

And those trains are going to be over a mile long, too. I mean, *eighteen* coal trains in one lousy day?"

Rubbing his hand across his face, Darwin shook his head. "Did you see that bullshit about not having to worry about the coal dust getting in people's lungs? Those open-top railcars are going to pass right through downtown, and they won't have any tarps on 'em."

"Diapers. That's what they call those covers. Diapers."

"Diapers, huh? You've done your research on this, haven't you?"

"Yeah, I've talked to a few people about it," Moon said, glancing over at the blinking light on Darwin's cable modem. "Oh, I guess you, like, heard the rumor about what ELF wants to do about the trains, huh?"

"No."

"Someone said they're gonna jimmy the tracks."

"Jimmy the tracks?"

"Uh-huh. That's what I heard."

"Well, that'd certainly get the railroad's attention, that's for sure. But it'd be pretty damn risky. Somebody could get hurt. Passenger trains run on those same tracks. I hope The Elves don't try anything stupid like that. I know there's no chance in hell the Flock would ever okay that sort of crazy stunt. No way. A locomotive jumping the tracks might kill its crew. ELF is going to make a lot more enemies than friends if it does something stupid like that. A wreck might even cause a few of our members to give it up and stop working with us."

The Earth Liberation Front was always a touchy subject with Darwin. On one hand, he seemed to understand why The Elves were doing what they were doing; whereas on the other hand, he appeared to harbor some sort of grudge against them. Numerous times, over the many years that Mooney had known him, Darwin had complimented the subversive group on their ballsy activities, while at the same time he had also cursed them out for having put so many innocent lives at stake. Like numerous other activists, Darwin knew that The Elves were damn lucky that no one had ever gotten killed per their last series of firebombings that had generated so much press coverage. So each time the ELF topic would come up, Darwin would always warn Mooney to avoid having any contact with that particular fringe group of dangerous radicals. Indeed, Darwin seemed to have some sort of passive-aggressive/love-hate struggle going on inside himself when it came to ELF's ecoterrorist tactics. And he was also the type of activist who could be quite blunt when it came to speaking his mind, too. He didn't mince words. At six foot three, he had a commanding presence. His frankness was rarely muzzled when he shared his enthusiasm with other environmentalists, and that in and of itself could've been why Darwin Digbee was so good at what he did. He wouldn't back down when it came to the really important stuff that he truly believed in. He was seriously passionate about helping Mother Nature and stopping the rape of the wilderness by the greed-is-good corporate assholes.

Seeing his subcommander's face tense up as he expressed his worries about what ELF might or might not do, Mooney thought it'd be best if he mellowed out the mood a bit by downplaying his own concern. "Well, y'know, that rumor's probably not even true. I'm always sort of leery of anyone who claims to know what The Elves are up to. I mean, as far as I know, I don't know anyone connected to the Liberation Front."

"So where'd you hear the rumor?" Darwin asked in a slightly agitated tone.

"Some lurker, who was using one of those Guy Fawkes masks as his avatar, posted it on an anarchist blog down in Seattle."

"Yeah, okay. So it could've just been a kissy-face nobody wanting some attention. Whoever wrote such stupid shit probably wouldn't even know a real elf if he was looking him straight in the eye and the guy was wearing a pixie hat from Santa's workshop."

"More than likely, you're right."

Now seeming to realize that the rumor had weak bona fides, Darwin scratched the back of his neck. "I guess it's something we need to watch out for, but I don't think we need to worry too much about it. Of course if a damn coal train does get derailed anywhere near here, the feds are going to be all over this damn town like bees on honey. We don't need heat like that. I'll ask around to see if anyone's heard anything." Darwin then glanced back down at his laptop and began rapidly typing away on his keyboard. Mooney could see that he was composing a short email, which only took him a couple of minutes to bang out. Then once he had finished writing the string of sentences, he quickly massaged his text through a pop-up window, turning what he'd written into coded gibberish. He next clicked down a list of addies – carefully picking and choosing which ones he wanted to select – before he hit the send button. To Mooney, it looked as though Darwin was configuring blind copies to a small group of Flock members. He only wanted those particular individuals to read what he'd written.

And since Mooney knew his subcommander was a stickler for following protocol, he understood why the emails were being protected by what appeared to be an updated encryption software – before they were being forwarded into a loop of hacked servers that would then bounce the digital gobbledygook through a series of IP switches and untraceable host computers . . .

Eventually delivering Darwin's typed-out message into whatever inbox. So if the recipient on the other end had been compromised and the right encryption key wasn't used to un-shred Darwin's text, the email wouldn't be readable, nor would there be a verifiable IP address that could be traced back to his laptop.

Watching his subcommander surf through this series of clicks, Mooney was reminded that he needed to do a 5.2 reinstall as soon as possible in order to replace his deleted encryption program since he didn't want to miss out on such an info blast himself.

Never-ending software updates. Gotta love 'em, huh?

21

Anyway . . .

As Mooney was patiently sitting across from Darwin, watching him perform this feat of cyber skullduggery, his own memory circuits, for whatever reason, began to wander back to the first time they'd ever met. That was when Mooney was a sophomore in college; and he was standing on the shoulder of a highway, hitchhiking to Austin after his Harley had been stolen in San Angelo; and a guy wearing a Panama hat (and hiding his bloodshot eyes behind dark sunglasses) had stopped his VW van to give Mooney a ride. The guy introduced himself as Darwin Digbee, and he looked to be about ten years older than Mooney.

Once underway – as the green microbus cruised along the highway just under the speed limit – it didn't take long for the proverbial ice to melt; and the two strangers were soon delving into a lengthy conversation about everything from nuclear energy to whatever happened to the hippies . . .

As they shared a fat joint and tooled their way through several small towns in the Hill Country. Back then, listening to Darwin philosophize on the rape of the environment, Mooney had quickly come to the conclusion that he was in the presence of a kindred spirit, a.k.a. –

A radical environmentalist.

Thereupon, when they'd finally made it to Austin, Darwin had graciously gone out of his way to hook Mooney up with one of the coeds he knew who worked for a eco-friendly nonprofit, and thus the situation had soon proceeded to become more and more involved from that point on. Of course, it had taken Darwin about two months before he'd been able to fully vet Mooney and officially accept him into a loosely affiliated group of Earth lovers. They called themselves L.E.A.F., and it was somewhat debatable as to what the four letters actually meant. As best as Mooney could ever figure out, the four letters were either an acronym for Lifesaving Eco Activist Flock; or L.E.A.F. didn't really mean anything at all. Some members had even told Mooney that anyone could plug in any set of words they wanted to so as to make the lettering fit whatever phrase that suited their fancy. It was that type of laid-back group.

And needless to say, considering the alternative-lifestyle habits of its members, the interpersonal vibe in L.E.A.F. was cliquey tribal, yet also quite welcoming when Mooney had first been recruited into the Flock. Indeed, what had initially made the social dynamic of the group so appealing to Mooney was the emphasis on the organization's nonviolent goals and positive social values. L.E.A.F.'s mission statement specifically forbid any of its members from destroying property if there was even the faintest possibility that someone could be harmed by such an action. Yet monkey-wrenching a tree-killing bulldozer or a crooked corporation's voicemail system – as long as no one would get hurt and as long as such a deed was justified in helping sustain the habitat against further harm – was quite acceptable.

Of course, there were also limits to such tactics since getting L.E.A.F.'s eco message out to the masses was a top priority, whereas crossing the Maginot line into any sort of life-threatening violence wouldn't be tolerated. Darwin had repeatedly told Mooney that the Flock wasn't a hormonal group of zealots who wanted to grab attention by burning things down or blowing things up. He'd said that L.E.A.F. wasn't an eco-terrorist organization, in the strict sense of the term. If it had been, Darwin swore that he never would've joined up himself. He didn't believe in that type of aggressive no-holds-barred activism. To him, such violent stunts did more harm than good. He'd told Mooney that he didn't want the public reading about such activities in the newspapers and then branding all environmental activists with a negative image. The last thing Darwin wanted was for the public to be turned off by a long paragraph in a news article about some disturbing event that was being blamed on a bunch of eco-warriors. He didn't want people to associate such activism with any sort of violent act that might harm an innocent bystander who just happened to be in the wrong place at the wrong time. If the public were to ever categorize the Flock's activities in that fashion, then he thought the PR message would boomerang and the positive image that the environ-mentalists had been trying so hard to achieve would decay into a negative.

Yet on the other side of the coin, even though the

higher-ups in L.E.A.F. had clearly stated that they summarily shunned any violence which had the slightest chance of harming anyone, the group certainly wasn't a wussy social club by any stretch of the imagination. Its members were very serious about changing the status quo when it came to helping save planet Earth from further harm. And though the group shied away from doing any sort of property damage that might put a human being at risk for physical harm – L.E.A.F. had become quite adept at employing less obvious subversions to attain its goals. Such behind-the-scenes *indirect* tools (as opposed to direct-action sabotage) . . . included disseminating anonymous press releases which highlighted the environmental damage that was being done by egregious corporations . . .

And also included performing undercover operations so as to bring to light the hidden evidence that would prove the legal culpability of the habitat-destroying actions of numerous unethical polluters . . .

By employing a broad proactive net that was supportive per a willingness to engage in stealth fund-raising campaigns which had the shadowy safety of untraceable money trails. In other words, all of L.E.A.F.'s public activities were performed in a nameless manner. The Flock went out of its way to avoid publicity. The underground cells flew under the radar. Only a very few people even knew that they existed. And it was this subversive aspect to the group's design that had so greatly appealed to Mooney when he had first joined up. He liked the anonymity. He thought that more good could be done vis-a-vis the implementation of uncredited subversions as opposed to such an underground group using heavy-handed law-breaking efforts. He knew the media spotlight could, in fact, cut both ways. Why take a chance on getting bad press coverage; why risk having an eco operation turn into a big win for the opposition? That would be counterproductive. "Environmental change through hidden action" was L.E.A.F.'s motto, and Mooney felt that those five words, rather clearly, proclaimed the organization's well-intended goals.

And so . . .

As the years progressed, Mooney had stayed a loyal member, always doing his part to help as much as he possibly could. He'd even given the Flock a good bit of money when he barely had enough to pay his rent. He'd also gone undercover and taken menial jobs that he absolutely hated to get involved with . . .

So he could get the inside scoop on the exploitative corporations that were spewing cancer-causing carcinogens into the environment.

But still, Mooney had his limits. He could only assume the role of a so-called "good ol' boy" for a relatively short period of time. Punching the time clock at a job that he found totally repulsive would quickly start to eat away at him. Some of the undercover assignments he'd been given had been agonizingly hard, and he would always have a tough time keeping his mouth shut when he had to work with right-wing yahoos who had absolutely no regard whatsoever for clean air and safe drinking water.

So once he was able to document the specifics of an environmental malefaction that the higher-ups had asked him to hunt down, he would then quit the dreadful job and disappear back into the shadows . . . after having surreptitiously handed the evidence off to a more visible group of activists such as Barking Earth. Sometimes it would only take Mooney a few weeks to recharge his batteries after he'd finished one of these assignments, whereas other times his undercover work would be so gut-wrenching that he'd have to go dark and hibernate for several months because he'd become somewhat shell-shocked by the type of work he'd been asked to do.

And such was the case when Mooney had picked up and moved to Bellingham per Darwin's prodding. Mooney had been dormant for three months after having worked as a roustabout on an oilrig that had been engulfed in a fireball by a high-pressure blowout in South Texas. If he hadn't've been on his lunch break in a nearby trailer, sneaking a look at the list of toxic chemicals that a service company would be using to frack the well, he might have lost his life. The hellish job had pretty much soured him on ever taking another assignment such as that again. Being burned alive wasn't worth it. He had his limits.

So even though he had gotten the dirt on the oil company, the emotional price he'd had to pay had taken its toll on him. Having to act like a right-leaning

EPA hater for 24 hours a day, 7 days a week – had sucked way too much joy out of his soul for Mooney to ever want to repeat the experience ever again. And so that's when Mooney had started writing his eco blog, and that's why he had remained unencumbered (marriage wise), during all of those years of his undercover work since he didn't want an oil-patch gal to get too close and figure out his true identity, i.e., realizing what he was really up to . . .

And that was also why he was able to move to Bellingham on such short notice. He had parted ways with Darwin two years before when his mentor had taken a L.E.A.F. assignment traveling from state to state, having agreed to work the enviro circuit in order to bring in new recruits; and Mooney had stayed back in Texas. Of course at the time, Mooney had thought it'd been a bit strange, in a serendipitous sort of way, for his sister to have enrolled in Bellingham's local university only a few months before Darwin had called and asked Mooney to come up and work with him. But then again, there weren't that many environmentally-friendly places that such a dedicated activist could live within the borders of the continental U.S. and still look themselves in the mirror; and so for Darwin and for Mooney's sister to both have discovered "little nirvana" was probably nothing more than random synchronicity.

Probably.

Yet there was also the hard to explain *un-explainable* that sometimes happened when a do-gooder was fighting the good fight for Mother Nature.

"Moon? You okay?"

Blinking his eyes, Mooney jiggled his head. "Yeah, I'm fine. I guess I was daydreaming or something."

"You're not stoned, are you?"

"No, I gave up pot years ago. I like to keep a clear head."

"Well, it doesn't hurt to get a buzz on every now and then, as long as you don't do it every day. Medicinal Mary Jane loosens up your synapses and keeps you grounded." Standing up, Darwin grabbed a table napkin and used it to pick up a brown-paper lunch bag that was sitting next to his laptop. He then handed the bag to Mooney, stepped over to the window, and peeked out the Venetian blinds.

Opening the bag, Mooney pulled out a brand-new computer mouse that was still packaged inside an unopened clear-plastic clamshell, along with its two-inch-wide/foot-long proof-of-purchase receipt. Turning the sales slip over, Mooney smelled the back. As he had expected, his nose dedicated the slight odor of invisible ink. It was a smell he easily recognized.

And so . . .

Knowing it was best not to ask any questions, Mooney then put both items back in the bag and carefully stuffed the bag in his coat pocket. "I guess I better get back home before it starts raining," he said as he stood up.

Nodding, Darwin slowly turned around, stepped over to Mooney, and hugged him. If there had been any listening bugs hidden in the room, the electronic devices would not have been able to record the upper-committee's secret instructions, i.e., the compartment-talized walls of their L.E.A.F. cell would not have been breached, and there would not be any fingerprint evidence leaving his subcommander's travel trailer.

Chapter Two

Zetty Hart wasn't the type of person to let some little something upset her. If a friend wanted to get an awful-looking tattoo . . .

Then that was her friend's problem, not hers. Zetty would, more or less, always give someone the benefit of the doubt, even though she thought that tattoos were quite ridiculous. It didn't matter if the person intended to get a winged angel, a horned devil, or a butterfly inked into their arm. The thought of suffering through all of those tiny little needle pricks for a permanent souvenir that could never be washed off . . .

So they could gloat over having put up with the agonizing pain . . .

Was one of the most immature ways of showing off – just to be showing off – that Zetty knew of.

"Hey, I have a cool tattoo. Wanna see it?"

"No, I don't want to see it. I don't like tattoos."

Yeah, well, needless to say, such lame-heads weren't the kind of friends Zetty wanted to hang out with anyway if she could possibly avoid it. She had learned a long time ago that it didn't do any good to get excited over such inconsequential stuff as a tattoo. No one really cared about someone else's ink job anyway. She thought that a lot of people simply wanted to be the center of attention, especially the duh-headed nincompoops who thought that a stupid tattoo made them a more desirable person than someone who had the proverbial blank canvas of untouched normal-looking skin.

What was wrong with plain skin?

And, of course, body piercings were even worse.

Way worse.

Gad.

Why go there?

Who cared?

What were such people thinking?

Didn't they know that when they turned eighty years old, if hepatitis from a dirty buzz needle hadn't killed them by that point in their lives, then surely a nursing home wouldn't want such a duh-brain with a bunch of wrinkled tattoos living down the hall from the little old ladies?

But still, that wasn't to say that Zetty was a dyed-in-the-wool fanatical prude. No, absolutely not. She wasn't a hopeless goody two-shoes. She didn't wear a nun's tunic. She wasn't a virgin waiting at the altar for some saintly betrothed to sweep her off her feet. That wasn't the way she lived her life. In fact, she'd only recently, and rather reluctantly, kicked her last boyfriend out of her bed because of his incessant consumption of beer, which had finally gotten the better of her. For the most part, Zetty pretty much believed in turning a blind eye if doing so wouldn't harm anyone else (or herself). *Live and let live* was her motto.

Hey, as long as no one stuck their nose too far into her private space with a harmful attitude, she was down with it. And even if someone did start to pester her for no reason, then just because she might not understand why they were rubbing her the wrong way, whether the person had an idiotic tattoo or not, that didn't mean she had to take their rudeness too seriously. For her, the glass was always half full. It was never half empty. Zetty thought that being reasonably tolerant of others, however misguided they might be, made the world a better place for all involved, as long as ignoring the misbehavior of others didn't cause her too much personal heartache.

So when a stranger had walked up to her and asked her where the post office was, Zetty hadn't given it a second thought. She was on her lunch hour, walking back from the Organic Only Café, and the stranger's demeanor had looked normal enough. Zetty hadn't noticed anything out of the ordinary about the guy, except that he was wearing a spiffy polo shirt – short-sleeved – and the weather was a bit chilly outside. Still, he was clean-shaven; he carried a leather briefcase; he didn't look like an ax murderer; and he only had one small tattoo of a maple leaf on the inside of his left arm. Rarely during the daylight hours in downtown Bellingham was there ever much to be concerned about when it came to muggers or pick-pockets. Nevertheless, considering the fact that every now and then there'd be a few felonious crimes perpetrated along the very streets that Zetty frequented, she thought she should err on the side of caution since she had never seen this particular stranger before.

To help him find his way to the post office – Zetty had simply pointed down the street, nodded her head, and left it at that. She didn't want to be rude, yet she told herself that this guy could easily find his way to wherever he wanted to go without her help.

But then, what the stranger did next gave her goosebumps.

"That's a very interesting bag you have there, little lady. I've never seen a fancy logo like that before." And, as he said this, the stranger began to slowly inch in closer . . . with his eyes glued to the satchel that she was holding in her hand. After an annoyingly long moment, he then suddenly glanced up, stared her straight in the eye, and said, "Are you married?"

"What?"

"Are you married?"

"Why are you asking me that?"

"Because you have such lovely blue eyes."

"No, I don't. They're green, not blue." She then pulled the satchel's strap up and over her shoulder. "Look, I've gotta get back to work."

"What type of work do you do?"

"Excuse me?"

"I apologize for being so nosey. I know it's a little odd, but I just moved here, and I don't know anyone in town. Right now, I'm living on my sailboat. I thought you might want to go get a bite to eat."

"Listen, I don't want to be impolite, but I've gotta go. I've already had lunch. Bye." And that was that. Having been as courteous as she possibly could've been, while still putting the kybosh on this weirdo's rather unusual pick-up line, Zetty hurried down the block and quickly zipped her windbreaker's zipper all the way up to her neck. She'd felt uneasy the whole time she'd been standing next to the guy. Looking into his beady eyes had made her stomach queasy, and she wanted to get as far away from him as she possibly could.

Luckily for her, there were a handful of people walking down the sidewalk; and no one else looked out of place. Bellingham had a relatively small downtown with quaint old buildings that had seen better days. There never was much foot traffic to speak of, so at least her timing hadn't been as bad as it could've been. A lot of the aging storefronts had "For Rent" signs taped to their doors, and there were dozens of empty vacancies throughout the Central Business District, which meant that a shopper never had to worry about gobs of people crowding around and checking out a window display, like tended to happen ninety miles to the south in Seattle.

After a few quick strides, Zetty swallowed hard, took a deep breath, and tried to calm herself down.

She didn't want to make a mountain out of a molehill since the stranger had probably been, more or less, harmless. Yet still, she'd had an icky feeling in the pit of her stomach that had warned her to flee from those beady eyes. There was something about the way he had looked at her satchel. When he'd gazed down at it, his face had filled with amazement. It had seemed as though he couldn't believe he was looking at what he was looking at.

So, having noticed his utter bewilderment, Zetty wondered why he had reacted the way he had, spending so much time fixating on her bag. What had grabbed his attention? Why had he stared at it like he had? It was just a simple linen satchel. If she'd been toting around a one-of-a-kind Birkin, she would have understood why he'd obsessed about it the way he had. But she wasn't carrying around that type of expensive bag since she couldn't afford to buy anything made by Hermes or Gucci or Armani. Hers was just an inconsequential blue carryall that had an unusual logo on its side.

Of course, what made the situation even more unsettling was the fact that Zetty didn't know anything about the satchel herself. After her mother and father had passed away, Zetty had found it in the bottom of her mom's dresser, all those many years ago. It had been wrapped in white tissue paper, and the bag had looked as though it had never been used. Her mother had also left a handwritten note inside it. The note had read: "Please never give this away. I want it to always stay in the family."

And so, since her mom had treasured the hand-me-down as much as she had, Zetty considered the satchel to be a keepsake heirloom. She hadn't wanted anything to happen to it, and that was why she'd been reluctant to ever use it . . .

Well, actually . . .

She had never carried it with her until a few weeks back when she'd had the sudden urge to take it out of the box she'd kept it in all those many years because she needed a new tote bag. She'd been shopping for an inexpensive carryall with a strap that she could slide over her shoulder, and she'd wanted her new bag to be large enough to lug groceries around in. So that was when she'd had a flash of inspiration, remembering her mom's keepsake. She thought it would be the perfect size for a shopping bag, and she knew it would remind her of her mom every time she used it.

But as tempting as it was to free the bag from its cardboard box and thus not to have to buy a new carryall to lug groceries around in – there still was a slight problem. Zetty wasn't at all sure what to make of the satchel's unusual logo, which was a six-inch-by-six-inch raised image that had been embroidered into its side. She had no clue what the logo meant, nor had she ever seen it used anywhere else. To her untrained eye, the needlework looked handstitched. But what was even more striking was the image itself. The logo depicted a leafy tree surrounded by a squiggly circle of gold snakes. Try as she might, she hadn't been able to figure out why her mom had liked the bag so much. It was one of those motherly mysteries that Zetty couldn't help but think about but which she probably would never be able to understand.

Of course, the mysterious satchel wasn't the only puzzle Zetty had struggled with after she had lost her parents. There were quite a few other unanswered questions that had haunted her. Yet since Miss Pineford, her foster mom, was the only person who actually knew the truth about what had happened all those many years ago – Zetty had been reluctant to bring certain subjects up. She was worried that she might say something which would upset Miss Pineford. For some strange reason, her foster mom had never wanted to talk about Zetty's mother and father. When Zetty would inadvertently mention something about her deceased parents, Miss Pineford's eyes would always mist over and her right hand would start to shake with a slight tremor. It obviously wasn't a subject she wanted to be reminded of. Her foster mom, for whatever reason, didn't want to discuss the past. So having learned not to bring it up, Zetty had stopped asking Miss Pineford about her parents.

And sadly . . .

As the years had slipped by, it turned out that Zetty began to realize that she might never be able to find out the truth. A few months after she'd graduated from high school, Miss Pineford had been diagnosed with Alzheimer's disease, and her memory had slowly begun to fade. So even though Zetty had been patiently hoping that her foster mom would one day feel comfortable enough with the past to explain more about what had gone on all those many years ago, the sweet lady was simply growing too old to be bothered with such nagging questions. Having first moved in with Miss Pineford when she was twelve years old and having stayed with her until she'd turned eighteen, Zetty had only been able to discover a few tidbits about her family's past during that whole time. Yet these were rare moments which had happened quite infrequently, and most such conversations had occurred when Miss Pineford would, somewhat unconsciously, begin to reminisce about her younger days, not even realizing what she was saying . . . and Zetty would be all ears. One time Zetty had, quite surprisingly, been told that her parents had moved to Bellingham from Canada soon after they'd gotten married. And that was a big shocker because her parents had always hinted at having friends up in Canada but had told their daughter very little about why they knew so much about the other side of the border.

Indeed, there was a great deal about her parents that Zetty would never fully understand. Her curiosity as to why her family tree hadn't been discussed at the dinner table was an unexplainable secret that she knew would forever haunt her. Yet still, she had, over the years, been able to fit together a few pieces of the puzzle, figuring out that she didn't have any living relatives since Miss Pineford had once told her that all of the members of Zetty's immediate family had tragically died in a wildfire which had swept through a farming valley in British Columbia.

So realizing what this meant, Zetty had come to accept the fact that she would never have any family to rely upon. No holiday gifts or birthday cards or wedding invitations would ever be arriving in the mail. It seemed she wouldn't have anyone to share her life with except Miss Pineford. And even though her foster mom had been a good bit older than Zetty's mother, the two of them had been the best of friends; and that's why Miss Pineford had taken Zetty into her home after her parents had passed away.

In a nutshell, this was about all that Zetty had ever learned in regards to her parents' past, which meant that she now just had her childhood memories to hold on to, which meant that she only had those first twelve years of living with her mother and father to forever treasure, hoping those early memories would last her a lifetime. Of course, she also would never have to worry about a long-lost relative ever showing up unannounced on her doorstep, either.

Then again, maybe meeting such a person wouldn't be as uncomfortable as she imagined it might be. Maybe having to deal with that type of an unexpected occurrence would turn out to be more of a godsend than a worrisome challenge.

Maybe.

It was hard for her to know for sure since she'd

never spoken to any of her relatives.

So living those six years with Miss Pineford had been pleasant enough. Zetty knew that her foster mom truly loved her. Zetty was exceptionally thankful to have had Miss Pineford in her life when she really needed her. In a way, it had been somewhat like living with the grandmother she had always wanted to hug and share her life with but had never met.

And so . . .

It was only later, when Miss Pineford's condition had worsened and she'd begun having more and more trouble remembering things, that Zetty had had no choice but to move her into a nursing home. Sometimes Miss Pineford would hardly be able to even remember what they had talked about several days before. That's how serious the disease had progressed.

Therein, with help from social services, the arrangements had been made, and Miss Pineford was placed in an assisted-care facility that specialized in such memory-lost cases. Then, as the years ticked by, they both settled into their new lives. This took a bit of an adjustment for Zetty to get used to since she had never lived on her own before, but that was what she had to do. And it wasn't that bad, really. Social services had done their part to help her as much as they could with the transition, which meant that Zetty had had to grow up somewhat faster than most girls her age, but she'd learned to relish her independence. She liked the challenge of having to cope with the day-to-day responsibilities. Living by herself wasn't so terribly awful. To her, it was better than having to stay with people she didn't know.

As for Miss Pineford's deteriorating condition – well, every now and then, when the weather turned stormy or when her doctor would put her on some new medicine, sometimes her mind would come back into focus, and she would remember a few things about Zetty's parents that she had forgotten to mention.

But this didn't happen that often.

So, having accepted her life for what it was, Zetty tried not to dwell on the past. She knew that there was nothing she could do to change anything anyway. Worrying about what had happened all those many years ago wouldn't improve her present circumstances and make her life any better. As her mother had always told her, "When someone dies, you have to take care of the living. There's nothing you can do for the dead. Take care of the living." And since Miss Pineford was the only family Zetty had left, that was what Zetty did. Every week she'd go and visit her foster mom at the nursing home and make sure she was being properly cared for.

Looking back, Zetty was glad that her mom had had the foresight to share such wonderful pieces of advice with her since her mom knew so much about so many things. There were a lot of growing-up lessons that her mom had been able to teach Zetty before she had passed away. And maybe if her mom had lived longer . . .

Maybe she would have eventually gotten around

to explaining an easy way to avoid strange men.

That would have been quite helpful to know.

Yeah, well, there was so much Zetty didn't understand as to why guys did the stupid things that they did.

Anyway, after looking over her shoulder to make sure the weirdo with the beady eyes wasn't following her, Zetty had finally made it back to the flower shop where she worked. Briskly walking in the front door, she nodded at her boss who was standing behind the counter. "Hey."

Briefly glancing up with a concerned look on her face, Casey finished writing out a delivery order. Then, in a concerned tone, she said, "Zetty, a guy just called and asked about you. He said he'd met you in front of the bank. He also said he'd forgotten to get your name and phone number."

"What'd you tell him?"

"I told him I don't give out that type of information."

"Oh, wow. Thanks, Casey."

"So, like, who is this guy?"

"I don't know. He just walked up to me and started asking me a bunch of questions. I think he's some sort of weirdo who lives on a sailboat. He had a tattoo on his arm. If he calls back, tell him I don't want to talk to him, okay?" Pausing for a second, Zetty then suddenly realized that there was something else she hadn't thought about. "I wonder how he knew where I worked?"

"Sounds like a stalker, if you ask me."

"A stalker? Why would anyone want to stalk me? Stalkers don't, like, live on sailboats, do they?"

"Well, anything's possible. I mean, there's no telling what a guy will do to get a girl's attention these days. You can't be too careful."

And of course Casey was right. Being too helpful and trusting of strangers might one day get Zetty into a load of trouble. She really did need to be much more cautious since "stranger danger" wasn't just for the little ones these days. Sometimes bad things happened to mature grownups in Bellingham. The downtown area wasn't immune from such stuff, although most of the criminal acts tended to happen at night when the drunks started roaming the streets several hours after the workaday downtowners had pretty much disappeared from the sidewalks and were safe and sound in their apartments with two deadbolts securely locked on their front doors.

Anyway . . .

As tended to happen when such a disturbing event proceeded to impinge upon her comfort zone, Zetty began running the what-if consequences of what could've occurred through her mind, wondering if the beady-eyed stranger could possibly be someone she should seriously be worried about. After all, he did have a tattoo, which was a red flag. And he obviously was a weirdo. That was undeniable. Yet she didn't know if he was a weirdo pervert or a weirdo purse-snatcher or some other sort of criminally motivated weirdo.

So for the next ten minutes – after Zetty had taken off her windbreaker, put on her apron, and had begun snipping the stems of a floral arrangement – she stood at her workbench and listened to Casey talk about her many run-ins with sex-crazed mashers. Her boss seemed to be a magnet for such guys, much more so than Zetty. Casey was five years older and was quite good looking. It didn't seem to matter that she had a wedding ring on one of her fingers, either. Of course, Casey wasn't at all shy about wearing sexy tight-fitting outfits that tended to accentuate her rather shapely body, whereas Zetty's wardrobe wasn't so showy. She tried to downplay her bodily assets so as not to attract too much attention.

Anyway . . .

Casey's venting as to why so many men were complete idiots soon faded, and the rest of the afternoon was pretty much uneventful. There were orders to be filled, which meant that Zetty's thoughts had soon returned to the same ol' same ol', with nothing else of any real consequence happening to distract her from her work.

Why waste time thinking about a lame-headed weirdo she hoped she would never ever see again?

When six o'clock finally rolled around – Zetty had pretty much put the guy out of her mind. She had more important things to think about than some nosey jerk she had met during her lunch break.

Hanging up her apron next to the time clock,

Zetty put on her windbreaker, said goodbye to Casey, and walked out the back door. As she stepped outside, she flipped the jacket's hood up over her head so she wouldn't get her hair wet. The sunlight was already starting to fade, and there was a light drizzle falling from the sky. But needless to say, that was so Bellingham. In this part of "The Evergreen State" – on the watery shores of the Puget Sound – when autumn arrived in early October, having a day without wet weather was the exception, not the rule. To her, the damp-and-dreary climate was part of the reason why she loved living where she was living. Rain, for her, was like a heavenly gift. Without the frequent showers, the tulips wouldn't be as colorful as they were, and the beautiful trees wouldn't grow as tall as they did. Stormy weather invigorated Zetty. She enjoyed looking up at the low-hanging clouds that were constantly hovering overhead. The gray sky seemed to keep her grounded. When it was sunny and bright outside, her mind would wander; and she'd start thinking about all of the worrisome things that she didn't want to think about. But when there were dark clouds in the sky, it perked her up and kept her out of the doldrums. One time she'd even heard a doctor on a talk-radio show label someone like her – "a contrarian."

So maybe that's what she was. Maybe she was a contrarian.

Or maybe she was just a person who liked stormy weather.

But whether she was or was not a diagnosable

contrarian, that actually didn't really matter to Zetty because she told herself that no one would be able to change her and thus keep the puzzling thoughts out of her mind anyway. In other words, she knew that a therapist couldn't just wave a magic wand and rearrange her thinking. No, it was up to her to take control of her inner mind. She had to do it herself. And she also knew that wallowing in her own gloom would only cause her to become more depressed, and that was an undeniable truth she would not be able to avoid. Indeed, after her parents had died, she had, for whatever reason, become a different person, learning that when too many sour apples dropped down around your feet . . . you had no choice but to pick them up, squeeze out the apple juice, and start adding in heaping spoonfuls of sugar in order to turn the bitter liquid into a healthy elixir. The three books she had read on the power of positive thinking had convinced her that her life would eventually turn out for the better if she could simply stay upbeat and not let the ill winds of fate turn her into a sourpuss. That was how a familyless orphan made sweet-tasting cider out of so many sour apples. The secret was to flip life's heartbreaking negatives into uplifting positives.

Think positive.

Be positive.

Stay positive.

And so . . .

That's what Zetty always tried to do. She was constantly telling herself that she had more to be happy about than she had to be sad about, even if it wasn't exactly true. Indeed, lying to herself was, in fact, a much more effective self-therapy than the alternative technique of telling herself the unvarnished truth, since being bluntly honest with herself would be way too hard for her to take. In other words, she felt a good bit better about herself if she avoided the awful darkness and didn't face her inner gloom head-on. Falsifying the truth actually allowed her to be more upbeat since being overly candid with herself in regards to her less-than-desirable circumstances would have been too much for her to take. So even though she told herself that there really wasn't any reason for her to be depressed – because she had so very much to be thankful for – she still knew that she had to be constantly vigilant so as not to let her guard down, so as not to let the emotional negativity get the better of her, telling herself she had to keep the sadness at bay since it always seemed to be lurking in the shadows, attempting to pull her deeper into the darkness.

Yeah, well . . .

Zetty did her best to be as optimistic as she possibly could be, knowing the limits of her own abilities. She told herself that something quite wonderful would soon turn things around . . . because she vividly remembered her mom once telling her that cupid's arrow had pierced her mom's heart right after she had turned twenty-six. That was when her dad had first asked her mom out on a date. And Zetty was now only a few months away from turning twenty-six herself.

So even if she was deluding herself with wishful thinking, she was convinced that staying positive was better for her than the alternative of being overly negative, telling herself that she had a lot of joy to look forward to, even though her life hadn't, up until then, been a bed of roses. Sure, bad things had happened. That was true. A train had killed her parents, and that had been terribly awful. Miss Pineford had had to sell her house and move into the nursing home; and that, too, had been hard on both of them. But still, deep down in her soul, Zetty knew that it wouldn't do any good to fret over the past. There was nothing to be gained by looking back and moping over things that she couldn't do anything about anyway. She had to look forward to the future. She was convinced that if she stayed positive, her life would eventually turn around and good things would come her way. She could feel it deep within her bones. Her future was bright. The heartaches of the past had come and gone. Her whole life lay ahead of her. She just had to think positive, be positive; and eventually everything would work out for the better.

Chapter Three

There never had seemed to be any rhyme or reason to his temper getting the better of him. Almost anything could set him off. That was just the way he was. And he'd been like that, going all the way back to when he'd gotten in a bloody fight in the fourth grade and had kicked an older kid in the face and busted the punk's nose. But hey, that dumb sixth grader shouldn't've said what he'd said. Little Edgar didn't like being called a momma's boy. So the older kid should've stayed outside with the other twelve-year-olds instead yanking Edgar's collar at the water fountain in the hall.

Stupid smartass.

Goddamnit.

School had been one fight after another for little Edgar; and he'd had his share of black eyes, busted lips, and broken noses. No other kid in his neighborhood had as many scars on his face as he did. Edgar would never chicken out. He would fight all comers, even if they were five years older and two feet taller. He didn't care. Balling up his hand into a big ol' fist came as natural to him as spitting.

By middle school, little Edgar's reputation had preceded him, and most of the smart alecks had wised up. They'd stopped messing with him. But then in the tenth grade, he'd gotten even more notorious when he was out playing baseball one day and a bigger kid had accidentally slugged him with a bat, planting the damn thing right up against the side of his face.

Of course, it was Edgar's own fault. He'd bullied his way into being the team catcher; and when he had squatted down too close to home plate, the older kid (who was up at bat) had taken a swing at a fastball, then had unintentionally brought the bat all the way around, hitting Edgar's catcher's mask and knocking him to the ground.

KA-BAM!

Sounding like a clap of thunder, the maple bat had instantly splintered apart.

Yeah, and that damn bat had hurt, too. Those old wooden bats could really wallop you.

Dammit to hell.

But Edgar didn't cry. No way. He wasn't going to let the other kids think he was a sissy. He wanted to be the meanest kid on the ball field, so he got up and kept on playing. And that's when a couple of the kids had started calling him "Stoneface" since he hadn't griped when his face had puffed up with a huge black-and-blue mark.

No, he'd kept his mouth shut. He didn't whine like a little girl. But still, he'd gotten really pissed off at the bigger kid who'd hit him with the lousy bat. Yeah, Edgar's temper had exploded like a goddamn howitzer; and once he was back up on his feet, he'd grabbed a piece of the broken bat and had busted the batter in the balls with it. Edgar "Stoneface" Sakowski couldn't help himself. He had a godawful short damn fuse.

So the nickname had stuck, and being called "Stoneface" had stayed with him throughout high school. Also, as strange as it may have seemed, Edgar always told himself that if he'd never been called "Stoneface," then he might not have ended up with a stonecutter's chisel in his hand.

Why?

Because he'd come to that conclusion based upon what had happened to him later in the eleventh grade. That was when his shop teacher, Mr. McTanker, had begun calling him by his nickname . . . and somehow a connection had been made, and the lanky hot-tempered kid with the big burly hands and fearless sneer had been matched up as an apprentice to a stonemason, with the apprenticeship eventually turning into a paying job after Edgar had graduated from high school. So having a wooden baseball bat smack him upside the head had actually helped Stoneface find a job he could make a living at. If he'd never been called Stoneface, then Mr. McTanker might not have hooked him up with the stonemason who needed an apprentice. And considering what the possible alternatives might've been, Edgar thought that pounding away at slabs of marble was certainly a lot better than working as a grease monkey replacing sparkplugs or freezing his damn butt off yanking in crab pots on a gut-wrenching fishing boat.

Chapter Four

And they say you can never go home. Well, in all honesty, Mooney sort of felt as though he had finally come home – even though, until he'd picked up and moved to Bellingham, he had never actually set foot in Whatcom County before. So to him, it certainly felt like home. It may not have been the place he'd been born, but he had a sense of being at peace in the Pacific Northwest. He didn't feel as though he stood out like a sore thumb. Living in Bellingham, he felt as if he at least halfway fitted in. No other place he'd ever lived before had given him such a sense of belonging. In his mind, he had finally come home. The town might have a few warts, but it was a darn good place to live compared to all of the other places he'd inhabited per the dozens of odd jobs he'd had since leaving the orphanage.

You see, Mooney had started life having been dealt a losing hand. As a young kid, he was left with his sister on the doorstep of the Knights of the Kingdom Orphanage in Bogalusa, Louisiana. Their mother had driven them to the facility in the middle of the night, pinned notes on their T-shirts, and driven away. For a six year old, that had been a hard goodbye to understand, which meant that Mooney's struggle to right the wrongs of the world had begun at a very early age. He had always felt like an outsider, never thinking he belonged wherever he was. So even as a child (and this probably was at least partly true because of what had happened to him at the orphanage), he'd never liked living in the Bayou State. Growing up in the Deep South, he'd been constantly picked on for his non-conforming thoughts, having learned early on that most of the so-called *good ol' boys* thought "liberal" was a four-letter word.

Yes, indeed. It had been a very hard row to hoe. Angry rednecks were a cruel bunch. Having been around quite a few of them growing up, Mooney had learned how their meanspirited minds worked. Each time he'd seen a black kid being bullied and had quickly stepped in to defend him, the name-calling would start . . . with Mooney soon finding himself in a knock-down-drag-out fistfight. In that part of the country, the hatemongering was nothing to be taken lightly. For a progressive-leaning kid stuck in an orphanage, it could get pretty dangerous real darn fast.

Thereupon, as soon as he could, Mooney had split and moved to greener "liberal" pastures, taking his sister with him. He was glad he had made it out of that particular part of Louisiana alive, having once been shot in the leg when he had tried to stop a drunken redneck from cutting down a two-hundred-year-old oak tree.

The KKK's Deep South.

A right-wing infested Louisiana parish simply wasn't his type of place.

Anyway, as strange as it may have seemed, the truth was that Mooney did, in fact, have a mom and a dad, even though he'd, for whatever dysfunctional reason, ended up at the orphanage. Having one time sneaked into the headmaster's office and read his abandonment file, Mooney found out that his parents had decided that they didn't want a son and a daughter because they'd been too poor to take care of two little kids, and that's why his parents had left Becky and him at the Knights of the Kingdom Orphanage in Bogalusa, Louisiana . . . with his mom having later called the headmaster to explain why her two little kids had been ditched on the building's doorstep.

Yes, it was hard to fathom; but some children, through no fault of their own, really got dealt raw hands. Mooney's childhood had been one big train wreck after another. Living with a bunch of strangers, while trying to acclimate into an institutionalized regiment . . . had made for a melancholy upbringing. And what had added to the heartbreak was the fact that his own parents had done what they had done, leaving his little sister and him to have to grow up in such a coldhearted place.

So . . .

Being placed in the orphanage had been a

defining moment in Mooney's life; and, without a doubt, it had warped his thinking, messed up his social skills, and given him a unique perspective on the depraved manifestations of human nature. Looking back, he never could figure out what crime he had ever committed to deserve such filial rejection. Couldn't his parents have done something else besides leaving him at the orphanage?

Indeed, this question would haunt him throughout his life. He never could seem to heal that emotional wound from his early childhood. All the psych books and Freudian interpretations he'd read on the subject hadn't given him a solid answer. So he'd never been able to find anything definitive in a textbook in regards to an effective way of coping with the internal damage that such parental rejection had caused. He had only been able to smooth over the problem with make-do fixes. The hole in his heart was still there, and he thought it would always be there. But he had learned what not to do. He had learned that drugs and alcohol only gave him a short reprieve from his distress, yet these numbing substances would also take away more joy than they would give him. It had taken him a number of years, but he had finally come to the conclusion that substance abuse wasn't the answer. It was a short-term, unsustainable self-medicating remedy. The ingestion of mind-numbing chemicals did a good job of clouding his brain and diluting the traumatic memories, yet the resulting stupor never actually cured the deep-seated pain that was forever following him around.

And so . . .

It was only when he had begun a daily exercise routine that a sustainable self-healing had eventually started to take hold, which allowed him to accept his social disconnect for what it truly was. Mooney had come to realize that he would never be normal and that he would always be an outsider and that he would forever be a rebel activist, looking in from the outside. He also knew he would go to his grave fighting for the underdog, fighting for Mother Earth, fighting for the tall trees that he had come to love so very much.

Yeah, well, that was just the way his DNA was configured. Mooney Waters would never be a go-along-to-get-along conformist. He was damaged goods. There was no way his neural circuits could ever be rewired. He knew the drumbeat of conventional thinking would, for him, always be an unrelatable mindset. Life might be a lovey-dovey field of four-leaf clovers for the kids who grew up in well-off middle-class brick-veneer homes in the ubiquitous suburbs, but that wasn't true for a poor kid who'd grown up in a creaky-old orphanage with bad plumbing, no A/C, and little heat in the winter. So even though there were a lot of goodhearted people who tried their best to help the disadvantaged when they could, there still was not enough social work being done to balance out all of the inequities in regards to those who had been dealt bad hands from the get-go. For such a wealthy country, there continued to be too much poverty and way too much disregard for the environment. A long list of *inconvenient truths* was still not being acknowledged. There was a huge chasm between the fat-cat rich and the food-pantry poor, between those who wanted to protect Mother Nature as opposed to those who had no qualms about polluting her wondrous beauty via the abusive ways of the narrowly educated.

Hence, having had the childhood he'd had, Mooney's formative years had, unequivocally, turned him into a questioning cynic. At an early age he'd learned how to spot the self-serving flaws of the greedy alphas who were running the human circus he'd been relegated to join. He'd found out that not everyone was warm and caring. Not everyone was well meaning. Not everyone was concerned about what was happening to the planet. And if someone lived on the wrong side of the tracks and was downwind of a toxic petrochemical smokestack, which was quite common in Louisiana – then life could be a harsh bed of nails that was constantly being made worse by the unfettered cancerous pollution. He knew if the environmental activists didn't push back and draw a line in the sand, then nothing would ever change. The rich would get richer, and the corporate crooks would continue to pick the pockets of the American public, while turning a blind eye to the terrible harm that they were doing to the Earth's ecosystem.

Thereupon . . .

Mooney had made a decision, at a relatively young age, to stand up to the profit-comes-first injustices and to fight the good fight. For him, eco activism had become a career path just like any other job; and to that end . . .

He was now out the front door, off to do his research. He wanted to check on the biodiversity of the local habitat, hoping the woodland in the nearby park would share a few of its hidden secrets. With so much wildlife living in and around the protected green space near where he lived, he knew he wouldn't be disappointed. He would usually always see a variety of free-living species each time he frequented Arbor Falls Park. It was an animal-friendly forest that had an abundance of free-ranging vertebrates. The birds were especially numerous – which included crows, wood-peckers, sapsuckers, eagles, owls, ducks, seagulls, blue herons, and geese. The large pond, near the first waterfall down from the lake, was a favorite hangout for a variety of waterfowl.

As for the other animals, Mooney had seen several different types of squirrels, rabbits, raccoons, and deer inhabiting the park. Off and on, he had also seen a few garter snakes slithering about, too. One time he'd even seen a coyote trotting across a trail right in front of him, looking not to have a care in the world. Another time he had walked up to within a few feet of a hungry beaver that was chewing its way into the bark of an old cedar tree that was growing next to the creek. And after having been told about the two otters by his sister, Mooney was now anxious to see if she had gotten it right as to there being a new species inhabiting the duck pond.

All in all, Arbor Falls Park was a healthy eco-system that was teaming with a broad diversity of flora and fauna. And since it also had so many species of trees – including Douglas fir, bigleaf maple, red cedar, cottonwood, spruce, and hemlock – it was the perfect place for an eco blogger, such as himself, to do his research. Jogging underneath the tall evergreens was a wonderful luxury that few got to experience on a daily basis. Many of the park's conifers were over a hundred and fifty feet in height. Plus, there were thousands and thousands of trees since the park spanned over two hundred acres. At times it almost felt as though he was in an outdoor cathedral, which Mother Nature had designed and built herself, in order to be able to share her abundance with the locals. Some naturalists might even go so far as to refer to it as a spiritual experience. And rarely did a day go by that Mooney wouldn't come across some snippet of environmental interaction that he could use in his blog. Of course, it might only be the inconsequential way an animal reacted to his presence, like when a inquisitive crow would calmly hop along the trail in front of him, looking to be as tame as a house pet; but still, each such encounter was valid research that he would later write down in his journal. And whether he used one of these visuals in his blog, or simply kept what he had experienced filed away in the back of his mind, his time in the park was never wasted. The inviting wildness of the woodland was constantly offering him fresh ideas since he was always looking for new and interesting ecological insights to share with his readers.

Crossing the pedestrian bridge over Arbor Creek, Mooney looked down at the fast-moving water that was madly rushing toward the bay. It was crystal clear, and he could actually see all the way down to the creek's bottom, being as it was only several feet deep. This was mountain snowmelt, which had migrated down from the higher elevations into Lake Whatcom, and now this runoff was draining out of the lake and into the creek. It had about four miles to go until it escaped into the Puget Sound.

Continuing ever deeper into the woods, Mooney only noticed a couple of hardy souls braving the elements on that rather chilly afternoon. The people traffic was relatively light, and this was possibly due to the fact that yet another rain-heavy cold front, like the one the day before, was due to pass through within the next hour or so, which tended to keep most of the park regulars sitting at home in front of their fireplaces.

Yet still, this being Bellingham — there would always be the outdoor fanatics, like himself, who rarely ever curtailed their park excursions unless there was a serious threat of high-velocity wind gusts and unrelenting heavy rain. If just a light downpour was in the forecast, then that was what water-repellant hoodies and rain slickers were for.

So . . .

Having acclimated to the seasonal weather pattern, since he had been doing his research in this locale for as many months as he had . . .

Mooney wasn't at all surprised when he soon came upon a park regular who was out walking her dog. This outdoor buff seemed to enjoy getting away from her indoor nest and, in the process, being able to spend some quality time with her pooch. Carol was in her thirties; she had a kid in kindergarten; and she loved to talk about the wild animals she would frequently see hiding up in the trees. Almost every time Mooney would run into her on the trail, she'd have a new story to share with him about something she had recently seen.

"Hey," Mooney said, stopping to pet her wolfish-looking Siberian Husky.

"Hi. I haven't seen you in awhile."

"I don't jog as early as I used to. Been kinda busy. What's up?"

"Nothing much. Remember that owl nest I told you about?"

"Uh-huh."

"Well, the two baby owls flew away."

"Wasn't that nest on the lower trail?"

"Uh-huh. A little ways up from the falls."

"Okay, I think I know where you're talking about. They really fattened up fast, didn't they?"

"They had a good mom. She was all the time flying in with stuff to feed 'em."

"What happened to the baby squirrels?"

"They're still getting bigger and bigger. They're running up and down that hemlock tree over near the stone bridge."

"Did you hear about the otters in the duck pond?"

"No. How many are there?"

"Two, I think."

"Cool. I hope they're a mating couple. Maybe in the spring we'll have some baby otters."

"How are you doing?"

"Okay, I guess." Carol then looked down at Mooney's bare legs and shook her head. He was wearing running shorts, which he did year round – except for on the coldest of winter days. Wanting to soak up as much sunshine and vitamin D as he possibly could, he hardly ever wore long pants in the park. He chose to dress in this particular way since Bellingham was notorious for its cloudy weather, and he wanted to expose as much skin as he could to the subdued sunlight, which meant that he kept his legs and arms uncovered for as many days as he possibly could.

"Aren't you cold?" Carol asked.

"No, I'm fine. I actually like chilly weather."

And though she proceeded to leave it at that, not saying anything about him being eccentric due to the fact that he was wearing running shorts, it looked to him as if she was somewhat puzzled by his unusual behavior, possibly thinking that he was a little weird. He had also spoken to her enough times to sort of be able to read her moods. When she would shake her head and have a slight glint of wariness in her eyes, this usually meant that she was about to blurt out something judgmental. Nevertheless, this time she'd held her tongue. And since she hadn't said anything negative, maybe this meant that she was trying not to come across as being too overbearing and bossy. In other words, Mooney had sensed, weeks back, that Carol was starting to get a wee bit interested in him, seeming to want to get to know him somewhat better. One time she had even said that she was thinking about getting a divorce. So when she had coyly begun flirting with him, flashing that lovely smile of hers, he couldn't help but become a little suspicious of her intent.

Yet still, as far as he knew, she was *sort of* married; and Mooney wasn't the type of guy who wanted to get involved with a married woman. He had learned a long time ago to avoid such soap operas. But if Carol hadn't've been married, he would've handled it quite differently. He would've asked her out on a date, even though she looked to be several years older than he was. Her shapely bod and pleasant personality were seriously attractive.

Romance. It was never easy.

Anyway . . .

Not wanting to lead her on (and preferring to keep their infrequent chats as platonic as possible), Mooney then excused himself from the conversation, gave her quick wave, and continued on his jog. Hooking up with the right woman was on his to-do list, yet the operative word was "right" – as in a good match. Mooney wasn't much for one-night stands.

So . . .

Having found out what he wanted to find out about the owlets, Mooney zoned back into his jog. Getting outside and away from his desk, he relished the exercise. It helped him focus his thoughts and clear his mind. He couldn't understand why anyone living in outdoorsy Bellingham would pay a membership fee at a health club since the great outdoors was free and available to all who had the good sense to partake of it.

Most people don't think outside the box. They're easily buffaloed by the herd mentality of their social programming and don't even realize it.

Anyway . . .

After having spent an hour revitalizing his soul in the park . . .

Mooney, once he had made it back home and was sitting down at his desk in the alcove, had been able to flesh out the approach he was going to use on the assignment that Darwin had handed off to him the night before. Having sorted through a variety of possible scenarios, Mooney had selected the one that he felt the most confident with, thinking he would be able to configure a bonding strategy that he hoped would be effective in persuading a new recruit to come onboard and fulfill a task that L.E.A.F. had uniquely designed for him. The guy's codename was ArticGecko, and he worked on a drilling rig in the Bering Sea off Alaska's coast.

As to how ArticGecko had first made contact with a Flock operative, Mooney wasn't exactly sure since the particulars of the introduction hadn't been explained to him; yet he knew that the upper committee must have parsed the guy's bona fides by having him cough up some vital intel on the oil company which he was working for. A L.E.A.F. hacking team then would have proceeded to use that insider information to fashion the malware virus that they had embedded inside the computer mouse (which Mooney had been given) so as to be able to take advantage of a specific network vulnerability that the newbie had tipped them to. And, in this regard, for the assigned group of higher-ups to have gone so far as to have implanted corrupting code into such an unrecognizable Trojan horse, i.e., to have programmed the malware into such a standardized device that could easily be plugged into any USB port so as to facilitate a debilitating data migration through a drilling rig's command-and-control system . . .

Had to have involved a serious amount of techno-savvy expertise. Of course, actually hiding a miniaturized flash drive inside the guts of the computer mouse probably hadn't been that hard to pull off, whereas to have had the epiphany of making such a Trojan "rodent" appear to be nothing more than an innocuous computer accessory . . .

Was near genius.

Who would ever suspect that a normal-looking mouse had been tampered with, especially one that was still encased inside an unopened clamshell package? The device actually looked exactly like any other fresh-from-the-factory accessory that anyone could buy at whatever big-box electronics store. There were no tattletale signs that it wasn't what it appeared to be. The plastic packaging had no irregular marks on it. It simply looked like a brand-new computer mouse.

And so . . .

Needless to say, Mooney had been quite impressed by the well-conceived intricacies of the overall mission. The Flock had taken its sneaky skullduggery to an even higher level than he'd expected. And now the ball was in his court. It was up to him to either close the deal or to nix any further contact with ArticGecko. A rendezvous point had been set up in Fairhaven, near where the guy would be getting off the Alaska Ferry. That was the location of the Bellingham Cruise Terminal, which was the southernmost termination point for passengers disembarking from the ocean-going vessels that serviced the Alaska Marine Highway System. The BCT was a convenient transit point for the U.S. travelers who were visiting the lower 48 from Juneau since Bellingham's ferry dock was right next to the Amtrak station (a facility which also housed an interstate bus station). Plus, up the hill from this travel hub was Fairhaven Village proper, with its relatively small historical district that looked out over the bay. And since this location had such a minuscule urban footprint, there were only a handful of cross streets that delineated a tiny nexus of city blocks in this part of Bellingham's south side. Most of the three- and four-story brick buildings that anchored Fairhaven had first been built back in the late 1800's, and so the whole area had an old-fashion feel to it, and this seemed to help attract a touristy crowd to the small mom-and-pop shops that catered to the passengers coming off the ferries, trains, and buses . . . along with those who would drive over from the Seattle-to-Canada corridor via Interstate 5 (which was only a few miles to the east).

Hence, as one might imagine per all of the comings and goings, Fairhaven Village was the perfect locale for operational intrigue. New faces were constantly arriving and departing; and two inconsequential strangers meeting for the first time in front of a bookstore certainly wouldn't draw any undue attention.

Or so Mooney hoped.

Chapter Five

In the six months after her new roommate had moved in, Zetty had learned a lot about a bunch of stuff she hadn't known before. Having never had a sister to share her life with, it had been a real eye-opener. Zetty had seen and heard things which were quite shocking; and so now she wished, with all her heart and soul, that she would have picked someone else to be her roommate. But Zetty also knew, even though she very much longed to forget the last six months, that the icky improprieties she had so reluctantly become acquainted with . . .

Weren't going to go away since they were forever stuck in her mind. There was no going back to the naiveté she'd had before she'd agreed to share her apartment. Zetty had come to realize that there were defects in human nature, which she wished she had never become aware of. Living in the small apartment she called home, even though she had her own bedroom, had her hearing torrid conversations and bodily noises that a nun would have run screaming out the front door from, if the nun had heard what Zetty had heard. The apartment walls were thin, and her roommate had no qualms about rocking her bedposts when she wanted to get it on.

Yes, that was so Edna-Ney Bunsey. Edna-Ney was one of the most uninhibited women Zetty had ever met. Edna-Ney was a flirt, and she made her living as a bartender. She liked to have fun, which meant that she would sleep with almost any Tom, Dick, or Harry who came along. She wasn't picky. That was just the way Edna-Ney was. But she also wasn't an out-and-out slut, either. No, Edna-Ney actually had good intentions. She wasn't coldhearted, although after she had gulped down a couple of cocktails, her ability to make rational judgments was pretty much toast.

At the man-hungry age of 36, Edna-Ney was a Roman candle that would just keep lighting up the night sky, with fireball after colorful fireball, when she jumped in bed with a guy. During the six months the two of them had roomed together, Zetty had learned more about human intimacy than she had ever needed to know for a lifetime. Their less-than-desirable living arrangements, per being crammed so close together in the pint-sized apartment, had opened Zetty's eyes and ears to so much stuff. Living with a nymphomaniac had taught Zetty that she absolutely didn't want to be an exploding firework when she got to be Edna-Ney's age.

And so . . .

On that particular Sunday morning, Zetty was

sitting in the kitchen at the Formica-top table, reading the weekly newspaper . . .

When her free-spirited roommate had walked into the room wearing her fluffy house slippers and a tight-fitting pink kimono.

"Morning," Edna-Ney said as she stepped over to the stove and poured herself a cup of coffee.

"Did you know that our neighbors to the north are snatching up houses down here?" Zetty asked, looking up from the news article she had just read.

"You mean, the Canucks?"

"Uh-huh."

"Yeah, I heard about that. Glad someone can afford to buy a house in this stupid town. Wish I could."

"But they're not from here, Edna-Ney. They're Canadians. I don't understand how they can do that."

"Zetty, no one's going to stop anyone from coming here and buying anything they want. Houses, boats, cars − or our cheaper gasoline. If they can afford it, we'll sell it to 'em. And they're not coming down here 'cause they like us, trust me. They're coming down here to save money. Up in Canada, they have to pay a lot of taxes on everything they buy."

"Oh, I see."

"Wish I had their free healthcare, I can tell you that. Maybe I should marry a Canuck, huh?"

"I thought you said you never wanted to get married."

"Well, I'm thinking about changing my mind. If I could hook up with a rich Canadian who wanted to buy a house – and if I could get their free health insurance – I mean, I'd seriously think about it. But, y'know, I still don't want kids, that's for sure."

"I want kids."

"I know you do, Zetty. But you didn't grow up the oldest in a family of six, having to change stinky diapers for all of your little brothers and sisters. Babies are a pain."

Knowing this was a touchy subject that Edna-Ney could get seriously perturbed about since she had already had her tubes tied, Zetty thought it would be best if she changed the subject. "Oh, your dad called. He wants you to call 'im."

"Did he say why he wanted me to call him?"

"No, but he said his operation didn't kill him. I told him to call your cell phone, but he said he didn't have that number."

"You didn't give it to him, did you?"

"No. You told me never to give it out."

"I bet he wants to borrow money. He always wants to borrow money." Shaking her head, Edna-Ney then took another gulp of coffee.

"He can't get a job?"

"No, he has a job, but he spends all his money at the casino."

"So, like, why'd he have to get an operation?"

"To fix his knee. He pulled it out when he was crabbing."

"Oh."

"If he hadn't've gambled all his money away, he

wouldn't be calling me. But that's my dad. I don't know how my mom puts up with him."

"What about your brothers and sisters? Can't they loan him some money?"

"They all know better. They're not stupid. He never pays anyone back."

"Oh."

"Uh-huh." And with that bit of disparagement, Edna-Ney refilled her coffee cup and toddled out of the kitchen. Talking to her about her family always made Zetty wonder what it would have been like to have grown up with a couple of brothers and sisters to share such things with. And sure, sometimes the family stuff could get dicey. Zetty knew that. But she'd rather have those types of problems than not having any family around to talk to at all.

Chapter Six

The morning the Alaska ferry was due to arrive, Mooney had gotten up early and had taken a city bus to Fairhaven. Riding mass transit with the morning commuters had allowed him to keep a low profile. There wouldn't be a license plate number or a mountain bike description to detract from his anonymity. And the weather had also turned out to be somewhat accommodating with its habitual gloom. The sky was overcast with a hint of rain, which tended to keep certain folks inside.

Checking his watch, Mooney made it to the historic district about ten minutes early. The only problem was . . .

He had forgotten that the bookstore didn't open for another hour, which meant that he now had to find an out-of-the-way place to burn some time while he waited. Yet, in that part of town, there wasn't much of a selection to choose from. He didn't want to stand in the doorway of one of the nearby shops and draw any attention to himself.

Looking around, he finally noticed a wooden bench on the sidewalk in front of a hair salon. So to keep a low profile, he slowly walked across the street and sat down. The bench offered him a good vantage point from which to reconnoiter the foot traffic and thus watch for any unusual activity around the bookstore. He tried his best to appear distracted and uninvolved, not wanting to look as though he was casing the street or overly analyzing his surroundings.

And given that nothing caught his eye, he took a deep breath and leaned back on the bench. Everything seemed to be, more or less, quite normal . . .

With only a few people walking along the sidewalk, appearing to be on their way to an appointment or possibly strolling to one of the nearby shops. No one was loitering at the street corner, and he didn't notice a surveillance van or any unmarked cars staking out the place.

After about five minutes or so, a guy (with a small knapsack slung over his shoulders) . . .

Walked around the corner at the far end of the street. He was wearing a yellow rain hat and carrying a Rubik's Cube in his hand. Those were the signals that Mooney had been instructed to look for.

Slowing his pace, the guy stopped at the bookstore's front door and tried to open it. When he realized that it was locked, he then stepped back and stared in through the plate-glass window, appearing to be looking to see if anyone was inside.

Not wanting him to stand there too long, Mooney got up from the bench and strode toward him. He crossed the street midway down the block and approached the guy just as he was turning around. "Did you see a malamute run down this way?"

"What happened? Did you lose your dog?"

Uh-oh.

That wasn't the password response Mooney was expecting to hear. Unsure of what to say next, he then rubbed his hand across his mouth and ad-libbed the first thing that popped into his head. "No. I didn't lose my dog. It's a friend's dog. Sorry to have bothered you." And as Mooney said this, he slowly turned to walk away . . .

And the guy suddenly snapped his fingers. "Oh, wait. Sorry. I forgot." The guy then pulled a small slip of paper out of his pocket, held it up to his bifocals, and began to read it out loud to himself. "I heard some barking down the street. I can help you look for the dog if you want me to."

Sighing, Mooney shook his head. "So why'd you have to read it to me?"

" 'Cause I didn't want to make a mistake."

Whoa.

In all the years he'd been sneaking around in back alleys to avoid the cops, Mooney had never seen a new contact act so nervous before. The guy looked to be about twenty-five years old, and he hadn't shaved in several days. The stubble on his face seemed to exaggerate the lost look in his eyes. "Just relax, okay?

We don't want anyone to think something's wrong."

"Oh, okay. Sorry."

"Look, let's go for a walk." Mooney then pointed down the sidewalk and proceeded to lead the guy around the building's corner.

"So, like, what happens if we get stopped by the police?" the guy asked, stuffing the Rubik's Cube in his knapsack.

"Why do you think we'll get stopped by the cops?"

"Well, I just thought they might be looking for you, that's all."

"C'mon. Chill, alright? Don't be so paranoid."

"Well, y'know, this is the first time I've ever done something like this. I didn't get much sleep last night."

"Look. I understand. But just be cool, okay? We're not breaking any laws or anything. You're not going to get arrested," Mooney said as they walked past a parking lot and toward the gravel path which connected Fairhaven Village to the South Bay Trail.

"Right. Just be cool. Gotcha."

And hearing him say this, Mooney fought the urge to roll his eyes. "Okay, so . . . you, like, work on an offshore drilling rig, right?"

"Yeah. I'm a subsea engineer. I work on the Oceanic Venturer for Stentung Oil."

"Do you like your job?"

"I like the money. I like having fourteen days off. But the fourteen days straight I have to work on the rig start to get to me when I'm working a lot of overtime."

"So how long have you been doing it?"

"Six months."

"Are you planning on quitting?"

"Yeah, I think so. That's why I hooked up with you guys. I don't want to, like, do it anymore. I don't want to die in a blowout."

"So what changed your mind?"

"What do you mean?"

"Seems like you should've thought about that before you started the job."

"I did, but I needed a paycheck. Then once I was working offshore, I began thinking about what happened out in the Gulf of Mexico when that deepwater rig exploded and those workers got killed and all that oil was spilled in the water." Slowly shaking his head, the guy appeared to be sincerely disappointed with himself. "In college, when I was studying to get my engineering degree, I guess I just sort of blocked out the environmental stuff. I got too caught up in doing what I was doing and didn't ask enough questions."

"Yeah, I get it. You were thinking about all the money you'd make, right?"

"Yeah, that's true. I wanted to make the big money."

Pausing to give the guy a little time to ponder what he had just said, Mooney let the conversation ebb a bit as they continued along the gravel path . . .

Which soon came to an abrupt end at 10th Street. They then moved onto the pavement and followed the sidewalk to the pedestrian bridge that crossed over the train tracks, walking a few yards above the rail corridor that ran along the edge of Bellingham Bay. Below them was the freight route that the coal trains would be using to haul their cargos up to Cherry Point.

From the elevated view of the bridge, they could see the San Juan Islands off in the distance. It was a vista that Mooney always found to be utterly captivating. The beautiful expanse of water, framed by Mount Constitution looming over Orcas Island, was a sheer joy to gaze out at. "Great view, huh?" Mooney said as he led the guy off the pedestrian bridge and down to the long boardwalk, which had been built on piers a few hundred feet out in the bay.

"Yeah, this is really nice. I noticed it when we came by on the ferry. Cool stuff."

"Have you ever been here before?"

"No, this is my first time. I wanted to bring my truck down from Juneau 'cause I'm driving over to Idaho to see my sister. There's also a professor who teaches at the university here who I'm going to drop by and say hello to. A friend of mine studied with him. He's a really great guy."

Then, as a jogger hurried past them, Mooney stopped and leaned against the wooden rail. There were pockets of walkers coming and going on the boardwalk, and he wanted to wait until there was a lull in the pedestrian groupings in order for the two of them to have more privacy in their conversation. He also wanted to see if anyone was following them.

Satisfied that they didn't have a tail, Mooney then

turned to the guy and said, "You know there's no money in doing what we're asking you to do. I hope you know that."

"I know. I'm not doing it for the money. I'm doing it because it's the right thing to do." And as he said this, his demeanor didn't waiver. There didn't seem to be a disconnect between his words and his thoughts. His nervousness had now somewhat faded, and he appeared to be genuinely expressing himself. Per a quick read of his body language, Mooney sensed that he was, indeed, who he said he was. If he hadn't've been nervous and somewhat clumsy in his initial attitude, Mooney would've had more reason to be concerned. In other words, if the guy had come across as overly confident and too bubbly, his vetting process would've had to have been extended. But this guy looked nerdy enough (with his dorky glasses, grass-stained khaki pants, and yellow rain hat) . . . to actually be a disenchanted rig worker who wanted to join the do-gooder side. The deciding factor was his unsure ego. He obviously was a follower and not a leader. Most federal agents had strong overbearing wills, which were hard to hide under a disguise.

But still . . .

Mooney knew that he had to be careful what he said. It was possible he was being conned. There were chameleon informants who were so good at what they did, that even their own mothers probably wouldn't be able to know for sure which side of the fence they actually were working for on any given day. Such nefarious characters could flip-flop faster than rats chasing cheese. Without a conscience to weigh down their web of lies, these types of operatives could easily fool almost anyone. And that's why the Flock was well compartmentalized. Losing Mooney wouldn't jeopardize any of the other L.E.A.F. cells in Bellingham.

But considering the fact that ArticGecko had scored more pluses than minuses up until that point in the vetting process, it was time to move on to the next level. "You want to work with us, right?" Mooney asked.

"Yeah. That's why I'm here. That's why I got in touch with you guys."

"Alright, let's say we decide to use you; and, hypothetically, you fulfill a certain objective for us. Then what."

"I don't understand what you mean?"

Pausing, Mooney glanced, yet again, at the pedestrian bridge. Now he only saw a handful of elderly strollers slowly ambling along its length . . .

With nothing appearing to be out of the ordinary. Mooney then motioned for the two of them to continue down the boardwalk toward Boulevard Park. "Let's keep walking."

"I thought you said you weren't worried about getting arrested."

"I'm not. But I am worried about being followed," Mooney said, looking down at the saltwater below them. "It never hurts to be careful."

"Y'know, it kind of sounds like you don't trust

me."

"Do you trust me?"

"Sorta, I guess."

"Okay, so – it's the same with me."

"Yeah, I get it. I see what you mean. You're trying to figure me out, huh?"

Mooney nodded his head. "I'm sure you realize we don't just work with anyone who comes along."

"Sure, I understand. You're, like, the fourth guy in your group that I've had to talk to get this far. And, like, all of 'em have asked me a bunch of questions, too."

"Well, just so you know, I'm the last gatekeeper you'll have to deal with. If we end up on the same page, you'll walk away with a clear understanding of what you're being asked to do. You won't have to jump through anymore hoops, okay?"

"That's good to know. I'm glad to hear that."

And so . . .

With little foot traffic on that part of the board-walk, Mooney slowed his pace and patted the brown-paper bag he was carrying in his coat pocket. "Just a couple of more question. What are you planning on doing after you complete your assignment?"

"What do you mean?"

"I mean, what if the rig you're working on stops functioning?"

"Oh, I see what you're saying. Well, I'll probably quite my job and go back to college. That's why I want to talk to that professor. I mean, like – I never want to have anything else to do with messing up the environment ever again. On YouTube I saw what happened with the Exxon Valdez. All those birds dying in that gooey oil. And a few months back, my girlfriend made me watch a documentary about that oil spill in the Gulf. The dolphins, the pelicans, all of those oily beaches. I never want to be a part of something like that."

"Grad school?"

"Uh-huh. I'd like to get a master's in environmental engineering and go work for Greenpeace."

Stopping, Mooney turned and looked ArticGecko straight in the eye. His face didn't display any signs of dishonesty. In fact, his eyes had a bit of sadness in them. It appeared as though he was struggling to be as helpful as he could be, and he seemed to be expressing what Mooney had come to refer to as an elevated amount of the martyr syndrome – which, of course, was quite different from the more common, and pejorative, martyr complex. The guy was languaging the same caring attitude that concerned greenies were known to express when they talked about putting Mother Nature first, above their own welfare. Plus, this new recruit also had that "I-don't-want-to-be-a-bad-guy-anymore" look in his eyes, too.

"Greenpeace, huh? Good for you," Mooney said.

"Thanks."

"Okay, so – you know not to talk about any of this or to admit to having ever met me, right?"

"Yeah. I've been told the rules. I know the risks."

84

"You absolutely can't discuss this stuff with anyone else, understand?"

"Yeah, I get it. I swear I won't say anything. I don't want to get anyone in trouble."

Good. Those were the words I've been waiting to hear.

So . . .

Having not detected any dishonesty in the guy's tone, Mooney stepped over to the railing and gazed out at Orcas Island. Its tree-covered little mountain – with its humpbacked shape, looking somewhat like the humongous backside of a giant whale – was a sight to behold. The wind had just begun to pick up, and Mooney watched as a cabin cruiser bounced its way over the choppy whitecaps a few hundred yards in front of them. With the sky growing ever darker, it looked as though a storm front was quickly moving in. Soon the rain would start blowing sideways across the bay.

"Wouldn't it be really awful if a place like this was ever polluted by an oil spill," Mooney said, nodding down at the water.

"Y'know, I don't think that will ever happen. They'd never let 'em drill here."

"True, but we have some oil refineries just north and south of here. A tanker ship could hit some sort of something, and the tide might push a spill right into this shore. It's a long shot, and let's hope it never happens, but it could actually happen."

"I guess you're right. I'd really hate to see an accident like that spoil these beaches. But I know I won't have anything to do with it if it ever does happen, that's for sure."

Mooney smiled and patted the guy's shoulder. "I believe you." He then slipped the paper bag out of his pocket. "Look. This is a new fresh-off-the-shelf computer mouse. What we need you to do is plug it into your rig's main computer network that works the important stuff like the values, pressure gauges, and stabilizing pumps."

ArticGecko stood there quietly for a long moment as he processed what he had been told, seeming to extrapolate the implications. He then swallowed hard and bit his lower lip. "You guys want me to infect the command-and-control system."

"Yes, that's right. Just plug it into a USB port. You won't have to do anything else after that. The mouse will do all the rest on its own."

"Oh, man." Shaking his head, ArticGecko looked down at the paper bag. "You guys are heavy-duty, aren't you?"

"Uh-huh."

"Well, I hope you don't hold what I've done up until this point in my life against me. Like, I'm sorry I ever got into the oil business, okay?"

"No, we won't hold it against you. We know your heart's in a good place . . . now that you've evolved your thinking."

Taking in a deep breath, ArticGecko then looked up and down the boardwalk. They were pretty much alone since the darkening sky and blustery wind seemed to have scared away the other outdoor enthusiasts. Now there was only one lone runner jogging on the boardwalk, coming toward them from Boulevard Park; yet it looked as though it would take her half a minute or so, at her present pace, to get to where they were standing.

Continuing to shake his head, ArticGecko took a step closer and used his body to block the jogger's line of sight . . .

As his hand quickly grabbed the paper bag and stuffed it in his coat pocket. "So, like, am I gonna die or something?"

"No. Nobody is going to die. The mouse won't sink the rig. It'll just screw up the control software and incapacitate some of the drilling operations. No one will be harmed. We don't do things like that."

"Oh, wow. That's good to hear."

"Any questions?"

"Yeah. What do you want me to do after I get it hooked into the network?"

"Nothing. Just act normal. Go with the flow."

"You don't think they'll figure out what happened?"

"Nope. You'll have nothing to worry about. They won't suspect a normal-looking computer mouse. The software code is designed to appear as though the infection was caused by some sort of internal malware that came embedded in the last operational update."

"Oh, okay. I get it. I follow that logic. Sounds probable, I guess."

"None of the life-support systems will be harmed. The infection will simply migrate to all of the hard drives and eventually crash the drilling operation within a week or so of its introduction."

"Which means, I might not even be onboard the rig when it happens, huh? Maybe I'll be on my fourteen-day off-cycle."

"Could be. But still, you shouldn't do anything out of the ordinary to attract attention. Before you resign your job, you should wait until the rig has to be towed into shore."

"Right. Wait until they want to transfer me to another rig, then bail."

"Exactly."

"What about future contact?"

"You mean, with us?"

"Uh-huh."

Now the female jogger was only a few yards away; and before Mooney proceeded to answer the question, he waited until she had run past them.

Nice legs.

Mooney then stuck his hands in his pockets. The wind chill was quickly dropping the temperature down to a lower level, and the humidity on the water was making it feel even colder than it actually was. "Look, don't try to contact us. Go dormant for six months after you resign. Then, when you get settled in wherever you end up, try to reestablish communication with the first member of our group that you hooked up with, doing whatever you did to get her attention."

"So, like, what if she changes her email address?"

"If she changes her email addy, then go to the second member you met with. And keep moving up the ladder, if you have to, until you work your way back up to me."

"But, like, I don't know who you are or your email or anything about you."

"Don't worry. It'll work itself out. Just keep using your same screen name when you start posting on the environmental blogs after staying quiet for six months. We have a long memory."

"Okay, if that's what you want me to do, that's what I'll do."

"Good. Now you should go back the way we came. I'm going this direction," Mooney said, nodding toward Boulevard Park. He then gave the guy a quick hug, turned, and began briskly walking away.

It was a risky way to live, but someone had to do it.

After striding a few yards, Mooney suddenly heard the horn of a slow-moving locomotive. A freight train was rumbling north along the shore with a long string of boxcars. The diesel-burning mechanical serpent appeared to have the unfettered energy of a nearly unstoppable force. Depending on its speed, Mooney knew that such a lengthy behemoth could take up to a mile to come to a complete stop. Fairytale dragons were wimps compared to these modern-day iron horses. Such heavy tonnage couldn't be slowed very quickly, and the loud blaring horn was the final warning to people to stay clear of the tracks . . .

Or suffer the deadly consequences.

Mooney told himself that it would take a tremendous amount of courage for anyone to lie down in front of such an unforgiving monster.

Playing chicken with a locomotive wasn't for the faint of heart. But if all of the deaf-dumb-and-blind naked apes sold their money-grubbing souls to the highest bidder, Mother Nature was charred toast, for sure.

Chapter Seven

Standing beside the railroad tracks, he could hear the loud horn of an approaching train. Rain was pouring down on his head, and it felt as though he was being hit by the slobbering spit of a thousand demons. But what was even more repulsive was having to listen to their godawful screeches.

Damn them to hell! Why can't the goddamn evil spirits leave me the hell alone?

If he took five steps forward, Stoneface would be right in the middle of the train tracks. And if he timed it right, the locomotive would be rounding the curve and unable to stop when the damn thing got to where he was standing.

Sayonara.

Taking a swig from his whiskey bottle, Stoneface turned toward the dirtied-up window that was facing out from the warehouse that he called home. His angel was standing inside, on the other side of the fogged-up window, staring back at him. Her face wasn't finished yet, so it was hard to tell what she was thinking. But he knew she wouldn't want him to die. She was much too nice to want something evil like that. So if he did, for whatever reason, get it into his head to step out in front of the approaching train, he at least hoped she would come to his rescue and bring him back to life.

Hey, that's what angels did, right? Weren't they put on Earth to help people when they needed help?

Again . . .

The locomotive's horn squealed out another warning. In a few seconds, the speeding train would be right there, and his angel hadn't moved a muscle. Her wings hadn't fluttered a single beat.

"Stoneface!" someone called out from behind him.

Turning around, he saw Bragg Gartok holding an umbrella over his head near the garbage cans by the side of the warehouse. Muttering under his breath, Stoneface told himself that he didn't want to tempt fate in front of a sleazy bastard like Gartok. He knew his angel wouldn't transmutate if such a scumbag was standing there, being as the no-good shithead wasn't the nicest pup in the litter. Gartok could get real mean real fast when he wanted to.

Taking another swig of whiskey, Stoneface then stepped back away from the tracks just as the freight train sped by.

CLINKETY-CLANK, CLINKETY-CLANK . . . CLINKETY-CLANK!

"What were you doing over there?" Gartok asked as Stoneface walked over to him.

"Just goin' for a walk."

"In this damn rain?"

"Yeah, in this goddamn rain, okay? If I waited for this shit to stop, I'd never get out and get some fresh air. What brings you over here?"

Puffing on his cigar, Gartok gave him a hard look. "Come over to tell you somethin'. Want to move inside and get out of this downpour?"

"Yeah, sure. Come on in."

Leading Gartok around the corner, Stoneface turned the cold-to-the-touch doorknob on his front door; and the two men entered the warehouse. Gartok had been there a number of times before, so he didn't flinch when he saw how unkempt the small art studio was. He knew Stoneface was a drunken slob, and it didn't seem to bother Gartok when he saw all of the trash that was cluttering the floor. There were crumpled-up hamburger bags, paper coffee cups, and empty bottles of whiskey littering the place.

Leaning his umbrella up against an empty crate, Gartok looked across the room at the unfinished angel. "Working on a new one, huh?"

"Yeah. She's gonna have bigger wings."

"You better not make her too top-heavy. You don't want her tipping over."

"Listen, I know what the hell I'm doing, alright? I've got her standing on a damn heavy pedestal, like the Statue of Liberty."

"Oh, yeah. I see what you mean." Taking a puff of his cigar, Gartok then walked over and lightly patted the angel's smooth derriere. "Nice butt."

"Dammit, you son-of-a-bitch. Don't you be touching her. She doesn't like it. So keep your goddamn hands off her."

"Oh, sorry. I forgot. There's no need to get mad at me."

"Look, I got things I gotta do. What'd you come here to tell me?"

Stepping away from the angel, Gartok moved over to the window and watched the last freight car clatter by outside. "Noisy as hell in here. I don't know how you put up with all that racket."

"Hell, it ain't like I have much of a choice. You get used to it. So what did you come here to tell me? Spit it out."

"Well, what I came by to tell you is . . . a few days ago I was up in the cemetery, and I talked to a gal about buying one of your angels."

"Yeah? What'd she say?"

"She said she couldn't afford it, didn't have any money. Ever heard the name Pineford?"

"Nope, I don't think so."

"Well, let me tell you, the Pinefords have a big family plot up there in the cemetery, and I noticed that this young gal had buried her parents in it."

"So?"

"Okay, here's the interesting part. I've seen her walking around downtown. A really nice looking gal. Too nice not to be married. She didn't have a ring on her finger. Oh, I even took a picture of her on my phone when she wasn't looking. Take a look." Gartok then pulled out his smartphone from his pocket, thumbed the screen, and turned the device around to show Stoneface the photo of the girl.

"Yeah, she's pretty. Nice face."

"Sexy bod, too, let me tell ya."

"Uh-huh. So why are you wasting my time with this shit, Gartok?"

" 'Cause it's something to think about." He then put the phone back in his pocket.

"What-da-ya mean?"

"Okay, let's say I get a guy to hook up with her. Then he, y'know, wants to do the right thing, and the guy takes out a life insurance policy on his new wife, if you get my drift. You interested?"

"No."

"Ten thousand dollars, easy money."

"Nope, I ain't gonna do it. A big payday won't do me no good if I'm sittin' in jail." Stepping over to his workbench, Stoneface then set his whiskey bottle down and picked up his wooden mallet. "You're not trying to double-cross me, are you, Gartok?"

"What are you talking about? You know me better than that."

"You didn't sell me out to the cops, did you?"

"Hell no. C'mon. I'd never do something like that. We're tight, man."

"Don't give me that bullshit. You better not be tryin' to make a lousy buck off me." Staring him straight in the eye, Stoneface then began banging his mallet against the palm of his hand.

FLUMP, FLUMP, FLUMP.

"Look, calm down, okay? It wouldn't make sense for me to go to the cops. You know that. Hell, you've got a bunch of shit on me. I mean, if I did do something stupid like that, then we'd both end up on death row."

"Don't screw with me. I don't like to be messed with, you son-of-a-bitch. Just you remember that. I don't take crap from nobody."

"I swear, you've got nothing to worry about, alright? I'd never go blab anything to the cops. I'm not stupid, okay?"

"I know. You're damn smart. Too smart, sometimes. If anyone could set up a dumbass plea deal and get himself off, it's you."

Taking one final puff off his cigar, Gartok stepped over to the workbench and extinguished the stogy in an empty sardine can. There was a faint sizzling sound as the decrepit smell of burning tobacco and dead fish filled the air. "C'mon, you know me better than that, Stoneface. I ain't ever gonna flip on ya. You don't got nothin' to worry 'bout." Swallowing hard, Gartok then wiped his hand on his pants and took a step back, seeming to want to put some distance between the two of them. "Oh, if you want to make a few extra bucks, I have another proposition for you."

"What is it?"

"You know that park up there next to the cemetery?"

"Yeah, I know where you're talkin' 'bout."

"Well, when I was walking through there the

other day, I noticed some six-foot fir trees. They were just the right size for Christmas trees. Really nice ones. A guy could sneak in there at night, drag 'em out, and no one would be the wiser."

"Yeah? And who'd want to buy 'em? Santa Claus?"

"I'll buy 'em. I have a connection down in Seattle who'll take 'em off my hands."

"How much?"

"Twenty dollars a tree. But that's only for five-, six-foot noble firs. All the dude wants is noble firs, nothing else. My friend's real picky about what he'll take. He only buys the really good ones."

Putting down his mallet and picking up his whiskey bottle, Stoneface took a long gulp. He needed a moment to think about it before he committed himself. Looking over at his angel, he waited to see if she was going to move her wings. If she had, that would've been a bad sign. But her wings didn't move. She stayed frozen in place. "Yeah, okay. Why not? I'll do it. I need to make some goddamn extra money. Sounds easy enough."

"Okay, just let me know when you have five trees, and I'll come by and pick 'em up."

Nodding his head, Stoneface shuffled over and opened the front door. It was obviously time for Gartok to leave.

Getting the hint, his partner in crime quickly grabbed his umbrella and hurried out into the rain, seeming to be glad he hadn't said anything that would have pushed Stoneface over the edge.

Damn bastard. He smelled sissified, like a French perfume bottle.

Yeah, Bragg Gartok was one sleazy character. If someone got it into their head to whack the guy's legs off, the no-good scumbag would probably still be able to slither away like some sort of cold-blooded snake. The shithead never seemed to walk in a straight line. His feet would sidewind their way across the floor. Only a weak-minded fool would trust a venomous reptile like that. Anyone with any goddamn sense – who wasn't hopped up on goofballs – knew that old saying about "honor among thieves" was pure unadulterated bull-shit. A lousy snake like Gartok would stick a shiv in his best friend's back if it would get him a wad of cash. His fangs were deadly poisonous.

Chapter Eight

After he had handed off the computer mouse to ArticGecko, Mooney returned to his normal routine. His blog was getting a lot of Net traffic; and he had to constantly diddle with its format and update its embedded links in order to keep his website fresh and engaging. Over the last few weeks, there had been a steady stream of hits, incrementally increasing each day. Of course, it wasn't as if Mooney was completely clueless as to what was causing the flood of new eyeballs. He actually had a vague idea as to why certain people were frequenting his website. It didn't take an exceptionally high IQ to figure it out. His hot-topic post about stopping the coal trains had obviously hit a nerve with a broad segment of the environmental activists. Yet because Mooney didn't want to ask too many questions as to why he was getting so many web hits, he preferred not to know who was who and why they were clicking on the banner ads that were helping him pay his monthly bills.

Mooney liked doing what he was doing; and he, of

course, liked getting paid to do what he was doing – so he was simply glad he had as many regulars as he did who were reading and responding to his online articles. And since he was also in the eco underground, he had a sneaky suspicion that he would be better off if he didn't delve too deeply into the particulars of why he was garnering so many clickthroughs. He might have his weaknesses and social limitations, but he certainly was at least sharp enough to know that it wouldn't be wise to mess with a World Wide Web cash cow when it came along. The last thing he wanted to do was to rock the kayak. He was relieved that the stuff he was publishing on the Internet was, in fact, interesting enough to keep his readers coming back for more. And thanks to his sister, if she hadn't've talked him into giving the blogosphere a shot, years ago – then Mooney never would have set up his website in the first place. Publishing his own eco blog had been her idea. Becky had been confident, from the get-go, that his emphasis on saving the environment would be quite popular from its very start.

And she was right, too.

Within six months of his blog's creation, Mooney was making a fairly steady income as a self-employed commentator, which meant he had been able to stop bouncing from job to job. And though his sister and him might not always agree on everything, it was nice having a younger sibling who was of the same persuasion as he was when it came to doing what was best for planet Earth. Using Becky as a sounding board had been a huge plus for him. At times her take on things could be much more advanced than his own. And, in the grand scheme of things, this was partly due to the fact that Becky was working on a master's degree in Environmental Studies at the local university and partly because they were housemates.

Sharing a place with another sentient being was always a bit of a gavotte for a guy like him. So at least it was somewhat easier on his worry circuits knowing the backstory on the person who was hogging the bathroom at all hours of the day and night.

Indeed, there were numerous pluses . . .

When it came to their one-on-one socializing and what-if brainstorming, being as the two of them could always do so without using any form of fossil energy, which meant that their exchange of ideas didn't gobble up any carbon at all. They only had to sit down at the kitchen table whenever they wanted to flesh out the pros and cons of sustainability and/or how they might better be able to help people wean themselves off of fossil fuels. Living in the same house was an easy way for the two of them to do this, since neither of them had to charge up a cell phone battery, nor did they have to turn on an electricity-sucking computer to dash off an email. Mooney and Becky could just sit down at the kitchen table when they wanted to discuss whatever thoughts they had on a variety of subjects when the mood hit them.

And so . . .

Since Becky had made him breakfast, that was

what she was proceeding to do. Over two bowls of steaming oatmeal, with a side order of wheat toast, they sipped their coffee and segued into a morning pow-wow.

"Moon, remember when they made us eat those cold scrambled eggs with ketchup on the yokes at the orphanage?"

"Yeah, I remember. You were five or six."

"I hadn't even started school yet."

"I know. It was pretty bad. They said if we didn't clean our plates, we wouldn't get to go see the movie that was showing that weekend. That was when they'd bus us into town for those Saturday matinees."

"Uh-huh. So maybe that's why I don't like eggs."

"Could be."

"Oh, I heard something interesting you might want to use in your next blog. You know those home fuel cells out of Silicon Valley that everyone's talking about? The ones you put in your backyard to get off the grid?"

"Okay."

"I did some research and found out they're not really that sustainable since they have to use some sort of hydrocarbon, such as natural gas, to generate the electricity."

"But you're off the grid."

"So? I'd rather be on the grid and getting my electricity from a non-polluting hydroelectric dam than having some oil company polluting the aquifers with their godawful fracking fluids so they can pipe in the natural gas to feed a fuel cell."

"Like in that magazine article?"

"Yeah, like in that article I stuck under your door. The greedy oil companies don't know what they're doing. Their science is so lame. If they really knew what they were doing, they wouldn't have to clean up all the messes they have to clean up."

Mooney couldn't argue with his sister's logic. And, needless to say, she wasn't actually aware of how truly informed he was in regards to the dangers of fracking. He had always bent over backwards to keep her in the dark about his Flock undercover work, not ever telling her about the job he'd had on the oilrig down in South Texas. She thought he had been off working on a research project for a nonprofit, back when they both were living in Austin and he'd had to make his frequent trips out of town. Becky had no clue he was a L.E.A.F. member, nor did she know the group even existed.

In any event, she had brought up a good point in regards to the California startup that was attempting to market a techno device that was being hyped with green branding and which some scientific types considered to be inherently unsustainable. Such a subject was one that seriously interested him. It had the smell of a win-lose that would resonate with his readers. Now he'd have to do some research and see what he could dig up. More than likely, he would be able to write something halfway compelling and post it. He was always looking for new material.

Giving him a supportive pat on the back, after having tipped him to her latest eco gripe, Becky placed her empty bowl in the sink and scooted out the door. She was on her way to class.

For Mooney, it was an eye-opening start to another day via having had a few minutes of sibling sharing. He was glad they got along so well, and they were lucky to have such a functional relationship. And since Becky was all the family he had, their emotional bond was the anchor that he could always rely upon.

It'd just been the two of them for all those years.

So now . . .

With the house all to himself, Mooney took a little time to reconnoiter his thoughts and plan out his day. He usually began his morning regiment by looking out the sliding glass door at Lake Whatcom, telling himself how truly fortunate he was to be able to have such a beautiful view. He couldn't complain about his circumstances, even if he was on a tight budget. The quality-of-life benefits of living where he was living were quite exceptional. Their cozy rent house was smack-dab in the Cascadian foothills, and the two of them had the unbridled joy of being surrounded by an abundance of tall trees, which guarded over the habitat as far as the eye could see. Plus, Mooney was his own boss and got to do what he wanted to do when he wanted to do it . . .

More or less. He didn't have to punch a corporate time clock. He didn't have to drive a lengthy commute in rush-hour traffic. He didn't have to waste his time with busywork, nor did he have to wake up early; nor did he have to keep a regular schedule, per se.

So, when it came to the big-picture macro, Mooney knew that he had it extraordinarily good. There were so many reasons for him to be happy. His laidback lifestyle was nothing to sneeze at. Few guys his age had the great fortune of being able to live the way he was living, unless they had compromised their values and sold out. But that wasn't the way it was in his case. The last thing he'd ever want to do would be to hurt someone else or join the conglomerate rat race.

No way.

Mooney might have his flaws, but he wasn't a selfish me-me-me scoundrel who was only out to feather his own nest. That wasn't how he wanted to live his life. He had a strong moral code that he tried his best to adhere to. His mantra was "do no harm to the planet," and that also included making an effort to do no harm to his fellow human beings, too – if he could absolutely avoid it.

Moreover, since he wasn't a naïve innocent – Mooney was well aware that there were millions of earthly inhabitants (walking around in expensive three-piece suits) who actually didn't deserve much compassion at all. And this was especially true in regards to the way so many money-hungry individuals abused the planet. Such myopic greed made an activist's blood boil. How dare they think they could get away with it? So when it came to disrespecting the environment, there was no wiggle room in regards to

Mooney's own personal beliefs. Yet because he was nothing more than a tiny minnow in a vast ocean of sharks, he was cognizant of the fact that his blog would never make the national news. He only hoped that his eco activism would help mitigate, at the basic level, a few of the glaring climate injustices when it came to saving the environment from further harm.

Indeed, he had to try. His conscience wouldn't let him sit on the sidelines. He felt compelled to fight the good fight, compelled to do what he could to right the many wrongs that were being foisted upon Mother Nature each and every day.

And so, being the dedicated activist that he was, Mooney was willing to bear the burden of nonconformity in order to achieve his goals. He was determined to go the extra mile, giving the save-the-planet cause as much time and effort as he possibly could. He would do what he had to do to get the word out in regards to the tragic inequities which were harming the natural balance of the Earth's ecosystems. As a self-employed blogger, he had committed himself to investing as many hours as it would take, for as many years as would be needed, to educate his readers about the injustices that were being inflicted upon planet Earth. And though he would have preferred to keep a low profile vis-a-via using a fake name when he posted his opinions on the Internet, he refused to be intimidated. He had always used his real name. Yet still, he also had been careful enough to never upload a photo of himself and had, for many years, refused to let anyone take a snapshot of him.

So that's how Mooney had ended up living the life he was living; and that's how his rather atypical career had swerved off the beaten path, branching away from the 9-to-5 norm. He had done what he had to do, knowing full well the risk he was taking. And even though he was walking a slippery tightrope without a safety net underneath him, he was at least getting to enjoy the wonderful beauty of the Pacific Northwest while, at the same time, having the exceptional joy of residing between the Puget Sound and the Cascade Mountain Range in an ecosystem that had huge swaths of conifers. Getting to breathe the fresh oxygen that was being generated by so many tall evergreens (which he could hug and commiserate with on a daily basis) – inspired him to no end. For Mooney, this was his ideal biosphere. His "green" banner ads paid the bills, and he got to do what he loved to do. The fear of serving a long jail term might have prevented a less determined activist from getting involved in some of the shadier activities that Mooney had allowed himself to get sucked into; but since he was good at avoiding detection by the authorities, he had been able to manage his anxiety and not let it become too debilitating. Mostly, he had accomplished this by convincing himself that as long as he mitigated the physical evidence which could tie him to an illegal action, then he would never be caught and locked up.

Thereupon . . .

As he attempted to compartmentalize his

thoughts in order for his mind not to be overwhelmed by the near-term uncertainty of yet another assignment that his subcommander would be handing off to him in the next few days . . .

Mooney sighed and continued to stare out the glass door at the lake. He tried to stay focused on how good he actually had it. Being able to gaze out at such an amazing view, each and every day, was a rare treat that few would ever have the chance to experience. The edge of Lake Whatcom was only twenty yards from the bungalow's back deck; yet what made the location even more appealing was the fact that this was one of those expansive bodies of water where the opposite shore was far enough away, maybe three quarters of a mile or so . . . which meant that when nighttime fell, the lights from the homes on the other side of the water sort of twinkled with cutesy auras.

For Mooney, this truly was paradise. Having grown up in Louisiana, he reveled in the fact that this type of hilly terrain was completely different than anything he had ever experienced before. Besides having a pristine body of drinkable water only a few yards from the back deck, he could also peer up at the looming foothills. And not that far away, he knew there was a beautiful snow-capped mountaintop (that was out there somewhere, but he couldn't actually see it from the bungalow's rear door due to the close proximity of the opposing foothill).

So . . .

This wasn't one of those high-priced vacation

views which an escapee from rush-hour traffic only got to experience for two weeks out of the year. No, not at all. This was 24/7. The tall trees and the hilly terrain would (hopefully) always be there for him to enjoy. Mooney was seriously smitten. Indeed, this was the very first time he had ever lived in a place where he could actually drive half a mile and look off in the distance at a dormant volcano shrouded in snow.

Oh, wow. Talk about the great outdoors being right outside my door.

Yes, indeed. Mooney savored the remarkable scenery, knowing that it was a rare gift. So each morning, before he sat down at his desk, he would always have to pull himself away from the sliding glass door and, rather reluctantly, plop himself down in the alcove in front of his computer in order to decide what he wanted to blog about. Most days he would be inspired by some sort of something and simply start typing away, using the notes that he had jotted down in his journal from the day before. But sometimes, if he didn't think his notations were worthy enough or if Becky hadn't tipped him to some sort of something, like she had done that morning, or if the cobwebs continued to cloud his thoughts before he had finished his second cup of coffee – he would get up from his desk and go back and look out the glass door for inspiration, hoping to see something of interest.

Yeah, well, it was a rather uncommon way to start a workday, but it tended to be quite productive for his needs.

Chapter Nine

When business slowed down, there wasn't much to do
but to wait for it to pick back up. Sometimes a whole
day would creep by without anyone calling and
ordering flowers, and other times they would have way
more customers than they could handle. Having
worked for Casey for almost two years, Zetty was glad
she was such an easygoing boss. When there weren't
any pending orders that needed their attention, they
would pass the time by talking about whatever they
wanted to talk about. Sitting behind the counter next
to the cash register, it wasn't as if they had to worry
about saying anything that might upset anyone else,
because when a customer did stroll into the flower
shop, the little bell above the front door would ring,
and they would then change the subject, if need be, so
they wouldn't get themselves in trouble.

And since there weren't any floral arrangements
that had to be rushed out the door that particular
afternoon, nor was there anyone browsing the display
shelves – this meant that they had the little shop all to

themselves.

"Casey, do you ever have weird dreams?" Zetty asked as she doodled on a notepad.

"All the time."

"Like, nightmares?"

"No, most of my dreams are kind of, I don't know, kind of mixed up TV commercials with a bunch of funny-looking people I've never met before. So, y'know, it's not like I see horrible things and wake up sweating or anything like that, if that's what you mean."

"TV commercials?"

"Well, I mean, they're not real TV commercials, of course. They're just these little moments of people doing dumb things, and I don't have any idea why they're doing what they're doing."

"Strangers? People you don't know?"

"Yeah, most of the time. But every now and then I'll dream about someone I know. But those don't make any sense, either."

"Like what?"

"Well, a couple of weeks ago I dreamed I was floating in a swimming pool that was filled with ice cubes, and my mom suddenly jumped in with her clothes on. Then I looked down, and I saw I wasn't wearing a swimsuit, and she took off her coat and handed it to me."

"Oh, wow. That's pretty weird. So what do you think it meant?"

"I don't know, Zetty. I couldn't figure it out. It was just a dumb dream."

"I had a strange dream last night."

"I hope I wasn't in your dream."

"No, no one was in my dream, 'cept me. But it was kind of strange, and I don't know if I should tell you or not."

"Oh, c'mon. You can tell me. I promise I won't tell anyone."

Sighing, Zetty thought about it for a moment, then decided to only tell Casey part of her dream because she didn't want her boss getting the wrong idea in her head. "Okay, well, it started off foggy. I was walking along this damp sidewalk, and I came to this huge tree that was growing out of the concrete, um, right in front of me."

"A tree?"

"Uh-huh. A really big tree. It had flowers blooming on its branches."

"What kind of flowers?"

"Birds of paradise."

"Yeah, that is kind of weird."

"Uh-huh. That's what I thought. But then it got even weirder when the tree started walking along the sidewalk in front of me."

"The tree had legs?"

"Uh-huh."

"What kind of legs?"

"Well, to me it looked like it had short stubby legs with web feet, like a giant duck."

"No way."

"Hey, I can't make these things up, Casey. I saw a

bunch of bird of paradise flowers growing on the tree's branches, and she had web feet like a duck."

"Wait. How'd you know it was a girl tree?"

" 'Cause she had long blonde hair and wore a pink dress."

"Oh, wow. That's really strange."

"Uh-huh. That's what I thought. But then it got even weirder. When I asked her if I could pick some of her flowers – she, like, got all mad at me and said her flowers were her babies, and then she started to cry 'cause she didn't want me killing her babies."

"My gosh. You really do have strange dreams. I never have dreams like that."

"It was sort of disturbing. I've been thinking about it all day. I was wondering what it meant."

"Zetty, it's just a dream. I don't think you should worry too much about what it means. It's not like it really happened or anything." And, as she said this, Casey leaned over and looked down at the doodles that Zetty had drawn on the notepad. Taking up most of the page, she had sketched out a sad-looking tree with three doves perched on its branches. "Interesting."

"But that's not what it actually looked like, of course. The tree in my dream didn't look like that 'cause she was in a dress, and I also penciled in real birds instead of the orange flowers."

Pointing, Casey saw something in the doodling that caught her eye. "Okay, so, what's that?"

"What?"

"Right there. Those two thingies under the tree."

"Oh, those. I didn't even realize I'd put those there. Huh, what do you know?"

"They look like . . ."

"Gravestones."

"Uh-huh. That's what they look like to me, too."

"Well, a few days ago I went up to the cemetery to visit my parents. Maybe that's where those came from."

"Oh, I get it. You mean, like, a Freudian slip, huh?"

"I guess so. But I left something else out, too."

"What did you leave out?"

"I didn't draw the strange man who wanted me to buy a statue of an angel. He told me I should put an angel next to my mother's grave. Talk about a weirdo."

"Another stalker?"

"No, I don't think so. He was just trying to sell me a statue, that's all. But he was, like, really creepy. I've never liked guys who smoke cigars."

"I hate that smell."

"Yeah, well, but nothing happened. He didn't ask me out on a date or anything. He just wanted me to buy a statue of an angel, that's all."

"Sounds like he was a salesman."

"Maybe so. I don't know."

"Men."

"Uh-huh. Anyway, I'm glad he wasn't in my dream."

"It was just a dream, Zetty. I wouldn't worry too much about it."

"I know. But, I mean, because it was so weird, it

did get me to thinking about what plants must, y'know, think about us when we pick their flowers."

" 'Think about us?' They don't have brains, Zetty. They're just dumb plants."

"But, like – what if they're actually smarter than we think they are? What if they don't want us killing their flowers?"

And just as Zetty said this, the bell above the front door tinkled, warning them that a customer had entered the shop. It was a middle-aged lady carrying a nearly dead fern in her hands. At first glance, it looked as though the plant's fronds had turned brown from over-watering. So it was quite possible that the poor fern was being tortured by too much love.

Watching the lady walk toward the cash register, Zetty motioned to Casey, letting her know that she would be in the backroom if her boss needed her for anything. She didn't want to have to stand there and make small talk with the lady since Zetty always got a bit emotional when she saw one of the plants she had cared for end up in such bad shape. Casey could do the honors of telling the lady what she was doing wrong.

From a quick glance, it looked as if the fern was lucky it had been brought back into the shop. Its discolored fronds probably wouldn't've lived another couple of weeks. Such critical-care emergencies never ceased to amaze Zetty. She absolutely couldn't understand why so many plant owners were completely dysfunctional when it came to the simple care and feeding of a potted plant. It seemed as though everyone wanted to think of themselves as having a green thumb, but few were actually smart enough to follow the easy-to-read instructions which came with each plant that was sold in the shop.

More was not better when it came quenching a plant's thirst.

Chapter Ten

Having received yet another set of orders from Darwin, Mooney now had to decide how to implement his new assignment without telling his sister why he was doing what he was doing. Darwin's note, written via invisible ink inside a ramen noodles cartoon, had instructed him to be prepared to hide a higher-up in his home. The Flock needed an out-of-the-way safe house, and they needed it to be move-in ready by the end of the month. This was an upper-committee top priority. Yet the problem was, Mooney would have to come up with a believable cover story (which would pass muster with Becky) so as to explain why a stranger would be moving in with them.

So . . .

Having spent the last few days, on and off, sorting through a handful of possible scenarios, Mooney finally had come up with a viable lie. It was the best fabrication he could think of to fit the situation considering the gotta-get-it-done circumstances. Yet because he had a slight bit of trepidation – since he was somewhat unsure if his lie would, in fact, be believed – he had decided to wait for the most opportune moment to spring it on his sister. And fortunately, this was his night to cook dinner, and so he hoped his subterfuge wouldn't be challenged, thinking that it might not cause a stir if it coincided with Becky having a full stomach. He told himself that by spinning his lie when she was in a good mood, then – more than likely – she would be a bit more receptive to what he was telling her and less likely to pick up on his falsification.

Thereupon, after having whipped up a one-course meal of organic veggies and pasta, Mooney bided his time and didn't say anything, thinking he would wait until they were halfway through their meal. For the first ten minutes, their conversation had simply plodded along through inconsequential exchanges of little importance, mainly focusing on the sudden turn in the weather and the diminishing harvest from their garden. So the initial part of his plan had gone off without a hitch. They were sitting at the kitchen table, eating a leisurely meal, and Becky seemed to be in a good mood.

"What spice did you put in the sauce?" she asked.

"Garlic olive oil and lemon juice."

"Tangy. I should get you to cook all my vegan dishes."

"You wish."

"Well, one of these days you're going to come around. They say once you go vegan, you'll never go back."

"Uh-huh. Sure. Seems like I read somewhere that a lot of people backslide all the time. They have these uncontrollable cravings for red meat and then pig out on animal-protein binges."

"Traitors. Vegetarianism is not a fad you can turn on and off, Moon. It's sustainable living, and it's just as important as eating local."

"I know."

"You'll come around one of these days. Another big E. coli scare, and you'll change your tune."

Sensing that he may have waited too long to explain to her what he needed to explain to her, Mooney then sucked in a deep breath and went for it, hoping the carbs from the pasta were still flooding her brain with their feel-good serotonin. "I guess this is as good a time as any to tell you the bad news. I'm not making enough money, Becky. My ads aren't pulling in as many clickthroughs as they used to. So I don't know how I'll be able to pay my half of the rent."

"Oh, no."

"Yeah, it's pretty bad."

"What are you going to do?"

"Well, I thought about getting a part-time job to bring in some extra cash. Y'know, keep the blog going and also have a regular paycheck."

"That might work, huh?"

"Yeah, but there's the problem of finding a job that someone will hire me to do. The unemployment rate is kinda high right now. And, like, I really don't want to stop writing this blog series I've been working on. I think convincing people to stop the coal trains is way too important not to finish."

"Yeah, I can understand why you feel that way. It is pretty important." Becky then stabbed the last piece of pasta on her plate and lifted the fork up to her mouth. "For sure. I don't think you should stop writing it."

"Well, I certainly don't want to put it on the backburner, but I still have to make enough to pay the rent."

Chewing her food, Becky swallowed and took a sip of water. "I tell you what. I have a little money saved up. I can loan it to you if you want."

"Thanks, but I don't want you burning through your savings. You might need it for a rainy day, and we both know how much it rains around here."

"Oh, stop. I'm serious."

"I know you are. And, like, I appreciate the offer, but I was thinking about doing something that's actually more sustainable. I wanted to pass it by you first . . . see what you think."

"Hey, you know I'm all for sustainability."

"Okay, so – what about we take in a roommate, and the roommate helps us pay the rent? Problem solved."

"Moon . . ."

"What?"

"Where are they going to sleep? We only have two bedrooms."

"In my room. I'll sleep on the sofa."

"In your room?"

"Uh-huh."

Giving him a quizzical look, she repeated herself. "In your room."

"Un-huh – 'cause I'm sure you don't want anyone bunking with you, right? And, y'know, I don't see how we could make much money if we offered to let our new roomie sleep on the sofa."

Becky blinked her eyes and shook her head. "Moon, a roommate? You know how I am about that type of stuff."

"Look, it just depends on the person, okay? Oh, and I forgot to tell you that an old friend of mine from college just sent me an email, asking me if I knew of a place in town that wouldn't be too expensive to rent."

"Like, he's moving here? Who is this guy?"

"No, he's not looking for a place for himself. He's not the one moving here. It's for a friend of his."

"A friend of a friend?"

"Look, I know it sounds a little sketchy, so that's why I'm having his friend drop by to make sure it'll be a good fit."

"Is this, like, a he or a she?"

"I don't know. My friend didn't say."

"Moon . . ."

"Hey, look. It'll be fine, okay? My friend's a nerd. He doesn't even drink, so it's not like he's hooking us up with a party animal. I was surprised he even asked me. The guy only had a couple of friends in college.

Most of the time he had his head stuck in a textbook."

And thus . . .

The deed had been done, the lie had been told, and Becky had gone along with the plan, not asking any more questions and agreeing to give it a shot. Nonetheless, Mooney regretted not being able to tell her the truth; but still, it was for her own good. He rationalized his shading of the truth by telling himself: "What she doesn't know can't get her in trouble."

Life was complicated, especially when it came to flat-out lying to your sister.

Anyway . . .

The next day UPS delivered a small nondescript package to their door. It was the encryption update he had been anxiously waiting for, having placed a back-order request over a month ago. Not wasting time, Mooney immediately loaded the CD into his optical drive and clicked through the install instructions. The pop-up menu on the 5.2 software matched what he had seen on Darwin's computer when his subcommander had performed his own sleight-of-hand encryption all those many weeks ago.

So now . . .

With his desktop finally integrated with the updated cryptography program and his IP identity safely hidden from the invasive authorities, Mooney could again securely communicate with the Flock via email.

Then . . .

Three days later, when Mooney was coming back

from his afternoon jog, he saw a stranger waiting on the steps of the bungalow's front porch. She had a checkered scarf around her neck. A carry-on suitcase and a backpack were sitting beside her. It was quite obvious that this was the Lifesaving Eco Activist Flock operative he had been told to expect.

"Hey."

"Hi. I hope I don't have the wrong address."

"Are you here to meet someone?"

"Are you Mooney?"

"Yeah, that's me. Wanna come in for a cup of tea?"

"Okay."

And with that exchange of pleasantries – he smiled, strode up onto the porch, and unlocked the front door. "Did you have any trouble finding the place?"

"No, a friend dropped me off. He had a pretty good map." Standing up, she grabbed her backpack and suit-case.

Turning to help her, Mooney reached down to pick up her carry-on bag. "Here, let me get that for you."

"No, it's okay. I've got it."

Noticing her independence streak and not being at all surprised, Mooney then led her inside. "Your room is down the hall. You can drop your bags in there."

"Nice place. I love old houses."

"Me, too. I think this one was built in the 1930's."

"Cool. The older the better." Smiling, she then followed him to his vacated bedroom, which he had already prepared for her arrival. He'd boxed up his stuff and had moved most of it into the living room.

"It's not anything fancy," he said, stopping in the bedroom's doorway.

"Oh, wow. It has a view. No one told me about the lake," she said as she eased her suitcase down next to the chest of drawers and dropped her backpack on the bed.

"Lake Whatcom," he said, nodding at the window. "On the other side of that foothill is Mount Baker."

"What's Mount Baker?"

"That's our local mountain with snow on top of it."

"Nice."

"Do you ski?"

"Cross-country."

"Then you're in the right place. Baker gets a lot of snow. Of course, it's not a biggie like Aspen or Snowbird; but it doesn't take that long to drive up there from here."

Hearing him say this, her body language tensed up ever so slightly. "I guess you know some environmentalists think ski resorts damage the ecosystem."

"I know. It's a tough one to rationalize. But I don't think there are any easy answers when it comes to the pros and cons of land usage. You have to pick your fights."

"Do you ski?"

"I used to. Gave it up. Ski slopes kill too many trees."

"Oh, so you were testing me, huh?"

"You might could say that, I guess."

Hearing him admit his hidden intent, his new housemate then offered him her hand. "I'm Tammy Treadwell."

"Mooney Waters. Nice to meet you, Tammy," he said, shaking her hand.

"So, are there any other roommates?"

"My sister Becky lives here, but she's not in the info loop, if you know what I mean. She has the other bedroom."

"Oh, she's your sister, but she's not . . ."

"No, I've never told her anything about any of this. So we have to be careful what we say."

"I understand." Tammy then nodded her head, turned, and glanced down the hall. "There's only two bedrooms?"

"Only two, which means I'll be sleeping on the sofa."

"Oh, c'mon. I can't let you do that. I can't let you give up your bedroom."

"Hey, don't worry about it. It's okay. I don't mind. I told Becky you'll be paying your share of the rent as a way to explain why you're here. I mean, I had to tell her something. So now the only logical thing for me to do is to sleep on the sofa. That way she won't get suspicious."

"Oh, I see." Tammy then stepped over to the bed and pressed her hand down on the mattress, looking as though she was checking out its comfort level. "What does your sister do?"

"She's in college, working on her master's at the university. Environmental Studies."

"I like the sound of that."

"Yeah, she's trying. She means well. She's off at class right now and won't be back for a couple of hours."

Grabbing her backpack, Tammy unzipped one of its pouches. "So have you ever thought about bringing her into the Flock?"

"Yeah, I've thought about it. But I think she's too, I don't know how to say it. She's too . . ."

"Too normal?"

Chuckling, Mooney couldn't help but smile. "Yeah, something like that. Too normal. That pretty much describes her."

"Hey, it's okay. I know I'm not normal by most people's standards. But we all can't be like everyone else, can we? Diversity is a good thing, right?"

"That's true. A good habitat needs biodiversity, that's for sure."

" 'I will follow my instincts, and be myself for good or ill,' to quote John Muir."

Mooney couldn't help but smile. "Cool. I like that. Maybe I'll use it in my next blog."

"I'm looking forward to reading it."

"Well, y'know, I guess I should, like, go take a shower. Please, make yourself at home. Glad you're here. If you need anything, just let me know." Mooney then excused himself and retreated down the hall.

Then a bit later . . .

In the shower, as the warm water splashed down on his shoulders, he ran the particulars through his mind as to what the two of them had said, wanting to make sure he had covered all of the important details, hoping that he hadn't missed anything crucial. Tammy Treadwell looked to be close to his own age, give or take a few years. She had arrived with a grungy, outdoorsy look – seeming to appear as if she had spent the last couple of months camped out in a rainforest. Her long black hair and piercing green eyes reminded him of a black panther. She even moved with the confidence of a big cat, displaying a relaxed willfulness. On first impression, she definitely appeared to be seriously focused. She certainly didn't come across as a namby-pamby.

A beautiful woman with a strong will. Always a challenge.

As he scrubbed his face with soap, Mooney suddenly realized that he had forgotten to tell her about his nerdy friend from college (the one he'd mentioned to Becky). Not wanting to leave a gapping hole in his cover story, he would have to remember to tell Tammy a few of the missing details so as to pacify Becky if the topic ever came up in a conversation. It was always the little stuff that would come back and bite you if you weren't careful. A good falsifier had to be prepared for the unexpected in order to avoid any unforeseeable missteps. In the eco underground, an activist could easily stumble and break something, like his own neck, if he didn't constantly stay on his toes.

Mooney pretty much knew that he would have some challenging months ahead of him if Tammy decided to stay around for very long.

Chapter Eleven

If he hadn't been so far in the hole, with only ten dollars in his pocket, he certainly wouldn't be driving up the hill, intending to check out what Gartok had told him a couple of days ago. Stoneface didn't like doing this type of stuff, but he also didn't have much of a choice. He desperately needed the money.

After turning off the paved street and parking in an out-of-the-way clearing down at the far end of the park . . .

Stoneface hiked through a patch of thorny brambles and began to make his way into the woods. Once he was under the canopy of the tall trees, it wasn't long before he found one of the many trails that snaked through the towering branches.

For the first hundred yards or so, it was all uphill. There was a steep incline, and he had to stop to catch his breath. Stoneface was out of shape. Living the way he was living, he never did much outdoor exercise or, for that matter, any sort of exercise at all. He'd had his fill of strenuous exertion in high school after having played football for three damn years. All of those repetitive workouts had pretty much soured him on boring calisthenics. He thought life was too short to waste his time on such stuff. He would rather be chiseling marble and clogging his arteries.

Anyway . . .

As he continued up the hill, sucking in as much oxygen as he could, Stoneface was suddenly startled when he saw a speedy runner come whooshing down the trail in front of him. She was decked out in tight-fitting spandex. Her boobs bounced up and down like cantaloupes. Yep, she was a real sight to behold. And from the expression on her face, she seemed to be totally zoned out . . .

With her mind on more important things, other than what she was doing.

Sexy women. Bellingham could always use more sexy women.

But then . . .

As she hurried lickety-split past him, she didn't acknowledge his presence or even seem to notice him at all. It was as though he wasn't even there.

Checking out her backside, Stoneface couldn't help but get an eyeful. Her red running outfit clung so snugly around her butt that it seemed as though he was staring at a nude body.

Almost, but not quite.

Too bad this wasn't a nudist park. If it had been, then maybe Stoneface would've had a reason to start partaking of some sort of regular exercise himself. With shapely gals like that bouncing their bods in the great outdoors, it would be tempting to take up hiking. Her legs, shoulders, and behind were exceptionally well proportioned. He thought her curvy dimensions would make for a very sexy statue.

But then . . .

Feeling a slight muscle ache in his legs, Stoneface told himself that he hadn't come there to find a woman. And so, once this hottie had trotted far enough away that her jiggling butt couldn't be enjoyed anymore, Stoneface turned his gaze back to the trees that were growing next to the trail. Having not been to the park in a few years, he had forgotten how mature the woodland actually was. Many of the trees were over a hundred feet tall, and most were Douglas firs. He didn't know the names of the other trees, but they certainly didn't look like noble firs to him. And since his hunt was limited to six-footers, he suddenly realized that finding himself some cuttable Christmas trees wasn't going to be as easy as he'd first thought.

Moving ever deeper into the park, he turned off the main trail and strode onto a thin side trail, walking under the green branches and peering into the underbrush for any signs of new growth. After about five minutes, he finally stumbled upon a couple of young trees. The only problem was . . . they were the wrong type of evergreen. They weren't noble firs. But still, it was an encouraging sign. Now he would just have to find the right location, find some older noble firs; and he was pretty sure he'd eventually come across some young'uns growing nearby.

After another twenty minutes of scrounging back and forth through the forest . . .

Then backtracking into the deeper, thick brush per an overgrown path that narrowly wove its way into the dense woods – Stoneface soon began to second-guess himself and was just about ready to call it quits. He thought his chances of finding any six-foot-tall Christmas trees were about as good as stumbling upon a needle in a haystack. But then he remembered that Gartok had mentioned something about the cemetery, which meant that maybe his partner in crime had seen the little firs over in that particular part of the park.

Not wanting to squander anymore of his time, and having now realized that he might have been searching in the wrong spot, Stoneface decided to go back down the hill and walk over to where the trail meandered by the graveyard. Yet remembering what had happened to him once before, he told himself that he didn't want to cross into the actual cemetery because he wanted to avoid talking to a certain concrete angel which a sleazy knockoff artist had, for some stupid reason, birthed from a lousy form-fitting mold. Fifty years ago, some jerk had sold that ugly-looking angel to a grieving family; and the poorly done statue had then been used to mark the interment where the grieving family had buried one of their dearly departed relatives. So whoever the guy was who had made the cheapo angel – well, he hadn't done a very good job. He'd scrimped on the statue's height, which meant that his bastardized concrete angel was a good bit smaller than an average-size person. Her pint-sized wings looked like pigeon feathers, and her nose was way too long. Her presence in the cemetery was an insult to all of the hardworking stonecutters who still did their work the hard way with a chisel and mallet. In other words, no legitimate artist with any integrity would ever have cut corners by being so cheap as to use a poured-cement mold. Such dumbass knock-off artists absolutely had no scruples whatsoever. They really didn't care about what type of life their mutant creations would have to live once they'd been placed in whatever location. All these shady characters cared about was making their money as quickly as they could.

Goddamn them to hell.

And so . . .

As Stoneface crossed back over to the main trail, he was heading back down the hill when he heard some joggers coming up behind him. The two were blabbering on about how they needed to find a way to stop an oil company from strip-mining the tar sands in Alberta. When they got to within a few yards of him – they hushed up, seeming not to want to spill the beans and have him hear what they were talking about, acting as if it was some sort of big secret or something.

Damn environmentalists. They were so jackass uppity. What did it matter if someone overheard their conniving plans to save the goddamn planet?

And, y'know, just because he wasn't wearing a fancy jogging suit, that didn't mean they were better than him. His khaki overalls were probably a hell-of-a-lot more comfortable than the clingy polyester outfits they had rubbing up against their inner thighs.

Getting pissed off (as they hurried around him), Stoneface spit on the ground . . . just missing the running shoe of the taller dude. The guy probably thought he was being so cool wearing his putrid green Day-Glo sneakers. He was lucky Stoneface didn't puke on them.

What a stupid imbecile. There was nothing worse than a snooty tree-hugger, and there seemed to be more and more of them moving to Bellingham every year. They were all over the damn place.

Anyway . . .

It then took Stoneface another ten minutes to walk down to the lower end of the park . . .

Slowly trudging along without overexerting himself . . .

When he eventually came around a bend . . .

As he made his way through a dense stand of trees . . .

And he suddenly gazed upon what he had been looking for. Looming upward as tall as a four-story building, he stopped and stared up at the branches of three noble fir trees. They were growing in a small clearing, which was a little ways off the trail. Their trunks looked to be several feet wide. Striding closer, Stoneface then spied two young trees that were sprouting up out of the ground on the other side of the clearing.

Bingo!

The two young'uns looked to be the right height. They couldn't've been more than six-feet tall. It looked like he was going to make a few bucks after all.

Hoping to find more Christmas trees, Stoneface then spent the next ten minutes scouring the woods near the big firs. He thought for sure there would be more little ones growing nearby. He circled around this way and that; but for the life of him, there weren't any more to be found. It appeared as though the proud evergreen parents had only conceived two little bambinos.

Shaking his head at the prospect of only making forty bucks, Stoneface wasn't sure if he wanted to take the risk and go through the effort of cutting the trees down. The odds of him getting caught weren't that great, but that wasn't what really concerned him. He was instead trying to decide if it actually would be worth it for him to exert the needed energy and come all the way back up there, late at night, and waste his time just to make a few measly dollars.

Scratching his chin as he took a moment to think about it, he turned and looked down the trail. He was now standing near the edge of the park and was only yards away from the cemetery. A long grassy lawn, wider than a city block, covered that part of the graveyard. Looking across the fence at the rows of headstones, his eyes were drawn to the hellish concrete angel with the awful-looking pigeon wings. There she was, right where she had been the last time he'd seen her, guarding the graves that surrounded her. Her ugly face hadn't change a bit. Yet what was even more disturbing was the way she stared straight back at him.

What impudence. The gall she had to look at him like that, giving him the evil eye.

But that was the way cheap imitation angels were. They were notoriously two-faced, and many of them had an angry demon living inside them. Blinking his eyes to make sure he was seeing what he thought he was seeing, Stoneface was certain he saw her wings flutter for a brief second . . . and her nose twitch.

Uh-oh. That wasn't a good sign. The damn demon inside her looked as though it was itching to cause some trouble.

And that's exactly what proceeded to happen when . . .

Ever so slowly . . .

The angel's whole body came to life; and she turned a crimson red, which meant that she was definitely possessed. When she raised her hand up in front of her face and shot him the bird, he had no doubt that the dark side was in control of her devilish soul.

How dare she do such a thing?

To him, it looked like she was going out of her way to provoke him. And try as he might not to, he couldn't help but get mad. She obviously was toying with him. Now, of course, he had no choice but to walk over there and put her in her place and to give her a piece of his mind. He wasn't about to let some deformed concrete atrocity insult him like that.

And so . . .

Unable to control his temper, that's exactly what Stoneface did. He quickly strode down to the steel gate, swung it open, and walked into the cemetery . . .

Making his way over toward the angel. "Hey, what the hell's wrong with you? Don't you have any goddamn manners? Why are you trying to make trouble?"

But she didn't flinch. She didn't respond to his taunts. She just stood there and acted as if she was a deaf mute.

Hurrying up beside her, Stoneface stopped and stared straight into her piercing eyes. "Oh, c'mon. Don't play games with me, goddamnit! I know you're an incubus. It won't do you any good to try to hide it." And as he said this, he reached his hand out and touched her stomach. He could feel a vibrating warmth emanating from her evil body . . .

As a whiff of brimstone hit his nostrils. Moving his hand up to her chest, he slowly rubbed his fingers across her bosom.

Then . . .

Faster than a dropping guillotine, she slapped him across the face. "Get away from me, you lousy bastard! Don't you dare touch me again!"

"You're a damn demon, aren't you? You're not an angel. I know what you are."

"I said, get the hell away from me! I don't want you touching me!"

"Dammit! You're the one who started this shit. So don't you try to tell me what to do. I'll do whatever I wanna do, goddamnit."

Fluttering her wings and baring her pointy teeth, she curled up her toes and pointed toward a nearby old cherry tree that was growing on a small hill all by itself. "Go talk to her. See what she tells you. I don't want you anywhere near me. Leave me alone."

"I hope your wicked soul ends up in hell. You're lucky I don't knock you to the ground. Don't you ever mess with me again, understand?" Stoneface then took a step back and glanced over at the cherry tree that was several hundred feet away. He had never spoken to a goddamn tree before, and he knew better than to believe what the angel had told him. Talking to a reincarnated statue was one thing, but trying to have a conversation with an old tree would be absolutely asinine. No tree had ever spoken to him before, and it didn't look like this one had a face, two ears, and a mouth, as far as he could tell.

Not wanting to look like a complete fool, and being unpersuaded it would do any good to walk over to where the tree was, Stoneface decided to call it a day and hike back to his truck. He'd wasted enough time hunting down the stupid Christmas trees, and he didn't want to tempt fate by prolonging his stay in the cemetery. The last thing he needed was for something dreadful to happen to him. He already had one feisty demon mad at him, and there was no telling what the other creatures of stone might get it into their heads to do if he lingered around too long. He knew he would be better off if he didn't press his luck. He also had a thirsty date with Miss Bourbon that he had to keep.

Chapter Twelve

So far, so good. His cover story had worked. Becky hadn't asked any hard-to-explain questions about Tammy. Nothing of consequence had come up. Mooney's sister had fallen for his little web of falsifications – hook, line, and sinker. She had assumed that Tammy Treadwell was who she said she was. If Becky had any suspicions that something was amiss, she hadn't said anything to Mooney.

Of course, maybe one of the reasons why the introductions had gone so smoothly was because Becky and Tammy had, relatively quickly, found common ground upon discovering that they both were vegetarians. That alone had them talking on and on about their protein intake and favorite foods. They seemed to obsess on sharing their to-die-for recipes, getting into long conversations with regards to the intricate veggie picks that they both were choosing in order to make sure that they were getting enough of the needed minerals in their diets.

So Tammy's first day had gone much better than

Mooney had hoped. He hadn't sensed any sort of personality conflict. He'd breathed a sigh of relief when he was finally able to snuggle sideways into his sleeping bag in the living room and turn out the end-table light.

The next day, after Becky had gone off to class – Mooney gave Tammy a tour of the neighborhood, thinking it would help her acclimate to her new surroundings. He showed her where the bus stop was, pointed at the convenience store down the street, and took her to the trailhead that led into the park. Their walkabout gave them a chance to interact, and it also facilitated his understanding of how her mind worked. For the most part, they both seemed to be cut from the same cloth. She had asked question after question about the habitat, appearing to want to learn as much as she could as quickly as possible.

And this was quite typical for a L.E.A.F.-er. The group's uniting philosophy, since its inception, had always centered around the practical application of activism. Theoretical perspectives were studied, but the core emphasis was tilted toward giving ecosystems the hands-on assistance that specific locations needed in order to help such habitats become as balanced and healthy as possible.

Hence, Mooney's explanatory tour had pretty much stayed on topic . . .

Until they were returning home and walking past a two-story split-level down the street. That's when Joe, an unemployed neighbor, had moseyed out of his brother's garage. He was wearing a faded flannel shirt and sporting a buzzcut. With a beer in one hand and a cigarette in the other, Joe shuffled up to them and began making a nuisance of himself.

"Hey, bud. Who's this?"

"She's our new housemate."

"Nice to meet you, new housemate. I'm Joe."

"Hi," Tammy replied, quickly waving her hand back and forth in front of her nose . . . trying to keep the cigarette smoke away from her nostrils.

"How's it going, Joe? Did you find a job?"

"Still looking." Joe then took a sip of beer and turned his attention to Tammy. "Welcome to the neighborhood."

"Would you please not smoke in front of me? I'm allergic to cigarettes."

Uh-oh. Not good.

Instantly sensing where this was going and knowing it would be best if he quickly ended the conversation before an argument broke out, Mooney cleared his throat. "Well, we gotta go. Take it easy, Joe."

"Man, what's the rush? Thought you two might want a beer."

"No, thanks. We need to get home before it starts to rain."

"Aw, c'mon. Cool your heels. A few raindrops ain't gonna hurt ya." Joe then pointed down at Tammy's hiking boots. "Nice damn boots. Where'd you get those?"

"Look, Joe. We really gotta go. Take it easy." And saying this, Mooney then tugged on Tammy's arm and pulled her toward the bungalow. He knew that if he didn't break off the one-sided exchange, Joe would continue with his twenty questions, and Mooney was sure that Tammy didn't want to waste any of her time since Joe obviously wasn't the type of human specimen that she would want to chitchat with.

Once they were out of earshot, Tammy finally said what was on her mind. "Who was that guy? Couldn't he see I didn't wanna talk to him?"

"One of our neighbors. He's living there with his brother. He's out of work. A few weeks back he tried to get me to pay him to cut a tree down in our front yard."

"Oh, now I get it. What a sleazebag."

"I've only spoken to him a few times. He's not a friend of mine."

"I would hope not," Tammy said, glancing up at the bungalow's trees. "He wanted to cut down that cedar?"

"No, the Douglas fir."

"Why?"

"I think he needs the money. And maybe he just likes cutting trees down. His dad's a logger."

"A logger? That really makes my blood boil."

"Mine, too. So that's why, if he ever comes up and talks to you – you should just tell him you have other things to do and you're not interested in talking to him."

"Tree-hater."

"Tammy, I probably don't need to tell you this, but neither one of us should do anything that'll attract any undue attention around here. The last thing we need is for a guy like that to get a bead on us."

"Well, I really am allergic to cigarettes, okay? And, like, I think he was hitting on me, too."

"I know. I saw the way he looked at you."

"Oh, great. That's just great. Mooney, what are you doing living in a neighborhood like this?"

"Hey, they're everywhere, okay? Not all northwesterners love trees. Some of them actually come from families that pioneered this area, going all the way back to when they migrated here to clear-cut the old growth and fish out the salmon."

"And, like, here I thought I was moving to eco-ville."

"Well, I kinda thought the same thing, too, when I first moved here. Wish it was true. You just have to know what's what and who's who, that's all. Me, I never assume too much when it comes to people I don't know very well. Takes time to figure out who you can really trust around here. There's plenty of good people in Bellingham, but there's also a bunch of bad apples, too."

Mooney then led her around to the back of the house to show her their vegetable garden. It still had a half-dozen producing plants. He was hoping the little patch of soil would keep supplying them with edibles up until the first frost, thinking that some of the more robust veggies might even hang on until Thanksgiving,

144

if it didn't turn too cold too early. So far, their fall harvest had been well worth the effort.

"Nice. Looks like someone knows what they're doing," Tammy said, walking down one of the rows of greenish plants.

"Becky's the gardener. She likes getting her hands dirty."

"Broccoli, pole beans, carrots. Yummy. What's this?" Tammy asked, pointing to a line of vegetables.

"Mustard greens."

"Oh, mustard greens, huh? I thought Southerns liked collard greens."

"You grow what you can. I like mustard greens, collard greens, and poke salad. But my favorite is turnip greens, actually. How'd you know I was from the South?"

"You have a slight accent."

"Oh, shucks. I thought all those years watching TV as a kid had spared me from having much of a drawl. Hardly anyone ever says anything about it."

"I also read your dossier."

And hearing her say this, Mooney was put in his place. Tammy Treadwell – if that was, in fact, her real name – probably wasn't a low-level worker bee after all. More than likely, she was a L.E.A.F.-er higher-up. As far as he knew, only the higher-ups had access to the membership info. Now he wondered how important she actually was. "Dossier? I was told that no one keeps a background file on anyone. I thought each cell was insulated from all the other cells, so if there ever was a security breach, the names of those in the other cells won't leak out."

"Yes, that's true. But you misunderstood what I meant. There's this website called 'Dossier Search' that anyone can plug a name into, pay a fee, and read a quick background report on whomever. It's culled from a few databases. So I checked you out."

"Oh, okay. That's the first I've ever heard of it. It's 'Dossier Search' dot com?"

"Dot net."

"Dot net. So if I enter your name, what's going to pop up?"

"Well, I wish you wouldn't do that. All the search engines and websites like that . . . they all data mine the stuff that's keyed into their search windows. In your case, your name was already out there in the public domain 'cause you have a blog. So it didn't take much snooping."

"Visibility."

"Exactly. But to answer your question, if anyone does a search of my name – I mean, like, nothing will pop up. I never use my real name on the Net."

"Smart."

"Can't be too careful these days." Bending down, Tammy then pulled a carrot out of the ground and brushed the dirt off it. "Have you ever wondered why carrots stay fresh for so long?"

"No, I've never thought about it before."

"I have. You can put carrots in the fridge, and they'll last for months and months, and you can still safely eat 'em. They don't seem to ever go bad."

"Maybe it has something to do with their orange color."

"Maybe so. Or maybe there's some sort of genetic life force that we're not aware of." Having finished cleaning the foot-long orange root, she smiled and bit into its tip. "Tasty. You can't get much fresher than that."

"You can pick whatever you want for dinner. That's what it's here for."

"Who's cooking tonight?"

"We thought we'd let you have all the fun. Right now I'm behind on my blog, and Becky won't be back 'til late."

"Sure, I don't mind." Nodding, Tammy unzipped her coat and lifted up the front of her loose-fitting blouse, turning it into a basket, of sorts. She then began rummaging through the garden, picking a variety of ripe vegetables. "Oh, I wanted to ask you. How'd you find this place?"

"You mean, this rent house?"

"Uh-huh."

"Becky found it. One of her professor's told her about it."

"Yeah, well, it helps to know the right people, huh?"

"That's true. We really lucked out. I'm surprised the rent isn't higher than it is." And as Mooney said this, it began to rain, ever so lightly. Quickly pitching in, he bent down and helped her glean enough veggies to feed three hungry stomachs. Once they had harvested a sufficient amount for dinner, they hurried up onto the deck and inside the house.

By the time Becky had walked in the front door, well past sunset, the kitchen was filled with intriguing aromas. "Something smells good," Becky said, entering from the living room.

"Your brother talked me into cooking dinner," Tammy said as she slowly stirred a spatula in a wok that was simmering on the stove.

Over at the sink, Mooney was busily washing a head of lettuce. "Becky, I think you said something about being late. So, like, I didn't want her to gag on my cooking."

"What is that?" Becky asked, nodding at the wok.

"Bengal curry. A yogi from India taught me how to make it."

Hearing her say this, an astonished grin washed across Becky's face. "Cool."

Then . . .

In less than half an hour, the three of them were sitting down at the kitchen table with two candles burning in front of them. To mark the occasion, Mooney had uncorked a bottle of French wine and had poured each of them a glass. The dinner plates brimmed with the homegrown bounty, and they began their meal.

After a couple of forkfuls, Becky expressed her utter delight. "It's really good. This tastes like something you'd get in a gourmet restaurant."

"Not too much curry?"

"No, not at all. It's very tasty."

For the first few minutes, Mooney simply sat there and listened to their banter, letting the two of them talk their foodie talk as he ate. He knew when to keep quiet. And since they both were well versed in the intricacies of flavorful ingredients, there was little he could have added to the conversation because his expertise with food preparation was exceptionally limited. Mooney was more of a connoisseur of what tasted good after it had been cooked than being a skillful preparer of a three-course meal. So it was only when Tammy veered the discussion away from food that he broke his silence. This happened when she, yet again, mentioned the South.

"Well, to be honest, I've never known any Southerners before. In fact, I've never ever been to Louisiana."

"Why not?" Becky asked.

"Good question. I guess I just never had the time or the inclination. It's not like the Deep South is known to be a hotbed of bleeding-heart liberalism."

"Well, it used to be much worse than it is now. It really has gotten better in the last twenty years," Mooney said.

"Okay, so – you, like, grew up down there, right? That's where your parents are from?"

"Not exactly. We actually don't know for sure. We were put in an orphanage when we were little kids. The people running the place never told us anything about our parents."

"Oh, sorry. I didn't know you guys had gone through that."

"Bogalusa. South Louisiana. The Knights of the Kingdom Orphanage. And I hated every minute of it. Where are you from?" Mooney asked.

"New York."

"City?"

"State."

"How was that?"

"You mean, growing up?"

"Uh-huh."

"It was okay. A small town. Nothing much to do."

Becky stared over at Tammy with an inquisitive look in her eyes. "I've always wondered what it'd be like to grow up in New York City. I can only imagine how hard it'd be to raise little kids in a place like that."

"I have a friend who grew up in Brooklyn. I don't think it's much different than any other place . . . except you kinda grow up pretty fast, is what I hear happens."

"I guess you have to grow up fast, huh?"

"I guess so. Y'know, you two aren't at all what I thought Cajuns would be like."

"Cajuns?"

"You said South Louisiana, right?"

"That's right. But as far as I know, we're not French Canadian," Mooney said. "At least, I don't think we are. There's a lot of people who live in South Louisiana who aren't Cajuns. And the truth of the matter is, we were actually brought up by redneck

Bible thumpers. The orphanage was run by conservative Protestants, and they're a heck of a lot different than most Cajuns."

"Wait. You mean, right-wing conservatives?"

"That would be a polite term for it, I guess. I don't think you can get anymore right wing than the people who were running that orphanage. They'd read the Bible to us everyday. And we were just little kids, too."

"So, like – what turned you into a bleeding-heart liberal?" Tammy asked, refilling his wineglass.

Mooney glanced over at his sister. "What do you think, Becky? You want to answer this one?"

"Moon thinks our parents were hippies. That's why we have so much nonconformist blood in our veins."

"She's pulling your leg, Tammy."

"No, I'm not. You just don't want to admit it. You said that for years and years. I'm not making it up."

"Hippies? Way down there?"

Sipping his wine, Mooney nodded his head. "Sure. Janice Joplin was from Port Arthur, which is in southeast Texas, right on the border with Louisiana. Or, y'know – maybe our parents were Mississippi freedom riders. Wish I knew what really happened."

Glancing down, Tammy then moved her fork around her plate, seeming to take a moment to digest what she had just been told. From her body language and facial expression, it appeared as though she was struggling to understand something which she wasn't willing to share with her housemates. But seeming to not want to draw attention to herself, she didn't stay mum for very long. Her next question was directed at Becky. "So how'd you get into ecology? Why a master's degree?"

"Moon got me into it. I was a happy-go-lucky conscientious consumer until he changed my thinking."

"Well, actually, you were always into it, Becky. I remember when the other kids were running around catching frogs after that big hurricane blew through, and you got upset 'cause they were torturing the cute little amphibians. You even yelled at them, if I remember it correctly. You threw a fit 'cause you wanted 'em to let the frogs go. You couldn't have been more than five years old."

"Well, y'know . . ."

"Then in elementary school, one time you went out trick-or-treating in that tree costume you made for yourself. You said your arms were branches, and you had those green pieces of construction paper cut in the shape of leaves stuck to them."

"She went trick-or-treating in a tree costume?"

"She looked like a tree to me. But some of the other kids thought she was a swamp monster."

"Stupid dummies. They needed glasses. What did they know? All they wanted to do was get as much candy as they could in their plastic jack-o-lanterns. But Moon, you're the one who was always reading all the nature books and telling me about how the grownups were destroying the planet."

"At least someone listened to me." Taking a sip of

wine, he then slowly looked over at their new housemate. "So how'd you get into the ecology thing, Tammy?"

"Happenstance, I guess. I'm sort of a late bloomer. I think it started when I began reading your blog," she said in a facetious tone.

"Yeah, uh-huh. Like I believe that. Right."

"Well – it's not that far from the truth, actually. It sounds like you two are much more serious about saving the planet than I am. I mean, I wouldn't call myself a real activist or anything like that," Tammy said in a sly tone.

Uh-huh. Right.

Trying not to roll his eyes, Mooney suddenly realized that Tammy wanted to stay deep undercover and didn't want his sister to know what was really going on, which was as it should be. And since L.E.A.F. had a strict protocol about keeping everything buttoned up, he thought it would be best if he changed the subject before Becky suspected anything. "Tammy, feel free to cook anytime you have the urge to toss something together. This is the best curry I've had in a long time. If you can whip up meals like this on a regular basis, I might think about becoming a vegan."

"Don't listen to him, Tammy. He's been eating my meatless dishes for years, but he still won't give up his animal protein."

"Oh, he's one of those, huh? Well, flattery doesn't work with me, Moon. You don't mind if I call you Moon, do you?"

"No, I don't mind."

Tammy then pushed away from the table, stood up, and picked up the empty dinner plates. "You know what, Becky? If the vegans do the cooking, then he won't have a choice but to eat what we cook, right?"

"Sounds like a good plan to me."

Chapter Thirteen

With the rain pouring down, she was glad she wasn't riding her bike. She would have been soaked if she'd been pedaling her two-wheeler. A passing car, speeding through a mud puddle, might have splashed a glob of dirty water up onto her face. Of course, since she was having to travel all the way across town, she never would have taken her bicycle that far anyway. The city bus was just fine with her . . .

Because when she let someone else do the driving, she didn't have to worry about maneuvering her bike around the exhaust-pipe-spewing cars that were clogging the streets . . .

And also because she actually liked looking out the window as the bus driver steered through the traffic snarls. It seemed as though there was always something new to see when Zetty gazed out from a bus window.

And so . . .

Trying her best to stay as upbeat as she could, even though a bunch of thunderclouds were eerily dark up in the sky — Zetty told herself that she needed to think of her trip to the nursing home as a grand adventure. Lying to herself in such a way gave her a good reason to get out of her apartment, in that it allowed her a chance to check out what was going on around town, which meant that she refused to think of her bus trip to see Miss Pineford as an unwelcome chore. Indeed, sometimes a lengthy bus ride could even be quite entertaining if she was lucky enough to get to eavesdrop on a few of the conversations that the other passengers might be having with their fellow seatmates or with a friendly bus driver. And since she'd ridden with this particular driver a number of times before, Zetty had discovered that a lot of people really enjoyed talking to such a gregarious character, i.e., they enjoyed talking to a guy who couldn't seem to shut up for more than half a minute. When he was sitting behind the oversized steering wheel, he seemed to always be in a good mood. At almost every stop he'd crack a joke and get some laughs. The guy truly seemed to relish entertaining the passengers. So it was quite nice that such a transit employee cared enough to want to break the monotony of such a long bus ride.

So Bellingham.

Anyway . . .

After Zetty stepped off the bus, she hurried along the sidewalk. Underneath her raincoat she was carrying a bouquet of flowers in her mother's blue satchel, and she didn't want the blossoms to get wet. Walking as fast as she could, she hastily made her way toward the nursing home, which was a half a block down the street.

Entering the front door, she flipped back her coat's hood, nodded at the receptionist, and quickly strode down the hall to Miss Pineford's room.

Zetty found her foster mom sitting up in bed, looking out the window at the rain. "Hi," Zetty said as she gently eased the door open.

Turning her head, Miss Pineford blinked her eyes and gave her a blank stare, not seeming to recognize her.

"I hope I didn't wake you up. I brought you some flowers." Taking off her raincoat and hanging it on the doorknob, Zetty walked over to the bed and pulled the flowers out of the satchel. She then held up the bouquet so her foster mom could see the colorful blossoms.

Nodding her head, Miss Pineford now seemed to understand what Zetty had told her. This was a good sign since Miss Pineford's mind would oftentimes come and go. Some days her Alzheimer's would be completely debilitating and the disease would keep her from remembering even the simplest of things; but then on other days her memory would actually be fairly good, and she would be able to recall many of the important events in her life that had happened to her years ago.

"Want me to put them in the vase?"

Turning her head toward the bedside table, Miss Pineford looked confused. "The . . . vase? I don't know where it is, sweetheart. Maybe someone took it."

"Well, I'm sure it's here somewhere," Zetty said as she glanced around the room. "Oh, there it is." The vase was sitting at the far end of the windowsill. Stepping over, she picked it up. "I'll go put some water in it." She then went into the adjoining bathroom and filled the flower vase with water from the sink's facet. Sliding the stems of the bouquet into the mouth of the vase, Zetty walked back into the room and placed the vase on the bedside table next to a tissue box.

"That was your mother's."

"No, Miss Pineford, I gave you this vase for your birthday, remember?"

Lifting her wrinkled hand up off the quilted bedspread, the old lady pointed at Zetty's blue satchel. She was staring at the logo of the leafy tree that was embroidered inside the circle of gold snakes. "I remember when they gave your mother that bag."

Realizing what she meant, Zetty smiled. "Yes, ma'am. You're right. This was my mom's. I thought you were talking about the flower vase."

"Did your mother ever tell you where she got that bag from?"

"No, ma'am. She never told me."

"Well, maybe it's time you were told." Coughing, Miss Pineford covered her mouth with her hand. She then turned and, once again, looked out at the rain. Growing outside her window was a small maple tree. And from Miss Pineford's expression, it looked as though she was trying to remember something that she had, for whatever reason, wanted to forget. Her eyes dimmed into a deep sadness.

Giving it a few minutes – since Zetty had learned not to rush the sweet lady – she patiently waited for her to find the right words as she continued to stare out at the maple tree.

But the words never came.

"Miss Pineford, are you all right?"

"Yes, sweetheart, I feel okay."

"You were going to tell me about my mom's blue satchel," Zetty said, sliding the bag off her shoulder and gently laying it on the bed beside Miss Pineford's hand.

Turning her gaze away from the window, and with a slight smile on her face, Miss Pineford pulled the satchel up onto her lap and rubbed her shriveled-up fingers across its logo. "Your mother got this up in . . . up in . . ."

"Canada?"

"Yes, up in Canada. It was given to her near where she was born. I had one just like it."

"Oh, so you had one, too, huh?"

"Yes, that's when we both had gone to the . . . to the . . ."

"You both had gone to the same store to buy it?"

"No, we both had gone to the . . . to the same meeting . . . when we'd joined a group of people who'd come down out of the mountains to save the trees."

"You mean, like the Sierra Club?"

"No, sweetheart. Back then, we didn't know anything about the Sierra Club. Your mother was just out of high school."

"Oh, okay. So I guess she must've been about eighteen years old or so, huh?"

Not seeming to hear what Zetty had said, Miss Pineford slowly turned her head and, yet again, began to stare out at the maple tree. Now the rain was blowing sideways through the tree's branches; and as the wind quickly picked up, two of the tree's golden leaves suddenly floated down to the ground. These were rather large leaves because this was a bigleaf maple tree.

Softly raising her voice in order to get her foster mom's attention, Zetty tried again. "Miss Pineford, you were telling me about when my mom got her blue satchel."

Blinking her eyes, the old lady looked down at the bag's logo. "Well, like I was saying, the man who was leading our group, he liked to make things with his hands. He made these bags himself, and he gave each of us one to take home."

"Oh, so I guess it was sort of like a social club, huh?"

"No, it wasn't a social club, sweetheart. We were . . . we were darn serious about what we were doing. A month earlier, a big fire had burned down a lot of the homes up there."

"That's right. I remember you telling me about that fire once before. You said it had quickly swept through the valley and had killed a lot of people. It was a huge wildfire. And you said the survivors had been mad at the loggers for starting it. There was something about the loggers burning brush so they could move higher up a slope to get to the big trees and cut them down."

"Yes, it was the greedy loggers who started the fire. And it was real bad, too. A lot people lost everything they had." Coughing, Miss Pineford then picked up the satchel and handed it back to Zetty.

"What happened after that?"

Covering her mouth with her hand, Miss Pineford shook her head. It looked as though she didn't want to say anything else about what had occurred all those many years ago, and this may have been because she didn't want to re-experience the painful memories. Or maybe she just needed a nap.

Slowly rubbing her fingers across her forehead, Miss Pineford closed her eyes. Now Zetty wasn't sure if she should ask any more questions or not. She thought it might be better if she just let her foster mom drift off to sleep.

"What were we talking about?" Miss Pineford abruptly asked, opening her eyes.

"My mom's blue satchel."

"Oh, that's right. Well, once we joined that group of mountain folks, and your father joined the group, too, of course – we were sworn to secrecy. So that's why your mother probably never told you about those people."

"Secrecy? Why? What was that about?"

"Sweetheart, I wish I could tell you, but I can't. I

swore I wouldn't ever tell anyone. And since I've kept the secret this long, I guess I'm going to have to take it to my grave."

"Miss Pineford, what was the name of this group?"

"Their names?"

"The name of the group that you joined."

Pausing, Miss Pineford clutched the bedspread and took a moment to think about how she should answer the question. "I'm sorry. All I can tell you is . . . some of their children, or maybe it was their grandchildren . . . well, later on they changed the group's name. It was always a secret, and so they didn't want anyone else to know the name of the group. And I also remember a few of them would come down here and meet with your mother and father, and that went on for a very long time."

"You mean, they'd come down from Canada?"

"Yes, that's when they went under . . . under . . ."

"Underground?"

"I think so. I think that's what they called it. But I want you to promise me that you won't ever tell anyone else that I told you about any of this, okay?"

"No, ma'am. I won't tell anyone. I promise."

"Oh, and before I forget, if anyone ever asks you about your mother's bag . . . you just tell them that a friend of mine gave it to your mother, alright? That's all you should say. But, um, if anyone ever uses the pass . . . the pass . . ."

"Comes over the mountain pass?"

"No, a word."

"A password?"

"Yes, a password. If anyone ever whispers the password in your ear, then it's okay for you to tell them your parents' names and were they're buried in the cemetery."

"Miss Pineford, my mom never mentioned anything about any of this. I don't know what it all means. Are you sure you have this right?"

"Sweetheart, I know I have trouble remembering things. And I wish we had talked about this sooner. But, for the life of me, I'd forgotten about it until I saw your mother's blue bag. I . . . I don't remember you ever having it with you before."

"That's true. For years I kept it in a box, and I just started using it when I bought some new sneakers that sort of matched it." Saying this, Zetty then lifted up her leg to show off her shoes. "See?"

"Oh, look at that. My, my. I don't think I've ever seen shoes that color before."

"I found them at a store in Fairhaven."

Nodding, Miss Pineford again closed her eyes. And, as she did so, the rain began pounding up against the window. Turning to look outside, Zetty noticed a man she'd never seen before . . . suddenly leave the sidewalk, walk over to the maple tree, and reach down to pick up one of the leaves that had just fallen to the ground. Putting a finger up to his lips, he stared straight at Zetty. If the window had been open, she was pretty sure she would've probably heard him *SSSSHHHHING* her.

"Miss Pineford, do you know who that man is out there under the tree?"

But Miss Pineford didn't respond. Zetty's question went unanswered. There was no reply because the old lady's head had slowly nodded forward, and it looked as though she'd fallen asleep.

Taking the hint, Zetty slid the strap of her mom's satchel up across her shoulder and put on her raincoat. It seemed as though she'd worn out her welcome, and it was time for her to go.

"Sweetheart, are you leaving?"

"Yes, ma'am. I think you need a nap."

"Well, I'm glad you dropped by. It's always good to see you. Don't forget the password."

"Oh, wait. You never told me what it was. I don't know the password."

"Yes, I did. I told you the password."

"No, ma'am. You only told me *about* the password, but you never said what it actually was."

"Oh, maybe I forgot."

"You mean, you forgot the password?"

"No, of course not. What I meant to say was . . . I guess I forgot to tell you the password. It's right inside your mother's bag."

"Where?" Zetty asked, opening up the satchel and looking inside.

"Sweetheart, do you see a handmade label in there?"

"Oh, yeah. There it is. I guess that's a label. I've never noticed it before."

"What's written on the label?"

"It says, 'Made in Canada.' "

"It does?"

"Yes, ma'am."

"Oh, I forgot about that. Well, is there anything written on the other side?"

"Yes, you're right. There is something written on the other side."

"No, don't tell me. Keep it a secret. And please don't ever tell anyone else, alright?"

"I won't. I promise."

"Good. Your mother would be very proud of you. I know she'd want you to keep the secret to yourself."

Smiling, Zetty then stepped over to the hospital bed and kissed Miss Pineford goodbye. "I love you."

"Bye-bye. I love you, too."

Turning toward the door, Zetty flipped off the light switch and eased the door closed behind her.

Chapter Fourteen

Having spent their first few days discussing the life-cycles of the local flora and fauna, with Mooney pointing out what he thought could be done to improve the biodiversity of the vast woodland that surrounded Lake Whatcom, he was a little surprised when Tammy began to ask questions about the urban habitat. Specifically, she wanted to learn more about down-town, the harbor, and the rail lines. She seemed to be especially interested in the Central Business District.

So, having been persuaded to share what he knew, Mooney offered to take her on a walking tour of the CBD. An eco activist had to stay up to date on the particulars of the nearest asphalt jungle since the commercial segment of the human habitat was a vital part of the biotic community. The more intel the underground was able to gather as to the big-picture complexities of an economic structure's inner workings, the better the Flock's prognostications would be in regards to what the future might bring vis-a-vis the politics of sprawl management and the associated degradation of the environment. And to this end, Mooney certainly didn't want to come across as a do-as-I-say-not-as-I-do hypocrite. Thus, he suggested to Tammy that they ride the bus downtown, which they did.

When they got off at the WTA station (i.e., at the main transfer hub) – and being as there was a small crowd of people milling about the boarding area between the arriving and departing buses – it took Mooney and Tammy a few minutes to acclimate to the city core. This slight bit of mental reconfiguration required an attitudinal adjustment because they were transitioning from the rather low people density that natural occurred around the lake . . .

Into the much higher concentration of humans in the downtown area. And though this wasn't much of a shock to Mooney's nervous system, Tammy appeared to be somewhat overwhelmed at first. An unpleasant expression immediately had formed on her face, and her body had tensed up. She was either suffering from indigestion, or she didn't like crowds.

But then . . .

As Mooney began leading her through the heart of downtown, her uptight demeanor soon faded once they'd moved away from the prying eyes of the coming-and-going bus passengers. Within a relatively short amount of time, Tammy had eased back into her "listening mode" . . . as Mooney began to explain his thoughts on the good, the bad, and the ugly of what they were checking out. And even though they weren't shopping to spend money, he also had found himself, somewhat reluctantly, referencing his personal-consumption habits as to which businesses were eco-friendly and which ones he thought she should avoid. Organic and sustainability were the catchwords he continuously repeated as he pointed to the storefronts that he felt she might want to consider frequenting during her stay in Bellingham. Between tips on where she could get the tastiest food for a reasonable price (or where she'd most likely meet a likeminded environ-mentalist), he also spiced his talking points with the various ways that a greenie, such as herself, could lower her carbon footprint by buying local.

"So, like, this is it?" Tammy asked after they had spent close to forty minutes strolling around the CBD.

"Yep, this is pretty much all there is to see. If you walk six blocks in either direction, you will have pretty much seen everything worth seeing. Years back, after they built the mega mall out in the suburbs, downtown Bellingham almost became a vacant ghost town. Most of the bigger stores, like the brand-name department stores, all picked up and moved to the mall . . . is what I was told happened when I did some background research for my blog. Then after a few years of ever-increasing blight, this part of the old downtown slowly began to turn around, and now the shopkeepers, if they're lucky – and I mean, really lucky – well, maybe some of them are making just enough to keep their doors open. Most of these places are locally owned. There aren't any big-box stores down here."

"It's quaint, that's for sure. These brick buildings must be over a hundred years old. Feels sorta like going back in time."

"True. And that's what I really like about it. They hardly ever build anything new down here. So to me, it's like stepping into a time warp, in a way."

"I wonder why it hasn't really changed that much after all this time? I mean, this is right next to the bay. Usually people will pay a premium to have a view of the water."

"Good question. Let's walk over here, and I'll show you what's going on." Mooney then led her to the end of the block and pointed toward a humongous industrial eyesore that was pockmarking a sprawling swath of land, which was spread out below them. Four or five blocks away, over at the water's edge, they gazed down from the heights of the CBD toward acres and acres of decrepit factory buildings. "That's downtown's future. The city and the port got together and took control of that old mill site, and now they're planning on bulldozing those buildings. That's a huge hunk of prime real estate because it's right on the waterfront. But get this. The big problem is . . . it might take them twenty years to redevelop it because they first have to spend millions to clean up the heavy metals. The whole area is laced with deadly carcinogens. And the word on the street is, there aren't any deep-pocket investors who are willing to take it on, which means that it's highly unlikely anything's going to happen anytime soon."

"Why will it take so long?"

"Because land-development money has dried up. To flip such a big footprint into condos and office buildings is financially risky. That's over one hundred and thirty acres. See how flat it is? From there to there, that whole mill site runs all along the shore. So if and when they ever turn all that land into a grid of streets, you're probably looking at close to thirty or forty city blocks."

"Which means downtown would double in size."

"Yeah, something like that. Of course, if that much undeveloped land were near the core of a big city like Seattle, then the profiteers would probably be willing to gamble their money on a flip. But since this is Bellingham, the demographics are way too small. For them to demolish that old paper mill, clean up the water bottom and the tainted soil, redevelop the land into a grid . . . that's going to cost a huge bundle 'cause the insiders want to make a fat profit off it."

"Politics."

"Exactly."

"So that used to be a paper mill, huh?"

"Actually, for over a hundred or so years, there were paper, pulp, and timber mills all along this part of the bay. A ton of pollution."

"I wonder how many trees they killed to feed those monsters?"

"Millions. It was really, really bad. They clear-cut and shipped trees in from all over. And, y'know, because it went on for so long, a lot of mercury seeped down into the ground and also built up on the water bottom."

"The greedy crooks. They cut the old-growth, raped the land, made their money, and passed the problem off to someone else."

"Yeah, exactly. But those days are finally over. No one with any sense wants another factory built anywhere near here. People don't want to live downwind of a smelly smokestack that spews stinky fumes in the air. Most of Bellingham has gone green when it comes to the really important stuff like this. The voting public wants fresh air and clean water."

"Thank goodness. It's about time."

"Well, it took them long enough. Let's hope it stays that way."

Tammy sighed and shook her head. "Y'know, except for that hellish lump of cancerous land, it looks like a pretty funky downtown to me. I like the mix of boutiques, little cafes, and the old-timey buildings. But I can't understand why there's so many banks."

"Oh, you noticed, huh? There are a lot of banks, aren't there? There seems to be one on almost every block."

"So, like, what's up with that?"

"I don't know. Maybe it's a cheap place to have a branch office. Or it could be because there's a bunch of retirees who cashed out of California and moved here to get away from the rat race."

"Sounds like fertile ground for fundraising, if you ask me."

And when Tammy said this, her comment instantly caught Mooney's attention. Up until that point, he hadn't pressed her as to why she was in Bellingham hiding out in a safe house. He thought it would be better for both of them if he didn't know what she was up to since some L.E.A.F. members were way more radical than others. Certain aggressive activists also had a tendency to ignore the group's more restrictive protocols. So not being the type to ever want to be *caught* conspiring to commit a violent act (if he could help it), Mooney knew that if he was kept out of the loop as to why someone like her was keeping a low profile, then a jury wouldn't have grounds to convict him as an accomplice since he would've successfully avoided being directly complicit in the other person's criminality (if and when someone such as herself ever did cross the line and conspire to do something that they shouldn't be doing in the eyes of the law). And though Mooney was willing to put his neck on the line when he was interfacing with a complete stranger like ArticGecko, he was savvy enough to only do so if he could control the circumstances and thus be able to quickly disappear without a trace; whereas with Tammy, she knew too much about him, which meant that his risk of being caught was quite high if things went awry.

"Fundraising? Is that why you're here?"

"Actually, I'm always fundraising. It takes money to do what we do," she said with an edge in her voice.

Hearing the tone she used, per sounding a bit

agitated that he had even asked her such a question, had persuaded him not to ask a follow-up. She obviously didn't want to talk about why she was in Bellingham. So, suspecting that there was a good reason she was being closemouthed, in that it was obvious she didn't have a desire to explain the specifics of her assignment – he dropped it.

And since they had already seen most of the important stuff that downtown had to offer, Mooney now only had one more street to show her. "Oh, before I forget, there's something else I think you might want to take a look at."

"Not another coffee shop."

"No, not another coffee shop. I thought you might wanna check out where the bookstores were."

"Nah, that's okay. I never buy books anymore. I have an e-reader."

"No books?"

"To print a book, you have to kill a tree."

"What about used books? These are used book-stores."

"Oh, used, huh? Well, if I can't find a download – maybe I would read a used book if it's been recycled."

"Used bookstores are great places for research. The two we have here are right across the street from each other; and there's all kinds of books on ecology and planting a garden; and they also have a bunch of how-to books on living off the grid."

"It's called a library."

"We have one of those, too; but the bookstores

have a better selection, and you don't have to give them your name. You can pay in cash. The library's a couple of blocks over there," he said, pointing down the street.

"Okay, whatever. I'll take a look at the book-stores."

Thereupon . . .

As they continued their stroll over toward another street, walking past a vacant storefront that had a "going out of business" sign plastered across its plate-glass window, Tammy abruptly stopped and gazed down at a disturbing graffiti tag. A malcontent had spray-painted an anarchist "A" inside a red circle on a brick wall.

"Looks like someone's not happy with capitalism, huh?"

"Seems that way," Mooney said, letting her soak in the ambience.

"Have you ever met any of the local anarchists?"

"Not that I'm aware of. I'm not into that type of activism. I try to avoid street violence."

"Yeah, they do sometimes push it too far, that's for sure. But, I mean, to really change the system, people have to be willing to storm the Bastille and do a few things that not everyone is going to agree with."

"Maybe as a last resort. Maybe if nothing else works. But I think Gandhi's path of nonviolence is actually much more effective, if you ask me."

Shrugging her shoulders, Tammy then turned her eyes back down the street; and they continued on toward the end of the block. For whatever reason, she didn't say anything else about the anarchist movement. Instead, she proceeded to change the subject. "You know, it seems to me, since this part of town has all the essentials – that it'd be the perfect place for central-core living. A person could live downtown, work downtown, buy their groceries downtown . . ."

"Drink downtown."

" . . . and not need a car. Looks like a fairly good habitat for an alternative lifestyle."

"A lot of the locals think the same thing. Even the money-grubbing developers have been ballyhooing core living. That's why they swooped in a few years back and bought up all of the cheap real estate. They were planning on building some pricey high-rise condos, but then the money dried up."

"I don't think you need a fancy condo to live smart."

"I know."

"Simple is better. Rehabbing an old building saves on material."

"Tammy, you're, like, preaching to the choir."

"So I guess you also know that cutting out the long commute is what makes core living so sustainable, right? I mean, we just walked by an apartment building; and living in a downtown apartment is a lot more affordable than buying a new downtown condo."

"Yeah, I know. But affordable housing isn't the real problem. What downtown really needs is more jobs and more places for people to work. That's the problem."

"Well, unless I'm missing something, this whole town isn't really that big. There must be jobs here somewhere."

"Not enough. When the paper mill went belly-up, that threw a lot of people out of work. So now, y'know, most of the jobs are at the university, on the fishing boats, at the hospital, and in retail at the mall."

"I hate malls."

"Tell me about it."

"Moon, from looking at the map, seems to me that many of the jobs which you're talking about would be within biking distance of downtown, or at least near a bus route."

"Yeah, they sorta are. That's true."

"Okay, so – doesn't that mean that a lot of people should be able to live downtown and ride their bikes or, like, take a bus to get to work somewhere that's not that far away?"

"Everyone knows that, Tammy. This is Bellingham, not a hick town out in eastern Washington. We have plenty of serious cyclists who've already given up their cars. Some of them even use their bikes to pull go-along carts when they move their furniture."

"You're kidding me."

"No, I saw it with my own eyes. A caravan of bicyclists hauling a guy's furniture on lightweight tag-alongs."

"Wow."

"Yeah. That's some serious eco, huh?"

"So what you're saying is . . . a lot of people here

176

get it, is that what you're saying?"

"Many do. That's true. Maybe not all of 'em are tuned into the eco channel, but many of 'em are, in fact, down with doing the right thing."

"Except for Joe, right?"

"Except for Joe. There's always going to be exceptions. But still, there are some very determined activists living in Bellingham. We're not the only ones who've flocked into this habitat."

"Be careful," she said, lowering her voice.

"I know. No one can hear us."

"I hope not." She then checked over her shoulder to make sure he was right, but there wasn't anyone on the sidewalk on either side of the street.

"It's cool."

"Okay, so, why aren't you living downtown? I mean, why are you living up on the lake? Don't you think you should be living down here in the core?"

"Yeah, I was wondering when you'd ask me that. And the only excuse I have is that Becky wanted to rent a house with a yard so she could have a garden; and that was the cheapest place she could find. When she came here to start school, I wasn't planning on moving in with her. This place wasn't on my radar. But then after a certain feathery friend asked me to come up here . . ."

"Did you even try to get her to think about downtown?"

"No, because I'd never been here before. I had no clue where she should or shouldn't live. I was living in

Texas. What did I know?"

In front of yet another bank branch, they crossed the street and headed up the sidewalk toward the CBD's tallest building, which was a vintage 1930's high-rise. At thirteen or fourteen stories, this art deco behemoth was a downtown landmark. Most of the surrounding buildings were only two stories high. And because this piece of grand architecture from the Great Depression clearly dominated the skyline, the building's New Deal design loomed somewhat like a bloated Egyptian obelisk over the city streets.

Turning the corner, Mooney and Tammy continued on down the street and walked past a small flower shop. The splashy multicolored lettering on the glass window read: "Stormy Day Flowers."

Then . . .

In mid-stride (as if a light bulb had suddenly clicked on inside her head), Tammy stopped and backtracked to the flower shop's front door, looking as though she wanted to check out a display of poinsettias. But, as it turned out, it wasn't the red-colored potted plants which had caught her eye. Instead it was a six-foot-tall noble fir that was sitting outside on the sidewalk next to the door. "Oh, no. Look at that."

Retracing his steps, Mooney walked up beside her. "What's wrong?"

"That container's too small for a tree that size."

"Yeah, I think you're right. It does look pretty darn small, that's for sure."

"It's like they're torturing the poor plant. That's so horrible."

"Anything to make a buck, huh?"

"It's criminal."

"You know what? I think we should go in there and tell them they need to put it in a bigger container," Mooney said, stepping over and lightly rubbing his fingers across the tree's needles.

Appearing to be getting increasingly upset (yet looking as though she was doing her best to stay calm), Tammy slowly shook her head. "Rule number four. 'Members should not cause a disturbance in groups or in pairs. Only one person at a time is authorized to protest in public. We do not want cell members being recorded together on surveillance tapes.' "

"You have the protocol manual memorized."

"As should you."

"Well, I know what it says, okay? I just thought in this case we could . . ."

"Mooney, there are no exceptions." Tammy then stepped away from the front of the flower shop and quickly moved a few feet down the sidewalk. "You go in and talk to them. I'll wait for you inside that bookstore down the block."

"Okay, use the one that's on this side of the street with the cardboard boxes out front."

"Right, the bookstore that's on this side of the street."

"I'll meet you down there in a few minutes, okay?"

Nodding and waving, Tammy then hurried away.

Sucking in a deep breath, Mooney once again ran his fingers across the needles of the little tree. It was so disturbing to see a plant mistreated like that. The baby fir needed to be in a larger pot so its growth wouldn't be stunted. If a tree that size stayed in too small of a container for very long, its roots wouldn't have enough room to grow, which would eventually turn it into a mutant bonsai.

Opening the flower shop's door, Mooney heard the tinkling of a bell as he stepped inside and walked over to the counter . . .

But there wasn't anyone standing at the cash register. "Hello? Is there anyone in here?" he called out.

"I'll be there in a second," a female voice shouted from the backroom.

Impatient, Mooney turned his back to the counter and scanned his eyes across all of the greenery that was cluttering the shelves along the walls. Stormy Day Flowers had dozens and dozens of potted plants, hanging ferns, and assorted knickknacks. Helping to light the interior, its plate-glass window faced north, so most of the plants were probably only getting a few hours of indirect sunlight each day during the fall months (when there wasn't an overcast sky blocking the solar rays from coming inside). But that wasn't saying much since weeks could go by in Bellingham without any nourishing sunbeams ever breaking through the low-hanging clouds.

Thinking that he must have walked by this place numerous times before without ever stopping to come inside, Mooney was now trying to control his displeasure, which was verging on animosity, because he told himself that he would never buy anything from an establishment such as this. If what was happening inside these walls wasn't a form of plant cruelty, he didn't know what was. And to make matters worse, he was fairly sure that only a few people would even be aware of how awful it was for a potted plant to have to live in such a dimly lit room. Most people thought of flower shops as pleasant retail businesses, fulfilling a public need. But what many didn't realize was that the poor plants (which were being sold out of such storefronts) had, in fact, been uprooted from their natural environments and were simply being trafficked by florists to make a quick profit. Many of the blooming perennials that were being sold in such places would have their reproductive flowers shorn off, while others would be stuck in cheap plastic buckets to live out their lives, being forever imprisoned in shadowy rooms without enough sunlight and thus forced to live under the thumbs of the adoptive humans who had carelessly bought them from such a place and who, many times, wouldn't water them enough or would water them way too much. So for the imprisoned leafy adoptee, such a business transaction would soon turn into a slow, painful death since many well-meaning people didn't know the first thing about properly caring for a potted plant.

To Mooney, the place was a repulsive torture chamber that facilitated horrible suffering.

"Hi, how can I help you?" the store clerk asked, entering from the backroom.

Turning around, Mooney saw a young twenty-something walking toward him at the other end of the counter. She gave him a weak smile as she stopped at the cash register and picked up an order book.

Surprised by her good looks and soft voice, Mooney steadied his temper. He didn't want to overreact and get into a heated argument with an innocent employee. "Is the owner here?"

"No, sorry. Casey had to go make some deliveries. Our driver called in sick today. Is there something I can help you with?"

Looking at the clerk's nametag, Mooney blinked his eyes to make sure he was, in fact, reading it correctly. "You're, um . . . Zetty?"

"Uh-huh."

"I've never heard that name before."

"I know. People tell me that all the time. It was my grandmother's name. She was from Canada."

"Oh, I see."

"You're not some sort of salesman, are you? If you are, you'll have to talk to Casey. But I doubt she'll want to buy anything. Salesmen come in here all the time, and she never buys anything from 'em."

"No, I'm not a salesman. I was just walking by, and I saw that tree sitting outside."

"Oh, the noble fir. That's the only one we have left."

Mooney took a deep breath and steeled himself to

say what he had to say. "Do you know it needs a bigger pot? For a tree that size, that little bitty tub you guys have it in is way too small."

"You think so?"

"I know so. Its roots don't have enough room to grow. You're torturing the poor thing."

Hurrying around to the end of the counter, Zetty quickly walked toward the front door. "I thought it was big enough. Let's go take a look."

Watching her stride through one of the display aisles, Mooney had no choice but to follow behind her.

When she got to the front door, Zetty swung it open and pressed down on a latch, which kept the door from closing. She then stepped outside, bent down, and checked the potting soil of the little fir . . . taking out a smidgen of dirt and rubbing it across her fingertips. "It feels like it has good moisture. It's not dried out. Looks healthy enough to me." Rising back up, she turned and nodded her head. "But, y'know, I think you're right. I guess it could use a bigger pot. I'll talk to Casey and see if she'll want to replant it. The larger-sized ceramic pots cost more, and she has it priced kind of low right now."

Uh-huh. Mooney had expected as much. It always seemed to be about how much extra profit could be squeezed out of a customer. Rarely were people ever focused on the ethics of what was the right thing to do. "Well, if you ask me, that's plant cruelty. No one should mistreat an innocent little tree like that. And all of your other plants are suffering, too. It's absolutely not right."

"What are you talking about?"

"I'm talking about you cutting the stems of the flowers and mutilating them. That's what I'm talking about. And you're also growing potted plants in conditions they don't want to live in. They're not getting enough sunlight. You're slowly killing 'em. Have you ever thought about it from their point of view?"

"Wow. Why are you so upset?"

"Because it pisses me off to see innocent plants harmed by people like you. There should be a law to stop this type of stuff from happening."

Standing in the doorway only a few feet away from her, Mooney watched as a deep regret instantly flooded across Zetty's face. Her eyes began to well up. It appeared as though he'd hit a nerve.

Sniffling, she wiped a tear from her cheek. "I love plants. I really do."

And when Mooney heard the honesty in her voice and saw how unraveled she'd become so quickly when he'd made his accusations, he instantly regretted having said what he'd said. He had obviously misjudged her, and now he wasn't sure how he should proceed. After all, she didn't own the flower shop. She was simply working there. So, in her mind, she had probably never even thought that much about what she was doing. "How much do you want for the tree?"

Reaching down, Zetty turned the price tag around and showed it to him. "Eighty dollars. It's on sale."

184

"Eighty dollars? Are you kidding me?"

Again, she sniffled and wiped her cheek. "Look, I know it's a lot of money; but I swear, we really are trying to do the right thing . . . hoping someone will buy it instead of purchasing a cut Christmas tree that's going to die and get tossed out after New Year's. We never sell dead trees. So if someone buys this live one, they get to keep it inside for the holidays – y'know, like, way early; and then afterwards they can plant it outside in their yard."

"Okay, I'll take it. I can't stand to see it suffer like that," Mooney said, pulling his wallet out of his jeans. "Look. I'm sorry I upset you. I know it's not your fault. You're just doing your job."

Hearing him say this, Zetty brightened her face ever so slightly. "Thanks. I appreciate you telling me that. I honestly do. But, um – you did give me some- thing to think about, that's for sure," she replied, glancing back down at the noble fir. "I mean . . . I never realized I was hurting the plants . . . 'cause, like, I've never thought that much about it before."

"So now you know, huh?"

"Yeah, now I know. I just wish someone would've told me sooner."

Sensing the sincerity in her tone and in the words she was using, Mooney thought she had potential to one day evolve her understanding. So regretting having said what he'd said, Mooney made a snap decision to go out on a limb and offer her a personal tidbit that he normally wouldn't've told a complete stranger. "Listen, if you're really serious about wanting to help plants and do what's good for the environment, there's this eco blog I think you might find interesting. It explains what I'm talking about. I'll write the Web address down for you."

"Okay. Thanks. I appreciate it."

He then pulled the required cash out of his wallet, followed her back to the counter, and paid her for the tree. On a slip of paper, he wrote down his blog address (not telling her his name, of course) . . .

Then he went outside, picked up the tree, and walked down the block toward the bookstore. Try as he might to be strong in the face of adversity, he was still a big softy when it came to crying women. He didn't have it in him to argue with such a sweet person. It seemed that Zetty was clearly quite naïve in regards to the gruesome dark side of the floral business. But then again, if he'd pegged her right, it wasn't her fault. Every day hundreds of thousands of people went out and bought cut flowers, and rarely did anyone ever stop to think about how such a purchase actually facilitated plant abusive.

It was insidious.

Buying a dozen roses was so terribly cruel. And educating the masses was a near impossible task because such ritualized habits were exceptionally hard to change. Yet maybe Zetty would now at least spend a little more time thinking about what she was doing to the innocent flowers. Mooney could only hope she would. He felt, if nothing else, he'd gotten her attention; and he also knew that this was how evolutionary thought, toward a more enlightened understanding, tended to work. Reconfiguring a person's perception of reality was never easy. Getting people to rethink the basics of ecology was a humongous task that few had the skills to achieve.

Anyway . . .

As Mooney slowly made his way down the sidewalk, lugging the noble fir in his arms, he began to wonder if a bus driver would even let him get on a bus with a tree that size. Having been unable to control himself when he had blurted out that he was going to buy the evergreen, Mooney hadn't actually thought it through as to how he was going to get the tree home. And since he was stuck in the situation that he was in, per acquiescing to Tammy's concern for the required protocols, the reason he hadn't asked to have the tree delivered was because he didn't want to give Zetty his name and address. In other words, via adhering to "rule number six," Mooney hadn't wanted his name written down on a receipt and thus have his identity breached via his face being recorded on a possible surveillance tape.

Cameras were everywhere these days.

And so . . .

Having impulsively done what he'd done (without taking enough time to think it through), he now began to realize that his trip home might have a few unexpected hitches, which he hadn't planned on.

Chapter Fifteen

Instead of driving his pickup truck into downtown, Stoneface told himself that he should be headed home. Yet for some damn reason, he had this urge to get in trouble. He was in a bad mood. He felt like slamming his fist into someone's face. And the best place to start a fight was in a bar. But since he only had ten dollars in his pocket, he was also pissed 'cause he knew he wouldn't be able to get really liquored up unless he could talk a barkeep into running a tab. In the last three months, Stoneface had been kicked out of a half-dozen barrooms, having been told not to come back until he had the money to pay what he owed.

So now, if he wanted to lie his way into some free booze, he'd have to find a watering hole where they would still serve him and, hopefully, he would also be able to get an unsuspecting bartender to put it on his tab. And considering how small Bellingham actually was, that left just one place, which he hadn't burned his bourbon bridge at. It was called The Boat Dock; and he was sort of friends with a couple of the bartenders who worked there. As far as he knew, his name wasn't on their do-not-serve blacklist. Moreover, The Boat Dock wasn't a sleazy drunk-infested dive, although it certainly wasn't too fancy, either. It was a working-man's blue-collar bar where thirsty fishermen, hardhat plant workers, and an occasional cheating wife would hang out.

As its name implied, the barroom was located right down on the edge of the water where Arbor Creek flowed into the bay. Sitting high and dry on wooden piers above the tidal flow, the place had a distinctive salty smell to it, sometimes even having a hint of wet seaweed in the air, reminding those who entered its doors as to what was ebbing and flowing only a few yards underneath their feet.

Parking his truck in the gravel lot down the street, Stoneface walked towards the bar's front door . . . passing a panhandler who was spread-eagle on a bus bench, sound asleep. Lying next to the guy was a hand-scribbled cardboard sign which read: "Work for food." So this wasn't the brick-veneer suburbs by any stretch of the imagination. This was a part of town that the homeless folks frequented quite a bit since it was only a few blocks from the Save the Souls Rehab Center. Stoneface knew it well. After having served his time in jail for public drunkenness on a number of occasions, and then having been sent by an old-lady judge to that goddamn get-sober clinic that was only a few blocks away – he'd sneaked out the backdoor of that lousy rehabilitation clinic more than once . . .

Only to be quickly rearrested yet again.

Entering the barroom, Stoneface eyeballed the crowd to see if he knew anyone who might want to buy him a glass of whiskey. Not seeing a familiar face, he walked down to the far end of the bar. It took a couple of minutes for the bartender to make her way over to him. When she did, the neon glow from the beer sign that was hanging in front of the back mirror hit her face, and he recognized who she was. Months back, this same gal had worked at one of the bars he had gotten himself kicked out of.

"What can I get you?" she asked.

"Double shot of bourbon. Put it on my tab."

"You don't have a tab here, Stoneface."

"You know I'm good for it . . . Edrena."

"Edna-Ney."

"Sorry. Edna-Ney. I'm not good with names. I forget names, but I never forget a pretty face. Double shot of bourbon."

"I guess you also forgot what happened at The Blue Goose, huh?"

"That was you?"

"Uh-huh. That was me. You up and skipped out on a sixty-dollar bar bill, and you put that poor college kid in the hospital."

"Hey, c'mon. It was a fair fight. He took a swing at me. Self-defense. The cops didn't arrest me."

"You broke his nose."

"He punched me upside the face."

"Well, as I remember it, you called him a lazy

190

momma's boy. That's why he hit you."

"So? The little pipsqueak looked like a damn momma's boy to me. You could tell he hadn't worked a goddamn day in his whole life."

"It was his birthday. He'd just turned twenty-one. He couldn't hold his liquor."

"So? That was *his* goddamn problem, not mine, Edrena."

"Edna-Ney."

"Hell, that's a hard one to remember, sweetie pie. Like I said, I'm not good with names."

"Look, if you try anything like that in here . . ."

"C'mon. Just one lousy drink. I promise I won't hit nobody." Stoneface then glanced around the room. "Y'know, even though it's kinda dark in here, I don't think I see anyone who'll give me much trouble, 'cept you."

"Yeah, uh-huh. That's real funny, but the owner won't let me run a tab."

"Just one drink, alright? I promise I'll pay my tab by the end of the month."

"Cash upfront. No money; no service."

"Damn." Squinting at her, Stoneface reluctantly pulled out his ten-dollar bill, kissed Alexander Hamilton's face, and slapped it down on top of the counter. "Okay, goddamn it. I'll pay for it. You talked me into it."

Giving him an unpleasant look, Edna-Ney shook her head. "Alright, but just one. Then you've gotta leave." Turning, she walked over to a shelf of whiskey bottles, which was at the other end of the bar.

Leaning forward, Stoneface eyed her backside. She wasn't as well proportioned as the sexy jogger he'd seen up in the park, but Edna-Ney's butt was pleasant enough to look at. Too bad she didn't like him since it would've been nice to have a girlfriend who poured stiff drinks with some extra booze in 'em.

Twiddling his thumbs, he watched as she reached up and grabbed a bottle of bourbon. The gal had boobs that Michelangelo would've loved to have gotten his hands on. But then, just as the hormones were starting to flow, Stoneface heard the legs of a nearby barstool scrape across the floor; and he shifted his eyes back to the mirror and watched as a stranger plopped himself down next to him. This kid couldn't have been more than twenty-five years old. He had a clean-shaven face, a barbered haircut; and he was wearing namby-pamby country-club clothes. He looked like he was on his way to a candyass frat party.

"This seat isn't taken, is it?" the kid asked.

"Nope."

Nodding at Stoneface, the lame-o then leaned across the bar and waved at Edna-Ney.

Now . . .

At first she didn't seem to notice the anxious kid since she was busy serving another customer. But the youngster was damn persistent, and he continued to wave his hand, trying to get her attention . . .

Until she swung around and picked up the glass of bourbon she'd already poured and proceeded to walk down to their end of the bar. That's when a what-are-you-doing-here expression jolted across her face.

"Hi, Tom. Haven't seen you in awhile," Edna-Ney said, placing the glass of bourbon in front of Stoneface and setting down his change next to it.

"I've been out of town. Went down to California. Just got back."

"What's in California?"

"My brother lives down there. Runs a restaurant. How's Zetty doing?"

"She's doing okay."

"Is she, like, seeing anyone?"

"No, not that I know of. I'm pretty sure she would've told me if she was."

"That's good. Do you think I should call her?"

"Well, if you want to know the truth, Tom, I think it's best if you just leave well enough alone."

"You do?"

"Uh-huh."

"But you said she wasn't seeing anyone."

"Tom, I don't think she wants to get back together with you. That train's left the station."

Then, from out of the shadows – a raspy voice shouted, "Barkeep! I need a beer!"

"Can I get you anything, Tom?"

"A Singapore Sling."

"You got it." Edna-Ney then gave him a nod and a smile and hurried away toward the other end of the bar.

Gulping down a healthy swig of his bourbon,

Stoneface wasn't sure if he should mess with this Tom kid or not. But since there wasn't anyone else to pick on, because all of the other barroom patrons looked to be older coots – Stoneface thought he'd have a little fun just for the hell of it. "Having girl trouble?"

"My ex."

"Women. You can't live with 'em, and you sure as hell can't live without 'em, that's for sure."

"Tell me about it. They're, like, really hard to understand."

"You young guys just don't know how good you have it."

"Why do you say that?"

" 'Cause a guy your age doesn't have to get married to get a gal to put out."

"I wish it was that easy."

"Don't we all. I've been divorced two times; and hell, I don't ever wanna go through that shit again, let me tell ya. So if you're smart, you'll never let yourself get pussy whipped . . . never let one of 'em put a ring on your damn finger. That's when they've gotcha by the friggin' balls, legal and all."

"I guess."

Knocking back another hit of bourbon, Stoneface could feel the alcohol tease his gullet and tickle his innards. A warm carefree feeling began to whack-a-mole his brain. And since he was just getting started and didn't want to stop, he took a moment to size Tom up, thinking that he might be able to con the stupid kid out of some drinks. "Look. I tell you what, compadre.

Let me buy you that first drink, and you can buy the next round, okay? Then we'll just keep 'em comin'."

"Sorry, but I've gotta drive home. I might get a DUI if I have more than one."

"One? Hell, that ain't no fun."

Walking back down to their end of the bar with the Singapore Sling, Edna-Ney tossed down a paper coaster in front of Tom and sat the girly concoction on top of it. "Here you go."

"Thanks."

Finishing the bourdon in his glass, Stoneface banged it down on top of the counter. "Another round, sweetie pie."

"I told you, only one."

"C'mon. Give a guy a break."

"I have to see the money first."

"My friend here is gonna pay for it."

"Tom, do you know him?"

"No, I've never met him before. I told him I was only having this one drink and that's it."

Snarling, Stoneface had trouble controlling his temper. "Damn it to hell. There's no need to lie about it, twerp. I heard what you said."

"I'm not lying. Honest to God."

Getting a worried look on her face, Edna-Ney reached across the counter and picked up the Singapore Sling. "C'mon, Tom. He's just trying to pick a fight. There's an empty stool down at the other end of the bar. Just ignore this guy."

Looking a bit befuddled, the kid got tongue-tied;

and a fearful expression tightened across his baby-bottom face. Maybe he thought he was sitting next to the creature from the black lagoon and was about to have his jugular ripped out. (Little did he know that it wasn't his imagination.)

And so . . .

When Stoneface saw how frightened the son-of-a-bitch had gotten, that's when he knew the kid wasn't a scrapper. The candyass, more than likely, had never been in a fistfight in his damn life. Dumbass sissy. He just didn't have any balls.

What was the world coming to? A goddamn hell-raiser couldn't even stir up a good ol' knock-down-drag-out bar fight anymore.

Heaving a sigh of frustration, Stoneface watched as the two of them retreated to the opposite end of the bar. There wasn't much of a crowd inside the place, so Stoneface could pretty much see what they were up to. After Edna-Ney had found the kid a safer place to sit, she then pivoted around and picked up the phone. And since Stoneface still had his wits about him, it didn't take a genius to figure out who the hell she was calling.

Not wanting to find himself on the wrong end of a billy club, Stoneface eased off the barstool and moseyed his way toward The Boat Dock's front door. He'd had his little bit of fun, and he didn't want to push his luck. He also knew that his angel would be waiting up for him back at the warehouse, and the last thing he needed was for her to start nagging him about where he'd been. Like he had told the goddamn twerp, "You can't live with 'em; and you certainly can't live without 'em."

Chapter Sixteen

It was late. She was tired. And she knew if she crawled into bed, she'd fall asleep . . .

But she absolutely, positively needed to stay awake. She didn't want to drift off into beddy-bye land until she'd had a chance to tell Edna-Ney what had happened. Zetty had to tell someone. She didn't want to hold it inside. And since it was a Tuesday, soon to be a Wednesday, she seriously hoped that her roommate wouldn't be bringing a man home with her.

Yet anything was possible, considering the circumstances. Knowing Edna-Ney as well as she did, Zetty told herself that the likelihood her roommate would be coming home with a guy wrapped around her arm was pretty much dependent upon the fickleness of flirtation. In other words, it more or less boiled down to Edna-Ney picking the right guy to flirt with at the bar that night. Also, if she did, like, have a horny guy tagging along with her, then Zetty knew her oversexed roommate wouldn't be in a talkative mood. And since Zetty wasn't the type of person to bother someone when they were having a fling with an inebriated stranger – her own impulsive whim to stay up past her bedtime would have been for naught.

So . . .

Fighting back sleep and knowing that she might be wasting her time, Zetty was patiently waiting in the living room. To while away the time, she had set herself down on the sofa and was reading a book which she had accidentally stumbled upon at the library. Someone had left it in a chair; and when Zetty had seen the photo on the dust jacket – a photo of a beautiful wedding dress hugging a tuxedo – she had immediately felt an overwhelming urge to take the book home with her. The author had a Ph.D. from Harvard, and the lady claimed to offer advice on how to meet the perfect guy.

But . . .

As tended to happen with so many so-called self-help books, Zetty hadn't been that impressed when she had started reading the first chapter. By page 15, she was almost ready to put it aside since she simply didn't have the gobs of money that this well-educated self-help guru was recommending that a single female needed (to spend) so as to buy all of the fashionable clothes and the pricey jewelry, along with all of the other gotta-have extras which this East Coast author claimed were prerequisites for an unattached female to attract a perfect match. Maybe there were women in Cambridge who had that type of money to spend on wooing a guy, but Zetty certainly wasn't about to squander all of her hard-earned savings on a bunch of expensive stuff that she really didn't need.

Closing the book, she stared at the wedding dress on its cover. A professional photographer had obviously been hired to take the photo, but Zetty couldn't help but wonder why there wasn't a bride wearing the lovely white gown. The chest, waistline, and sleeves were perfectly filled out, so it appeared as though that someone had actually modeled inside the frilly linen when the photograph had been taken, yet later, for some reason, the bride-to-be had been erased from the final picture.

It was disconcerting, to say the least.

So, having read the pages that she'd already read . . .

Maybe in this case a person could, in fact, judge a book by its cover. How was it possible that an empty wedding dress, without a bride; and an empty tux, without a groom; would be able to live happily ever after? It didn't make any sense to her. Surely it wasn't the clothes that made a wonderful marriage. Anyone could rent a fancy outfit. In other words, Zetty believed that it was the loving personalities of the betrothed couple who were wearing the wedding clothes that really mattered, not how fancy the outfits appeared in a touched-up photograph.

Marketing.

Yeah, well, she should've known better than to get her hopes up, thinking she was going to find the secret to happiness in a how-to book. There hardly ever was an easy answer or a quick fix when it came to such matters of the heart. Usually, the flavor-of-the-month/be-all-to-end-all/fad-fueled advice . . .

Never actually lived up to its expectations. Rarely was such a book as good as the snappy claims that were printed on its dust jacket. There always seemed to be something missing. Most books weren't at all what they appeared to be; or, in this case, the advice was as empty as the high-priced wedding dress.

Oh, well.

But at least she hadn't wasted any money buying the stupid book. Yet still, she could understand why it was available at the local library. For certain types of debutants from well-off families, that type of book did offer a few tips on how to splurge on the pricier accoutrements that such upper-crust gals could possibly use to attract a fast-lane preppy. But the eligible guys in Zetty's rather limited social circle weren't in that league, even though a couple of them might have foolishly acted as if they were. She didn't have any friends who had gone to a snooty private school, and she wasn't one to put on airs, either. She didn't think it would do any good to act like someone she wasn't. Zetty simply wanted to meet a handsome guy who had a warm heart and a well-paying job.

Was that too much to ask?

Hearing the footsteps coming up the hallway stairs, Zetty brushed her hand through her hair and anxiously hoped that she didn't look like an old maid whose days had come and gone. She was prepared to make a beeline for her bedroom if Edna-Ney had a man with her. Zetty had even preplanned what she would say if a guy walked through the door. Doing her best Meryl Streep imitation, she'd first act surprised, then yawn . . . and to win the Oscar she'd nonchalantly say, in a barely audible voice, that she hadn't been able to sleep and had gotten up to have a glass of milk and was just doing a little reading to put herself in the mood to go back to bed.

So . . .

As she nervously sat there, listening for a male voice . . .

Zetty heard the jingle of keys and the lock being turned. Quickly opening the book, she stared down at a random page and tried to look relaxed, telling herself that she was on stage and that she had to act the part as best she could.

When the door swung open . . .

Zetty was quite relieved to see that Edna-Ney was alone.

"Hey, you're up."

"I couldn't sleep. Thought I'd do some reading."

"God, what an awful day. I just want to take a hot bath and go to bed. I don't even have the energy to make a sandwich," Edna-Ney said, closing the door behind her. She then quickly took off her coat and hung it on the coatrack.

"Edna-Ney, I need to tell you something."

"Oh, you do, do you? Well, I thought you might have something on your mind. You never stay up this late."

Swallowing hard, Zetty closed the book. "I know you're not going to believe me, but I think I'm being followed."

"What do you mean, you're being followed?"

"I know it sounds weird."

Making her way across the room, Edna-Ney stopped at the door to the kitchen. It appeared as though she couldn't decide if she wanted to get something to drink or if she wanted to keep listening to what Zetty was desperate to tell her. "What are you talking about?"

"Okay, here's what happened. Yesterday, when I went to see Miss Pineford, she told me some things about my parents which she'd never told me before."

"So, like, what does that have to do with you being followed?"

"Wait, let me finish."

"I thought you said she had trouble remembering things."

"She does. Most of the time. But yesterday her mind was as clear as a bell."

"Oh, so her memory had sorta come back. What did she tell you?"

"Well, that's the problem. I promised to keep it a secret."

"Zetty, have you been drinking?"

"No, of course not. You know I don't drink."

"There's always a first time."

"Look, I'm not making this up, alright? It really

happened, okay?"

"I believe you."

"You don't sound like you do."

"Look, it's been a long day, alright? I'm exhausted. Go ahead and finish what you were saying."

"Okay, so, anyway – when I was talking to her, what happened next was . . . there was this man outside watching us. He was looking in through the window. That's when it got weird."

"Who was this guy?"

"I don't know."

"Zetty, maybe it was just your imagination playing tricks on you."

"No, I don't think so. I know what I saw. There was this guy standing outside in the rain next to Miss Pineford's window. I saw him with my own eyes. But at the time it happened, I didn't think that much of it. Then today, another stranger came into the flower shop and told me how we were mistreating plants and that we shouldn't be killing flowers and that we should stop selling Christmas trees."

"What?"

"Yeah, I know it sounds weird, but that's exactly what happened. I can't, like, make these things up."

"Was this a homeless guy or something?"

"No, and that's the really strange part. He looked pretty normal, and he was sorta good-looking, too. Oh, and he didn't have a wedding ring on his finger."

"Love at first sight."

"Edna-Ney, I'm being serious, alright?"

"Hey, don't get upset. I'm just teasing you."

"You don't believe me, do you?"

"I didn't say I didn't believe you; but I'm a little confused. The guy at the nursing home . . . was he the same one who, like, bugged you at the flower shop?"

"No. They were two completely different guys."

"Okay, so – why'd you say you were being followed? It sounds to me like it was a coincidence. Happens to me all the time."

"Look, I swear I'm being followed, okay? Remember a few weeks back when I told you about that guy who was living on his sailboat."

"Uh-huh. But I thought he was hitting on you."

"Well, y'know, I never figured out what he was actually up to. That's what I'm saying. These weird things keep happening to me. It seems like I'm having way too many coincidences, if you ask me. So, y'know, that's why I'm pretty sure I'm being followed, which makes me wonder if Miss Pineford was right."

"Right about what? I don't understand what you're talking about, Zetty."

"I wish I could tell you, but I can't."

Softly sighing and slowly shaking her head (and looking somewhat like a high school teacher who'd heard one too many tall tale from a student who hadn't done her homework) – Edna-Ney turned and stepped into the kitchen. "Stay right there. I need a beer."

Rolling her eyes, Zetty waited as her roommate raided the fridge . . . then she watched as Edna-Ney came back into the living room with a can of beer in one hand and a sack of potato chips in the other.

"Want some?" she asked, sitting down on the sofa and offering Zetty the open bag.

"No thanks."

"Comfort food. I think you could use some comforting, Zetty."

"But, like, I'm trying not to eat any carbs. I don't wanna gain anymore weight."

"Okay, suit yourself." Taking a sip of beer and munching on a potato chip, Edna-Ney then changed the subject. "Oh, before I forget, Tom came by the bar tonight. He asked about you."

"Tom? What'd he say?"

"He asked me if you were seeing anyone."

"So, like, what'd you say?"

"I told him you were dating a deputy sheriff."

"No way. You didn't really tell him that, did you?"

"Well, I thought about it. That's what I should've told him. But I didn't actually say that. He wanted to know if it'd be okay for him to call you."

"Oh, no. So then what did you say?"

"I told him that you never wanted to talk to him ever again."

"Edna-Ney, I never said such a thing. You know that. I wish you wouldn't've told him that."

"Well, I'm sorry if I said something I shouldn't've said. I thought I was doing you a favor."

"You know I still care about him. I just don't want to date him anymore, that's all."

"If you care about him, then maybe you should

call him."

"Call him? I can't call him. I don't want him getting the wrong impression."

"Zetty, it sounds to me like you don't know what you want. I think Tom's a nice enough guy, if you ask me. I never did understand why you dumped him."

"I dumped him 'cause it wasn't working out, that's why. He's, like, so immature. I want a guy who's serious about getting married, and Tom just wanted to have sex."

"Sex? Well, I mean, most guys are like that. But if you're lucky, it's not mutually exclusive."

"What does that mean?"

"It means, once you get Mister Right kinda used to sleeping with you . . . then if it feels warm and fuzzy, that's when you start dropping hints about getting a marriage license."

"Yeah, uh-huh. Thanks for telling me . . . like the umpteenth time, Edna-Ney."

"No problem. Good advice never grows stale. Sometimes we just have to hear it over and over again before it finally sinks in."

"If you say so."

"No worries. I think I pretty much scared him away anyway. I doubt Tom will call you." Taking another sip of beer, Edna-Ney yawned.

"Oh, I bet you're tired, aren't you? Sorry if I'm keeping you up. I'm sure you want to go to bed, huh?"

"Nah, it's okay. I understand." Edna-Ney then reached inside the bag and grabbed another potato chip. But instead of tossing it straight into her mouth, she sat there staring at it. "So, um, tell me again why you think you're being followed."

Laying her book down on the coffee table – Zetty reached over, stuck her hand in the potato-chip bag, and pulled out a handful of chips. "Well, it's like I have this icky feeling I'm being watched all the time. It started when that beady-eyed stranger, weeks back, came up to me and wouldn't take *no* for an answer."

"A totally different guy from these other two, right?" Edna-Ney said as she dropped the crispy-looking potato chip that she'd been staring at back in the bag.

"Yeah, totally different. That first guy – he's the one who said he lived on a sailboat, remember? And he's also the one who called Casey and asked her what my name was and, like, wanted to know my phone number."

"You never told me that."

"I guess I didn't tell you 'cause, when it first happened, I didn't take it that seriously since Casey didn't think it was anything to worry about 'cause she thought the guy was just hitting on me."

"You make it sound like that's a bad thing."

"Edna-Ney, you're not me, okay? We don't think the same way. You do things I'd never do."

"I'm a bartender, okay? I know what guys want."

Munching on one potato chip after another, Zetty wasn't hungry, but it was hard to say no to a bag of salty potato chips. "Anyway, I had to tell somebody. It's really been nagging me. But, y'know – now that I've talked about it – I guess it does sound pretty stupid, huh?"

Taking another sip of beer, Edna-Ney nodded her head. "I wouldn't exactly call it stupid; but, if you ask me, I think it's just horny guys hitting on you. That's all it is." Standing up, Edna-Ney then offered her the bag of chips.

"No, thanks. I've already had way too many already."

"Look. I'm going to take a hot bath and go to bed. I don't think you have anything to worry about, Zetty. It's just guys being penis heads. That's all it is. Good night."

" 'Night."

Sucking in a deep breath and exhaling through her nose (like she'd read in her yoga book), Zetty slowly reached over and turned off the lamp. Sitting there in the dark, she closed her eyes and tried to calm herself down. Edna-Ney was probably right. Why would anyone want to follow Zetty around? What reason would they have for doing something weird like that? The only logically explanation was – it was just hormonal guys being horny. That's all it was. It was nothing more than a series of unexpected stupid coincidences.

Maybe so.

And, of course, it was also possible that Miss Pineford could've been confused. The medication she was taking might have clouded her mind, and what she thought she was remembering wasn't what had actually happened all those many years ago. So that could explain why she had said what she'd said.

And given that Edna-Ney knew a lot more about men than Zetty did . . .

The most sensible conclusion seemed to be that there was nothing out of the ordinary going on at all. As her mom had always told her, "Don't be a worry-wart. Don't make a mountain out of a molehill." And her mom was rarely ever wrong. Zetty's mother was so smart when it came to figuring out what to ignore and what to take seriously when something totally unexpected would come along.

Don't be a girly-girl drama queen. Don't make a mountain out of a molehill.

And so . . .

Trying not to let her imagination get the better of her, Zetty told herself that she would just have to learn not to let such things upset her. She told herself that it would all work itself out if she simply didn't take any of it too seriously. It wouldn't do any good for her to assume the worst and let a series of unexpected coincidences spook her into worrying about stuff that wasn't true.

"Things always work out for the best. It may not seem that way at the time, but eventually you'll look back and realize that things always do work out for the best." And that was another one of her mom's favorite pieces of advice. Zetty had heard her repeat those exact words over and over again. "Don't be a worrywart.

Don't be a drama queen like Mrs. Wilson down the street. Things will always work out for the best. You just wait and see. Think good thoughts; and wonderful blessings – like falling leaves – will come your way."

Chapter Seventeen

Maybe he shouldn't have done what he did, but at the time it felt like the right thing to do. He couldn't help himself. His conscience had nagged him to do something . . .

And so he felt an overpowering urge to free the noble fir from its flower-shop prison. If he hadn't've forked over the cash to buy the little tree its freedom, Mooney would have gone home ashamed of himself.

Yet strangely enough, Tammy had a different opinion. When they'd met up later at the bookstore, she'd told him that he shouldn't've made such a big deal out of it. She said he was attracting way too much attention, and she was concerned about protecting her anonymity. So, not wanting to be seen with a guy walking around with a Christmas tree, she explained to him that she thought it would be best for both of them if she took a separate bus home . . .

And then she proceeded to hurry off down the street by herself.

Of course, she was right about people stopping

and staring. Mooney did look pretty peculiar walking down the sidewalk with a Christmas tree in his hands. At one point a blue-haired punked-out teenager had even come up to him and asked where Santa Claus was.

Then later . . .

When a bus pulled up to the bus stop . . .

No one was joking when the driver told Mooney that he couldn't bring the tree onto the bus. It had taken quite a bit of cajoling to get the driver to change his mind. Being a stickler when it came to what could or couldn't be carried onto the bus he was driving, the guy only relented after Mooney had politely explained to him that he was on a mission of mercy, pointing out that the baby tree needed a bigger plastic container to grow its roots in.

Unusual things can happen in a town where people have subdued egos.

The likelihood that a transit passenger would have been allowed on a city bus anywhere in Texas with such a potted tree would have been highly unlikely, to say the least.

Anyway . . .

By the time Mooney had made it home, he'd had one heck-of-a workout. The tree was much heavier than it looked. It had been a long afternoon.

Lugging the plant inside the bungalow, he sat the noble fir down in the living room, right in front of the doublewide window, trying his best to pick a spot where its leaves would be able to soak in the utmost sunlight. Then, stopping to catch his breath, he stood there for a long moment and admired his handiwork. A feeling of well-being instantly washed over him as he gently ran his fingers along one of the fir's little sprigs.

"Isn't it kind of early for a Christmas tree?" Becky asked as she crossed toward the kitchen from the hall.

"It's not a Christmas tree."

"It looks like one to me."

"Well, maybe it looks like one to you, but you know I'd never buy a Christmas tree. Have you ever seen me do something dumb like that before?"

Stepping back into the living room – Becky walked over, lowered her nose to a limb, and smelled the tree's scent. "Yes, I have, actually. I remember when you were ten years old, and I saw you decorate a Christmas tree with some aluminum icicles. Does that count?"

"Someone else cut that tree down and gave it to the orphanage. I was just doing what everyone else was doing. I was a stupid little kid."

"Okay, but what about when you came to see me that time in Baton Rouge, and you had a tree on top of your van?"

"Yeah, that's true. But like I told you back then, I found the poor thing lying on the side of the road. Best as I could figure out, it'd probably fallen off a truck since it had that bailing wire wrapped around it."

"Uh-huh. And if I remember it correctly, I told you I didn't believe you 'cause I thought you'd made that story up as an excuse for showing up with such a big

Christmas tree. Then you grinned at me and dragged it inside my friend's house and gave it to her."

Mooney knew his sister was a fanatic when it came to remembering such things. It was always hard for him to slide a white lie past her. "Hey, what was I supposed to do with it? I mean, your friend said she was going to go out and buy a Christmas tree anyway. So, like, I thought I'd save another tree from getting cut down by giving her that one."

"Yeah, if you say so."

"It's true. You know I wouldn't lie to you, Becky."

Puffing up her face at his dry wit, she then turned to the window and looked outside. "So, like, where's Tammy?"

"She said she had some shopping to do. She's taking a later bus."

"The landlord dropped by."

"Yeah? What he'd say?"

"Not too much. He said he was just coming by to say hello and see how things were going. He asked me if we had anything that needed to be fixed."

"That's weird."

"Yeah, I thought so, too. I mean, I've never rented a place where the landlord, like, wants to fix things that aren't even broken yet."

"He was probably just making sure we didn't have any pets and weren't growing anything illegal in the garden."

"I guess."

"You didn't tell him about Tammy, did you?"

"No, of course not."

"Good. Our lease says something about having to notify him if anyone else moves in."

"Yeah, I know. You told me. But I think it's going to be harder to hide Tammy than a cat, if you ask me."

"Well, if it ever comes up, we'll just say she's here for a visit. No big deal."

"I'm not going to lie to him, Moon."

"I didn't say you had to lie to him, Becky."

"You said tell him she's visiting."

"Well, y'know, when you really think about it, she is just visiting. It's an extended visit of sorts."

"Oh, c'mon. I don't see why we can't just tell him the truth. What difference does it make?"

"Because if we did that, we'd have to pay him more rent, that's why. It goes up when there's three people living here."

"Oh, okay. I guess you're right." Shrugging it off, Becky then disappeared down the hall, leaving Mooney alone with his thoughts.

Not having wanted to say anymore than he should, considering the circumstances – Mooney knew he couldn't exactly explain what the real reason was why they needed to keep Tammy's living arrangements under wraps, since that would've made his sister a coconspirator. So he had to hide the fact that Tammy didn't want her name listed on the lease because she was adamant about not having any sort of documentation in regards to her whereabouts floating around. And Mooney also thought that if he kept Becky

216

completely out of the loop, then her ignorance as to the facts would grant her some legal cover if anything ever did come back to bite them.

So under the circumstances, Mooney had to always be careful and watch what he said. And it wasn't easy, by any means. He was constantly walking a fine line, wanting to do whatever he could to prevent his sister from having any sort of connection to L.E.A.F. – while at the same time, also doing his best to protect Tammy from the authorities. And in order for him to juggle these two divergent objectives, there were a number of considerations that he needed to factor in so as to equalize the equation, being as it was somewhat complicated to achieve both priorities at the same time. Indeed, it was a constant balancing act that kept him on his toes.

Never easy.

Thinking that Tammy would, more than likely, have taken the next bus out of downtown, Mooney began to get a little worried when, after an hour, she still hadn't showed up, and it had already turned dark outside. He had been typing away at his computer in the alcove, trying to catch up with the work he'd put off earlier that day, when he noticed how late it was getting. Worried that Tammy might've run into a problem, Mooney was almost to the point of calling her on her cell when he finally heard the plop of footsteps on the front porch.

Feeling a sense of relief that nothing had happened, he glanced over at the door and watched as

Tammy inched it open and stepped inside. "Hey. I thought you might've gotten lost."

"Why would you think that?"

"Because I thought you said you were taking the next bus."

"I went to the library. Free Internet," Tammy said as she walked over to the alcove.

"Oh."

"Is Becky here?"

"In her room. We're having sandwiches tonight."

"Works for me." Tammy then lowered her voice, leaned in over his shoulder, and looked down at his computer screen. "You got what I meant by free, huh?"

Following her lead, he kept his voice to a whisper. "I know. Untraceable."

"Exactly. Everything you type on this high-speed connection is logged. All of your search-engine entries, all of your emails . . ."

"Yeah, I know we have to be careful, like you said before about the data tracking. But at least I've installed the 5.2 encryption update for the important stuff."

Then . . .

From down the hall, Becky chirped up behind them. "So, like, what are you two whispering about?"

Turning his head, Mooney saw that Becky only had a pair of socks covering her feet, and that's why she had been able to silently walk down the hall from her bedroom without being heard. Her shoeless feet hadn't made any sort of pitter-patter on the hardwood floor. "Tammy was asking me when your birthday was."

"My birthday?"

"Yesterday he said something about it being this month, and I was just wondering what day it actually was, that's all."

"You don't have to get me anything for my birthday, Tammy. C'mon, don't worry about it, okay?"

Wanting to shift the attention to another topic, Mooney then abruptly turned his head back to his computer and began typing away. "Sorry, but I have to finish this. I'm right in the middle of writing a post, and I'm under deadline."

"I think he's trying to tell us something, Tammy."

"You think?"

As expected, his distraction worked. Getting the hint, the two of them then retreated down the hall to finish their conversation out of earshot.

Then later that night . . .

After the veggie sandwiches had been consumed and the three of them were sitting in the living room, talking about what Mooney should do with the rescued fir tree, Becky offered up an easy-to-accomplish suggestion. "Hey, I have an idea. What about planting it in the backyard next to our garden?"

"Yeah, I guess we could do that. But, like, we'd have to check with our landlord to make sure it was okay with him."

Tammy then offered her opinion. "Well, if you ask me, I think the only decent thing to do, since it's so young, is to plant it next to some other noble firs out in the woods. If I was a baby tree that size, I know that's what I'd want you to do."

Hearing Tammy say this, Becky scrunched up her face and looked to be somewhat surprised by what she had just heard. "Y'know, I never thought about that. I guess a baby tree would want family nearby, huh?"

"I know I would. I'd want to grow up next to my own species and not have to live out my life all alone in a small backyard, having to put up with pesky humans all the time."

"Me, too," Becky replied.

Slowly unzipping the front of her sweater, Tammy then looked over at the tree. "I saw some mature firs growing down in the park."

"You mean, those nobles down by the cemetery?"

"Uh-huh."

"Okay, that might work," Mooney said, warming to the idea.

"But isn't the park owned by the city?" Becky asked.

"Yeah, it's a city park. The taxpayers own it. That's true."

"So, like, doesn't that mean you'll need to get permission or a permit or something? Moon, you can't just go plant a tree on public land."

With a mischievous grin, Tammy then leaned forward and looked as though she was having a flash of inspiration. "Wait, I know. What if we do a creepy-crawly late at night and secretly plant it in the park? I mean, what are they going to do? Dig it up?"

"Yeah, that's true. I doubt anyone would even notice it. It'd just be another tree in the park," Mooney said.

"But wouldn't you be breaking the law?" Becky asked.

"More like bending it. I don't think planting a tree on public land would be considered an out-and-out felony."

"Well, I know what my ecology professor would say. He'd want you to fill out the proper paperwork first," Becky said.

"Okay, and what if we did that, and what if they said 'no?' Then what?" Tammy asked.

Not knowing how to answer her question, Becky sat there with a puzzled look on her face.

"Listen, it's just one tree, Becky. It's not like we're messing with the whole ecosystem or anything," Mooney said, glancing over at the noble fir.

Tammy then got up off the sofa, walked over to the little tree, and gently rubbed its leaves. "Maybe we could start a new fad. You could, like, post it on your blog and try to get people to go out and plant hundreds of Christmas trees in a bunch of parks all over the country."

"That's an idea. 'Save a Christmas tree. Keep it alive. Plant it in a park. Take pictures and post them on the Net,' " Mooney chuckled, riffing off of Tammy's brainstorming.

"Viral videos."

"Yeah, wouldn't that be way cool? Becky, can we borrow your camera?" And when Mooney suddenly blurted this out, he was only halfway joking, having been caught up in the hilarity of the camaraderie. He hadn't actually thought through what he was saying. But still, he'd put his foot in his mouth and had said it anyway, so now it was too late for a do-over. He couldn't crayfish out of it.

Giving the question some serious thought, Becky sat there with a solemn expression on her face. At first it appeared as if she would be the odd person out since she always preferred to avoid breaking any rules and wasn't the type to express an activistic point of view. For her whole life, Becky had tried to be a goody two-shoes, never wanting to do anything that would ever get her sent to the principal's office or, heaven forbid, arrested. She wasn't a radical environmentalist. She didn't want to go to jail. She thought she could change the system by working from withinside the system.

So, after having patiently endured their spirited enthusiasm – Becky crossed her arms in front of her chest and finally said what she was thinking. "No way. I'm not loaning you my camera." But then, quite unexpectedly, she flashed a big smile; and it looked as though their devil-may-care eagerness had been contagious. "Are you kidding me? I'm not letting you two have all the fun. I'm going with you. I want to shoot the video myself. You talked me into it. Why not? What could it hurt?"

Hearing her say this, Tammy then did a one-eighty and glanced over at Mooney with an apprehensive gaze. He could easily guess what she was worried about. In the heat of the moment, they had somehow painted themselves in a corner, not realizing what the ramifications would be if Becky decided to tag along. So now they were stuck. If they didn't follow through with their plan, Becky might get suspicious.

Yet, needless to say, the baby tree did need a new home. There was no arguing that point. And, without a doubt, the perfect place for it to be replanted would be in the park because there was little chance the noble fir would ever be cut down if it was residing within that greenspace's protective boundaries. Also, since this would be a benign act of environmental activism, the proposed caper wouldn't be that hard to pull off. Nonetheless, there were L.E.A.F. protocols that had to be adhered to, which meant that any evidence, such as a digital recording of the two Flock members involved, would have to be erased. So Mooney told himself that he would have to make sure that the images on Becky's camera never got uploaded to the Web. The last thing L.E.A.F. needed was for Tammy and him to be videotaped doing something unlawful and having such a prank generate a ton of hits on the Internet.

Big Brother was always watching, even when you didn't think he was watching.

Chapter Eighteen

There wasn't much food left in his kitchen. When he opened the cabinet door, he only saw a tin of tuna and a few slices of bread. A can of beans sat on the counter. That was it. The fridge was completely empty.

Stoneface had to figure out a way to scrounge up some money, or he wouldn't have enough food to keep his energy up to swing his mallet. But running out of edibles wasn't the worst of it. He only had half a bottle of bourbon left, and it'd be way too much agony for him to bear if he couldn't smooth out his nerves with regular sips of whiskey. He'd suffered through delirium tremens a few times before, and he sure as hell didn't want to get walloped by the damn shakes again. So it was time for him to call his ol' high school buddy Ken McGardy.

McGardy was a no-good lowlife, and Stoneface would only call him when he was flat broke and needed some quick cash. So if it took breaking the law to keep liquor and food in his damn stomach, Stoneface was willing to do whatever he had to do. When the wolf was sniffing at your door, you didn't have much of a choice. Him and McGardy went way back. Stoneface had known the sleazy bastard even before McGardy had turned hardcore. Years ago, Stoneface had pretty much seen the writing on the goddamn wall when McGardy had flunked out of the eleventh grade after he'd skipped three weeks of class. Then, with nothing else to do, the crazy son-of-a-bitch had gotten himself hooked on boosting cars, which meant he'd eventually ended up rotating in and out of the penitentiary with the regularity of a migrating buzzard.

Dialing his phone number, Stoneface could only hope that McGardy was out on parole and not pacing back and forth inside a 9' by 12' cell. Stoneface hadn't spoken to the scumbag in about eight months, so it was highly possible that McGardy could've already done something illegal and been re-incarcerated.

"Hello?"

"Ken, it's me. Edgar."

"Yeah, what's up, Stoneface?"

"Why don't you come over to my place? Let's go make us some money."

"Sorry, no can do. I got a court date comin' up. If I get caught doin' something I shouldn't be doin', they're gonna lock me up and throw away the lousy key. Six strikes, and I'm out."

"I thought it was three strikes."

"Got lucky with a few plea bargains."

"Look. This is easy money. It'll only take us a couple of damn hours. No way we'll get caught."

"Where?"

"Gotta come over to find out 'cause I ain't gonna get into any of the details on the damn phone."

"Yeah, I hear ya."

"Come on over, and I'll tell you what you need to know."

"Okay, I'll be there in a few hours."

"Alright, see you then." Hanging up the receiver, Stoneface wasn't sure if the bastard had told him the truth or not. From what McGardy had said, and from the way he'd said it, Stoneface was sort of suspicious. It was possible the sleazebag had turned into a goddamn snitch. That six-strikes bullshit was hard to believe.

To steady his twitches, Stoneface lifted up his bottle and took a swig of whiskey.

He knocked back just one quick gulp since he had some worked he wanted to do.

Talk about putting hair on your chest.

He then picked up his chisel and mallet and began chipping away on his angel. He'd been furiously working on the face, and the statue was now almost finished. He only had a little more work to do on the lips and ears.

As he stood in front of her, looking into her beautiful eyes, he hoped she wouldn't mind the smaller bosom he'd given her. Of course, if she did feel gypped, there was nothing much he could do about it now. The block of marble (which he'd bought at half price because there was a hair-thin crack running through the slab) . . . had less workable stone in that part of her torso. So Stoneface had had to cut away a good bit more from the angel's front side than he normally would've done on an unblemished piece of rock. Also, to compensate for her petite boobs, he was spending more time working on her face, trying his best to make it as lovely as he possibly could. He didn't want her mad at him. He told himself that the extra effort he was taking to smooth in the fine details would hopefully prove to her that he'd done all he could to make her as pretty as possible.

Between a few more swigs of booze and the demands of his work, he soon lost track of time. He was doing what he loved to do, and he never thought about anything else while he was swinging his mallet. If he had his druthers, he would always stay zoned out in his art. The only time he was ever at peace with himself was when he was chipping away at a slab of marble. The cares of the world seemed to disappear, and his anxiety switch would click itself off, and the nagging worries would fade from his soul.

After a couple of hours ticked by . . .

Stoneface was making fairly nice progress on the angel's protruding lips . . .

When . . .

Lost in his chiseling, he heard a loud knock at the door. Glancing over at the clock, he saw that it had been over four hours since he'd called McGardy. Putting down his tools, Stoneface quickly wiped the dust from his face, stepped over, and swung the door open.

Ken McGardy stood outside in the rain.

"It took you long enough to get here, goddamnit."

"Had to find some jumper cables. My car wouldn't start."

"You didn't steal it, did you?"

"No, I told ya, I stopped jackin' 'em two years ago."

"Get your ass in here before you shrivel up," Stoneface said, giraffing his head outside to see if anything looked out of the ordinary. But thankfully, there was nothing of consequence that caught his eye, except the heavy rain pounding down on top of the warehouse's corrugated roof.

Slamming the door, Stoneface followed McGardy over to the marble angel. Like molasses attracting flies, everyone who came by his studio always wanted to get a closer look at the newest angel coming to life.

"Nice. Looks like she's almost finished," McGardy said as he reached out his hand to touch her chin.

"Hey, get your goddamn hand away from her! Don't you dare put a finger on her!"

"Oh, sorry. I forgot."

"How many times do I have to tell you, goddamnit? Never ever do that."

"Man, don't get so upset, alright? It's just a piece of stone."

"No, dammit. She's not just a piece of friggin' stone. Get away from her."

"Okay, okay. Chill out, man. You asked me to come by and talk to you, remember?"

Reaching for his bottle of bourbon, Stoneface grabbed a glass and poured a few fingers in it. He didn't want his temper getting the better of him. He told himself that he had to calm himself down because he needed McGardy to help him make some money. "Here. Drink up," he said, handing him the glass . . . hoping to smooth things over.

"Thanks."

"Make it last, 'cause that's all you're gonna get."

Grinning with a half-ass smile, McGardy took a gulp and smacked his lips. "Yes siree. There it is. Liquid sunshine."

"Well, it ain't hooch out of a thumper, but it's almost as good." Rubbing his hands together, Stoneface then stared McGardy in the eye, taking aim at him like a hunter would with a rifle. "Look, this caper's gonna be a piece of cake. No alarms. No cops to worry 'bout. Quick money like we did last time."

"Scarp metal?"

"Yeah, a few hundred pounds of the shit."

"Damn."

"It won't take us five minutes to load up my truck with it."

"Where?"

"A construction site over off the river. They're building a new bridge across it."

"Won't there be a security guard?"

"He falls asleep. An old man who can't keep his damn eyes open."

"I don't know, Stoneface. Sounds kinda risky, if

you ask me. He's gonna have a friggin' cell phone on him."

"C'mon. I'm telling you, it's easy money. There's a bunch of rebar and cut-up support beams. The old man sleeps in his damn car a little ways up from where they're doing the work. We'll drive in on the dirt road that runs along the river, get the scrap, and he won't even see us."

"You sure?"

"Yeah, dammit, I'm sure. I've watched him two nights in a row. But it looks like they'll probably have the metal hauled off pretty soon . . . so I'm thinking we better get our asses up there tonight before it's up and gone."

"Shit, man." Knocking back the last of his whiskey, McGardy pulled out his cell phone and flipped it open. "I've got a woman I need to go see."

Grabbing the phone, Stoneface quickly slapped it closed and stuck it in his back pocket. "Hell no. No way. Stand the bitch up. I don't want you making no friggin' calls."

"What are you talkin' about? Give me my damn phone back."

"Ken, I'm calling the shots on this goddamn job. I don't want you making no damn calls, understand? I'll give you your stupid phone back after we get the money from the junk buyer."

"Yeah? And when the hell will that be?"

"Well, if we get up to the river tonight, we can cash the metal out in Tacoma tomorrow."

Having listened to Stoneface's proposition, McGardy didn't appear to be too happy with what he was hearing. And it didn't help that he wouldn't look Stoneface in the eye, either. McGardy kept glancing over at the door, acting as if he might be planning a quick escape.

Sensing his friend's hesitancy (and halfway trying to keep his temper in check, but not trying too hard), Stoneface then picked up his mallet and chisel and lightly tapped the two of them together. He wasn't out-and-out threatening McGardy, but still he thought a little reminder as to what he was capable of . . .

Might help the son-of-a-bitch comprehend the seriousness of the goddamn situation. If the bastard didn't get the lousy hint, then it'd be his own goddamn frigging fault as to what might happen next.

"Okay. You talked me into it. I need the money. Let's do it."

And so . . .

That's what they did. They went outside, hopped into Stoneface's pickup truck, drove up to the river, and stole the scrap metal from below the bridge. The heist went as smooth as glass. The old man who was guarding the construction site never got out of his car. It was easy pickings. The only problem they ran into occurred the next morning at the junkyard when the one-eyed guy who was running the lame place . . .

Started questioning Stoneface about where they'd gotten the cut-up metal from. The bastard said it looked to him like they were trying to get rid of stolen property.

What the hell?

The last thing they needed was for the scrap guy to call the cops.

Why was he saying that shit?

They'd even gone out of their way not to look too scuzzy by stopping at a pump-it-yourself convenience store and shoplifting a disposal razor and a can of shaving cream. Using a sink in the men's restroom, they'd shaved off their stubble, thinking their porcupiny whiskers made them look suspicious.

So what was up with this son of a bitch? Couldn't he see they weren't grubby-looking thieves?

Nevertheless, and luckily for them, being as the one-eyed asshole wasn't too smart, he'd also made a stupid mistake. He should've kept his suspicions to himself and waited until after he'd asked Stoneface for his driver's license. Instead, the guy had blurted out his inflammatory accusation before he'd even asked to see an ID.

Dumb shit.

Yeah, presumably . . .

With all the rotten-toothed scrap-metal pilferers stealing everything in sight to feed their addictive meth habits, law enforcement had recently started cracking down; and now every Tom, Dick, and Harry was having to cough up an ID so as to prove who was selling what to whom.

And so . . .

Considering the shadowy circumstances, Stoneface had barely avoided a pair of shiny handcuffs since the stupid junkyard guy had said what he'd said before he'd first asked to see a proof-of-ID driver's license. So not wanting to take a chance on getting caught, Stoneface had, of course, immediately known he'd come too damn close to getting himself in trouble. It was a squeaker, to be sure. Standing right across the counter from the one-eyed shithead when he'd asked to see his friggin' driver's license – Stoneface had stiffened into his best poker face and had acted as if he'd been insulted. He then proceeded to yell at the idiot, cursing him out. "Nobody calls me a goddamn thief, you son of a bitch!" Spitting on the counter – Stoneface quickly turned and hurried out the door . . .

Shouting over his shoulder that he'd go sell his goddamn scrap somewhere else.

Then . . .

A couple of minutes later, after they'd driven away from the junkyard – McGardy got cold feet. He told Stoneface that he didn't want to take any more chances on getting caught because he didn't want to go back to the slammer. He'd had enough shit for one day. He said he wanted to throw in the towel and ditch the stolen metal. He said he didn't need his name on another arrest warrant. He was a little jittery, thinking that the one-eyed ratfink might have written down Stoneface's license plate number and called the cops.

Unable to talk McGardy out of his paranoia, Stoneface relented, and they ended up dumping the hot metal in the woods in an out-of-the-way spot a few miles south of Bellingham, up along a logging road that ran into the foothills.

After they'd ditched it, Stoneface started to get worried that McGardy might snitch him out to the cops as a bargaining chip; but since the stupid score had only been a pipsqueak petty larceny, Stoneface told himself that the odds were in his favor that his pal in crime wouldn't squeal. A known criminal with a lengthy rap sheet wouldn't be able to get much of a plea bargain if he coughed up a lame petty larceny on someone else.

So . . .

Keeping his word — because he didn't want to give McGardy a reason to flip on him — Stoneface handed the bastard back his cell phone. Their easy-money payday had been a complete flop, and Stoneface now was up a creek without a paddle. He had to figure out another way to make some quick cash, or the hungry wolf would get evermore aggressive and go from just sniffing at his door to clawing his way inside.

It looked as though Stoneface had no other choice but to take his hacksaw up into the park and cut down those two Christmas trees. Forty dollars was better than nothing. Two twenty-dollar bills would be enough to get him a couple of bottles of bourbon and a bite of food.

Chapter Nineteen

She was trying her best not to think about it; but for some reason she couldn't get it out of her head. She told herself that Edna-Ney was probably right. There was no reason in the world for anyone to be following Zetty around town. So most likely it was just her overactive imagination playing tricks on her.

But still, Zetty couldn't dismiss what had been said to her when that good-looking stranger had come into the flower shop and bought the Christmas tree. His attitude towards helping plants had hit a nerve. To Zetty, it felt sort of like slipping on a banana peel and landing face down in an ants' nest of biting lies, not knowing what was, in fact, true . . .

And what other people simply wanted you to believe because they'd falsely been convinced it was undeniably true . . .

When it was actually nothing more than a big fat stupid lie.

"You haven't said much all morning. What's wrong, Zetty?" Casey asked as she walked into the shop's backroom.

Zetty was standing at her workbench, snipping the ends off a dozen roses that she was carefully arranging into a floral bouquet. "You don't think plants feel things, Casey?"

"Feel things? No, I don't think so. I mean, they're alive, of course, but they don't have brains or hearts or anything like that. They're just plants, Zetty. Why are you asking me that?"

"Well, yesterday – when you went out to make those deliveries, a guy came in the shop and bought that noble fir. I was going to talk to you about what he said, but then you didn't get back 'til late, and so we didn't have time 'cause you had to rush home."

"We had theater tickets."

"Oh, that's right. I heard it was a pretty good play. Did you like it?"

"Sort of. It was entertaining. But we didn't stay for the whole show 'cause Dan started to fall asleep."

"In front of everyone else?"

"They have him working the first shift, and he has to get up at four."

"Oh, no wonder he fell asleep, huh?"

"So what did that guy say to you? The one who bought the noble fir."

Sticking the last rose in the arrangement, Zetty slowly turned it around to make sure she had balanced out the bouquet and hadn't put too many flowers on one side since she didn't want it to look lopsided. "Well, I'm not exactly sure why he said what he said,

236

but he told me that we shouldn't be killing flowers."

"Killing flowers? Who was this guy?"

"I don't know. That was the first time I'd ever met him before. Like I told you, for some reason, I keep meeting strange men who say weird things to me."

"They're just hitting on you, that's all."

"Yeah, that's what Edna-Ney said when I told her about it, too. But, like, I'm pretty sure this guy wasn't hitting on me. I think he was actually mad at me 'cause I was working here. I don't think he was trying to get me to go out with him."

"Are you sure he was mad at you 'cause you worked here?"

"Uh-huh."

"Well, that is a little strange, huh?"

"Yeah, that's what I thought."

"Okay, so, why'd he buy the Christmas tree if he was mad at you?"

" 'Cause he said he didn't want to see it suffer. Those were his exact words. He didn't want to see the little tree suffer. He said we had it in too small a pot."

"Oh, he did, did he? As if we'd do something dumb like that."

"Well, the tree was getting pretty big. He was right about that. And, I mean, I'd already thought about repotting it. Anyway, he also said no one should cut down Christmas trees. He said plants shouldn't be killed."

"Oh, now I get it. This guy sounds like an environmental activist. Those dingbats will say anything to stop people from cutting down trees."

Finishing off the bouquet with some baby's breath, Zetty wasn't sure if she should be completely honest and go ahead and say what she was about to say; but then she went ahead and said it anyway. "Well, you could be right, Casey. He, like, did sound like a tree-hugger. But the problem is, I don't think he's actually wrong. What he said made sense to me. And that's why I'm thinking about quitting."

"Are you serious?"

"Casey, the last thing I want to do is to hurt anything. I know I wouldn't want to have my feet cut off. I think plants feel things just like we do."

"C'mon, Zetty. The guy obviously didn't know what he was talking about. Flowers and trees don't have feelings. That's impossible. They don't feel things like we feel things. I mean – you know we have to cut down trees to build houses and do stuff like that. And we also use wood to make a lot of things. So, I mean, what he said absolutely didn't make any sense."

"But trees are alive. They grow, and they change, and they have baby trees. They're not brainless rocks, Casey. People could use bricks and steel and, I guess, maybe plastic to build a lot of the things they build instead of having to kill so many innocent trees."

"That's ridiculous. You're worrying about something that doesn't matter one iota. Trust me. We're not hurting plants because plants don't feel anything. They're just mindless plants."

"Casey, it matters to me, okay? What if you're

wrong and he's right?"

"Listen, even if there's something to what he said – you yourself are not actually killing anything, are you? You don't actually pick the flowers out of the ground, do you? So you're not actually killing the flowers. They come to us already picked, right? So *we're* not killing any plants. It's total nonsense."

"But it's the same thing. We're part of it."

"Okay, if you want to think like that, then go ahead and think like that. And if you're serious about quitting, I'm not going to try to talk you out of it. But, I mean, you need to seriously think about what you're going to do for a job. Where are you going to work? Zetty, you have to have a job, right?"

"I know. And that's what worries me. I don't know what I'll do to pay my bills."

"Look. I think you're just . . . confused. And I can understand why what he said is upsetting you. I understand that. So, I tell you what. It's slow right now. We don't have any more orders to fill. Why don't you just take the rest of the day off and go home and think about it, alright?"

"Okay."

"Tomorrow you can call me and let me know what you decide."

Having said what she needed to say, Zetty nodded her head, took off her apron, and hung it on the wall. She then wrote down her time on the timesheet, put on her coat, and walked out the back door. She thought it was nice of Casey to give her the rest of the day off so she could think through her decision. And Casey was right, of course. Zetty was confused, and she wasn't sure what would be the best thing for her to do. The ants' nest was stinging her brain. There didn't seem to be an easy answer to her dilemma.

Stepping outside into the fresh air, Zetty thought that a bit of exercise might help clear her head and give her a better idea as to what would be the appropriate choice for her to make. And since she didn't have to hurry off to be somewhere at a certain time and was free to do whatever she wanted to do with her afternoon, she turned and began walking toward the bay. She had a few extra hours on her hands, and she knew that taking a long walk always helped her sort through her thoughts when she had something important to think about. There was nothing like an invigorating stroll to put things in perspective.

It took about fifteen minutes of brisk walking for Zetty to make her way down to the edge of the shore . . .

Where she stopped to look out at the sailboats which were bobbing up and down on the waves off in the distance. If only she could sail away, she thought. If only she could travel from place to place and not have to worry about all of the stuff she was worrying about. Wouldn't that be a fun, carefree way to live? She so wanted to escape her troubles and leave them far, far behind her. But she also knew she wasn't that type of person. She told herself that it never did any good to run away from a problem. Trying to hide from her responsibilities would just make things worse. She wasn't naïve. She knew she had to be strong and face life head-on. Somehow, if she simply gave it time, she knew she would get through this rough spot; and, in the end, it would all work out for the best, like her mom had always told her it would.

So, even though running away would be the easiest thing to do – there was no way she could just up and leave Bellingham. She had to be there for Miss Pineford. It would break the old lady's heart if Zetty deserted her. And Zetty also didn't want to leave all of her high school friends behind, regardless of the fact that most of them had already moved out of town. But a lot of them still came back for short visits, especially during the holidays.

No, she told herself that she couldn't just pack up and leave on a whim. If she quit her job, she would still have to figure out something else to do so as to be able to stay in Bellingham and have enough money to pay her rent.

Life wasn't as easy as some people thought it was.
And so . . .

As she stood there staring down at the water, Zetty struggled to decide what she should do. Then, hearing the puttering sound of an outboard motor, she glanced up and looked out at the bay. A small dinghy was pulling away from one of the sailboats, and it was headed toward the shoreline. The guy steering it was the same weirdo who'd asked her about her mom's blue

241

satchel weeks back on the sidewalk in front of the bank.

Oh, no. Why was this happening to me?

Zetty had gone for a walk to calm herself down and sort through her thoughts; but now she was getting anxious all over again. And what made it so terribly disturbing was . . .

The stupid guy was staring straight at her and waving his arm.

Covering her face with her hands, Zetty turned around and quickly hurried back up the hill toward downtown. The last thing she wanted to do was to have to talk to this weirdo. And she knew that this wasn't another coincidence, either. Something definitely was up for her to have so many complete strangers going out of their way to strike up a conversation with her. Something way out of the ordinary was happening. It wasn't her imagination; and it wasn't guys just wanting to hit on her, like Edna-Ney and Casey had said. But Zetty had no clue why these guys were doing what they were doing. She couldn't understand what she'd ever done to cause them to come out of the woodwork and start bothering her. Every time she turned around, there was another strange man trying to talk to her; and now she felt as if all of this unasked-for attention was getting to be too much for her to deal with. She just wanted to go home and pull the covers up over her head and hope it would all go away.

Chapter Twenty

Everyone was on the same page (or so they thought). They'd waited until a few hours after dark, and now the three of them were going to trek into the park and plant the baby tree. To make it easier on Mooney's arms, since he didn't want to have to lug the noble fir so far, Becky was letting him use her little red wagon to roll the tree to its new home. When they had first moved into the bungalow, she'd found the toy wagon in the basement and had promptly commandeered it, claiming "finders, keepers." She'd told Mooney that it would make the perfect wheeled transport for her garden tools. And later, when there was eventually enough produce sprouting in their garden to harvest, Becky had also ended up using the wagon as a gathering basket to bring the fresh veggies inside.

"Ya'll ready?" Mooney asked as he set the baby tree in the wagon near the front door.

"It looks pretty dark out there. Do you think it's too dark for me to use my camera?"

"I don't know. Maybe so, Becky. It is pretty dark."

"Well, I'll bring it anyway. It wouldn't hurt to try, I guess." Becky then strapped her fanny pack around her waist. Its zipper pouch was barely large enough to hold her video camera and a few extra batteries.

"Y'know, just make sure you don't shoot our faces, okay? Even in low light, you might get some clear images. So keep it pointed at the tree and down at our feet and, like, get a shot of the shovel digging the hole – but, like, don't shoot our faces, alright?"

"It's just a video, Moon. What's the big deal?"

Looking over at Tammy, Mooney could see her cringe ever so slightly. She was obviously having second thoughts, but for some reason his coconspirator was holding herself back, seeming to be reluctant to explain why she didn't want her face on camera . . . which meant that it was left up to Mooney to manage the situation. "Becky, if you get us on camera and it ends up on the Net, then that would be documenting a crime, if it is, in fact, a crime. Not too cool."

Buttoning up her coat, Tammy then quickly reinforced what Mooney had said. "I agree. I don't want to be filmed doing anything illegal."

"But, like, it was your idea, remember?"

"I know it was my idea." Tammy then reached inside her coat pocket and pulled out a pair of gloves. "But now that I've had more time to think about it, I'm not sure using the camera is such a smart thing to do. When we first talked about doing this, I kind of thought it'd be an anonymous video to inspire other people to plant trees. And, y'know, I'm okay with that.

No problem. But I really don't want it to be in a video that can be traced back to me. I don't want to do something wrong and have it, like, live forever and ever on the Internet."

"Oh, wow. I can't believe how wimpy you two are. We're just planting a tree. Even some of my professors have told us in class that we should be doing more stuff like this. And a lot of my friends spend gobs of time watching videos, more than they do reading books. And, like, you're the one who said you wanted it to go viral, remember? So that sounded like a great idea to me."

"Becky, I think what Tammy's trying to say is that she's all for people grabbing their shovels and planting trees, but she wants to be careful and not have us uploading some sort of legal evidence that can be used in court."

"Okay, okay. I get it. No faces. Fine. Don't worry about it. Neither one of you will get a call from a reality TV show, I promise."

And so . . .

With the camera issue seemingly finally settled, the three of them then moved out the front door. Having planted many trees before, Mooney had put a bag of mulch and a milk jug full of water in the toy wagon with the little tree. So now, with the added weight, one of the wagon's wheels had begun squeaking as he rolled the wagon across the front porch. The noise was just loud enough to be heard, but it wasn't annoying enough to cause too much concern.

Or so he thought.

"Look at us. It's like we're going on a make-believe safari," Tammy joked, appearing to want to lighten the mood as she grabbed the shovel that was leaning up against the front porch.

"Yeah, a video safari," Becky snickered, checking the battery light on her camera. "I've always wanted to do a photoshoot."

"Wishes can come true," Tammy replied, moving down the walkway and over to the street.

Keeping his mouth shut, Mooney let the two of them have their fun. He was glad to hear them mellowing out the vibe. The last thing he wanted was for them to get mad at each other and stay mad at each other.

Making their way along the street, the wagon wheel continued its squeaking. It was somewhat noisy, yet Mooney still didn't think it would attract any undue attention.

But then . . .

As they passed Bob's house, the porch light suddenly came on.

"Uh-oh," Mooney said.

"What's wrong?" Becky asked.

"I was hoping we wouldn't run into Joe. He's the guy who lives there with his brother. So, like, if he comes outside, just let me do the talking, alright?"

But as it turned out, Mooney's concern was for naught. For as quickly as the porch light had been turned on, it had hastily been flipped back off. It seemed as though the noise from the squeaky wagon wheel had only been bothersome enough to get a pair of eyes to glance out the blinds of the window in order to check to see what was going on outside; yet since there wasn't much to gawk at, the porch light had quickly been turned back off. Maybe if there had been a bunch of gang members pulling up to the house in a lowrider for a home invasion, then the light would've stayed on, and maybe someone would've had a reason to pick up the phone and call 911. But since it was only the persnickety neighbors pulling a Christmas tree in a toy wagon – who cared?

So, continuing down the block, they crossed the highway and slowly squeaked their way toward the trailhead. "If it was any darker out here, we wouldn't be able to see where we're going," Becky said, leading the way.

"It'll brighten up once the moon comes out," Mooney said, glancing up into the trees.

"It's not a full moon, is it?"

"No. Only a half-moon. But that'll be plenty of light."

Pulling a small flashlight out of her pocket, Tammy turned it on. "I came prepared, just in case."

"I think you might want to turn that off, Tammy. We don't need to attract any more attention than we already have."

"Yeah, I know. I'm just checking to see if it works, that's all. I know we need to stay incognito." She then scanned the light beam across the trail . . . before she pressed the "off" switch.

"Tammy, if you're out in the woods at night with Moon, it's always a full moon," Becky said with a slight giggle.

"Okay, so – is that a good thing or a bad thing?"

"I guess it depends on who he's with."

"Oh, c'mon. That's just an urban myth," Mooney said.

"You mean, the part about you causing trouble or the part about the full moon? Which one's the urban myth?"

"The part about people ending up in emergency rooms when there's a full moon. Statistically, that's actually not true."

"But your own sister just said . . ."

"She's from Louisiana."

"So are you."

"Tammy, one time – not long after Becky graduated from high school – we went down to New Orleans, and she grabbed my arm and pulled me into this voodoo parlor in the Quarter; and she asked the lady running the place to sell her a love potion. I think she was trying to get herself a new boyfriend."

"Moon, you know that's not what happened."

"Yes, it is."

"No, it's not. I was just buying a gag gift for a friend, that's all. I didn't think it'd actually work."

"Full moon, voodoo hexes, ghost stories – none of that stuff's true. It's just superstitious gobbledygook," Mooney said, shaking his head.

"Well, I'm glad it's only going to be a half-moon tonight. I wouldn't want to be out in the middle of the woods with you two if there really was a full moon up in the sky."

"Tammy, you surprise me. I wouldn't've thought you were the type to believe in any sort of mumbo jumbo," Mooney said.

"I don't. Absolutely not. I want verifiable proof. I only believe in scientific logic. Or, as the Buddhists like to say, 'You should only believe what you can see and hear with your own eyes and ears.' What I was talking about was our visibility. If we had more moonlight shining down on us, then someone might recognize who we are . . . is what I was trying to say."

"Well, I wouldn't worry about it too much. I doubt we'll see anyone else in the park this time of night."

"Hey, y'know, this is starting to remind me of that time you were arrested, Moon."

"Arrested? So, like, what did you do to get yourself arrested?"

"It wasn't as bad as she makes it sound. The charges were dropped. I was a freshman in college. We were protesting wetland encroachment. An oil company was digging an access canal in a marshland. We went out late one night and did a sit-in in front of their equipment."

"Oh, okay. I guess that's a good reason to get arrested, huh?"

"Tammy, have you ever been arrested?"

"No, I try to avoid things like that. I have

claustrophobia . . . so I don't think I'd like being locked up very much."

"Well, from the way you talk, I thought you might've gotten involved in some protests or something such as that."

"No, not me. The last thing I want is an arrest record. Something like that can follow you around the rest of your life."

Hearing where this was going, Mooney was fairly sure that Tammy didn't want to discuss such things with anyone outside of the Flock. Ergo, he thought it was time to, yet again, change the subject. "Becky, are you going home with Ivan for Thanksgiving?"

"I think so."

"Is Ivan the one who's studying to be a marine biologist?" Tammy asked.

"No, that's Fred. Ivan's working on his Ph.D."

"Oh, he's the guy with the beard, right?"

"Uh-huh. From Portland."

As they crossed over the pedestrian bridge, and since there was a void in the overhead canopy at that particular spot in the woods, they now could see the moon reflecting off the creek several yards out from the bridge. Stopping, Tammy gazed down into the water. "It's running way higher than it was, and it looks like it's moving pretty fast, too."

"All that rain we've had."

"So, like, how far is it from here to the bay?"

"Maybe four or five miles, give or take a mile or two."

"Too bad you can't kayak it."

"You actually can if you want to portage around all of the thirty-foot waterfalls between here and there. But no one wants to do that. At least, not anyone I know wants to do that."

"Why not?"

"I guess 'cause it's way too much trouble. Most people just paddle out on the lake, or they put their kayaks in down at the bay."

Stepping away from the railing, Becky continued across the steel pedestrian bridge. "Yeah, and a couple of people recently got killed when they went canoeing out in the bay and a wave tipped them over."

"Hypothermia?"

"Uh-huh."

Pulling the red wagon, Mooney made his way to the other side of the bridge and onto the six-foot-wide trail of limestone gravel. Hanging back, Tammy lingered at the metal railing, seeming to want to soak in the sound of the fast-flowing current that was swooshing by right below her feet. It was somewhat obvious that Arbor Falls Park was casting its spell over her, as it seemed to do with almost all of those who came for a visit.

Letting their housemate enjoy her moment of contemplation – Mooney and Becky continued up the trail into the shadows. "Moon, how come she's so careful about what she says?"

"What do you mean?"

"She never talks about herself. And, like, when

something comes up in the conversation about her past, she clams up. I think she's hiding something."

"I don't think so, Becky. That's just the way she is."

"Well, I don't get it. She doesn't have a job; she's not in school; and she doesn't know anyone living here – so what's she doing here?"

"Why don't you ask her and see what she says?"

"I did. She said she's taking a year off and traveling around and thinking about what she wants to do with her life. But to me, that doesn't make any sense. If I was taking a year off, I'd go to some exotic place like Tahiti or Bali."

"Look, I wouldn't worry about it, okay? I think she's nice enough. We're lucky we didn't get stuck with a college brat who only wants to drink beer and party twenty-four/seven."

"Well, she's certainly not like that, that's for sure. She's soooo serious. And I thought I cared a lot about the environment. But, like, she has me beat hands down. Yet I swear she's hiding something. I mean, I don't think she's a criminal or anything like that. Well, at least, I hope not."

"Becky, I'm sure we don't have anything to worry about. You have to look at it from her point of view. She doesn't really know us. And, as you know, a lot of people are kind of careful about opening up to people they haven't known for very long. So she'll probably let her guard down and warm up to us once she sees we're outstanding citizens."

"Speak for yourself."

Chuckling under his breath, but still taking what his sister had said quite seriously, Mooney hoped he'd been able to mollify Becky's suspicions without sounding too protective of Tammy's hidden agenda since he didn't want to tip his hand. Being caught in the middle like he was, there wasn't much wiggle room either way. He knew if he said too much, Becky might be able to connect the dots and question his motives, which was the last thing he needed to happen.

Anyway, the rest of their hike into the park went smoothly enough. With the cover of darkness, and since it was as late as it was, they had the trail all to themselves, although a few times Mooney thought he had heard someone following them, yet each time he'd looked over his shoulder, there was no one there. So maybe it was nothing more than the wind in the trees.

After about twenty minutes, they had finally made their way to the black chain-link fence which separated the park from the cemetery. And by that time, the overhanging clouds had pretty much completely faded away, and the bright moonlight was now shining down in its full glory. On one side of the open area near the fence was a dense tree line of tall conifers. On the other side of the fence was a row of headstones that stretched for yards into the darkness, with only an old cherry tree growing on a small hill between the graves.

"It's getting cold," Becky said, still leading the way.

Without any leafy shrubbery to block the strong breeze that was blowing in from the bay on that part of the foothill – Mooney also felt the temperature drop. Zipping up his coat, he stopped to put on his gloves. "It's the wind chill."

Tammy, seeming to relish the cold, peered across the fence. "You know, at night that cemetery actually does look kind of spooky."

"I thought you said you didn't believe in stuff like that," Becky said.

"I don't. But you can see why people start thinking that way when the light's so dim. See that angel on the other side of that tree. It looks like it could almost flap its wings."

"That'd be really weird."

"Y'know, I think what's really sad is where they planted that cherry tree. It's had to live all alone on that hill its whole life," Mooney said, staring over at the old tree.

"That's a cherry tree?"

"Uh-huh. In the spring it has these really beautiful pink blossoms."

"Stupid cemeteries. People should just be cremated and not take up so much land with their dead bodies. Think how many trees had to be cut down to make room for all of those graves," Tammy said.

Squeaking along, Mooney then pulled the toy wagon off the trail and parked it in front of the grove of noble firs. "Are ya'll going to just stand there all night? We've got work to do."

"I think Tammy's waiting for that angel to flap her wings and fly over here to help you."

"Could you bring me the shovel?" Mooney asked as he unloaded the wagon.

"Oh, right." Swinging the shovel down from her shoulder, Tammy walked over to where Mooney was standing. "I tell you what. Why don't you let me do the digging, okay? Where do you want the hole to go?"

Moving deeper into the woods, Mooney stepped over to an empty spot between a pair of baby firs and the mature evergreens that towered over them. He kicked the heel of his boot into the ground to mark where he thought the orphan tree should be planted. "Here looks good."

Following behind him, Tammy glanced up at the limbs of the tall trees. "Yeah, I guess this is as good a spot as any. Should get plenty of sunlight. Not too close to the other trees."

Appearing to want to offer her opinion, Becky then walked over and began pushing buttons on her video camera. "Well, y'know, if I was a baby tree, I think I'd rather put my roots down a little farther into the woods and, like, not be right next to the trail."

"But if we do that, the little tree won't get much sunlight."

"Yeah, but it doesn't need to be that close to the trail, I don't think. You know how people are."

"True. But check out the other trees. So far those two six-footers seem to be doing fairly well where they are. I don't think anyone's going to bother them. Not in

255

the park," Tammy said.

"Hey, you never know. Not everyone's a saint around here. Just the other day they arrested three kids for setting fires in the cemetery," Becky said.

"Setting fires? Was that in the college paper?" Mooney asked.

"Uh-huh. They caught three high school kids with a box of kitchen matches and a can of gasoline, and they had pentagram tattoos on their arms."

Hearing this, Tammy shook her head. "Your brother warned me about how, um, things aren't always cool with some of the locals around here."

"Well, like everywhere else, we have our mutant dimwits, I guess. Too much genetically modified corn, if you ask me." Mooney then proceeded to tear open the sack of mulch.

"Or, y'know, as I like to call 'em, lame-o's," Becky replied, pointing her camera up at the moon.

Sighing, Tammy stepped back and stared down at the ground. "Look, I think right here is fine." She then plunged the edge of the shovel into the dirt.

"Go for it," Becky said, swinging her camera around and pointing it at the tip of the shovel.

"When you get tired, just let me know," Mooney said, stepping out of Tammy's way. "Two feet down should be good enough."

And so . . .

The digging had begun. Tammy worked the shovel like a pro. Watching her quickly cut open the topsoil, Mooney was impressed by how strong her arms were.

She shoveled out the dirt with a determined effort; and her spading only slowed for a few seconds when Becky, not realizing what she was doing, had moved in too close . . .

Trying for a low-angle camera shot, which had briefly crimped Tammy's rhythm. But then, seeing her mistake, Becky had quickly stepped back and gotten out of the way . . .

Pointing her lens at Tammy's anonymous waistline.

After about twenty minutes of serious effort, Tammy had dug the heck out of the hole. She was breathing hard, and her energy level seemed to be waning. "Want me to finish it?" Mooney asked. "Looks to me like you're down about two feet."

Stopping to replenish her oxygen intake, Tammy peered into the bottom of the hole. "Never hurts to go a little deeper so you can add in enough mulch."

Reaching over and sliding the shovel from her hands, Mooney nodded his head. "Yeah, that's true. I'll just widen it out a bit."

Then . . .

From off in the distance, a howl could be heard piercing the crisp air. Lowering her camera, Becky walked back over to the trail and stared off into the woods. "Oh, wow. Sounds like someone's hungry, huh?"

"A coyote," Mooney said between shovelfuls.

"In the park?" Tammy asked.

"Yeah, they come in here and use it as a safe harbor. When the neighborhood cats go missing, that tells you something's up."

"Coyotes eat the housecats?"

"They have to eat something. Not enough rabbits, I guess."

Walking back over to the toy wagon, Becky thumbed the buttons on her camera and flipped out its mini-screen. She replayed some of the footage that she had already recorded. "Wish I could get a coyote on camera. That'd be, like, sooo amazing."

"Back in the spring, I saw one trot across the trail down in that low spot near the stream. Didn't have much meat on his bones. Looked pretty scraggly. But the critter completely ignored me, as if I wasn't even there."

"I thought they avoided humans," Tammy said, again looking down in the hole.

"They do. But I guess he didn't smell me 'cause I was topping the hill, and he was already halfway across the open space. Just trotted right off into the woods."

"They're good diversity for the habitat. The more wild animals in here the better." Stepping over to Becky, Tammy then glanced over her shoulder at the playback of the footage that had already been recorded. "Not enough light, huh?"

"Yeah, it's too dark."

"Looks like you need a built-in spotlight."

"What about trying your flashlight?"

"I guess we could, but I doubt it'd work."

"It might work. You never know."

"Okay, if you wanna try; but, like, don't get too carried away and shoot a bunch of shots. You only need a few closeups of the tree and the hole. I think that's all you really need, if you ask me."

"I know, no faces. No mug shots. You want to protect your privacy." Then, swinging the camera around, Becky pointed the lens at her brother's hiking boot. "Tammy, why don't you shine your flashlight down in the hole? And, like, keep it pointed straight at the bottom for say ten seconds . . . then, like, shine it on the baby tree so I can get a shot of it sitting in its tiny container."

"Okay."

"So, like, after we do that . . . we'll then finish up with a shot of it being planted in the hole."

"You might also want to get a closeup of the mulch being poured in and the shovel mixing the mulch with the dirt before we put the tree in," Mooney said.

"Yeah, that's a good idea."

Thereupon . . .

Having come to a consensus, that's exactly what they proceeded to do. They plodded around in video mode, letting Tammy shine her flashlight at the various items so as to illuminate the agreed to shots. But since the intensity of the pint-sized light beam wasn't that bright, and since the recorded images could only barely be made out on the flip-out mini-screen – Mooney was skeptical that it was even worth the effort. Still, their staging of the camerawork hadn't taken up that much of their time; and the shot-by-shot coordination had given Becky something to do. Indeed, it was quite obvious to Mooney that his sister very much enjoyed the role of movie director, even if it was too dark for such a small camera to clearly capture anything worth recording.

Anyway, after the noble fir had been eased down into the ground and Mooney was carefully pouring the water from the milk jug around its trunk, having already leveled out the mulched-in dirt . . .

Becky finally turned off her camera. For a brief moment, it seemed as though she was happy with herself . . .

Until something suddenly caught her eye, and she quickly ducked behind a nearby tree. "Uh-oh. Turn off your flashlight. Don't make any noise."

"What's wrong?"

"I think I saw someone."

Heeding her warning, Mooney grabbed the wagon; and Tammy quickly picked up the other paraphernalia. They hurried out of the moonlight and into the shadows, darting under the tall trees. "Are they coming this way?"

"I don't know. It looked like the tip of a lit cigarette."

"Okay, just stay cool, alright? Let's keep our voices down and move a little ways off into the woods so we can put some distance between us and the baby tree. They won't notice what we've done if we're not standing near the fir," Mooney said in a hushed tone.

"Yeah, but what if it's the cops; and what if they come over here and ask us what we're doing?"

"If that happens, we'll just say we're taking a shortcut through the park. They might go for that."

"Yeah, right. Like they're going to believe we're out for a la-di-dah stroll with a squeaky wagon, a dirty shovel, and an empty bag of mulch."

"Well, it's not like we have a dead body with us or anything. And we're not carrying any weapons. So, y'know, just be cool. I'll tell them we're coming back from helping a friend do some gardening. There's nothing incriminating about any of this as long as they don't see where we planted the tree. Oh, and don't say anything about your camera, okay? That's the only evidence they'd have on us."

"Moon, you know I'm not a very good liar," Becky said as she stuffed her camera in her fanny pack.

"Look, all you have to do is keep your mouth shut and let me do the talking, okay?"

They then proceeded to sneak off along the edge of the woods . . .

With Mooney carrying the wagon in his arms and Becky and Tammy lugging the rest of the stuff.

After they had made their way through the darkness for about thirty yards, they looped back to the trail and stopped to see if there was anyone following them.

But it was totally quiet.

So at that point Mooney knew that it probably hadn't been the cops. If anything, it might've just been a cigarette smoker who, more than likely, hadn't even seen them. Or it was possible that maybe someone had been toking on something besides tobacco. It could've been a teenager trying to hide his dope smoking from his drug-sniffing parents.

And so . . .

Having done the good deed that they had set out to do, they high-fived each other and hiked back up the trail. But strangely enough, once they'd made it back to the warmth of the bungalow's living room, Mooney felt as though he'd left a little child alone in the woods. He knew he had only done what was best for the baby tree, but still there was a slight letdown. The tug on his emotions had stirred up some of the painful memories from the orphanage. He'd been reminded of how it felt to be left behind in a strange place without his parents to look out for him.

But thankfully, the reverberating gloom hadn't stayed with him for very long. By the next morning, his mind had refocused on his work. He had a deadline looming for an article he'd agreed to write for a blogger friend of his . . .

Which had been pitched to him as an investigative piece on why genetically modified corn, and its many variations in the food supply, was becoming the Achilles' heel of the American diet. Having done some in-depth research on the topic, Mooney had concluded that the public needed to be told why feeding corn to cows was one of the main reasons for there being so much deadly E. coli bacteria in the food system. Cow stomachs weren't meant to consume an unlimited diet of cheap corn. Their ruminant stomachs were better suited to digest grass and hay, not pounds and pounds of hybrid corn every day.

By late in the afternoon, Mooney had found and vetted much of the material he would need to write the article. Then, as he was taking a coffee break, he noticed Becky's camera sitting on the kitchen table. Knowing she'd gone off to class, he checked to see if there were any discernable faces on the saved video vis-a-vis the threesome's escapade in the park.

It only took him about ten minutes, per quickly skimming through the footage with the help of the fast-forward button, to review all of the scenes that Becky had recorded the night before. Having not seen any-thing of consequence that was uniquely identifiable, he rewound the tape and put the camera back on the table. Even with Tammy's flashlight illuminating the camera shots, there hadn't been enough light to make any sense out of what his sister had shot. So Mooney knew that his new housemate would be relieved to know that a traceable image of herself wouldn't be ending up on the Internet, if she hadn't already checked out the footage herself.

Now conceivably, if Becky's camera had somehow recorded a video sequence of a pair of playful otters romping near the baby tree, even in poor light . . . then Becky might've had a YouTube hit on her hands. Lovable animals acting like rambunctious kids seemed to always get a ton of "likes" on the Internet. But in this particular case . . .

Such popularized typecasting simply wasn't meant to be because it appeared that his sister's otter sighting had been a fluke. No one else had seen the furry animals, even though Mooney had repeatedly scouted the duck pond numerous times after Becky had told him she'd spied the two mammals at that location.

Yeah, well, maybe the cute furballs were just passing through the Arbor Creek habitat on their way to a less-humanized fishing spot . . .

Possibly looking for a much easier way to fill their stomachs than having to compete with a bunch of quacking ducks. So hypothetically, if a video lens had, in fact, been pointed at the visiting aquatics . . .

Then it was conceivable that such a pair of wild animals might not have wanted a camera capturing their images – somewhat like the two Flock members had shied away from the limelight, too – since the feral fuzzballs quite probably wouldn't've been in the mood to have their privacy pixelated for posterity.

Of course, the almost-tame mallards that Mooney frequently saw in the park's duck pond . . .

Certainly wouldn't have wanted any fish-eating competitors (such as a pair of hungry otters) . . .

Hanging around for very long, either.

Chapter Twenty-One

It felt like he was teetering at the end of a rickety gangplank . . .

Looking over the edge . . .

Wobbling back and forth . . .

With the tip of a sword nipping up against his spine . . .

As six-foot waves crashed around him. He only had a couple of dollars left in his pocket, and he was nearly out of bourbon. If he didn't come up with some damn cash pretty soon, he'd end up sinking to the bottom of the bay and be picked over by the hungry crabs. The loan sharks he owed money to would, more than likely, filet him into bite-size chum and toss his bloody appendages into the water after having used their razor-sharp switchblades to do their wicked handiwork to his flesh and bones.

For days Stoneface had been working feverishly to finish his angel. He'd even cut back on his drinking to keep his mind focused on the tiny detail work that needed to be performed on her face. Taking catnaps, he'd also been staying up most of the night, wanting to get the last bit of chiseling over with as soon as he could so he would finally be done with her.

And now, with only a dozen more swings of his wooden mallet, he was almost there. Taking a moment to admire her delicate features, he rubbed his callused fingers across her silky cheek. She was his pride and joy, and Stoneface desperately wanted her to like him.

But still, her lips wouldn't move. She just stood there, unwilling to acknowledge his presence. And that was just the way some angels were, so he wasn't at all mad at her for not talking to him. How could he be mad at her? He loved her more than he loved himself. She was as beautiful as any sculpture he'd ever made. She was a rare one-of-a-kind. An unbiased art critic might even call her his masterpiece. Her proportions were perfectly balanced with only a sly hint of sexy innuendo in her hips. Her powerful wings looked remarkably realistic, seeming to be able to float her up off the ground with little effort. Stoneface had spent hours and hours meticulously crafting each feather. And her breasts were the breasts of a saint. Their girly curves were as smooth as a baby's skin. Her eyes were the eyes of a morning dove. Her lips were as sweet as a passion fruit, ripe with a fullness that begged to be kissed. Even her feet were exceptionally gorgeous. He had worked diligently to shape the dainty arches and the lovely toes to make sure, when she floated above a field of flowers, that none of the colorful blossoms would be able to match the beauty of her tiniest parts.

Stepping back, he put down his chisel and mallet. His arms were tired from the incessant work. He needed a drink.

As he turned and walked over to the kitchen, stirring up the dust on the floor as he went, Stoneface suddenly heard a loud knock at the door. Stopping, he froze in place. Rarely did anyone ever come by so late at night. Cocking his ear, he listened for some sort of hint as to who it might be.

And then, yet again . . .

There was another rapping of knuckles against the outside of the door; but this time it didn't sound as threatening as it had the first time. So, not sensing any impending danger since most goddamn loan sharks would've just busted the door in, he concluded that it was probably someone he knew because they seemed quite determined to get his attention.

Striding across the room, he grabbed the doorknob, gave it a twist, and flung open his front door.

Ken McGardy was standing outside in the dark. He was holding a pistol in his hand, and he pointed it at Stoneface's stomach. "Give me my friggin' money."

"What money?"

"Damn it. You know what money." Pushing his way inside, McGardy closed the door behind him.

"Hey, c'mon. Put that damn thing down. I don't know what you're talking about."

"Look, cut the crap. I went back up in the woods where we ditched the scrap metal, and it wasn't there. So don't lie to me. You picked it up and sold off my half."

"No, I didn't."

"Yeah, you did."

"Wait a minute. Hold on. Why'd you get it in your head to go back up there? You didn't say nothin' to me about going back up there."

" 'Cause I found a guy in town who said he'd pay me good money for it, that's why."

"Are you crazy? If you fence that stuff here in town, they're gonna know where it came from. That's why we drove all the way down to Tacoma, remember?"

"Don't give me that bullshit. You double-crossed me. So where's my goddamn money?"

"You stupid son-of-a-bitch. You're standing in front of my face and calling me a goddamn liar; but you're the one who went down there to pick it up; and you didn't say nothin' to me about what you were doing, did you? I bet you weren't gonna pay me my half, were you?"

"It don't really matter, does it?"

"Yeah, it does."

"No, it don't 'cause you beat me to it."

"Look, Ken. I swear on my mother's grave I didn't double-cross you. I didn't go down there and get that goddamn scrap metal. Someone else must've gotten in there and picked it up. It certainly wasn't me."

"Bullshit! Don't lie to me," McGardy said, slapping the butt of his gun upside Stoneface's chin. "I hate being lied to, you thievin' bastard!"

Trying not to explode, Stoneface didn't strike

back. He didn't want to get himself shot in the belly. So instead of taking a swing at McGardy, he slowly slid his hand across his bloodied lip, biding his time until he could figure out a way to get the gun out of the bastard's hand. And yeah, he knew he was in trouble, but he also knew he might be able to calm things. The last thing he needed was for the gun to go off and have someone hear the shot and call the damn cops.

"Ken, stop and think, okay? Put yourself in my shoes. I've been working day and night, trying to finish my angel over there. That's why I'm all dusty and need a bath. You know I've never double-crossed you before. I know better than to do something disrespectful like that. I'm not stupid."

Spitting on the floor, McGardy kept the gun barrel pointed at Stoneface's gut as he proceeded to crab-walk his way over to the marble sculpture. "Yeah, right. You've been here the whole time workin' on your goddamn angel, uh-huh." With his left hand, McGardy then reached out and patted her derriere. "Y'know, it'd be such a shame if she accidentally fell over and broke into a bunch of pieces, wouldn't it?"

"No, don't you do that. Don't even think it. Get your hand off her."

"Then why don't you give me my damn money?"

"I told you, I don't have any goddamn money. I didn't hock that friggin' metal. I'm broke. I'm telling you the goddamn truth."

"Listen, damn it! Cough it up, or I'm pushin' her over, and you're gonna regret it, you lying scumbag."

"You stupid jerk. Can't you see I'm telling you the truth? She's my big payday. When I sell her, she's gonna make me plenty of money. If you knock her over, you'll have to kill me, 'cause I ain't got nothin' else to lose. And you'll be looking at murder one, too. So when they find you hiding in some cheap motel, as they always do 'cause you're gonna make a stupid mistake, they'll strap you on that goddamn hospital gurney, and they'll give you a friggin' lethal injection, and then you'll wish you'd never pulled the goddamn trigger."

Blinking his eyes like a flashing red light at a four-way stop, McGardy's head began to shake. "Are you swearing to me on a stack of Bibles that you didn't go back in there and pick up that metal we dumped in the woods?"

"I swear on my mother's grave. I'm not lying to ya. I'm telling you the honest-to-god truth."

Sucking in a deep breath, McGardy scrunched up his face. He looked like he needed to light a match under a spoon of heroin to calm his nerves. "Hell, you no-good shithead. I know I shouldn't believe you, but I guess I do. I tell you what. Let's let bygones be bygones. You sell your pretty-looking sweetheart, then you pay me for my time, and we'll call it even. No hard feelings."

"Even?"

"Yeah, even-steven. Or, y'know, if you don't want to patch things up, then I'll just knock her over right now, and you won't get squat, goddamnit."

"Okay, okay. Would a hundred dollars get us

straightened out?"

"Yeah, I can forgive and forget for a hundred bucks."

Stoneface was willing to bargain with the Devil if it would save his lovely angel from being harmed. But he also knew he couldn't trust McGardy as far as he could throw him. At the drop of a hat, the guy would turn on him. A drug addict like him would rat out his best friend to get enough money for a fix.

Damn slimebag.

So Stoneface agreed to the deal and got him to leave the premises. Then once the no-good bastard had left, Stoneface grabbed his whiskey bottle. His nerves were shot. He wanted to kill McGardy. Draining the last swig of bourbon into his mouth, Stoneface knew he was too upset to do any more work. His adrenaline was riled up. To simmer himself down, he told himself he had to shift his thoughts to something else. He had to vent his frustrations and not let his anger consume him. For days he had been putting off going up into the park, and now it was as good a time as any to get it over with.

Grabbing his hacksaw, Stoneface turned off the lights and slammed the door behind him. He desperately needed to make some quick money. Cutting down the two Christmas trees would be the easiest way for him to put a little bit of cash in his pocket so he could buy another bottle of booze.

A man would do things he never thought he'd ever do when he was broke.

It took him less than twenty minutes to drive up to the park since there wasn't any traffic to speak of at that time of night. Most folks had already gone to bed, and the streets were pretty much empty.

Parking in his out-of-the-way spot below the park, he checked to make sure his pickup wasn't too close to the road. He didn't want a nosey cop to get suspicious and stop to see what was going on.

Stoneface then walked up the slope through the tall weeds. The moonlight was just barely sufficient for him to see where he was going. He would've brought his flashlight with him, but the batteries didn't work, and he couldn't afford to buy any new ones to replace 'em with.

Soon, he felt the wind pick up and the temperate drop. A steady onshore flow was whipping in from off the bay. He began to get a little worried that he might get caught in a rainstorm, but he told himself that he should've thought about that before he'd left home. Now it was too late to turn around.

Hurrying his pace, it took Stoneface another five minutes to get up to the main trail and over to where the noble firs were growing across from the cemetery. And even though the chilly air was slightly invigorating, seeming to take the edge off his inebriation, he was pissed at himself because he'd forgotten to bring his damn gloves. His fingers were getting cold. The gusting wind had dropped the wind chill down to near freezing.

Huffing and puffing against the biting cold, he

stopped to catch his breath and pulled the hacksaw out of his coat pocket, rubbing his thumb across its blade. It was as sharp as a butcher knife. He always kept his tools in tip-top shape. He might be terrible with money, but he was a darn good stonecutter. Sawing through a pipsqueak tree trunk would be a piece of cake, whereas dragging the two goddamn trees back to his truck would be the real chore.

Steeling himself for what he knew he had to do, Stoneface then glanced up at the moon and noticed a dark cloud creeping ever so slowly across its face. It looked like he would need to hurry if he didn't want to get wet. There was nothing worse than getting soaked in a bone-chilling rainstorm with a strong wind frosting up your fingers and pelting you in the eyes.

Quickly making his way over to where the little Christmas trees were growing . . .

He at first was thrown for a loop by what he saw. Something was wrong. Why was he seeing what he was seeing? It didn't make any sense. He couldn't understand why there were now three six-footers growing in front of him, instead of two. Jiggling his head to clear out the cobwebs, he wanted to make sure he wasn't imagining something that wasn't there.

And no, he wasn't drunk; and no, the moonlight wasn't playing tricks on him. He was, indeed, standing in front of three Christmas trees, not two.

Three damn noble firs.

Scratching his head, Stoneface told himself that there had to be a logical explanation. Things like that didn't happen. A damn tree couldn't just pop up out of the ground and grow that goddamn tall that fast.

Bending down, he looked to see if he could figure it out.

What the hell is this shit?

And even in the dim light, it didn't take much of an effort to understand why there were now three Christmas trees. It was obvious that the third little fir had just recently been planted right there next to the other two.

Talk about good timing. This was like manna from heaven. Now it looked as if he was going to make more damn money than he'd first thought. So either his luck was finally changing, since he would soon have sixty dollars in his pocket, or maybe someone was messing with him. When Bragg Gartok had talked him into this two-bit caper, he hadn't said anything to him about anyone planting fir trees in the park. So it was possible that the extra little tree was nothing more than the happenstance of Lady Luck. Could be some dumbass was growing himself some easy-money Christmas trees and was waiting for the holiday season to come around, thinking he would then come back in there and cut 'em down and cash in on his illegal harvest.

Hey, anything was possible. Why else would someone plant a noble fir in the park? It didn't make any sense. And Stoneface was pretty sure that it hadn't been the Parks Department, that was for sure. With all of its layoffs and budgets cuts, the City Council surely wouldn't be wasting taxpayer money planting trees on public land. It didn't add up.

So, thinking the way he was thinking . . .

It must have been some dumbass doing something he shouldn't've been doing. And seeing as there wasn't anyone around to stop him – if this was, in fact, some sort of off-the-books tree-grow operation – Stoneface wasn't too worried about getting caught. The stupid idiot who was growing the noble firs should've been smart enough to know that a poacher like him might come along and steal the little tykes right out from under his damn nose.

Rubbing his hands together to warm them up, Stoneface then dropped down to his knees and leaned in with the hacksaw.

But then . . .

Just as he was sliding his trusty blade up against the trunk of the freshly planted fir – he heard a pair of wings flutter behind him. The noise sounded as though it was coming from the cemetery, and it piqued his curiosity. He wondered what size bird would make such a loud flapping commotion.

Standing back up, Stoneface turned around and saw the bastardized concrete angel hovering several feet up in the air. Her wings were beating as fast as a humming bird's, and she was slowly motioning to him with her right hand, trying to lure him toward her. It looked as if she wanted him to come over so she could tell him something.

But why? Why was she smiling at him like that

and waving him over?

The last time he'd tried to talk to her, she hadn't wanted to have anything to do with him. And, of course, he hadn't forgotten how hard she'd slapped him in the face, either. Yet now, here she was coaxing him to come closer.

Befuddled, Stoneface told himself that he still had enough liquor in his stomach to keep the d.t.'s from faking him out, so he didn't think he was hallucinating. If he had been imagining something that wasn't actually there, then most likely it would've been a funny-looking pink elephant with big floppy ears and not a poorly crafted statue which was flapping her wings as fast as she could in order to keep herself hovering above the ground. Plus, he didn't have the shakes. So the concrete angel had, indeed, come to life.

Of course, since he'd already had a spat with her once before, he knew he shouldn't do what he was going to do, but he couldn't help himself. When a transmutating angel – even a badly made knockoff – beckoned you over, it was almost impossible to ignore her. And such incarnations would rarely ever fly up in the air. There had to be something otherworldly going on.

Mesmerized, Stoneface walked over to the cemetery gate, *creaked* it open, and strode into the graveyard. Making his way between the headstones, he watched as the angel slowly drifted down to the ground and landed in front of a tree, just as the wind began to pick up. Even a giant pterodactyl would've had trouble staying aloft in the blustery gust that was now whipping in from the bay.

"Okay, so, what did you want to tell me?" Stoneface asked as he walked up the hill and crossed in front of the tree.

Laughing in a high-pitched chortle, the angel shook her head and pointed down at a grave that he was walking on top of.

"C'mon, I ain't got all night. It's fixing to rain, goddamnit. You called me over here, so you can at least be polite enough to talk to me." Stepping closer, Stoneface was now between the angel and the old tree, standing within several feet of its trunk. The wind was howling in his face, and its intensity was so tenacious that he had to lean into it just to keep himself from falling down.

It was also getting much colder by the minute, too. He was freezing his butt off.

Then suddenly . . .

He heard an eerie snapping noise, followed by a thunderous . . .

CRACK!

It sounded as though the old cherry tree was splintering apart.

Oh, no!

In a split second, he realized that the tree was coming straight down on top of him, looking as though its heavy trunk was going to kill him. And by the time this horrifying thought had jolted through him, he knew it was too late to get out of the way. He watched in disbelief as the tree upended, and its rootball quickly lifted up out of the ground.

KA-BAM!

The trunk smashed into his skull and slammed him down into the dirt. His body was flattened like a blood-and-guts pancake.

The pain was excruciating. Having a Little League baseball bat hit him in the face was small potatoes compared to being walloped by so much friggin' wood.

Unable to breathe, Stoneface's last thought was —

At least I won't have to suffer for very long, goddammit. Death will take me pretty quick. I just wish I could've had one more sip of bourbon.

Chapter Twenty-Two

After hiding in bed for two days, Zetty told herself that she had to cowgirl up and start asking more questions so she could figure out who these stalkers were and why they were doing what they were doing. There must be some sort of reason she'd become so popular with complete strangers. It had to be a mistake, which just needed to be cleared up. They obviously had her confused with someone else. She wanted to explain to them that she wasn't who they thought she was, hoping they would then apologize and her life would return to normal.

At least that was what she assumed would happen.

And so . . .

Once Zetty had come to this conclusion and had begun thinking about all of the unexplainable weirdnesses in that particular way, her resolution to straighten out her mistaken-identity problem had, in fact, helped her get out of bed. That morning she had even walked several blocks to a vending machine and bought a morning newspaper in order to read the classified ads so as to see if there were any jobs she could apply for. This was the first time in years she'd purchased a daily paper since she would always just read the free alternative-style weekly . . .

And since she didn't have any interest at all in reading what was in the regular paper anyway. But now Zetty needed to get a job, and so paying for one measly newspaper wasn't so bad as long as she didn't let herself get into the habit of buying a copy every day. She had her fingers crossed that someone might need an ex-floral arranger who'd decided, on the spur of the moment, that she didn't want to work with dead flowers anymore. She also still hadn't told Casey that she was quitting. After having spent hours and hours thinking about it, Zetty was pretty sure she wouldn't change her mind; but still, because her life had suddenly turned upside down, with all of the weirdos hitting on her, she had put off doing what she knew she had to do, wanting to give it a little more time before she talked to Casey. In other words, Zetty thought she needed to wait until she had built up her courage so she'd be able to squarely face the inevitable . . .

And thus have the strength to say what she knew she would have to say. Telling Casey why she was doing what she was doing wouldn't be easy.

Anyway, even though Zetty had bought a morning newspaper, hoping to find a job in the classified ads – she never did get to that particular section of the paper because of what she'd seen on its front page. A disturbing photo of a fallen tree had caught her eye. The headline read: "Man Killed by Tree in Arboretum Cemetery."

Quickly glancing through the news story, Zetty had instantly been shocked to find out that a tree had keeled over and killed a stonecutter. The facts were a little sketchy, but it appeared as though a strong wind had come up, and the poor guy had been in the wrong place at the wrong time.

It was quite sad.

But then . . .

Before she'd actually finished reading the whole article, she had again glanced back at the unsettling front-page photo of the dead tree, and that was when she'd noticed a familiar headstone.

Well, at least, it sort of looked like a certain headstone she'd seen before. Yet since the news photo had been taken from a good distance away, and since there were so many graves in the cemetery – she wasn't completely sure she was right, but it certainly did remind her of one of the small gravestones near her parents' cemetery plot.

And naturally, that got her attention.

Trying not to let herself get too upset, Zetty then thumbed through several pages of newsprint to read the end of the article . . .

And there it was. The reporter had actually written it out in black and white. The fallen tree was a wild cherry tree.

Oh, no. Zetty immediately knew what that meant.

There was only one wild cherry tree that she was aware of in the Arboretum Cemetery, and that was the hundred-year-old tree that was growing right beside her parents' graves.

For an agonizingly long moment, Zetty just sat there, unable to move, and continued to stare down at the newspaper photo. Tears came to her eyes. Seeing the dead tree lying on top of where her parents were buried brought back the heartwrenching memories. She had stood in that very same spot many times before, so she couldn't help but feel terrible about what had happened. Then her emotions got the better of her, and her right hand began to shake. She was devastated. The circumstances were hard for her to cope with.

Wiping back the tears, Zetty knew what she had to do. She had to go up to the cemetery and make sure that her parents' graves hadn't been disturbed. She also felt that she needed to take them something special, other than a bouquet of dead flowers, in order to make up for what had happened.

And so . . .

Wanting to do what her heart told her needed to be done, she decided to give her mom her favorite little toy which Zetty had been saving in her hope chest with some of her other keepsakes. On Zetty's sixth birthday, her mother had given her a cute plastic puppy; and so she decided that such a cherished memento might bring her mom some comfort if she placed the little toy on her mom's grave.

My mom really loved dogs.

Thereupon . . .

By the time Zetty had gotten out the door and caught the bus up to the lake . . .

Riding it all the way to the cemetery . . .

It was early afternoon. The sky was overcast, but at least it wasn't raining. For days, a torrent of showers had soaked Bellingham, with the heaviest downpours coming late at night. So even though the sun was now hiding behind a bank of clouds, not wanting to show its bright yellow face, Zetty was thankful that the rain had finally let up.

Walking up the trail from the bus stop, she clutched her toy puppy in her hand. Her tears had stopped, but she was still beside herself. She wasn't sure what she would find at her parents' burial plot. She just hoped that the old cherry tree hadn't damaged either of the headstones. From the newspaper photo, it had been sort of hard for her to tell if the tree had, in fact, landed on either of the graves.

Then . . .

As Zetty made her way into the cemetery and walked toward the small hill . . .

She saw the toppled tree tilted over on the ground. It was surrounded by broken branches. Having already shed its autumn leaves, the tree's remains reminded her of the skeletal bones of a dead bird. Sticking out from both sides were the featherless wings, and the long spine of the trunk kind of looked like the bird's neck. And for some reason, it didn't appear as though the groundskeepers had, as of yet, removed any of the debris. Maybe they had other things to do; or maybe they were waiting for a tree-removal service; or maybe the police didn't want anything disturbed until they'd had enough time to fully investigate exactly why the tree had fallen on top of the stonecutter.

In any event, there was no one around, which was also a bit surprising. Of course, in this particular part of the cemetery, there rarely ever was anyone doing anything, except for the occasional visitor solemnly laying flowers on a grave. With winter coming on, the groundskeepers had stopped mowing the grass weeks ago. And being the fastidious lawn-care workers that they were, it also looked as if they had already finished raking up most of the fallen leaves.

Steadying herself, Zetty continued forward and slowly made her way over to the dead tree. Now she could see what she was hoping she wouldn't see. A big branch had landed right on top of her mother's grave. But then, as she got closer, she breathed a sigh of relief when she saw that the weight of the tree's heavy trunk had actually fallen between the two headstones, which meant that neither of her parents' grave markers had been struck. In fact, for whatever reason, and quite remarkably, it looked as if the old cherry tree hadn't actually damaged any of the surrounding headstones at all.

Thank goodness.

Stopping beside a broken tree limb, Zetty stared

down at where the stonecutter had probably been standing. It appeared as though the body-recovery team, or whomever it was who did such stuff, had had to cut away part of the tree's trunk, along with some of its thick branches, to get to the corpse. Inching in for a better look, she now could see the red bloodstains on the grass. The poor guy must have been really clobbered pretty good because it was obvious that he'd lost a lot of blood.

Needless to say, it was disturbing to think about what had happened. The whole scene looked pretty macabre. It wasn't every day that someone got killed by a tree in Bellingham.

"Hey, what happened?" a voice called out from behind her.

Turning around, Zetty glanced across the fence and over into the park.

Oh, no. It was the guy who'd given her the stinging lecture on being nice to plants. What was he doing there? It seemed no matter where she went, these I-wanna-talk-to-you meddlers simply wouldn't leave her alone.

Not wanting to get into a conversation at that particular moment, even though she had told herself that she needed to start stirring things up if she was ever going to be able to figure out exactly what was going on with these nosey guys who seemed to be always hounding her and wanting to bend her ear . . .

Zetty shook her head and wiped her hand across her cheek. She wasn't in the mood to talk to anyone.

Straightening out someone else's rudeness could wait until a more appropriate time. She didn't want to have to explain why she was there doing what she was doing.

So, feeling uneasy – and thinking this wasn't a good time for chitchat – she turned back around and walked over to her mother's headstone, hoping the guy would get the hint and go away.

But that's not what happened.

He didn't get the hint.

He didn't go away.

Instead, Zetty heard the cemetery gate creak open behind her, and then she heard the guy's footsteps coming straight toward her.

"Look, I apologize if I upset you the other day. I hope you won't hold that against me."

Sighing, Zetty didn't know what to say; but she didn't want to be impolite, so she turned and faced him. "It's okay. I don't blame you for saying what you said."

"Oh, you've been crying."

"I have a lot on my mind."

"Well, if this is a bad time . . ."

Yes, of course this is a bad time. Can't you see I'm standing next to a grave?

Yet since she now had his attention, she decided to ignore his ill-mannered indiscretion and get it over with. "Look, since you walked all the way over here – I guess I'll just go ahead and tell you that I thought a lot about what you said, and I'm going to try to be nicer to plants, okay?"

Seeming to suddenly realize that maybe he shouldn't've come over and bothered her (possibly because of the agitated tone she'd used), the stalker began to anxiously rub his hands together. "Well, I'm glad to hear you're going to be nicer to plants. So, um, does that also mean you're not mad at me?" And as the guy proceeded to ask her this question, he continued on past her . . . walking over and staring down at the wild cherry tree's upended rootball.

"Quite honestly, I don't think I was ever really mad at you. If anything, I guess I was just sort of puzzled by what you did."

"Puzzled? What do you mean?"

"It's hard to explain. Let's just say I don't understand why I seem to keep running into strangers like you."

"Okay, now I'm confused. What type of strangers are you talking about?"

"Like I said, it's hard to explain. I was hoping maybe you could tell me what was going on."

"Tell you what's going on? I have no idea what you're talking about." And as the stranger said this, he then turned and peered down into a freshly dug grave on the other side of the rootball. "Y'know, this really pisses me off. Why the heck did they have to dig a grave so close to the tree's roots?"

"It's a cemetery. That's what they do in cemeteries. They dig graves."

"Well, I mean, they didn't have to go at it like butchers and cut through so many of the tree's roots.

They should've dug the grave farther away."

Stepping over to see what he was talking about, Zetty shrugged her shoulders. "Maybe the family that owns this burial plot; maybe when they first bought it . . . the tree wasn't that big and so maybe that was one of the spots someone wanted to be buried in. Did you ever think about that?"

"That's no excuse. The gravediggers should've known better than to do what they did. They should've thought about what so much digging that close to an old tree would do to it. They killed it." Then, shaking his head in disgust, the guy moved over and stared down at the bloodstains on the grass. "Uh-oh. Looks like someone got hurt, huh?"

"You didn't read about it in the paper? It was on the front page."

"No, I don't get the paper. What happened?"

"A gust of wind knocked the tree down. It fell on a stonecutter and killed him."

"Whoa. The tree keeled over and killed a guy, huh? I wonder what he did to deserve that?"

"What do you mean?"

"Well, it kind of looks to me like he must've been doing something he shouldn't've been doing since he wasn't able to get out of the way fast enough."

"Why do you say that?"

"Because I think most people probably would've been able to get out of the way of a falling tree."

"You think? Maybe it happened too quickly, and he didn't have time to get out of the way."

"Maybe so."

Shaking her head, Zetty told herself that this guy was a serious tree lover; and he obviously had a somewhat unusual perspective on things. He certainly seemed to have an atypical opinion about how people should treat plants, that was for sure. So, being in the mood that she was in, and being unable to think clearly, she let her guard down and pointed at the two graves. "That's where my parents are buried."

And when he heard her say this, he stood there for a brief moment and didn't respond.

Then, with an apologetic expression on his face, he said, "Oh, so that's why you came up here. I guess reading about it in the paper would be troubling, huh?"

"I had to see what happened. I'm just glad their graves weren't disturbed. And even though you're probably not going to believe me, I really did love that old tree. It certainly didn't deserve to die," Zetty said as she wiped back a tear and glanced down at the toy puppy in her hand, gently rubbing her fingertips over the dog's head and remembering back to when she was six years old and she had quickly torn the colorful wrapping paper off of her birthday present and had first seen the little pooch's loveable eyes. "So, I mean, I actually did listen to what you said about trying to help plants, and that's why I decided to quit my job, and that's also why I didn't bring any dead flowers with me when I came up here. I think flowers have every right to live long lives just like we do. So instead of bringing my mom a bouquet, I brought her this puppy."

Nodding his head, the tree lover's face melted into a subdued calmness. "Oh, okay. Um . . . would you like me to leave? Do you need some time to be alone?"

"No, you're not bothering me. I like talking to you."

And when she said this, his eyes slowly glanced down at the toy puppy. "Say, I tell you what. Why don't you go ahead and do whatever you were going to do, and then let's go for a walk in the park. I'd like to hear more about why you're quitting your job."

"You mean, so you can write about it in your blog?"

"Oh, you checked out that website, huh?"

"No, I think that piece of paper accidentally fell in the trash. I was just making a wild guess since you look like someone who might have some sort of blog."

"Well, y'know, I wouldn't want to impinge upon your privacy. I promise I won't write about it. We'll just talk, that's all. Off the record. Not for my blog."

"If you really want to know the truth, I wouldn't be offended if you wrote about any of this, actually. It wouldn't bother me. I mean, if you think it'd help convince people to stop hurting plants, then I wouldn't have a problem with it." Bending down, Zetty then placed the little puppy on top of her mom's headstone. "She always liked dogs."

And so . . .

Having done what she'd come there to do, Zetty turned and smiled at the tree lover. This rather peculiar fellow had such a pleasant demeanor. And his voice was strangely soothing. She sensed he was someone quite special. He might have an odd way of looking at things, but she didn't think he was a weirdo stalker. A weirdo stalker wouldn't've been at all interested in why the old cherry tree had fallen over and killed a man.

Walking toward the gate, the two of them left the cemetery and entered the park. "I read the names on the two headstones that were next to the old tree. You must be a Hart."

"Yes, Zetty Hart."

"I'm Mooney."

"What's your last name?"

"Waters."

Mooney Waters. It had a nice ring to it.

Then . . .

And as they walked along the trail, Zetty couldn't help but notice the grove of noble firs which was growing right on the edge of the woods. "Look. Your favorite tree."

"Yeah, you're right."

"Oh, and it looks like someone just planted one, too."

"Huh. Whad'ya know?"

"I wonder who'd do that?"

"Maybe the city has a new tree-planting program."

"Yeah, maybe so." Not wanting to pull the rug out from under his charade, Zetty left it at that. She might not have a college degree, but she certainly was smart enough to recognize the exact same noble fir which she'd sold him only a few days ago. She had watered the little tree for several weeks, so she knew the shape of its limbs and how its crown leaned slightly to the left. She had no doubt that it was the exact same tree. But since it appeared as though he didn't want to share the particulars of how the baby fir had ended up in the park, she wasn't going to press him for an answer. She'd let him keep his secret.

"You said you were quitting your job. Are you doing that because of what I said when we first met?"

Unsure if she would be able to explain why she was doing what she was doing – and since she also didn't want him to feel responsible for her leaving her job – she didn't know what to say. But then she realized that he might think she was being disingenuous if she didn't at least offer him some sort of explanation. She had never been good at hiding things. "Well, to be honest, what you said did get me wondering about some stuff I'd never thought about before. Like, y'know, the part about plants feeling things. The more I thought about it; the more it seemed to make sense. Plants are just as alive as we are. So, um, I guess they must feel things like we feel things. I don't see why they wouldn't."

"Of course they feel things. We evolved from plants. Plants have been around a lot longer than we have. But quitting your job's a biggie, don't you think?"

"Well, it's not something I wanted to do, that's for sure."

"So, like, do you have another job lined up?"

"I'm pretty sure I can find another job. There has to be something I can get paid to do besides arranging flowers. But, I mean, that's not my only problem right now. For some reason, and I have no idea why – weird stuff keeps happening to me."

"What do you mean?"

"I don't know how to explain it. It's just, I don't know, weird stuff."

"You mean, like that tree falling down?"

"No, I don't think that had anything to do with me. The stuff I'm talking about kind of started back when I bought my new shoes."

Looking down at her feet, Mooney seemed to be perplexed by what she meant. "Those shoes?"

"No, these are my clodhoppers. My other shoes. I'm talking about when I bought a pair of blue tennies."

"So what do you mean by weird stuff?"

"You know, weird stuff – like when a stranger comes up to you and starts asking you dumb questions. Weird stuff like that."

Again, he looked down at her shoes, seeming to think he had missed something. "You mean, someone said something to you 'cause you were wearing blue shoes?"

"No, it was because I bought the shoes to go with my mom's old satchel, and when I started carrying it around with me – that's when, for some weird reason, this stranger wanted to talk to me. Weird stuff like that."

"Zetty, maybe this guy just wanted to ask you out on a date. Maybe the blue tennies gave him an excuse to say something to you."

"So, you think it was my fault, and I should never have bought the shoes in the first place, is that it?"

"No, I'm just saying when a guy sees a good-looking girl like you, and if she's wearing some sort of something that gives him an easy excuse to break the ice, then you have to expect that that's what's going to happen, that's all."

"He was just hitting on me."

"More than likely, yeah."

"Okay, maybe so. I mean, that's what someone else said, too. They said it was just a guy being a guy. But, like, I don't think that's what it was. I think it was something else."

"Why do you say that?"

"Well, 'cause I thought – y'know, him coming up to me like that – might've had something to do with my mom's satchel. Nothing like that had ever happened to me before. But when I decided to use her bag to carry stuff around in . . . that's when it all started, right after I bought the blue shoes since they were the same color."

"Hey, maybe I'm wrong; but if you ask me, most guys really don't care about things like that. Women do, but guys don't. It doesn't matter if you're wearing high heels or if you're walking around in bare feet. That's not what guys look at."

Of course, Zetty knew what he meant; but it was

how he said what he said that made her realize that he was trying to be civil in polite companion. Without having mentioned any of her unmentionable body parts, Mooney had rather cagily focused in on the heart of the matter, so to speak, while, at the same time, sidestepping the obvious. And since he was a seriously handsome guy, he probably pretty much knew what he was talking about. "Well, maybe you're right. Maybe I'm wrong. Figuring out how guys think isn't that easy for me, that's for sure. But, like, I really thought the logo on my mom's satchel might've had something to do with that stranger coming up and talking to me. I mean, for some weird reason, he just kept staring at it. His eyes weren't looking at me. They were pretty much glued to the satchel."

"So why do you think he was staring at it?"

"Honestly, I don't know. Maybe it was because it's kind of unusual. No one else has one quite like it. It's a blue satchel, and it has a dark green logo of a tree inside a squiggly circle of gold snakes. My mom got it years ago, and I found it in her things after she'd passed away."

Why am I telling him this? I feel like I'm talking to a psychiatrist or someone who acts like a psychiatrist.

Anyway . . .

When he heard these words pop out of her mouth, Mooney tensed up. Zetty could tell she'd said something that had hit a nerve. The way he'd instantly reacted was a dead giveaway. Plus, to make it even more bewildering, it also looked to her as though he was trying his best not to appear to be too obvious about having been taken aback by what she'd said. In other words, it seemed as if he didn't want her to notice how startled he was about what she had just told him.

"Um, do you know where your mom got the satchel from?"

"I think someone in Canada might've given it to her."

"Oh, okay. That could explain it. Maybe it's a collector's item. Maybe that's what's going on. Maybe you unknowingly crossed paths with an antique collector."

"You think?"

"Could be. I'd like to take a look at it."

"Sure, okay. I'll show it to you. And if it turns out that's all it is – I mean, if it's some sort of antique, then that would explain a few things, I guess."

Stopping at the top of the trail, they turned and looked down at the bay. Two of the San Juan Islands could be seen off in the distance, looking like a pair of humongous humpback whales coming up out of the water for air. It was a gorgeous view, and it was also the perfect note to end their walk on because Mooney, after he glanced down at his watch to see what time it was, said he had to get back home so he could help his sister with a research project.

Oh, my. He has such a caring face.

Realizing that he had more important things to do with the rest of his afternoon, Zetty (feeling an overwhelming urge to get to know him better) . . .

Invited him to drop by her apartment at seven later that night, giving him her address. She asked him to come by and check out the satchel's logo. She thought that maybe he would be able to tell her if it really was a collector's item or not. Of course, she was also using the invitation as an excuse to see him again, too, since he seemed to be seriously nice and since she was already thinking ahead to the possibility of getting him interested in asking her out on a date, which meant that she needed a reason for them to spend more time talking to each other in order for that to eventually happen.

Hey, it never hurts to try. A girl has to try. As she'd often heard her mom tell her dad, "You can't just sit on your hands and wait for things to happen. You have to get out the door and go climb the mountain if you ever want to make it to the top."

Chapter Twenty-Three

Now he didn't know what to think. He had gone back to where they'd planted the baby fir in order to check to see how it was doing, and he'd ended up crossing paths with the girl who'd sold him the tree at the flower shop.

That was unexpected.

Plus, when he'd looked over the fence into the cemetery and had noticed the fallen dead tree, a deep sadness had overcome him. The old tree's tragic death had been quite disturbing. Staring down at the deceased remains of such a large tree was always tough on him, especially one which had been so badly mistreated. The cherry tree, from all appearances, had had a relatively hard life. It had grown up all alone on that small hill for those many years. And to add to the tree's never-ending woe, it'd also had to suffer through the repeated hardship of having its roots continuously surrounded by more and more coffins as the years had progressed.

Poor tree.

No wonder it had keeled over. Its roots had been

starved to death by the heartless gravediggers who'd kept shoveling out their countless buckets of dirt so they could plop in the six-foot-deep burial holes around its trunk. Mooney now regretted not having done more to help the old tree while it'd still been alive. But his focus had been on the wild plants that were growing in the park; and since the cemetery wasn't actually a part of the park, per se . . .

Mooney hadn't included the cemetery's fenced-in species on his watch list. In hindsight, there might have been something he could've done to alleviate the cherry tree's suffering if he'd only known that the gravediggers had been spading so much dirt so close to its shallow roots. Maybe he could've prevented it from toppling over.

The unfortunate incident had reminded him that no tree should be taken for granted. All living life was interconnected in ways that few humans understood. To him, planet Earth was a zoetic organism. It wasn't just a watery chunk of space rock spinning around the Sun. Some might call it the Gaia hypothesis, but Mooney didn't consider the complexity of the inter-connectedness to be a hypothetical hypothesis at all.

No, to him it was quite real.

So, all in all, it had been a somewhat strange afternoon. Hearing Zetty talk about her new concern for helping plants and then finding out that she was quitting her job because her conscience was bothering her (since she wanted to stop being a purveyor of dead flowers) . . .

Such a heartfelt divulgence, coming from someone he'd only briefly shared his philosophical concerns with – had been a bit of an eye-opener. It seemed that Mooney had wrongly misjudged her when they'd first met. She obviously was a well-meaning person. And the only reason he hadn't taken the time to ask her more about what had happened to her deceased parents was because his antennae had picked up on her emotional wobble. He could see that she'd been quite shaken up by the tree tipping over near their graves. So Mooney hadn't wanted to burden her with any troubling questions about how her parents had died.

Then . . .

When she'd mentioned the logo on her mom's satchel, that unexpected detail had really knocked him for a loop. It was as though a bizarre synchronicity had suddenly whirled its way into his human habitat, somewhat like an unseen funnel cloud.

But why?

Why had such a harmonization happened?

Had they simply met because the baby tree needed help, or was there more to it than that?

Of course, the possibility of there having been some sort of unforeseen hands bringing the two of them together would've been considered an outlandishly absurd thought to most people. Yet for an enlightened member of L.E.A.F., such a serendipitous occurrence would not have been labeled as being totally abnormal. There was, in fact, a logical explanation as to why what had happened had happened . . .

Which meant that Mooney now had to decide what he should do about it. Maybe Zetty deserved to be told what she didn't know.

Then again, on the other hand, there was the Flock secrecy protocol. It would be almost impossible to tell her the truth without him having to mention the unmentionable details.

It was a conundrum with no easy answer.

If you want to save yourself, you'll have to also save the planet.

Sitting on the back steps of the bungalow and gazing out at the lake – Mooney struggled with what he should do. He told himself that he needed to talk to Tammy about this unexpected turn of events; but she wasn't home when he'd returned from the park, nor was Becky. So to get his mind off of the discomforting uncertainty, Mooney sat there staring out across the water and breathing in through his nose . . .

Watching the sunlight begin to fade across the sky. A few hundred yards out, a small sailboat was slowly floating by.

The water was calm.

Up on land, there weren't any rabbits in the garden munching on their fall veggies; and except for his dilemma over what to tell Zetty, all was well in his human biosphere.

Ergo, it seemed like a good time to quiet his mind with some backyard meditation.

Om ah hum.

Ommm ahhh hummm.

Disconnecting from the constant tick of time, Mooney covered the face of his wristwatch with the palm of his hand and told himself: *There's no past; there's no future; there's just the calm serenity of the present moment.*

Om ah hum.

Ommm ahhh hummm.

Then . . .

After a few minutes of restful meditation . . .

And feeling as if he was being pulled back into reality from a sleepy daydream, Mooney heard the back door creep open. Turning, he saw Tammy's hiking boots standing next to him.

"Hi, I wondered where you were," she said as she moved down the steps and walked out into the chilly air.

"Did you go into town?"

"Had a few things I needed to pick up."

"Find what you wanted?"

"More or less. The only thing that's still on my shopping list is a brand of tofu I like."

"Did you try the co-op?"

"No, I'll check there next time, I guess." Tammy then plopped herself down on the steps. "Wow. That's such a beautiful view, huh?"

"That it is. That it is." Glancing down at her boots, Mooney suddenly noticed that there wasn't a speck of dirt on them. It amazed him how she could tool around town without ever getting her boots dirty since

Bellingham was notorious for its muddy sidewalks. Anyway, this was as good a time as any to bring her up to speed on what had occurred earlier that afternoon. "Tammy, there's something I need to tell you."

"Okay."

"I think I may've met the daughter of two founding members."

"Of the Flock? Are you sure?"

"No, I'm not positive, but I'm hoping to find out more pretty soon. She wants me to drop by her place later tonight."

"Wait. How'd she know who you were?"

"She didn't know who I was. And I don't think she knows anything about L.E.A.F., as far as I can tell. She seemed to be completely clueless about who her parents really were. They died years ago. So I don't think she's ever been told anything about any of it."

"Mooney . . ."

"Look. I know it's a problem, I give you that."

"When did you talk to her?"

"Earlier this afternoon. And it was the strangest thing, too. When I went down into the park to check on our baby fir, I noticed that an old tree had toppled over in the cemetery. She was standing right beside it. It was the girl from the flower shop, the one who'd sold me the noble fir."

"You mean, she was, like, waiting for you in the cemetery?"

"No, I don't think she was waiting for me. If anything, at first it looked as though she didn't even want to talk to me. She seemed to be upset 'cause that tree had fallen next to her mom's grave."

"Oh, so that's why she was standing there. But don't you think it was a bit of a coincidence to run into her like that?"

"Yeah, I thought about that. It was pretty weird. Really strange, actually. But, I mean – I don't think she knows anything about me or the Flock." Brushing a piece of grass from his pant leg, Mooney continued with his explanation of the unsettling events. "So anyway, when I saw the fallen tree, I was sort of curious as to what had happened, and I was also seriously surprised to see her standing there, too. I'd only met her that one time before. Then we started talking; and, for whatever reason, she opened up and told me something that there's no way she could've known unless it was true. I mean, she seems to be totally genuine. And it all adds up, too, because her parents' graves were right there, right next to that old tree which had fallen over. A Flock tree."

"C'mon. How do you know that? There's a lot of graves buried next to a bunch of trees in that cemetery."

"Yeah, that's true. But I checked the date they died. It was on their headstones with their birth years. The timeline fits. They were the right age. And they were buried under that old tree, i.e., a Flock tree to watch over their graves."

"Probably a coincidence."

"I don't think so."

"Did they move down here from Canada?"

"Yes, she did mention Canada back when I first met her at the flower shop, but I didn't want to ask her too many questions in the cemetery. I was worried she might get suspicious. Maybe she'll tell me more about her parents when I go see her tonight."

"Mooney . . ."

"Tammy, I know I'm not following the manual on this. I know the rules. But if this is some sort of coincidence, then it was meant to be, if you ask me. Like I said, I don't think she went out of her way to get my attention. You were there when I first ran into her, by happenstance, if that's what you want to call it. We were just walking by that flower shop. She didn't come out and talk to us. I'm the one who went inside and talked to her. So, I mean, I don't think she's working for the other side."

"Mooney . . ."

"Look, there's even more to it than that. Today she also told me she has her mom's old satchel. And get this, it has our logo on it."

"No way. C'mon. How could she have a Flock logo?"

"I'm telling you, from the way she described it, it's a perfect match."

"Would you please lower your voice?" Tammy then stood up and walked over to the corner of the house to make sure that no one was in earshot. Looking over at the neighbor's backyard as an extra precaution, she shook her head. It didn't appear as though there was anyone outside. Making her way back over to the steps, she leaned up against the house. "Moon, do you know why I'm here?"

"No, you never actually told me why you were here, and I never asked you. But you did say something about fundraising. So I figured maybe that's why you came here."

"Look, I'm sure you know there are several other cells in Bellingham that you've never been told about."

" 'What we don't know, can't hurt us,' right?"

"Exactly. So I shouldn't even be telling you this, but now I think you need to be brought into the loop." Pausing, Tammy sorted through her thoughts before proceeding in a near whisper. "One of our members saw a female walking around downtown with a founder's satchel. Then later, when we tried to track the intel down, it actually verified out as being true. Her name's Zetty Hart."

"You knew all along, didn't you?"

"Yes, I knew she was working in that flower shop, that's true. And yes, that's also why I didn't want to go inside. We've been following her for weeks, trying to figure out what she's up to."

"You could've told me."

"I was under orders not to tell you. 'What we don't know . . .' "

" '. . . can't hurt us.' "

"Look, I know it wasn't the best way to handle it, but I didn't have that many options since the assignment was being handled by another compartmentalized cell. They were trying to nail it down ASAP. We can't have someone walking around town advertising our logo. As you know, we only use the L.E.A.F. insignia on our internal documents as a certification mark. So, like, we absolutely don't want anyone using it for anything else."

"Oh, man. This is . . . this is . . . Well, I mean, it sounds like someone forgot to tell the founding members that their logo was a big secret way back when they first started the Flock. That's what it sounds like to me."

"Moon, I don't know what you do or do not know about some of this stuff; but as best as I can understand it, when the founding members first got together, they had no idea their little group would eventually evolve into as large an organization as it's become. Yet from the very start, they were always big on secrecy, which means we really don't know how many of them are still alive because, right from the beginning, they made sure they compartmentalized the L.E.A.F. cells and never let anyone write any of the membership names down."

"Tammy . . ."

"Look, I know I'm breaking protocol, but let me finish, okay?" She then quickly glanced around, yet again, to make sure that no one was in earshot before she lowered her voice to an even softer whisper. "Anyway, we both know the government has been trying to infiltrate us. They want to know how many cells we have, and they're desperate to get a list of all the names. Some of us think they may've even planted a few deep informants, trying to find out what we're up to."

"Saving trees. Stopping the crooks from polluting the air and the water. That's what we're up to."

"I know that, and you know that; but they want to look under all the rocks for a link to ELF."

"Well, if I was them, I'd be worried about another ELF, too."

"Hey, c'mon. ELF isn't the problem. They've done a lot of good. You know that."

"I just don't see how their type of violence sends the right message. It's counterproductive."

"I agree they've done some stupid things. We're on the same page. And that's why we don't do things like that, but we do have some of the same goals, as you are clearly aware of. Anyway, the reason we prioritized this can of worms is because we don't want the gov putting the pieces of our puzzle together. We don't want the FBI getting their hands on the satchel. So if there ever has been a leak and if the FBI happens to have an image of our logo in their database, assuming they do, then they would obviously use such a satchel to trace the names of our cell members, if they could get their grimy hands on it."

"But that means they might already know she has it, and so maybe they're using it as bait. Did you ever think about that? Maybe by you coming here and having the Flock put so much effort into this, the feds are getting even more names and info than they ever would've had if the alphas simply would've just let it go and turned the page."

"Hey, c'mon. We're not stupid, alright? We did, in fact, think about that. And that's why we had Zetty checked out. If the FBI had a file on her, they would've already have confiscated the bag, or they would've put a tail on her. But that didn't happen. She still has it, and we haven't seen any undercover guys wearing dark sunglasses following her around."

"Oh, man. This is a weird loop I'd rather not be in."

"Too late now."

"Well, I still don't get it. Why are you risking so much to get your hands on an old satchel? I mean, it sounds to me like there still might be something else you haven't told me."

"Look, I've already told you way too much, okay? We need to stick to the protocols. It's better if you don't know anymore than you already do."

"Why does that not surprise me?"

"Oh, wait. I almost forgot. There is something else I need to tell you. Since Zetty took it upon herself to open up to you, I want you to work your magic and sweet talk her into giving you the satchel."

Shaking his head, Mooney couldn't help but raise his voice. "Tammy, you know that's not going to happen. Why would she do that? She, like, inherited it from her mother. And unless I'm missing something here, there's no way I can explain any of this to her. So if I even hint at what her parents were really up to or try to explain why that logo was on her mom's bag, she might go to the cops. I mean, who knows what the heck she'll do."

"Moon, I've already thought about that. That's why when you go see her, I need you to take a picture of the bag. And I also need you to look inside it and check to see if it has a label that says it was made in Canada."

"Oh, right. Like she'll let me do that, uh-huh."

"Why wouldn't she? You just said she doesn't know what she has or why she has it. So if she's totally naïve as to what's going on, then I think you should be able to figure out a way to make it happen."

Pausing to think about what Tammy was implying, Mooney rubbed his hand across his face. "Well, I did tell her that it might be a valuable collectable. I had to tell her something to explain why it was attracting the interest of, y'know . . . *pushy strangers* who, as it turns out . . . you conveniently forgot to tell me were Flock members badgering her."

"Look, mistakes were made. I agree. True. But you were kept in the dark for a reason, okay?"

"Compartmentalization."

"Exactly. So, like, here's the deal. Get a picture of the satchel, check the label, and offer to buy it."

"Buy it? For how much?"

"A few hundred, tops."

"No, I don't think she'll go for that."

"Well, try, okay? Ask her how much she wants for it. We might could go a few thousand – if, like, y'know, push comes to shove."

"So what should I tell her if she asks me why I want to buy it?"

"Tell her the truth, but not the whole truth, of course. Tell her you know someone who's into collecting collectibles; and if she says she wants more money, then tell her you'll have to get back to her after you check with the collector to see if he's willing to up his price."

"Oh, man. I hope this isn't illegal."

"I don't think so. It's not like we're conspiring to commit a crime. We're just buying a satchel, that's all. Oh, and tell her the buyer also wants her to sign a confidentiality agreement, and see what she says."

"To keep it quiet?"

"Exactly. We don't want her blabbing about any of this to anyone else. That's the last thing we want. So, I mean, even if we use a fake name on the confidentiality agreement, she won't know it's bogus. As long as she thinks it's a legal document, maybe she'll keep her mouth shut."

"Well, it seems to me that it might be easier to talk her into joining the Flock and have her just give it to us. Less hassle, if you ask me."

"No way. That's absolutely not going to happen since she doesn't have that type of psychological profile. Her background report said she wasn't activist material."

"Could be the report was wrong. I think she has potential. That's the impression I got. But since I've only spoken to her those two times, we didn't talk that much about the environment, actually."

"Look, we don't want you trying to recruit her. We simply want you to get the bag and get this over with as soon as possible. We've already had way too much visibility on this as it is. It's only been by sheer dumb luck the FBI hasn't blipped her on their radar."

Chapter Twenty-Four

She knew she shouldn't have said what she said, but she couldn't help herself. Miss Pineford had asked her not to tell anyone where her parents had been buried unless they knew the secret password. Yet having no way of knowing if the stories that Miss Pineford had told her were true or not, Zetty wasn't sure if her foster mom's memory was reliable. It was possible that the Alzheimer's had already progressed too far. A lot of what Miss Pineford had said simply didn't make any sense.

So when Mooney had suddenly walked up to Zetty in the cemetery and had begun reading the inscriptions on her parents' headstones – being as she was standing right next to him – Zetty had decided that there was no reason for her to lie to him about who they were. It was obvious why she was there. Who else would she be visiting in the cemetery?

Then again, if Zetty hadn't've been so upset over the fallen tree . . .

Maybe she would've been able to hold her tongue.

She certainly hadn't intended to tell anyone where her parents were buried; but she also didn't think that there was any reason to lie about something that she wasn't at all sure Miss Pineford had remembered correctly anyway.

Of course, as it turned out, Zetty was actually glad that Mooney had come over and struck up a conversation with her, even though his timing had been somewhat unsettling, considering the circumstances. Their little chat had made her feel a good bit better about what had happened, and his concern for her welfare had seemed to be sincere. Also, knowing what she now knew, she certainly didn't want him to change his mind and decide to never see her again.

Yet still . . .

Deep down in her soul . . .

She was pretty sure he wasn't attracted to her – not even in the slightest bit – whereas she was seriously smitten with him.

But so?

So what?

They didn't have any common friends. And, as far as she could tell, he wasn't from Bellingham.

Hence, she told herself that she shouldn't be wasting her time even thinking about the possibility of Mooney Waters falling for her, because a guy like him was never going to ask her out on a date anyway. He was only interested in checking out her mom's satchel. For some reason, that was what had really grabbed his attention . . .

Much more so than anything else she'd said. It wasn't as though he was intending on starting a relationship with her. She was too plain and unassuming to catch the eye of someone like him.

Nonetheless, in preparation for their rendezvous, Zetty had stopped by the library to read his blog. Sitting at one of the computer stations, she had keyed his name into a search engine and had scanned her eyes down a list of links to a number of articles that he had posted online. And, quite surprisingly, it was an impressive list of titles, too.

Then, when she had clicked on one of the blue links, his bio had popped up via a sidebar. It said that after he'd graduated from college, Mooney had worked for a number of environmental nonprofits . . . before he'd finally found his true calling in life and had begun writing his own eco blog. And though she couldn't tell if he was famous or not from this quick bit of research, she did conclude that he certainly appeared to be somewhat well known, considering how many people posted comments on his webpage.

So, having read what she'd read on the Internet, Zetty now knew that she shouldn't get her hopes up. Being who he was, he might not even show up at her apartment because he probably had more important things to do than drop by for a visit. If anything, when he'd walked up to her at her parents' graves, he could've simply been concerned about what had happened to the fallen tree. Or maybe he was doing some research for an article he was writing. In other words, why would someone like her – or why would her mom's old satchel – matter that much to a guy like him?

Trying to stay levelheaded, Zetty told herself, having had some more time to think it through, that she really shouldn't let her expectations get the better of her by thinking that Mooney would even come by her apartment since she didn't want to be disappointed if he ended up breaking his promise.

Then later . . .

When she'd gotten back home and had had even more time to think about what it all meant, she wished that Edna-Ney hadn't've been at work. Zetty would've liked to have asked her what her opinion was in regards to what Mooney had said. But since her roommate was at the bar working her regular shift, Zetty knew Edna-Ney wouldn't make it home until much later that night.

Oh, well. Why should Zetty worry about something that probably wasn't going to happen anyway? Worrying about a handsome guy knocking on her door wouldn't do her any good.

And so, with that thought in mind, Zetty decided that she would just prepare herself for a letdown and try not to fret over being stood up by such a good-looking guy who she, more than likely, would never ever see again.

Now, despite having already suspected what the outcome would be – as 7 o'clock came and went, Zetty was, nevertheless, anxiously plopped down on the sofa.

Her head rested on a pillow, and she was comfortably snuggled under her mom's old comforter. In her hand she held the open pages of yet another library book. But thankfully, this time the picture on the dust jacket hadn't been a bait and switch. No, this time she wasn't reading a book which teased a person's eyes with false promises. This time it wasn't that type of book. Instead, she'd found a how-to hardback that clearly laid out the easiest way that an average person could simplify his or her life. The author had, quite remarkably, learned how to live on only $500 a month by constantly clipping coupons and compulsively pinching pennies. The photo on the book's cover showed a credit card being cut in half by a pair of scissors, along with a shot of the determined-looking young lady who was cutting up the credit card and who had, in fact, written chapter after chapter on the many useful tools that low-income people could apply to their personal lives in order to stop spending money on the unneeded luxuries that they really didn't need to be spending their money on in the first place. The author went on and on about how living a modest and simple life could be so much more rewarding than having to constantly worry about being able to make a big enough paycheck in order to have a big enough income to pay only the minimum amount due on an ever-increasing mound of credit-card debt.

Normally, Zetty wouldn't have even picked up such a book, preferring to spend her time reading almost any other topic than penny pinching. But since she had already quit her job and since her money was tight, she thought that she might be able to learn a few tips on how to cut back on her monthly expenses. And, somewhat surprisingly, the author's straightforward way of explaining what a *"necessity* cash purchase was as opposed to what a superfluous *luxury* debit transaction was" – really did connect with Zetty. By the end of the first chapter, she was already thinking about grabbing her scissors and cutting up at least one of her credit cards.

But then, just as Zetty turned the page and began reading the next chapter, she heard a soft knock on the front door. At first, she froze. She felt paralyzed by uncertainty. Unable to move, she simply lay there and waited, not knowing what she should do. She told herself that it couldn't possibly be Mooney. She told herself that it might, instead, be one of the weirdo stalkers, possibly attempting a godawful home invasion.

But after she heard yet another gentle rapping, sounding somewhat like the way her dad used to softly knock on her bedroom door – she bit her lower lip, marshaled her courage, and slowly eased off the sofa, trying not to make any noise. The walls were thin, and the living-room floor would oftentimes creak when people walked across it.

Not wanting to make the slightest of sounds, she quietly tiptoed over to the other side of the room and peeped out through the peephole.

It was Mooney.

"Just a second," she said, hoping her voice didn't sound overly nervous. Zetty then turned and hurried down the hall to the bathroom. She wanted to make sure her hair wasn't out of place.

Can't take too much time. Can't keep him waiting too long.

But then the mirror above the sink lied to her. She knew she didn't look as good as her reflection appeared to show because she hadn't flipped on the light switch. Hey, even tiny amounts of electrical usage quickly added up when you were pinching pennies. That was what she'd just read at the end of the book's first chapter.

Mirror mirror . . . why can't I ever believe you?

As she hurried back into the living room – she abruptly stopped, checked her clothing, and brushed a tiny goose feather off the bottom of her blouse. Her mom's down comforter was always shedding its fluffy innards at the most inopportune moments. Yet luckily, Zetty had noticed the little white plume before she had opened the door.

Now inspecting both sides of her sleeves and also quickly glancing down at the legs of her jeans, she wanted to make sure she didn't have any more pieces of lint stuck to her clothes.

Thank goodness there's not anything else clinging to me.

Sucking in a deep breath, she then proceeded to slowly swing open the door, trying her best not to look frazzled, trying her best to appear to be cool, calm, and collected.

"Hey. Sorry I'm late. I had to stop and get some new batteries," Mooney said, holding up a small camera in his hand. "You wouldn't believe the line at the checkout counter. There was only one clerk working the register, and she told me everyone else had called in sick with a stomach flu."

"Oh, I heard about that going 'round. It's really awful. A neighbor had it."

"Not something I'd want, that's for sure." Mooney then, for some strange reason, glanced down at the floor next to her blue tennies. "Is that a feather?"

Blinking her eyes, Zetty looked down and sighed. "Uh-huh. My comforter spurts one out every now and then. I think I need to sew up some of its loose seams."

"So it must be a goose feather, huh?"

"Uh-huh."

"Keeps you warm in the winter."

Nodding her head, she slowly reached down, picked up the feather, and put it in her pocket. "You know, you sort of, like, surprised me. I thought you weren't coming."

"Well, I'm sorry about that. I would've called and told you I was running late, but I didn't have your number."

"Would you like to come in? You're letting out the heat."

"Yeah, sure," he said, stepping inside the apartment.

Closing the door behind him, Zetty at first

couldn't decide if she should lock the locks or not; but since it never hurt to be extra careful, she turned the deadbolt and locked both of the locks. "Want some tea?"

"Okay."

"If you don't mind, we'll talk in the kitchen. It's warmer in there," she said, leading him into the other room.

"Nice location. So downtown."

"Yeah, I like it. But, y'know, it's pretty small. And I also have a roommate, too." Moving over to the sink, she picked up the teakettle and began filling it with water. "Is green tea okay?"

"That's fine."

Setting the teakettle on top of the stove, Zetty rummaged through the cabinet, found the box of tea, and pulled out two bags. As she did this, Mooney sat down at the kitchen table and looked out the window. It was dark outside so there wasn't much for him to see except the lights that were shining in from the windows of another apartment building, which was only a few yards away on the other side of the alley.

"So, you've already quit your job?"

"Uh-huh. I just couldn't go back," she said, turning on a burner.

"Good for you. If you don't mind me asking, what are you going to do now?"

"Like I said, I'm looking for another job. I have a little money saved up, so I guess I'll be able to get by for a while without a paycheck."

"What type of work are you looking for?"

"Well, I've only done retail; and, like, I don't wanna get stuck in a bar or a restaurant. I mean, I'm pretty sure I wouldn't like that type of work. I've heard so many horror stories about it."

"I worked as waiter one time. Some people won't even leave you a tip, or they'll just give you a couple of quarters."

"That's what I heard."

"Do you have any friends who might could get you hired doing what they're doing?"

"In Seattle. But I can't afford to move down there. And the rents are way high, too."

Then later . . .

After the tea had steeped, Zetty began to wonder when Mooney would start talking about the satchel. He'd obviously brought his camera to take a picture of it, and he'd even driven out of his way to buy new batteries. But as the minutes continued to tick by, they kept talking about her life and what she was going to do to make ends meet. When she tried to change the subject, he would keep coming back to the same topic with more questions about her plans for the future.

"What about college?"

"I wanted to go to college, but I couldn't afford it. After my parents died, there wasn't any way I could pay the tuition. Then when Miss Pineford lost a bunch of money in her investments, I had no choice but to go out and get a job right after I graduated from high school."

"Miss Pineford?"

"My foster mom. But, like, she's old enough to be my grandmother, really. Now she's in a nursing home, and that's another reason I have to stay in town so I can be here for her when she needs me."

"You don't have any other family?"

"No, not that I know of. When my parents immigrated down from Canada, all the rest of my family had died in a fire up there."

"Y'know, Zetty, you remind me of myself."

"Why do you say that?"

"I guess 'cause my sister and I ended up in an orphanage when we were kids. We didn't have any relatives to take us in."

"You lost your mom and dad?"

"No, they didn't die or anything. But we were pretty young when we got put in the orphanage, so I'm not exactly sure what happened, actually."

"Oh, my. I can only imagine what it must've been like to be carted off to an orphanage. I'm lucky I had Miss Pineford."

"It doesn't sound as if you had it that easy, if you ask me."

"I got by. You do what you have to do. Want to look at the satchel?"

"Sure."

"Okay, let me go get it. I'll be right back," she said, putting down her teacup. She then stood up from the table, walked into the hall, and retrieved the satchel from the dresser in her bedroom. Zetty kept the satchel wrapped in the same tissue paper that her mom had used all those many years ago.

Bringing it back into the kitchen, she unfolded the paper and handed the bag to Mooney.

"Do you mind if I take a picture of it?" he asked, slipping his wafer-thin camera out of his pocket.

"No, I don't mind."

"Y'know, it looks to me like it's in really good condition. Doesn't seem to have been used very much."

"I don't think my mom ever used it at all. For a long time, I just kept it in a box, hidden away."

Setting the satchel down on the Formica top in front of him, Mooney flashed four snapshots from several different angles. "I think it's handmade. Someone put a lot of work into it."

"Yeah, that's what I thought, too. I've never seen another one quite like it."

"Do you mind if I look inside?"

Remembering what Miss Pineford had told her, Zetty wasn't sure what she should say in response to his question. And, for some reason, she suddenly felt a slight tinge of trepidation about showing him the satchel since Miss Pineford had cautioned her against reveling too much about her family. But then, when Zetty stopped to think about it, Mooney seemed to be someone she could trust. He was so relaxed and appeared to be really nice. She knew in her heart that he wasn't there to do her any harm. He'd already seen where her parents were buried. Yet still, Zetty thought that it might be best if she didn't let him look at the label inside the bag. "Why do you want to look inside it?"

"Just to see how it was made. Check out the craftsmanship. Like I said, I think I might know someone who'd want to buy it."

"Buy it? But I don't want to sell it," she said, reaching over and plucking the satchel out of his hand. Trying not to appear too flustered, she then began rewrapping the bag in the faded tissue paper.

And as she did this, Mooney's eyes stayed glued to the satchel. "Y'know, I understand why you wouldn't want to sell it, but I can promise you they'd make it worth your while if they wanted to buy it. I could be wrong, but they could go as high as two thousand dollars."

"Two thousand dollars?"

"Like I said, I can't make any promises, but I think they might be willing to pay that much for it."

"Really? Two thousand dollars?"

"I think so. It looks like a one-of-a-kind collectable, if you ask me."

Pausing to consider his offer, Zetty was somewhat tempted to instantly say "yes" because she certainly needed the money. But still, the satchel's sentimental value meant so much more to her. "No, I can't sell it. Sorry."

"Look, I tell you what; and please don't hold me to this 'cause I'm going way out on a limb; but what if I could get you a lot more money than that for it? How much money would they have to offer you to get you to sell it?"

"Honestly, I really don't want to part with it. I can't sell it."

"Are you sure?"

"I think so."

"Okay, I understand how you feel. But let's say someone wanted to pay something like ten thousand for it. Now, don't hold me to that amount, alright? I'm just tossing out a guesstimate. But, I mean, hypothetically, if they did want to offer you a lot of money for it, would that interest you at all?"

Stunned by the large sum that had popped out of his mouth, Zetty at first had a hard time even contemplating being paid that much money for her mom's old bag. She was truly taken aback by his proposition. It was as though she had misunderstood what he'd said. Did he really say "ten thousand dollars?" Unable to give him a reply, she put the satchel in her lap and gently pressed down on the tissue paper. She then sighed deeply and put her hand over her mouth.

"Are you okay?" he asked.

She shook her head. She was at a loss for words.

"Look, you don't have to give me an answer tonight. Just think about it, okay? I can show the photos to someone I know who might want to buy it. We'll wait and see what they say. But, like, don't get your hopes up. That was just a rough guesstimate. I might be way out of line. They may not want to pay that much for it."

Nodding, Zetty again lightly brushed her hand

across the tissue paper. She didn't know what to think, nor did she know how she should react. She tried not to look too nervous.

"Listen, all I ask is that you at least think about it, okay?"

"Okay, I'll think about it." Then suddenly, and quite unexpectedly, there was a loud knock at the front door, which gave Zetty a start. "Oh, I wonder who that is? Is someone picking you up?"

"No."

"Well, I'm not expecting anyone." Getting up from her chair and placing the satchel on the counter next to the stove, Zetty quickly walked into the living room and looked through the peephole.

It was her ex-boyfriend. *What's he doing here?*

Unlocking the locks, she opened the door. Tom was standing at the top of the stairs.

"Hey."

"Tom, what are you doing here?"

"I came by to say hi."

"Tom, you know I don't want to see you."

"I thought maybe you'd changed your mind. I saw Edna-Ney the other night. We talked about you."

"Tom, someone's here. I really don't want to discuss this right now, okay?"

Sticking his head around the edge of the door, Tom glanced into the kitchen. "Oh, you're seeing someone else, huh?"

"Tom, I told you, this isn't a good time. Would you please leave?" And, as she said this, Zetty slowly began closing the door.

"Okay. I can take a hint." He then turned and walked down the hallway stairs.

Shaking her head, Zetty shut the door, locked it, and returned to the kitchen. "Sorry for the interruption. Tom's kind of impulsive. I've known him ever since the sixth grade."

"It's okay. I understand."

"So, um, what were we talking about?"

"Well, I think we've pretty much covered everything," Mooney said, glancing down at his watch. "I guess I need to go. I have to get up early tomorrow for a conference call from Boston." Standing up, he slipped his camera back in his pocket. "Oh, what's your phone number so I can call you when I find out if they're interested in buying your bag?"

"I'll write it down for you. It's listed in my roommate's name."

"You might also want to give me your email address, too. Just in case."

"Okay."

And that was that. After she wrote her phone number and email address down on a slip of paper and handed it to him, Mooney didn't linger any longer. With a quick goodbye, he was out the door.

Gathering up the teacups and saucers, Zetty placed them in the sink. She was still in a bit of shock at the large sum of money he'd mentioned. Ten thousand dollars would really come in handy, considering she was unemployed. If she couldn't soon find a job, she wasn't exactly sure what she'd end up doing once she had depleted all of her savings. Every month she had rent to pay and food to buy. Edna-Ney was an understanding roommate, but Zetty knew that she barely made enough money to pay her own bills. She was a terrible spendthrift. She would burn through her paycheck as fast as she made it on eating out and buying new clothes.

Standing at the sink, Zetty felt a cold chill run through her body. She stared over at the tissue paper. She almost could hear her mother's voice telling her that money didn't make the world go around. Life wasn't about money. Her mother had always put people first, not money.

But, then again . . .

If her mom had actually been there to offer her some advice, maybe she would've told her that keeping something for sentimental reasons might not be the smartest thing to do when a keepsake was worth so much money. Her mom had always been exceptionally practical when it came to financial matters. And given that her mom had been a stickler for saving her nickels and dimes for a rainy day, she might have told Zetty to take the money.

So, it was a decision that Zetty wished she didn't have to make, and it brought back the sadness that she didn't want to have to feel in her heart. Closing her eyes, she covered them with her hand and began to cry. She didn't know what she should do. Despite needing the money, she really didn't want to have to part with something that had meant so much to her mother. Zetty was being pulled in opposite directions. There wasn't an easy answer. She desperately wanted someone to hug her and make it all go away.

Chapter Twenty-Five

Walking down the stairs and out the building's front door, Mooney was worried that he might have said something he shouldn't've said. Tammy had only mentioned a couple of thousand dollars. She hadn't agreed to pay much more than that for the old satchel. But being the soft touch that he was, Mooney had felt sorry for Zetty; and he knew it was his fault that she had quit her job. He couldn't dissuade himself from empathizing with her hardship. And seeing how little money she had, and because she had lost her parents at such a young age – a flood of good intentions had overtaken him. He could only hope that he hadn't gone too far. Now he had no choice but to convince Tammy that paying such a large sum for the linen bag would be advantageous. Yet he also knew it wouldn't be easy since the Flock was notoriously tight-fisted when it came to spending money.

Moving along the sidewalk toward his car, Mooney was startled when he suddenly felt a hand tap him on the back of his shoulder. He hadn't heard anyone come up behind him, and it had happened quite unexpectedly.

Stopping, he slowly turned around, not knowing what to expect.

It was Tom, Zetty's ex-boyfriend. "Hey, got a minute?"

"Is there something wrong?" Mooney said.

"Yeah, sort of. So, like, what's up with you and Zetty?"

"Excuse me?"

"Look, c'mon. I know you're dating her, okay? There's no need to hide it."

"Sorry. I think you have me confused with someone else. I'm not dating her."

"Yeah, uh-huh, right. You wouldn't lie to me, would you?"

"No, not at all. If I was dating her, I'd tell you I was dating her; but I'm not dating her. I had the impression you two had broken up."

"We did. Months ago. She dumped me."

"What happened?"

"Heck if I know. I guess I did something she didn't want me to do. Maybe I got too wasted. She's not a big drinker."

Sizing Tom up, Mooney could see that he appeared to be pleasant enough. He didn't have an angry demeanor. "Well, we only recently met. I honestly don't know her very well at all. But I think she's a nice person, if you ask me. She must've seen something in you she liked. Want some advice?"

"Okay."

"Take her a box of chocolates. Try to patch it up. Tell her you're sorry and you're turning over a new leaf. You might also tell her that she means more to you than getting wasted does. But, I mean, whatever you do, don't take her any flowers."

"Chocolates, huh?"

"Exactly. I don't think she wants anyone to give her any flowers ever again."

"So, like, how do you know that?"

" 'Cause that's what she told me. She's not into dead flowers."

"Oh, okay. No dead flowers."

"Look, I gotta go. Take it easy." Mooney then patted Tom on the shoulder and turned to leave.

"Thanks," Tom said, waving goodbye.

Parting ways, Mooney continued on to his car. There was a chill in the air, and he hadn't dressed for the cold. He should've worn a sweater under his coat.

As he drove back up to the lake, he had a lot to think about. The moving parts inside his brain weren't all in sync, and keeping his center of gravity away from the edge of the cliff and on the middle path would take a bit of effort.

In less than ten minutes, Mooney had turned off the main boulevard and was now driving through the quaint neighborhood which ran along the edge of Arbor Falls Park. Checking his watch, he was hoping to make it home before Becky. On Tuesday nights she had her monthly Save the Whales meeting, and those get-togethers would usually last several hours.

But then . . .

When he finally pulled into the bungalow's driveway, he noticed that his sister's bedroom light was on, and he immediately realized that she must've come home early. He should've expected as much because his sister was constantly rearranging her schedule. She rarely ever stuck to the same routine for very long. Like him, she didn't like trudging away – day in and day out – in a repetitive rut.

Stepping inside the front door, Mooney was surprised to see Tammy sitting at his desk in the alcove, using his computer. Becky wasn't in the room. "Hey."

"How'd it go?" Tammy asked.

"Sorta good and sorta not so good." Lowering his voice, he walked over and glanced down the hall. "I don't want Becky to hear us." He then checked to see if his sister's bedroom door was open; and that's when he heard the shower running in the bathroom. Realizing that he'd have a few minutes to discuss the particulars of what had happened without having to worry about Becky overhearing the conversation, Mooney stepped back over to the alcove. "Sounds like she's taking a shower."

"She's shampooing her hair. Becky always shampoos her hair on Tuesday nights."

"Oh, okay. That should take a few minutes. So, um, here's the deal. The not-so-good news is – the girl with the satchel won't take a couple of hundred. She wouldn't even take a couple of thousand."

"Why not?"

"Because she wants to hold on to it, that's why."

"Moon . . ."

"Look, you had to be there, okay? The good news is – I got some pictures. Wanna check 'em out?"

"Of course."

He then nodded his head at the computer screen. "Okay, I need to load 'em into my hard drive."

"Oh, right. Just give me a second." Doing some quick typing and mouse clicking, Tammy exited an email she was composing and logged off. She then stood up, and Mooney sat down in front of the keyboard.

Reaching over, he opened the top desk drawer, pulled out his camera's accessory cord, and plugged one end of it into his computer and the other end into the side of his camera. Moving the cursor through the prompts, he transferred the pictures from the camera's memory onto his viewing app. He then opened the first photo. "There it is."

"Wow. It's larger than I thought it'd be."

"I think it's the real McCoy. It didn't look like a fake to me."

"Let me see the rest of the photos," Tammy said.

Complying, Mooney slowly clicked through the other three, lingering on each one until she nodded her head. "That's it. I only took four."

Leaning in for a closer look, Tammy stared intently at the last photo, which was a shot of Zetty sitting across from him at her kitchen table. "She doesn't look like a con artist to me."

"I doubt she's ever cheated anyone in her whole life. Zetty Hart. I couldn't help but feel sorry for her."

"Why? Why do you feel sorry for her?"

"Because it was rough losing both her parents. And she just quit her job, too. As far as I can tell, she doesn't have very much money."

"Okay, so – why wouldn't she take the two thousand if she needs the money?"

"I guess 'cause the satchel means too much to her. Since it was her mom's, she has an emotional attachment to it. She doesn't want to part with it."

"Did you look inside and check out the label?"

"No, she wouldn't let me."

"Why not?"

"I'm not exactly sure why she wouldn't let me look inside. I think maybe she might know more than she's letting on. But, like, it's hard to tell."

"You mean, about us?"

"Maybe; maybe not. I'm not exactly sure. I couldn't figure it out. But there did seem to be something about her foster mom that she was being a little coy about. She kind of danced around a few things. I also got the impression she really didn't know that much about her parents. But, y'know, I could be wrong."

"I hope you're not wrong. And I hope *we're* not wrong."

"I think maybe she probably just got a little suspicious when I mentioned how much the satchel might be worth."

"Well, like you said, it does look like an original, that's for sure. And the last thing we need is for the wrong people to see the logo and get their hands on it."

"You're worried she'll lead the authorities to the names of the founding members, aren't you?"

"If they figure out who her parents were, they might be able to trace some of the underground cells by metrical association."

"Group segmentation modeling."

"Uh-huh, which means we'll all be at risk."

"Like dominoes."

"Exactly. And that's the last thing we need. There were only a handful of originating members who came down from Canada. As far as I know, none of them have ever been ID'ed. We only know a few of the names ourselves. So if our intel is correct, then we're pretty sure each cell was reasonably well compartmentalized, but no one knows for sure since the founders were pretty good at keeping their secrets."

"You hope."

"Well, so far so good. But now they're getting old. A few of 'em have died. And the word is, they're paranoid about who they can trust."

"Infiltration."

"Yes, infiltration. There's also an internal power grab, too. Some of the younger radicals have already splintered off and started their own cells, or they've hooked up with other more aggressive groups."

"Such as ELF."

"Well . . . um . . . let me put it this way. No comment."

Shaking his head, Mooney looked Tammy in the eye, yet decided not to press her for a clarification. "Uh-huh."

"Look, I don't want you to get the wrong impression, okay? As I understand it, ELF's had us in their sights for a long time. So when one of the Flock splinter groups put the word out, some sort of arrangement was, in fact, made. It was kind of like a schism. That's why the FBI is now putting so much effort into hunting us down."

"And I guess that's also why the satchel is so important, right?"

"Well, if you ask me, someone made a huge mistake – way, way back – when they first made those bags for the founding members. I mean, we never should've continued using that image. I always said we didn't need an insignia, but no one would listen to me. Of course by then it was too late."

Hearing the shower turn off, Mooney quickly exited his desktop's viewing app and again lowered his voice. "So now we have our proof. And if I'm reading the tea leaves correctly, it sounds to me like we need to wrap this up ASAP, which means we need to offer Zetty a lot more money . . ."

"How much more?"

"Ten or twenty thousand."

"Are you serious?"

"I know the higher-ups are stingy with their

budgets. I know that. But I also know the Flock has access to some deep pockets in Silicon Valley."

"How do you know that?"

"Well, let's just say my blog has a big following down there."

"Oh, god. People shouldn't be emailing stuff like that. It's all traceable. Don't they know the feds have software that vacuums the whole Web?"

"C'mon. If anyone knows how to hide an IP address, it's hackers."

"Hackers?"

"Hey, I don't pick 'em, okay? They pick me. Nothing I can do about it."

"Mooney . . ."

"Look, I actually think the satchel is worth a heck-of-a-lot more than twenty thousand. Think about it."

Wringing her hands, Tammy heaved a nervous sigh and rolled her eyes. Mooney could tell she was stressing out. She wasn't trying to hide it. "Look, I can't make any promises, but I'll see what I can do. That's a lot of money."

From down the hall, they heard the bathroom door open. Turning in his chair to face Tammy, Mooney put his finger up to his lips.

Tammy nodded her head and backpedaled toward the kitchen. "Want a banana-strawberry smoothie?" she asked in a normal tone.

"Yeah. Sounds good."

Then . . .

For the rest of the night, nothing more was said about the satchel. Their cozy lair on the lake returned to its normal dynamic vis-a-vis the inconsequential interaction of three two-legged mammals going about their regular nesting activities.

Not surprisingly, it took over three weeks for Tammy to maneuver her funding request up the ladder of insulated safety warrens so as to get the allocation approved by the right subcommittee. Next, she had to travel out of town in order to meet with a certain someone, having been asked to verbally explain why she needed such a large sum of cash and also to clarify what it would be used for. In L.E.A.F., nothing ever happened quickly. The Flock was way too hierarchical for anyone to make a snap decision when it came to spending such a hefty sum of money.

As the weeks ticked by, Mooney returned to his daily regiment of research and blogging. A part of him was put off by L.E.A.F.'s petrified way of doing things; but there wasn't much he could do about it. He wasn't the type to make waves when it came to such concerns. Yet still, since so much mental energy had to constantly be invested into the financial side of the save-the-environment equation, it reminded him of what he found to be totally appalling about present-day American society. Over and over again, important decisions were simply coming down to the money involved. For decades, the power politics of the D.C. beltway had been spinning out of control. Critical ecological determinations were being hamstrung by the

Congressional clout that the mega corporations were bringing to the debate when they lobbied the masses in order to sway as many minds as they could to their side of an issue. The herded public appeared to have stopped caring about what was the ethical and moral thing to do. A certain segment of voters seemed to only be worried about their pocketbooks and showed no concern at all as to the science of saving whatever endangered species or of protecting whatever polluted habitat. It was blatantly obvious that the American dream had been hijacked by the greed of special interests. For Mooney, the unrelenting brainwashing by the corrupt politicians had become a worrisome state of affairs. Each time the fat cats were successful at hypnotizing enough eyeballs with their million-dollar media blitzes of false spin, a cadre of their lock-stepping corporate minions would then cheerfully swamp the Internet with another round of regurgitated lies and thus begin gloating over their so-called controlling voting edge. They would joyfully proclaim their Congressional wins by boasting that they had garnered enough ballots to defeat yet another climate-change decision . . . to the detriment of the environment.

And arguably, a similar winning-at-all-costs philosophy (per the opposite side of the coin) had also begun to impregnate L.E.A.F., too. Mooney had, quite regrettably, come to the realization that it was often difficult for such a diverse group of eco misfits to efficiently hone in on an achievable set of priorities when so much of the Flock's political effort depended upon having enough funding to successfully implement actionable responses to the never-ending lies being foisted upon the public. Yet still, at its core, Mooney also continued to believe that the organization's goals were sound and that such command-and-control hiccups would eventually self-correct. The Flock was, in his opinion, trying to do the right thing . . . most of the time. If it took shadowy activism to juxtaposition an important environmental concern into the glare of the media spotlight, then so be it. Maybe it didn't matter that some Flock members had lost their way by thinking that the ends (which they were so passionately working toward) did, indeed, justify what-ever means (that they were willing to use). Learning how to game the system via using the system's own innate flaws against itself, meant that an activist couldn't help but halfway agree that the lessons learned from Machiavelli, back in the Renaissance, might still be considered valid in the 21st century.

Yes, people would be people. Human nature was hard to change. Not everyone had altruistic DNA in their genome. A vast segment of the U.S. populace appeared to have an inherent weakness when it came to its demographic being duped by the siren call of self-serving greed. Many couldn't seem to clearly fathom what would, in fact, be best for their own long-term self-interest . . . since protecting planet Earth's fragile ecosystems required the application of objective foresight, along with a certain amount of sacrificial investment so as to counterbalance the voracious exploitation of the world's natural resources.

Harm not, sustain more.

In any event, being as Mooney was nothing more than an inconsequential worker bee, his input into the Flock's fundraising efforts was nil. The higher-ups never asked him for his advice when it came to making the big decisions. He wasn't involved at that level. And because he was well aware of his own imperfections, he tried his best to avoid such intrigues (when possible). In other words, he didn't have a desire to move up the pecking ladder. He wasn't at all ambitious when it came to networking the organizational chess pieces in order to feather his own cubbyhole. He already had enough on his plate. Simply finding the time to do his research effectively with as little hassle as possible was a big enough challenge for him as it was. The distractions of having to deal with his own dysfunctional interfaces in regards to his personal life were quite demanding. He needed another eight hours in the day to do all that he wanted to do, because sometimes his emotional baggage would mix in with his L.E.A.F. assignments . . .

Which was to say . . .

Mooney had, for weeks, been struggling to understand why he wasn't more attracted to Tammy than he was; whereas, for some hard to fathom reason, he found himself continually thinking about Zetty. Indeed, the reverse should have been true. Tammy was exceptionally bright; the two of them had a lot in

343

common per having compatible interests; and Tammy was, without a doubt, a dyed-in-the-wool dedicated activist.

But ironically, when Mooney did a gut check, he considered Tammy's blind obsession with trying to save the environment to be her Achilles' heel. Many times she came across as being too radical, i.e., as being too willing to run the proverbial bus over anyone and everyone who got in L.E.A.F.'s way.

Whereas . . .

Mooney refused to think like that. He believed in the Buddhist philosophy known as *The Middle Way,* which Tammy didn't seem to be a fan of, even though she claimed to be a Buddhist. Or, another way of putting it, Mooney tried to always keep an open mind and thus avoid the uncompromising end-game extremes, having concluded that the middle path held the most merit. Per his way of thinking, a do-gooder activist (of whatever stripe) shouldn't be too far to the left or too far to the right. Either scenario would be detrimental to a cause. On his blog he'd even once posted a sly paraphrase of his philosophical meditations vis-a-vis riffing off of the Goldilocks' nursery rhyme. "Not too much; nor too little. Strive for the compromise in the middle."

Yeah, well, maybe one day he would learn to take his own advice and apply such to his personal life. Ever since he'd moved to Bellingham, he'd been trying to find the right woman to steal his heart away; but because he worked at home and since he wasn't into joining any time-consuming social organizations, due to the fact that he was already so heavily committed to the Flock; and since he couldn't relate to the beer-induced bravado which tended to pervade the bar scene; and since his sister refused to play matchmaker . . .

Consequently, the sum total of these opposing variables meant that Mooney's infrequent hookups were dependent upon iffy chance, at best. His love life was regretfully relegated to running into strangers when he was out jogging in the park or when he was walking around downtown.

Slim pickings, to say the least.

But now there was Zetty.

Zetty Hart.

Of course, he knew he had to be careful . . .

Because it didn't appear as though they had that much in common. She didn't seem to have an inquiring mind, nor was she an intellectual. And given that Mooney had always been attracted to super bright females, what valid reason would he have for putting her on his to-date list besides the fact that she was quite pretty?

So, trying his best to be realistically objective, he told himself that her good looks shouldn't be the only reason for him to want to get involved with her since, if he were to start dating her, then surely after a few months of heated passion (and without the bonding magnetism of an inquiring intellect to keep him engaged and thus hold his long-term interest) – he would, more than likely, simply get bored and want to break it off.

With him, a beautiful face would catch his eye, but it took a sharp mind to keep him interested.

Ergo . . .

Knowing what he knew about her, Mooney certainly wouldn't characterize Zetty as being a member of the intelligentsia. Far from it. She hadn't gone to college, nor did she seem to have the personality of an activist. Yet having briefly glanced at her bookcase when he'd visited her apartment, he did suspect that she might have a passion for reading, although he seriously doubted that she had much of an affinity for great literature or classical philosophy. No, Zetty appeared to be more of a commoner when it came to her reading material, if the book he'd seen on her end table had been any indication of her taste in nonfiction.

But still, there was something quite appealing about her that had sparked a longing in his heart. Her naiveté was refreshing, and she didn't seem to be overly judgmental. Her default mode appeared to favor optimism over pessimism. And for a guy who was spending way too much of his time contemplating the interconnectivity of complex ecosystems, her simplicity was endearing. Or, as Rousseau might have said, Zetty was a naturalist in her own unassuming way.

Still, Mooney suspected that too much analytical analysis of anyone's personality might, in and of itself, be a flawed approach to figuring out compatibility.

Plus, if an uninvolved third party were to take into consideration Mooney's childhood (because he hadn't had loving parents to nurture him), then the emotional dysfunction that he had experienced growing up in the orphanage also needed to be factored into the computation. In other words, if a complex equation (with all of its plus-and-minus variables) was calculated in an attempt to define his psychological profile – and given that he had been socially warped at an early age – then balancing out the pros and cons for a precise Freudian quantification might be somewhat like trying to find dark matter in deep space. So it was possible that Mooney's tendency to dissect people the way he did (to vet their thinking) . . . would never give him a viable answer as to why certain individuals acted the way they did . . .

Including why he himself did what he did.

Not every problem had a scientific solution.

Or, another way of putting it, Mooney had come to the realization that his own self-awareness tended to be more of a liability than an asset at times. He knew that he was damaged goods. Years before, after he'd broken up with his fiancée, he'd even self-diagnosed himself as having a deep-seated fear of rejection. And strangely enough, as it turned out, his personal track record with various lovers over the years . . . had, indeed – and for whatever reason – proceeded to fulfill that self-diagnosis. Mooney wasn't good at bouncing back. Rejection would literally throw him into a heartwrenching tailspin. His coping mechanism was slow to kick in. He was the type of guy who would, after being dumped, retreat into a self-imposed hibernation and then endlessly contemplate what had gone wrong.

So, at a primal level, Mooney was way too cerebral for his own damn good. And given that this awful curse had possibly befallen him because he'd been yanked away from the bosom of his mother and deposited in a redneck orphanage at a young age, he knew that he might not ever be able to recover from such a traumatic debilitation. It was possible that he would have to forever live out his life, always overcompensating by repeatedly attempting to recalculate his perceived future (when it came to relationships), in order to hedge against any unfore-seenable downside, hoping to make sure that he would never again be walloped by yet another unbearable rejection. And maybe, deep down, the reason why two philosophical opposites were attracting in this case could have been because Zetty had such a loving nature to her personality. Maybe Mooney's fear of rejection was the real reason why he'd found her to be so appealing, beyond her remarkable good looks.

But . . .

If this was true, why had he egged on her ex-boyfriend, telling Tom that he should try to patch things up with her by taking her a box of chocolates? What had motivated Mooney to say such a thing?

In retrospect, he could only conclude that he'd been (in some sort of self-protective way), trying to make sure that Zetty wasn't whimsical when it came to the guys she wanted to date. Or possibly, Mooney was subconsciously trying to eliminate an emotional conundrum since, if Zetty and Tom did get back together, then Mooney wouldn't have to face yet another possible rejection. Indeed, he might have his flaws, but he certainly wasn't the type of lame-o who'd callously elbow his way in between a star-crossed couple who was trying to patch things up and get back together. He certainly didn't want to date a girl who was already hooked up with someone else.

Of course, when Mooney attempted to self-analyze his libido via questioning his own motives, he also knew that the process of pondering the inner workings of his subconscious mind never did much good anyway. It rarely ever helped. So he told himself that instead of wasting his time trying to figure himself out, he actually needed to be refocusing his thoughts on the functional doabilities of what could be accomplished, which meant that he should be targeting the more practical concerns of his life and thus should stop worrying so much about the what-if hypotheticals that he had little control over.

Thereupon, being fully aware of his own limitations and cognizant of what would, in fact, be a more efficient use of his thought time – he proceeded to do what needed to be done. He disciplined himself and began to laser in on his work, knowing that there never seemed to be any easy answers when it came to his personal life, whereas his undercover endeavors to lessen the environmental damage to planet Earth actually did reward him with winnable emotional dividends.

And so . . .

After numerous days of serious effort, and upon achieving some success at ignoring what he shouldn't be thinking about vis-a-vis having spent some serious butt-in-the-chair time plugging away on his blog in an attempt to get his mind off of his impaired social interactions . . .

Mooney was suddenly jarred out of his workaday zone by a seasonal transition. Late one afternoon, the first snowstorm of the fall had come barreling down out of the Fraser Valley, carrying with it an abundance of frozen precipitation. Wintry weather had finally arrived. To him, it was a welcome change. Mooney relished the drop in temperature. Tempestuous autumn, with its chilly windstorms, was his favorite time of year.

And, as tended to happen, with the falling snow also came a corresponding dead silence inside the bungalow. The outdoor hubbub had drastically quieted down. The abrupt change in weather was somewhat like having a mountain of fluffy soundproofing dumped down on every square foot of the habitat, which meant that the verbalizations within the walls of the rent house had now become somewhat amplified. From down the hall, Mooney couldn't help but be distracted by Becky and Tammy's endless chattering, hearing them go on and on about their follicle-protecting shampoos and climate-friendly moisturizing hair conditioners. And since Mooney didn't have any interest at all in what they were droning on about, their incessant prattle had pretty much sidetracked his focus and had gotten his mind off his work.

Thinking that a little time alone outside in the cold weather would be good for him – Mooney decided that such an escape would be the preferred alternative, as opposed to attempting to persuade his roommates to curtail their chitchat.

So, going with the flow, Mooney retreated from his keyboard, bundled himself up, and proceeded to trek out into the park to check on the noble fir. He wanted to make sure the little one was safe and sound, hoping the chilly air wouldn't be too nippy for the baby tree. With the thermometer having only dropped four degrees below freezing, Mooney didn't think the replanted fir would have any trouble acclimating; yet he also didn't want to take a chance on being wrong, so he decided to go and see for himself.

Crunching across the fresh snow, which wasn't more than a couple of inches deep, Mooney slowly made his way along the main trail, moving farther and farther into the woods. He savored the serene solitude. The air was crisp, and there was nary a sound. It was at moments such as this that he felt the most at peace. If more people could experience the revitalizing civility of the great outdoors or a regular basis, he thought that the masses might be able to evolve their thinking into a different perspective in regards to the rat-race lifestyle that so many of them were suffering through each and every day. The majestic tall trees, in their own unique way, seemed to offer unconditional comfort to all who sought it out. The beautiful evergreens, with their year-round green foliage, never appeared to get upset unless something exceptionally serious was threatening their lives, such as a rapidly spreading wildfire. They were always willing to share their oxygen with their animal friends, while at the same time, continuously scrubbing the carbon dioxide out of the air. Why more people weren't out hugging trees was beyond him. About the only chore a homeowner ever had to do in order to maintain a yard full of lovely trees was to rake up the leaves when they fell to the ground in the fall. If a sturdy tree had enough sunlight and water, it was pretty much self-sustaining. Year in and year out, the branches of a tree would offer cooling shade in the summer and wind-blocking protection in the winter.

What was there not to like about a beautiful tree?

Anyway, after hiking through the shallow snow for twenty minutes or so, Mooney finally made his way to the far side of the park and over into the grove of noble firs. The snowfall had dusted the baby tree; and the clumped-up snowflakes were weighing down a few of its limbs. Gently brushing off the white buildup, Mooney ran the tips of his gloves through the little plant's green needles. When he finished, the noble fir looked as spry as ever. It was such a lovely shaped tree.

Then . . .

Noticing how much of the fluffy stuff had piled up

on the ground around it, he got down on his hands and knees and slowly scooped the buildup back away from the tree's pint-sized trunk. He thought that since the baby fir was still adjusting to its new home, he'd try to help it along with an extra bit of TLC. Plants were much smarter than most people gave them credit for, and they enjoyed empathetic love just as any human would.

Pleased with his effort, Mooney got to his feet and stepped back to check out his handiwork. The baby fir now looked to be quite happy and appeared to be reasonably healthy in its new soil. Mooney was glad its relocation was working out as well as it was.

Feeling somewhat like a proud dad when a son grew up and was old enough to go camping on his own, Mooney smiled and took solace in his act of kindness. It was these small winnables which made it all worthwhile.

Waving goodbye, Mooney then turned and crunched his way through the wet snow and over toward the black chain-link fence that surrounded the cemetery. Opening the gate, he continued inside the graveyard . . .

Making his way to where the wild cherry tree had lived for all of those many years. And naturally, as he had expected, the groundskeepers had already hauled away all of the deadwood, along with the upended rootball. They had also done a fairly good job of releveling the ground where the accidental death had transpired. The family burial plot, which was now covered with a blanket of snow, looked as though the old tree had never even been there . . . since there wasn't the tattletale sign of a protruding stump. Nothing peeked out at him from where the tree had once stood, nor did a granite headstone mark the spot of the tree's passing. Sadly, Mooney could only hope that the remaining roots – hidden deep down in the ground – were at peace.

After pausing to contemplate the regrettable loss, imagining the tree's natural beauty as though it was still there . . .

Still tall and stout . . .

Still spreading its branches ever upward . . .

Mooney decided to check out the names on the headstones which surrounded the empty space where the tree had lived all those many years. Again, he read the born-and-deceased dates of Zetty's parents. Next he scanned the inscription on a taller tombstone that had been placed there to memorialize a man named Leif Ericson Pineford. And needless to say, Mooney found the guy's first name to be an interesting moniker per its phonic similarity to l-e-a-f. Also, what immediately got his attention was the finely crafted laurel that had been carved into the gravestone above Leif's name. The chiseled image, with its tiny little maple leaves, looked somewhat like a halo.

A leafy halo.

Thinking that he might be onto something, Mooney then walked around the burial plot and was surprised to see that none of the surnames matched any of the other surnames on the other headstones, yet all of them had the exact same leafy halo. Telling himself that such a graven display was somewhat peculiar for a large grouping of unrelated interments, since this set of burials was a good distance away from the rest of the other gravesites further down the hill, Mooney speculated on what it might could mean. Reading the various names of the deceased, he told himself that this clearly wasn't a case of a big family having only birthed girls, because the male first names easily out numbered the female given names. Of course, when a bride assumed her husband's last name and then proceeded to use her maiden name as her middle name, such a renaming would have been expected, although that wasn't what he was reading on the headstones. No, there were too many names that didn't match for this to be a family burial plot.

Thinking it through, Mooney then came to the conclusion that such a replicating series of laurel halos wasn't an instance of female siblings simply assuming the surnames of their husbands. That obviously wasn't what was going on. So the only logical explanation that Mooney could come up with . . .

Was that most, if not all of the members of this rather large family, or whatever type of social grouping this actually was, must have either been adopted (and thus they had retained their birth-father's last name), or maybe some charitable benefactor had, years ago, purchased this relatively large burial plot and had proceeded to offer these dozens of gravesites to a bevy of friends, letting them use the location for their dearly-departed family members, instead of keeping the hilly plot for the benefactor's own immediate relatives.

So it was possible that such an occurrence could've been a possible likelihood, although Mooney had never actually heard of anyone bequeathing gravesites to their friends before. Usually, when it came to burial arrangements, as far as he was aware of, most families didn't burden others with such concerns (outside of their immediate relatives) in regards to a deceased-person's interment.

Then again, there was also yet another possibility as to why so many different last names had been buried on that small hill. From the pieces of the puzzle that Mooney had been struggling to understand, he was fairly certain that Zetty's parents were two of the founding members of L.E.A.F. And if that was indeed true, then all of these laurel-tagged gravesites might, in some strange way, be connected to the Flock. In other words, Mooney could have stumbled upon the very spot where many of the pioneering first members had been buried.

Now, needless to say, considering the probabilities of this actually being true – Mooney told himself that the odds were infinitesimally small that this was, in fact, the burial site for all of the deceased founding members of L.E.A.F. It was a long shot, by any stretch of the imagination. The possibility that something such as that had occurred was highly unlikely. If anything, his own speculative nature was simply getting the better of him. How could he have ended up living so close to the graves of so many founding members?

Short of the *tree gods* luring him to this very location by some unknowable mystical power . . .

There actually was no logical explanation which would explain such an occurrence. And Mooney absolutely didn't believe that trees were any sort of gods, that was for sure. He might be a dedicated tree-hugger and an advocate for environmental activism, but his thinking was very much defined by the rationalism of verifiable science. Trees might be sentient beings pursuing their own evolutionary path, but he didn't believe for a second that they were angelic spirits who could willfully affect the lives of humans.

Now admittedly, it was true that a few of the L.E.A.F. members he'd had contact with over the years did have such bizarre thoughts. Indeed, there was no denying that this type of weird thinking had been discussed at a few of the group meetings. Nevertheless, these so-called tree-god believers were but a small minority of the membership. To him, any sort of superstitious thinking, such as a tree being an otherworldly god, was terribly flawed. Trees were not living gods, as some African tribes had characterized them to be. Trees were simply loveable plants. They were huggable life forms that had the ability to grow exceptionally tall and outlive most humans, if given the chance to fulfill their natural lifecycles.

That's all they were. Trees were not angelic spirits or godlike beings. No well-educated person could possibly think such a thing.

So, dismissing from his mind the wild idea that he had somehow discovered the burial site for many of the founding Flock members, Mooney zipped up his coat and walked back home. He already had enough to worry about as it was. The last thing he needed was to fall headfirst into a dubious rabbit hole and get bounced around by irrational thoughts. Maybe the snowstorm had briefly short-circuited his cerebral cortex; or maybe he was going through caffeine withdrawal since a certain someone had forgotten to replenish the bungalow's cupboard with a pound of coffee, and earlier that morning Mooney hadn't had his usual cup of joe since they'd been quickly snowed in and were waiting for the icy streets to be plowed.

Roommates.

It was always something. There never seemed to be a dull moment. Mooney's life was anything but ordinary.

Too bad the so-called tree gods didn't actually exist because if they did, in fact, exist; then maybe they would have taken pity on him and intervened in his messed-up life by blessing him with a bounty of riches so he could afford to buy a place of his own and not have to be distracted by hair-product conversations which he had no interest in hearing discussed at all hours of the day and night.

Yeah, well, as if that was ever going to happen,

huh?

Mooney wasn't holding his breath.

Chapter Twenty-Six

After biting her fingernails for a few days, which she did absentmindedly without even realizing she was doing it – Zetty had finally come to terms with her bothersome situation. She was determined not to spend another afternoon hiding underneath the covers, worrying about her problems. She knew it wouldn't do her any good to fret over the things she couldn't do anything about. She told herself that she needed to stop obsessing on the stuff she absolutely had no control over.

Standing in front of the bathroom mirror, Zetty wagged a finger at her reflection and admonished herself for wimping out. She told herself that she needed to start focusing on what she could do, such as getting serious about finding a job, and stop whining about what she couldn't do. She told herself that there was absolutely no reason for her to be biting her nails and letting her nerves fray since she knew she had enough money in her savings account to pay her rent and cover her bills for a few more weeks.

So, refusing to let the uncertainty get the better of

her, Zetty was just about ready to head out the door and go to the library to search the Internet for a job . . .

When she heard a knock at the front door.

Stepping out of the bathroom, she tiptoed across the living room floor and peeked out the tiny peephole. Tom was standing out in the hall, holding a box of chocolates in his hand. At first she didn't want to open the door; but she wasn't that type of person. Such a response would've been too coldhearted.

I'm better than that, she told herself. *My pride won't let me do something so inconsiderate.*

Trying to be polite and not ill-mannered, Zetty inched open the door, stuck her head out, and waited to hear what he had to say.

"Hey. I brought you a present."

"Tom, why are you bothering me like this? I told you it's over."

"I know, but I thought you might change your mind."

"No, I'm not going to change my mind. It's over, okay?"

"You like chocolates, don't you?"

And even though she did have a weak spot for French chocolate, Zetty wasn't going to let herself be bribed. She was stronger than that. Once she had dumped a boyfriend – that was it. She wasn't going to change her mind. There was no going back. She would never ever change her mind and reverse a decision she'd made because she'd already given Tom a number of chances to mend his ways, and he simply wouldn't make the effort to do what he needed to do to fix his many unfixable problems. "I'm surprised you didn't bring me flowers."

Hearing her say this, Tom's face scrunched up with a puzzled look. "Flowers? You wanted me to bring you flowers? I thought you had this thing about dead flowers."

"How'd you know that?"

"That guy I saw you with, the last time I dropped by, said you didn't want any dead flowers."

"You talked to him?"

"Yeah, we sorta bumped into each other. He's the one who told me you might wanna hook back up with me."

Oh, no. That was the last thing Zetty wanted to hear. Stunned by Tom's confession, she felt a sense of defeat fill her stomach. If he was telling her the truth, then that meant that Mooney was only interested in the blue satchel and not her.

Unable to hide her dismay, Zetty now wasn't in the mood to discuss such matters with Tom. She knew it would be hopeless to even try. "Look, I don't know why he told you that, but he doesn't know what he's talking about, okay? I don't want to get back together with you, Tom. That's not going to happen."

"So, like . . . I guess you're still fond of flowers, huh?"

"No, that part's true. I think people should stop killing flowers. But that doesn't have anything to do with us getting back together. You just need to go find someone else. And please, stop bothering me, okay? You're wasting your time."

"Zetty . . ."

"Look, I'm sort of busy, okay? It's over. That's the end of it. I don't have time for this. Bye." And with those curt words, Zetty closed the door and quickly locked it.

What else could I do? What else could I say?

Well, at least she hadn't yelled at him and called him names.

But then . . .

As she stood there with her back to the doorknob, holding her hand over her mouth, not wanting to make the slightest bit of noise . . .

She anxiously waited for his footsteps to retreat down the hallway stairs. At first there wasn't any sound of him leaving, and she began to get slightly peeved, thinking that maybe she'd been too nice. She wondered if yelling at him might've been the better way to go.

But fortunately, after a couple of minutes, which had seemed to drag on for an excruciating amount of time – she heard him tromp away. *Thank goodness.* She was greatly relieved that he had finally gotten the message.

Still, it would've been nice to have pigged out on yummy chocolates, but she had her standards of proper etiquette. A box of French bittersweets was hard to say "no" to, but all of those mouthwatering calories weren't enough of a bribe for her to overlook Tom's numerous personality flaws. If she wanted to gain weight, she could just go out and buy her own box of tasty chocolates.

Duh.

So now, maybe Tom would stop bothering her. Having heard her say what she had said, his ears should've perked up and the dim light bulb should've gone off in his thick head; and hopefully he had finally realized that she wasn't going to change her mind.

Yet, in a strange way, he'd also done her a favor, too. He'd told her something about Mooney which she hadn't known. When Tom had inadvertently mentioned what Mooney had said to him about the two of them possibly "hooking back up" – that little tidbit of information was the straw that had broken the camel's back. Zetty now understood that Mooney wasn't at all interested in a romantic relationship, and this was a hard pill for her to swallow.

It was now obvious to her that Mooney wasn't going to be her knight in shining armor. He wasn't going to ask her out on a date. His mind was clearly on other things.

Lying to myself won't do me any good. It'll just postpone the heartache and make it worse, not better.

So, if nothing else, Zetty knew she had to fess up and face reality. It was a sad lesson to learn, but she realized that she couldn't let wishful thinking get the better of her. She told herself that she couldn't allow her heart to be beguiled by a make-believe fantasy. There wouldn't be a Mr. Right riding up on a white

Clydesdale to save the princess who'd been locked away at the top of the bell tower. Such things might happen in fairytales, but they didn't happen in real life.

Oh, well. No one ever said life would be easy – except for those nincompoops who wrote the self-help books.

And so . . .

After a couple of weeks of filling out dozens of job applications and not getting a single callback for an interview, Zetty had awakened late one morning and wasn't able to make it to the library as early as she would've liked. By the time she did walk through the automatic glass doors, all of the computer stations were taken, which meant that the librarian working the desk had begun handing out little plastic cards with numbers on them. The nice lady told Zetty that she would have to wait until a terminal freed up.

Hearing this, Zetty glanced over at how many people were in line ahead of her. It was a motley group of twelve fidgety souls – most needing haircuts and some hiding their shaved heads under funky hats – but all of them looked as though they desperately wanted to check their email accounts one last time before the world unexpectedly ended since it was quite obvious that they wouldn't be able to live with themselves if the planetary jig was, indeed, up . . .

Without one last perusal of their inboxes and the corresponding deletion of nuisance spam. So seeing she'd have to bide her time for maybe thirty minutes or longer, because there were a dozen people in front of her – and not being the type of person who relished waiting in such a slow-moving line – Zetty decided to go over to where they kept the printed versions of the newspapers so she could at least read the local classified ads while she waited.

Walking to the far end of the periodical display, Zetty picked up a daily paper and noticed a headline on the front page that caught her eye. The FBI had arrested a professor at the local university, and there was a disturbing picture of him in handcuffs.

Oh, my. That was a shocker. She couldn't remember the last time she'd ever heard about the FBI doing much of anything in Bellingham.

Then, as she brought the paper up closer to her eyes, she recognized the professor's face.

Whoa! And that was an even bigger shocker because he was a customer who had come into the flower shop several months ago to buy ceramic pots for his houseplants. So now Zetty was seriously interested in finding out all of the sordid details as to why he'd been arrested.

Sitting down in an empty chair to read the news article, she was surprised to discover what had happened. It seemed the FBI had compiled a bunch of evidence . . .

And had collected tip-offs from several unnamed sources, which led them to believe that the professor was a direct-action environmental activist and a member of ELF. He was suspected of being an accomplice in an unsolved arson case that had destroyed a telephone-pole warehouse.

Dumbfounded to find out that the FBI had been tailing him and tapping his phone for several months, Zetty couldn't help but feel uneasy. She wondered what would've happened if he had decided to set fire to the flower shop? Letting her imagination get the better of her, she thought that the guy could've come in to buy the ceramic pots as a ploy, when in fact he was actually there to scope the place out with the intent of coming back later to burn the shop down.

What a horrible thought.

But then again, maybe she was getting too carried away by her own negative thinking since the news article wasn't really that clear about his subversive activities. There was nothing in the paper about why he'd done what he'd done, which meant for her to jump to any sort of conclusion in regards to him having any ill will toward the flower shop would've been a bit of a stretch, to say the least.

Yet still, why would a university professor be involved in such a crime in the first place? Surely he hadn't gone out and burned down a telephone-pole warehouse simply out of spite. And though no one had died in the fire, the authorities were calling him an ecoterrorist.

Wow. I'd actually talked to a terrorist.

Wanting to learn more about what it all meant, Zetty patiently waited until her number came up. Then, when she was finally sitting down in front of one of the computer screens, she quickly moved her fingers across the keyboard, typing the word "ELF" into the browser's search engine.

And there it was. That's why the FBI had spent so much time on the professor's case. The Earth Liberation Front had a long history of using violent acts in order to achieve their environmental goals. The authorities suspected that ELF had been involved in numerous arson cases spanning many years. Expensive houses, storage buildings, and even luxury cars had been torched.

Oh, my. Talk about being eye-opening.

Zetty'd had no idea that such stuff had been going on. She rarely ever watched the news on TV and had mostly only been reading the weekly newspaper, which was a relatively tiny local that pretty much never printed any national news stories . . . so this was the first time she'd ever even heard about ELF.

Ecoterrorism in Bellingham. Who knew? How come no one had told her about it?

Anyway, as she proceeded to read paragraph after paragraph about the Earth Liberation Front, she soon began to understand why the FBI had sent a cadre of undercover agents to arrest the professor, being as ELF was at the top of the FBI's list of homeland terrorist organizations. Of course, Zetty had known that the authorities were looking for foreign terrorists coming into the country from Canada, but she hadn't realized that there were any American terrorist groups burning buildings down, nor could she have ever imagined that one of their members would've nonchalantly walked into Casey's flower shop and spoken to her.

Who would've ever thought such a thing could have happened to Zetty? It seemed she'd actually met a guy whom the FBI considered to be a threat to the national security.

As she sat there trying to remember if the professor had said anything out of the ordinary to her, Zetty couldn't even recall a single word of their conversation . . . possibly because he had seemed to be so unassuming and normal. The only peculiarity that had jumped out at her at the time was his shaggy six-inch goatee.

Yet still, she had always been somewhat naïve when it came to university professors because she thought of them as well-intentioned eggheads who were several notches above everyone else. Professors weren't supposed to do anything wrong. Such people obviously had super-intelligent brains, which meant that they should be smart enough to stay out of trouble. Getting arrested by the FBI and carted away to jail was a really huge no-no.

Unable to stop reading about it, Zetty then clicked back to the first list of search-engine hits in order to check out yet another online news article so as to learn more about what had happened, hoping to understand some of the behind-the-scenes details in regards to how the FBI had been able to tie the university professor to ELF. And that's when she suddenly had a disturbing thought. In this second article, a Seattle reporter had stated that there appeared to be a very active group of

ELF members in the Puget Sound area and which the reporter had specifically referred to as an underground cell. And on the webpage that Zetty had found this intriguing tidbit on, there also were several blue links to other news reports about how ELF was extremely serious about "stopping the corporate exploitation of the planet."

"Stopping the corporate exploitation of the planet?" Wait. Hold on.

As strange as it may have seemed, having just read what she'd read, some of the background information she was uncovering had a familiar ring to it, reminding her of a few of the things that Mooney had told her during their walk in the park.

Hadn't he used that very same phrase?

And since she'd read his blog only a few days ago, she knew he devoted page after page to what he called the *"Corporate Greed"* topic, attempting to explain why millions of people were letting their gluttony for more and more money hijack their souls, which he claimed was causing the planet's human population, and most of the free-world politicians, to do a great number of things that were terribly harmful to the environment.

But come on. There had to be a reasonable explanation as to why Mooney's words were so similar to some of the ELF rhetoric. The likelihood that he was also an ecoterrorist was totally absurd. He was just a guy who was passionate about saving the planet. Surely the similarities were nothing more than sheer coincidences. That's all they were. She knew that there were a lot of environmental activists living in Bellingham. The whole Puget Sound area was full of greenies. And since this part of the state was so left-leaning on the political spectrum . . .

Then such save-the-world thinking was probably what had brought Mooney to Bellingham in the first place. Just because he was gung-ho about protecting the environment and had sorta stormed into the flower shop, wanting to complain about the mistreatment of a fir tree, that didn't mean that there was a connection between him and the professor.

No, that couldn't be true.

There was only a slim possibility that the two of them even knew each other. So it wouldn't be fair to paint them both with the same brush.

No, of course not.

There just couldn't be any sort of connection between the two of them. Mooney hadn't come across as being that type of person. He certainly wasn't an ecoterrorist. When Zetty had talked to him up in the park, she hadn't heard him say anything that would lead her to believe he had a criminal mind.

But still . . .

The more she thought about it . . .

Neither had the professor, as she remembered it, either.

So, if she ever did see Mooney again, then she told herself that she would have to remember to ask him a few probing questions about how far he thought people should go in order to save the planet, and she would also have to specifically mention ELF, just to see what his reaction would be.

In any event, having wasted way too much of her computer time on something that absolutely had nothing whatsoever to do with why she was at the library, Zetty finally got around to reading the online classified ads.

And, lo and behold, a job listing caught her eye. There was an employment opening that jumped out at her. A downtown thrift store needed a salesclerk; and Zetty knew exactly where the place was. It was only about five blocks from her apartment.

Thinking she wouldn't be the only applicant, she told herself that this wasn't the time to dilly-dally. So she quickly logged off the computer, hurried past the checkout desk, breezed through the automatic glass doors, and made a beeline to "Missy's Secondhand Store." She was sure if she had a chance to talk to Missy, then she would see that Zetty would be the prefect person for the job. Missy wouldn't be able to say "no" once Zetty had charmed her with her wonderful people skills.

Chapter Twenty-Seven

In Bellingham, the first snow of the season wouldn't usually stay on the ground for very long. And so, within a few days, the temperature had risen back up above freezing . . .

The icy slush had melted away . . .

And the human habitat had returned to its normal activity.

Well . . .

Except for inside the bungalow on the lake.

Hurrying in the front door, Becky had come back from a class in a distraught mood. Mooney could tell she'd been crying.

"What happened? What's wrong?"

"My professor got arrested."

"Arrested? For what?"

"The FBI thinks he's a member of ELF. They said he had something to do with a fire at a warehouse where a utility company stored its telephone poles."

Trying to mask his uneasiness at hearing his sister say what she'd just said, Mooney played it low key. He didn't want Becky picking up on his gut-churning apprehension. Yet, of course, he instantly knew that this FBI collar was way too close for comfort. If the government was out and about, casting its prosecutorial net around town to snare ELF members, then it was also quite possible that the feds might eventually stumble upon one of the L.E.A.F. cells. Mooney had always worried that some of the local activists who were advocating similar environmental philosophies might be involved in both organizations, although he'd never been sure that there actually had been any cross-fertilization, per se. "Was this the same professor who helped you get the scholarship, the one you said was a fan of my blog?"

"Yes, Wayne Billson. He's the reason I came up here in the first place. When he interviewed me for a slot at the university, he mentioned your website, wanting to know if we were related. He's the one who signed off on my funding."

"Oh, that is kinda disturbing, huh?"

"Stupid FBI. I don't care what they say. I don't believe for a minute Wayne did anything wrong. He wouldn't hurt a fly. I think they made, like, a huge mistake. They probably thought, since he's so vocal about saving the environment and since he knows so many activists, that he must've been involved somehow. It's not right."

"Becky, c'mon. The FBI doesn't arrest someone unless they have strong evidence."

"Well, maybe Wayne talked to the wrong person, or did something altruistic that he shouldn't've done;

and, y'know, they just misunderstood what he said. In class, he always tells us that we have an obligation to stand up and fight against planetary injustice, like the freedom riders did to help Martin Luther King. But, I mean, he never told us to break the law. He's not like that."

"Okay, then maybe you're right. It could be they got the wrong guy."

"They did get the wrong guy. I've taken two of his courses, and I've never heard him say anything about ELF. Never."

"From what little I know about The Elves — I think they're pretty tightlipped. I mean, I think they have to be. The FBI's been hunting them down for years."

"The Elves?"

"That's what they call themselves. The Elves."

"Okay, if you say so." Shaking her head, Becky sniffled and rubbed her hand across her nose. "Like, this is so stupid. Wayne isn't an arsonist. He simply has this thing about protecting trees, that's all. You should see the leaf collection he has on his office wall. I think he loves evergreens more than he loves people. I bet someone just made something up so they could get a reward."

Seeing how upset his sister was, Mooney fully understood why she was feeling what she was feeling. She had every reason to be frustrated and confused. But knowing what he knew, he wasn't too surprised that ELF was active at the university. That did sort of fit their M.O. And now, having heard what he'd just heard, the greater concern was the possibility that Becky's favorite professor might also be a member of L.E.A.F. If this was true, then Mooney might need a lawyer himself.

So . . .

Given that there was little more he could do to console his sister, he decided to let the conversation peter out. He didn't want to go into any more details in regards to his thoughts about ELF. He was already on thin ice. Feeding the conversation with more fuel would do little to help Becky cope with her discomfort.

Thereupon, like Becky would frequently do when the emotional carpet had been pulled out from under her, she went into the kitchen and poured herself a glass of soymilk. The white liquid seemed to calm her nerves. That was how his little sister would deal with life's tribulations. A glass of soymilk was her go-to pacifier.

Wanting to finish what he was working on, Mooney stayed in the alcove and continued plugging away on his computer. It was only later, after he'd had a little more time to ponder what had happened with Professor Billson, that he realized that Tammy had, for whatever reason, gotten up at the crack of dawn that morning and had quietly sneaked out of the house, not having said anything to anyone. Most days she'd be the last one to get out of bed. But today had been different.

Knowing how well connected she was, Mooney then speculated it was possible that Tammy could've been tipped to the news that something seismic on the Richter scale had gone down in town. And maybe, being as her departure had occurred quite early, maybe she hadn't wanted to say anything to Mooney because she thought he was still asleep and she didn't want to wake him up. But since he was such a light sleeper, he'd actually heard her mucking about right as the sunlight had begun peeking through the curtains; yet because he had gone to bed so late, he'd played possum, wanting to go back to sleep since he knew he needed to get some more shuteye to be completely functional.

Anyway . . .

Having finished the final paragraph of the commentary he'd been researching for the last three days, Mooney then pulled up the local newspaper's website.

And there it was. The first page had an article about Professor Wayne Billson being arrested. As Becky had said, this was quite a large earthquake. It seemed the FBI had no doubt that ELF was in Bellingham.

But this wasn't the only front-page article that had caught Mooney's eye. There was also another news report about an offshore drilling rig that was listing on its side in the Bering Sea, and the paper had published an online companion photo of the rig's phallic-looking derrick tilting precariously at a precipitous angle . . .

As the floating steel monster was being towed to shore. It appeared as though the contraption's stabilizing pumps had failed, causing too much seawater to flood into several of its flotation chambers.

Reading the details as to what had happened, Mooney learned that the Oceanic Venturer had had an operational malfunction while it was exploring for hydrocarbons off the Alaskan coast. Stentung Oil, the owner of the mammoth rig, had evacuated the crew and was now sending the semi-submersible in for repairs. There were no reports of anyone being hurt. A corporate spokesman had stated that the company was reevaluating its drilling plans and that it might be two years before there would be any new exploratory deepwater drilling that far north.

Needless to say, Mooney was now conflicted by the push/pull of opposing emotions. On one hand, he was glad his brown-bag assignment had achieved its goal of disabling the Oceanic Venturer; whereas on the other hand, he was worried that the two news events might somehow be connected. The timing of Professor Billson's arrest was somewhat suspicious. Yet Mooney also knew that such timing might be nothing more than a dumb coincidence. Maybe the FBI was only interested in tying Billson to the arson case. Both events could've occurred around the same time without there actually being any sort of connection between the two.

But then, as the photo image seeped ever deeper into his brain, Mooney's heart began to race. He remembered that ArticGecko had mentioned something about wanting to drop by and see a certain professor at the university. He'd said that a friend of his knew the guy.

Oh, man. If Wayne Billson was, in fact, that same professor . . .

So now there definitely was a reason for Mooney to be very concerned. When it came to the Federal Bureau of Investigation nabbing a suspect who was only a couple of degrees of separation away from his own underground cell, Mooney knew that he needed to proceed with extreme caution.

So considering how the circumstances were rapidly unfolding, Mooney wasn't at all surprised that no one in the Flock had contacted him about what had happened. His leafy cohorts had probably wanted to avoid computerizing an uptick in chatter volume, since a sudden spike in Internet activity, coinciding with the two news events, might be enough of a statistical anomaly to attract the FBI's attention. ELF was so radioactive, that every cell member knew that they had to steer clear of giving the authorities even the slightest appearance of an indirect association between the two groups. And if such a link had, in fact, occurred – then the L.E.A.F.-ers in his local cell probably had been smart not to want to lock in a digital record that could possibly be used to document any sort of increase in communication exchanges vis-a-vis the ELF arrest. And though Mooney contemplated reaching out to his higher-ups, he dissuaded himself from doing so via any electronic communication. He realized that he had to stay in quiet mode. The safest way for him to avoid a "Hoovering" dragnet would be to simply ignore the fact that the local arrest and drilling-rig malfunction had even happened . . .

And thus not to blog or to email anyone about what had gone down.

But then, having duly disciplined himself per coming to terms with his own deaf-dumb-and-blind strategy (and even doodling out a cartoon of three see-no-evil monkeys on his notepad) – Mooney was thrown for a loop when even more crud hit the fan. Walking down the hall to the bathroom, he all of a sudden had an urge to peek inside Tammy's bedroom . . .

Per having noticed that her environmentally-friendly hair products had disappeared from the shelf above the bathtub. So, not being one to dismiss such an intuitive impulse – Mooney slowly opened the door to her room, looked inside, and saw that all of her belongings were gone. Tammy had taken her suitcase, her backpack, and her clothes with her. The room was left the way it had been when she'd first arrived. It looked as though she'd never even been there. More than likely, she had even wiped it clean of her tattletale fingerprints.

Realizing the gravity of the situation, Mooney tried his best to stay calm. He didn't want to jump to a conclusion as to why Tammy had left so suddenly. He would first have to confirm the factual details before he began to assume too much. He also told himself that it would be better for all involved if he waited to tell Becky. He didn't want to add any more uncertainty to what his sister was already having to deal with, nor did he want to stick his foot in his mouth and say something which could come back to bite him. In other words, it was possible that the money had come through to buy the satchel, which meant that Tammy could've had to make a quick trip out of town to pick it up. And though Mooney doubted that that was what had actually happened, there still was at least a slim possibility that such an explainable circumstance could've been the reason why Tammy had up and left the way she had.

Living in the underground was fraught with jeopardy and uncertainty.

Anyway . . .

Taking into account the overall complexity of the situation, Mooney didn't want to go out on a limb and say anything to his sister until he'd had a chance to get a more definitive explanation from Tammy. And he also wanted to let things cool down a bit, too. He didn't think that Becky needed any more complications in her life. She already had enough to deal with as it was. Mooney also knew that he'd have to come up with yet another palatable cover story . . . if it did, in fact, turn out that Tammy had left prematurely with no intent of coming back.

Following Flock protocol, he walked back to the alcove and checked his desk to make sure that there weren't any incrementing scraps of circumstantial evidence lying about. Rarely did he ever write anything down that could get him in trouble, but he wanted to be sure he hadn't missed anything.

Flipping through his spiral notebook, he scanned his research notes. Nothing jumped out at him. He then looked through the slips of paper that he was constantly using to jot ideas down on. He only found a doodle of a baby tree next to a smiley face inside the outline of a maple leaf. Tearing it out, he ran it through the shredder. Even the slightest innuendo had to be erased. He even shredded his doodle of the three deaf-dumb-and-blind monkeys because he didn't want to have to come up with a believable lie as to why he had sketched such a cartoon image in the first place.

Satisfied with his effort, Mooney then put on his coat, strapped on his bike helmet, and walked out the front door. Unlocking his mountain bike from the porch railing, he hopped on the two-wheeler and rode away. It was time to check in with his subcommander. He felt an urgent need to talk to Darwin as soon as possible.

See evil. Hear evil. Stop evil.

And so . . .

Being super careful that he wasn't being followed, Mooney quickly rode into the park and down to the bottom of the foothill.

He then biked over to the hiking trail that ran along the creek and continued straight into downtown, weaving through the city streets and backtracking a few times . . .

As he made his way south toward the Happy Valley neighborhood. It only took him a few more minutes to make it to the backstreet alleyway, which ran all the way to the RV park. Per Darwin's work schedule, Mooney knew that he only had a brief window of opportunity to catch him at his trailer. And since it was standard procedure not to prearrange a rendezvous time, this meant that the Flock always shied away from phone calls so as to avoid tipping off the authorities. If a contact wasn't home, a return visit would need to be attempted.

Biking up to Darwin's travel trailer, Mooney saw that he had timed it well. The scarecrow in the vegetable garden was still wearing its green baseball cap, which meant that Darwin Digbee was home and not being watched. If there had been a blue baseball cap on top of the scarecrow's head, then Mooney would've known not to stop, i.e., he would've continued on down the street and returned an hour later. And if there had been a cautionary red baseball cap, then such a warning would have told him to never come back. The color red meant that a local cell had been compromised and that all future contact should be broken off until further notice from the Flock.

Leaning his 21-speed up against the side of the trailer, Mooney snapped on his bike lock. By parking it there, he was warning away the other cell members. The last thing Darwin needed was to have another L.E.A.F.-er show up at the same time as Mooney and thus accidentally cross-fertilize a heretofore unconnected group of activists.

Walking up the metal steps, Mooney pressed the doorbell button. The mechanical chime reverberated on the other side of the metal wall.

"It's open," he heard Darwin say from inside.

Entering the trailer, Mooney saw his subcommander standing beside his rocking chair, peering out the Venetian blinds. "Hey. I hope I didn't come at a bad time."

"No, I'm glad you dropped by." Darwin then turned and sat down in the chair. "Have a seat."

Easing down on the couch, Mooney wasn't sure how much Darwin knew about the situation with the FBI arrest. "I guess you heard what happened, huh?"

"You mean about the professor getting cuffed?"

"Uh-huh. And about what happened up north." And when Mooney said this, Darwin quickly touched his index finger to his lips, warning him that he didn't want to talk about the Alaskan news report.

Nodding, Mooney let him know that he understood.

"I saw the professor's photo in the paper," Darwin said.

"It's not good, is it?"

"Nope. That's way too close for comfort. Now they'll be digging into the backgrounds of anyone he had contact with."

"A big net."

"A very big net. No one's safe. For a town this size, it could be a problem for us. As you know, the gov has tried for years to tie us to ELF."

"Don't tell me he was in the Flock."

"You're asking me?"

"I know we're supposed to be compartmentalized, but considering the circumstances, if there is a direct link . . ."

"Actually, whether there is or there isn't – that's not your concern or mine. We have to assume the worst and continue on from there. Now it's all about damage control. Protect the Flock."

"Right."

Darwin then pulled his cell phone out of his shirt pocket. Pointing to it, he shook his head and slowly ran his finger across his neck, mimicking the cut of a knife. "Understand?"

Mooney again nodded his head. "Go dark."

"Absolutely no communication. Hibernate for the next twelve months and wait until we get back in touch."

Damn. It really was bad. The Flock had been spooked. The FBI was on their trail. And though Darwin wasn't clarifying, Mooney wondered if he knew about Becky's connection to the professor. That was a concern, but Mooney didn't want to say anything because telling his subcommander such a snippet of info might somehow boomerang around and possibly be considered, in a court of law, a conspiratorial means of linking two L.E.A.F. members to ELF, even though, as far as Mooney was aware of, there hadn't been any sort of actual physical contact between the two organizations except for the indirect circumstantial evidence of his sister being a student of the professor's.

Nonetheless, an aggressive prosecutor could conceivably stretch the facts and claim that his sister's student/teacher interaction was proof that there had, indeed, been a network of intrigue, even if she had no intent whatsoever to do anything wrong. Certainly, in Mooney's mind, it was nothing more than a mere coincidence that Becky had been studying with that particular college professor. Yet Mooney also knew that when the feds started one of their witch hunts, many times they would ignore the truth and would use whatever means was at their disposal to corral their list of suspects. J. Edgar's heavy-handed tactics were still haunting the halls of the Bureau.

Plus, there was the associated complexity of the computer mouse having been given to ArticGecko. That was the volatile fuel which might could be ignited and, once such a blaze got going, the flames had a chance of engulfing all involved in a fiery inquisition. If the FBI had connected the dots as to why a Stentung employee had met with an environmental activist several weeks before the drilling rig's software had suddenly gone haywire, then the possible bureaucratic mistake of pegging the monkey-wrenching to ELF and not to L.E.A.F. (if that was what had actually happened) – would quite probably only be temporary. Another investigative fuse could possibly be lit, and the hot-burning sizzle might quickly spread to anyone in the Bellingham underground loop.

So there were a number of combustible loose ends to clearly be worried about.

Sliding his cell phone back in his pocket, Darwin then reached down and pulled a half-finished scarf out of his wife's knitting box. "Y'know, Karen's been working on this for weeks. I don't think she's ever going to finish it."

"I like that color. Looks nice."

"Yeah, I could use it this winter, that's for sure. Lamb's wool." Darwin then dropped the scarf in his lap and reached his hand down inside the wooden box. He pulled out two fat envelopes and handed one of them to Mooney. "Here. Ten thousand. Try not to pay more than that for the satchel."

"Oh," Mooney said, having not expected his subcommander to do what he did. In other words, Darwin had totally surprised him. Mooney hadn't anticipated that his subcommander would be the intermediary to hand over the cash for the satchel's purchase.

And so it was then that Mooney immediately realized that Tammy must have delegated this handoff to Darwin. Mooney's earlier assumption that she had flown the coop, so to speak, had turned out to be correct.

With a perturbed look on his face, Darwin then glanced down at the second envelope. He paused for a moment, appearing not to want to part with it. "Now, if the young lady won't sell you the bag for ten thousand, you can go up another ten thousand if you have to go that high, alright?"

"Okay."

Shaking his head with an obvious sense of annoyance, Darwin then handed Mooney the second pudgy envelope. "This is a hell-of-a-way to tie up a damn loose end. I mean, if the security committee had simply asked me what I thought, I would've told them we didn't need to be spending so much goddamn money on an old satchel. But it's too late now. Any questions?"

Wanting to be sure that they were both on the same page, Mooney did have a question. "So, I guess I won't be seeing Tammy anytime soon, will I?"

"I would say that's a reasonable assumption. Her visibility was compromised. She was at risk. Too many breadcrumbs, if you know what I mean. She told me to tell you thanks for all of your help."

"That's all she said?"

"Well, y'know, she was in a bit of a hurry."

"I understand. Okay, so, if and when I do get the satchel, what do you want me to do with it? Do you want me to bring it here?"

"Hell no. Don't bring it here. Absolutely not. I don't need the headache. Put the satchel and any of the money you don't use in a safe-deposit box." Darwin then picked up the unfinished scarf. "Like I said, we won't be seeing each other for a while. So, y'know, just wait until I get back in touch with you. When you see me wearing this scarf, you'll know the coast is clear. If I'm not wearing it, act like you don't even know who I am, okay?"

"Okay."

"I also want you to use our regular color code the next time we see each other . . . if anyone comes along and knocks on your door and starts asking you about

The Elves."

"Follow the protocol. I'll wear an orange baseball cap if something like that happens."

"Good. That's easy to remember. And hopefully by this time next fall, we should be in the clear."

They then hugged each other, said their goodbyes, and Mooney pedaled away from the RV park. The impromptu rendezvous had been productive; but now Mooney had a lot to think about.

First off, he had to figure out a way to explain Tammy's unexpected departure to Becky, and he knew that wouldn't be very easy. He also told himself that he would have to come up with a believable lie, which would pass the smell test. It seemed the older his sister got; the harder it was for him to fool her.

Another birthday; another distracting lie to worry about.

But, of course, that wasn't Mooney's biggest problem. He also needed to think through what he should do if the FBI showed up at his door and started asking questions. If they had a search warrant, he wasn't exactly sure how he was going to explain the twenty thousand dollars he'd just been handed. He would also need to come up with some sort of halfway logical explanation if the FBI asked him about Tammy. Mooney would have to figure out some sort of something he could tell the special agents if they were savvy enough to connect the dots.

Yes, indeed. With the potential for so many feathers to be plucked, there were a lot of pieces of the jigsaw puzzle to consider. When a situation like this came along, a lowly worker bee could start to regret having been involved as deeply as he was in eco activism. Trying to do the right thing, was never easy. It was much more complicated than he ever thought it would be.

Anyway . . .

Having run the various scenarios through his mind as he quickly pedaled to the bottom of the northwest side of the foothill that encompassed Arbor Falls Park . . .

Mooney got off his bike and began slowly walking it up the steep incline. This part of the greenway trail cut through a sloping neighborhood, which divided downtown from the streets that dead-ended up at the lake. He preferred to walk his bike up this section since the pedaling was way too arduous. Plus, the plodding exertion was a nice change. It gave him a little more time to sort through a variety of gambits that he needed to think about before deciding on what he should do. There were a number of ramifications he had to seriously consider. He knew the best way to keep Becky out of trouble was to tell her as little as possible, but he still would have to come up with a believable explanation as to why Tammy had left without even saying goodbye.

As for the FBI, if any of their agents did, in fact, show up at his door – Mooney knew that he would have little choice but to clam up and ask for a lawyer. Short of telling them the truth, which he absolutely couldn't do, he didn't seem to have any other options. The last thing he needed to happen was to get caught lying to the feds, since he knew he wouldn't be able to talk his way out of their chokehold. He also didn't want to paint himself in a corner and then have to tell more and more lies, trying to explain the first poorly thought-out lie.

Yeah, well, such conniving wasn't as easy as some people thought it was.

Juggling so many China plates took a great deal of dexterity.

Anyway . . .

Once Mooney had made it back home, he was relieved to see that there wasn't a nondescript, official-looking sedan parked in the driveway.

So far, so good.

Then . . .

When he had safely made it inside the front door – and not knowing a better place to hide the twenty thousand – he stuck the two envelopes in a sock and stuffed the sock under the mattress in his bedroom. Where else was he going to put it? He couldn't take a chance on Becky finding it. That would be the last thing he needed. No, he certainly didn't want to have to try to explain to her why he had so much money after he had previously told her he was on an exceptionally tight budget.

Satisfied with his subterfuge, Mooney then put on his best poker face and knocked on Becky's door to see if she had heard anything new about her professor. He also wanted to nail down a preemptive falsification framework in regards to what had happened with Tammy, hoping that his sister wouldn't begin presupposing as to the highly unusual turn of events, i.e., he didn't want Becky's mind whirling with questions and coming up with answers that might cause either of them too much woe.

"Who is it?"

"It's me."

"Me who?"

"Becky, c'mon. Stop joking around. We need to talk. It's about Tammy."

After a short delay, the door opened. His sister stood there in her terry cloth bathrobe with a towel wrapped around her head. "So, like, what's up with her?"

"She moved out."

"Why?"

"Something came up. I think it might've been a job offer. I'm not really sure."

"She told me she had a trust fund and didn't have to work."

"Really? She said she had a trust fund?"

"Uh-huh."

"Well, I didn't know that. She never told me that, but it doesn't surprise me. Anyway, all I know is, um, she, like, up and left. And she also changed her cell phone number, too."

"Wait. Why'd she do that?"

"I don't know. I didn't ask her."

"Moon . . ."

"Look, I wish I knew what's going on with her, but I honestly don't have a clue, okay? Maybe she'll call and explain it to you. I never could figure out why she'd hardly ever text or email me. I mean, what was up with that, huh? Like, she only wanted to talk to people on the phone. She rarely ever would use email."

"I know. I thought that was kinda strange, too. But she could've at least have said goodbye."

"Stuff happens, I guess. Any news about your professor?"

Sniffling, as if she was going to sneeze but then repressing it, Becky rubbed her nose. "On Thursday we're having a protest rally at the federal building. A bunch of his students are going to show up. No one believes he did what they said he did. Everyone thinks he was set up or, y'know, whatever you call it. Like, no one ever heard him say anything about ELF. It makes absolutely no sense."

"Look. Please don't do anything you'll regret, okay? You know they take pictures at those rallies."

"I'm sure they do. So? I don't have anything to hide."

"That's true. But you don't want Big Brother putting you on his watch list."

"What do you mean?"

"What I mean is, you don't want the FBI opening up a file on you."

"I don't care. I haven't done anything wrong."

"Becky, even if you're not involved, they might

make a dumb mistake and think you are involved. Stuff happens. People screw things up all the time. And you don't want that hassle. You don't want to have to pay a lawyer to clear up something you didn't do. Like, it can get real messy real fast when the FBI starts digging around in people's garbage."

And when she heard him say this, she sucked in a deep breath, covered her mouth with her hand, and stared him straight in the eye. It was as though she was reading his mind, or maybe she was possibly using her feminine intuition to instantly guess at what he was thinking. "Oh, no. That's why Tammy left so quickly, isn't it? She's in ELF, isn't she?"

Say what? Why had his sister even thought such a thing? Yet her words hit him like a load of bricks. Here he was trying to spin the disinformation so as to protect Becky from getting involved, and she somehow sniffed out the worst-case scenario. "Why do you think that?"

" 'Cause you know something you're not telling me, that's why. Moon, you're a terrible liar. You always have been."

"Becky . . ."

"No, listen. Listen to me. Wayne gets arrested, and then Tammy splits. What's up with that? I mean, doesn't that sound a little too coincidental for there not to be some sort of connection between the two of them?"

"Hey, c'mon. Stuff happens like that all the time. You told me there's no way Wayne could be in ELF, right? And just because our roommate had to suddenly leave for some dumb reason . . ."

"Look, I'm just saying it seems a bit suspicious to me, okay? The cops must think someone's involved, or they wouldn't've . . . ." But then Becky didn't finish her train of thought. Her face morphed into a distrustful stare. "Moon, you're not in ELF, are you?"

Slowly shaking his head, Mooney knew that he had to appear as sincere as he possibly could, considering the question. "Of course not. C'mon, you know me better than that."

"Then what are you hiding? Why are you trying to protect Tammy like you're doing?"

"What do you mean? Why do you think I'm hiding something?"

" 'Cause I know you too well, that's why. When you get all serious like this, there's always something you're not telling me. And it really hurts when you start fudging and keeping your stupid secrets – like – to yourself."

"Becky, I'm not lying, okay? I'm telling you the truth. I'm not in ELF. You know I'd never have anything to do with a bunch of hormonals who'd, like, burn something down. You know me better than that."

"Well, I guess that's true. You don't like any sort of violence. But I still think Tammy could somehow be involved."

"Sure, I guess anything is possible. That's true. But I seriously doubt Tammy would've had anything to do with ELF. She didn't seem like the type of person who'd go around setting fires, if you ask me."

"I don't know. Maybe so. But it still sounds a little too coincidental."

"Granted. I give you that. But coincidences happen all the time. Stuff happens. Life is, like, way complicated these days."

"Sure, uh-huh. If you say so." Becky then sighed ever so slightly and sneezed into her hand. "So, like, what are you going to do about the money?"

"What money?"

"Y'know, for the rent. Since Tammy's gone and since you're not making enough from your blog to cover your half of the rent, how are you going to pay it each month?"

"Oh, the rent. Well, I guess we'll just have to get another roommate."

"Yeah, I guess so, too. Want me to ask around?"

"Okay, sure. See if you can find someone. But, I mean, it can't be one of your boyfriends, alright?"

"Why not?"

" 'Cause I'm still your brother and . . ."

"Oh, don't be so old school. Chill, okay?"

And since Mooney knew he'd already accomplished most of what he'd wanted to accomplish . . .

He left it at that. Shrugging his shoulders, he turned and walked down the hall, letting Becky return to doing whatever she had been doing before he'd knocked on her door. He told himself that it wouldn't do any good to try to talk his way around the problem more so than he already had done.

Retreating to his computer, and remembering

what Darwin had told him, Mooney wanted to check to see if there had been any more news updates about ELF. Also, having heard what his sister had said, Mooney now realized that she was onto him. Maybe she hadn't actually come out and accused him of breaking the law, but it was obvious that she at least sort of suspected he'd done something he shouldn't've done. He sensed that she was starting to question his honesty, possibly thinking he wasn't being as truthful with her as she thought he should be.

And, of course, she was absolutely right. He was feverously flapping his wings, trying to veer away from the blades of a prosecutorial jet engine in order to avoid a bird strike. In hindsight, knowing what he now knew, Money should never have let himself get talked into rooming with Becky. It had been a monumental mistake from get-go. He didn't like having to lie to her.

But still, there was little he could do about it now. It was what it was. In the future he would have to be a lot more careful so as to keep his sister better insulated from ever getting involved in his underground activities (as had happened this time). Money would never forgive himself if Becky, for whatever reason, ended up on the wrong side of the law because of something he'd done. The last thing he wanted would be to have her falsely accused of being engaged in any sort of subversive activities which she absolutely had nothing whatsoever to do with.

Chapter Twenty-Eight

At the secondhand store, Missy had told Zetty that the salesclerk position had already been filled. But still, all wasn't lost because Missy had also explained that the store might need someone else in a few months. So Missy had then asked Zetty if it would be okay to keep her application on file, saying that she would give her a call when she had another opening.

That gave Zetty a smidgen of hope.

Yet, of course, she knew that she certainly didn't want to have to wait another two or three months to start bringing home a paycheck. And Zetty also knew that when someone like Missy said such-and-such about a possible job opening – an unemployed person had to take that type of kissy-face talk with a big grain of salt. Missy was just being nice. She probably didn't want Zetty to get discouraged, nor did she want to lose her as a paying customer.

And – surprise, surprise – Missy's words had actually worked, too. After she'd shared that little bit of encouragement, Zetty had ended up buying a slightly used dress and paying more than she should've paid for it since it had been such a good fit. The dress was a cute nautical with off-white and coral stripes. To Zetty, it looked as though it would be the perfect outfit for summerwear.

But then . . .

Once she had returned home and had had some time to think about it, she asked herself why she'd wasted her money on something she wouldn't be wearing for all those many months. It truly hadn't made much sense for her to buy the dress except for the fact that the price was less than a third of what it would've cost her at a department store. The nautical was a steal, so when she saw it in Missy's secondhand store, she thought she absolutely had to have it.

But then her spending splurge had begun to nag Zetty once she'd gotten home and had seen herself wearing the dress in her own mirror.

What was I thinking? She didn't need a summer dress. She had plenty of summer dresses hanging in her closet.

With a clearer head on her shoulders, Zetty now realized that what she had done had been a mistake. She'd fallen prey to the instant gratification of an impulse buy. Purchasing the dress had simply made her momentarily feel good about herself, while it had also helped Missy ring up a quick sale. Zetty had fallen into the codependent trap of using her credit card to make two people smile at the same time.

Only spend money on the basic necessities.

Anyway . . .

As it turned out, Zetty was the one who actually needed a helping hand, not Missy. Zetty was scrimping to get by, and she knew she positively shouldn't have bought the dress since she really didn't need it. What she'd read in that self-help library book with the scissors cutting up a credit card on its cover . . . had now come back to haunt her.

Moping about in despair, Zetty spent the rest of the afternoon cleaning the bathroom. Scrubbing the porcelain gave her a way to punish herself for having forked over too much money on a dress she absolutely didn't need. She told herself that she should only spend money on the important necessitates such as chicken salad sandwiches and chocolate chip cookies. If she'd been a big drinker like Edna-Ney, Zetty probably would've gone out and knocked back several large glasses of hard liquor to get her mind off of her financial inadequacies. But since she was her mother's daughter and since she had been brought up better than that, Zetty knew not to let herself succumb to the chicanery of drowning her sorrows at a scuzzy bar. Luckily, neither of her parents had been drinkers; and Miss Pineford had been a strict teetotaler, too. Her foster mom wouldn't let anyone bring any sort of alcohol into her home.

With the rinse-off water *gurgling* down the drainpipe in the bathtub, Zetty was just finishing up her spick-and-span sponge out . . .

When the phone rang. Quickly pulling off her rubber gloves, she hurried into the hall and reached to pick up the receiver. As she did so, she suddenly felt a bit of optimism jolt through her. She thought that it must be someone calling about one of the jobs she had applied for; and, of course, they were probably calling to check in with her, wanting to set up a time for her to come in for an interview.

But no, she was wrong. That wasn't who was calling.

It was Mooney.

For the first few seconds, Zetty was tongue-tied and unable to say much of anything. She could barely even acknowledge he'd dialed the right number.

But then, as she got ahold of herself, trying not to hyperventilate, while she was also doing her best to concentrate on each and every word that he was saying as he quickly began to tell her that the buyer — who was interested in her mom's satchel — had actually come through with the money . . .

It felt as if both her lungs had completely emptied themselves of oxygen. Zetty didn't know what to say. Standing there with the receiver held up to her ear, she finally was able to mumble out a halfway audible response. "Yes, okay," she said.

Now thankfully, it hadn't seemed as though Mooney had picked up on her discombobulation because he then continued on with his one-sided conversation, telling her that he wanted to drop by and talk to her about what she wanted to do about her mom's bag.

Say what?

What she wanted to do?

She had no idea what she wanted to do.

Being caught off guard by his statement, Zetty stuttered out the first thought that had popped into her head and told Mooney that she still wasn't at all sure she would ever be able to part with the satchel. And that's when there was a long pause from the other end of the phone, and that's also when the tone of Mooney's voice abruptly changed and he told her that the buyer was willing to offer her five figures.

Hearing this, Zetty had to stop and think what Mooney meant by that.

Five figures?

Had she heard him correctly? Surely she wasn't hallucinating. Indeed, it had sounded as though he was talking about a considerable amount of money.

Pressing the receiver up closer to her ear, as she continued to listen to his soft-spoken pleasantries, she couldn't help but think that he truly wanted her to get a good deal.

But then . . .

He suddenly sneezed and said he had a busy schedule and was behind in his work. He asked if it would be okay for him to drop by in a couple of hours and talk to her about what she wanted to do. Strangely enough, she almost had the feeling that he was asking her to do him a favor.

Oh, my. Maybe she'd been wrong about him all this time. Maybe he was merely attempting to find an excuse so he could come by and talk to her. At least, that was the impression she got when she heard the soothing and almost buttery tone of his voice.

Swallowing hard, she muttered, "Yes, okay." But what else could she have said? She didn't want him to change his mind, and she certainly didn't want him to think that she was inconsiderate. No, she positively didn't want him to think that she was only interested in using him to make a lot of money.

So, trying to be as amiable as possible, she told him that he could come by her apartment and talk to her about the satchel. But still, she made sure he understood that she hadn't actually made up her mind as to whether or not she would be willing to part with it. She didn't want him getting the wrong idea. She wanted to be clear about her ambiguity as to what she intended to do.

Without hesitating, Mooney said he sympathized with her reluctance to make a commitment either way. Then, with a muffled cough, he thanked her for agreeing to let him drop by and proceeded to finish the call by saying he would see her shortly. Also, the whole time he was on the phone, she couldn't help but think he had a severe cold and shouldn't've even been calling her until he felt better. His concern to see her as soon as possible was a bit puzzling, to put it mildly.

Hanging up the receiver, Zetty thought about what had just transpired.

Then it hit her.

Oh, dear. She didn't have much time. He was actually coming by to see her.

Rushing to put away her cleaning paraphernalia, Zetty hurried to take a shower and spruce herself up. This wasn't exactly going to be a date, but it would be somewhat similar to a date, in a way. A handsome guy was coming over to her place; and they would, no doubt, be spending some time together, much like a real date.

During the whole time she was in the shower, she thought about what she should do about the satchel. It seemed as though no matter what choice she made, she quite possibly would, more than likely, regret her decision. She really needed the extra money, yet she also didn't want to part with something that had meant so much to her mother.

There didn't seem to be an easy answer.

As she put on a dress and a sweater, she still hadn't decided what she was going to do. But then, after she'd finished dabbing on her makeup, with her eyes staring back at herself in the mirror, she shook her head and knew what had to be done. She would do what her mother would've wanted her to do.

Hearing a light knock at the front door, Zetty glanced over at the clock and saw that it was still early. Mooney wasn't supposed to be there for another ten minutes. Flustered, she looked back in the mirror. She wanted to check to make sure nothing was out of place. She turned her head to the right and then to the left. Her makeup seemed to be fairly well balanced.

Satisfied with her appearance, Zetty hurried into the hall and made her way to the other side of the living room, hearing the floor creak under her shoes. Stopping at the front door, she peeked through the peephole.

It was Mooney.

She took a deep breath, unlocked the locks, and slowly eased the door open.

"Hi. Sorry I'm early, but the bus didn't take as long as I thought it would."

"That's okay. Come in."

Entering the room, he took off his coat and placed it on the coatrack. "Thanks for seeing me on such short notice."

"Well, I wasn't planning on doing anything this afternoon anyway, so I'm glad you called. We're out of tea, but I can make you a cup of coffee."

"No, that's okay. I'm fine."

"Have a seat."

Coughing in his hand, Mooney stepped over to the sofa and eased down onto its cushions.

Zetty then crossed in front of him and plopped herself down in the chair next to the window. "I wanted to tell you I've been reading your blog. You've written a lot of interesting articles. I think you do a pretty good job of explaining how so many things are interconnected, and you make it really easy to understand."

"Thanks. I try not to make it too complicated."

Nodding, Zetty was hoping she could just quietly sit there and give him a chance to say what was on his mind and thus let him start the conversation. Yet, for whatever reason, he seemed to be more uptight this time. He looked standoffish. His arms were crossed in front of him, and his body was tensed up. Zetty wondered if maybe she had misjudged her appearance. She wasn't sure, but she had a sneaky suspicion that she could've overdressed for the occasion.

With their conversational pause continuing on for an agonizingly long minute . . .

Or maybe even longer than that . . .

Zetty could feel an uneasiness begin to seep into her stomach. Mooney's visit wasn't going at all like she had expected it would. Something was definitely wrong.

So wanting to change the mood and not let her nerves get the better of her, Zetty decided to try another tack. "Are you feeling okay? You look a little under the weather."

"I think I'm coming down with a cold. I took some antihistamines, so I'm a little groggy." Mooney then pulled a handkerchief out of his pocket and sneezed into it.

"Oh, that's what's wrong. I was afraid it might have been something I said."

"No, it's nothing to do with you. I just have a sore throat, but I'll be fine."

"Y'know, I was wondering what you thought about that professor getting arrested. Everyone's been talking about it. Someone said they even saw a news crew from one of the networks interviewing a few of his students up at the university."

Mooney took a moment to gather his thoughts

before he answered. And, as he did so, his eyes wandered around the room. It seemed as if this might be a touchy subject for him and that he possibly didn't want to discuss what had happened. "A network news crew, huh? I hadn't heard that. But, I mean, I'm not surprised. The Earth Liberation Front is a big news story, that's for sure."

Seeming to have hit a nerve, Zetty was surprised by the change in the tone of his voice; but she couldn't tell if his edgy response was caused by his sore throat or by something else. "Well, from what I read in the newspaper, it sounds to me like ELF has done some really bad things."

"That's true. They're fire-breathing radicals, for sure. There's no doubt about that." Mooney then sneezed into his handkerchief yet again. Sniffling, it looked as though he was almost going to sneeze a third time – as he opened his mouth really wide – yet he somehow was able to stop himself from doing so. Lowering the handkerchief back down to his lap, he finished his train of thought. "I think ELF just wants to grab the public's attention; but I also think they're going about it the wrong way. Violence only gets people in trouble. It doesn't do much to save the planet."

"Do you know anyone who's in that group?"

"No, I don't think so. Why?"

"Well, one time I actually met that professor . . . the one who just got himself arrested. He came into the flower shop to buy some stuff."

"You're kidding me."

"No, when I saw his picture in the paper, I recognized him. It was the same guy."

"Do you remember what he said to you?" Mooney asked, coughing into his hand.

"Y'know, I honestly can't remember him saying much of anything. Seems like he just came in to buy two ceramic pots for his houseplants, is what I recall happened."

"He didn't try to recruit you, did he?"

"Recruit me? Don't tell me they do things like that."

"No, I was just making a bad joke," Mooney said, sniffling and rubbing his nose with the handkerchief.

"Oh, okay. If you say so. But it's sort of hard for me to tell when you're joking." And, in all truthfulness, Zetty sensed that he wasn't joking. She actually had thought he was being quite serious because of the way his eyes had narrowed and squinted. Seeing him react in that way, she couldn't help but think he wasn't joking, even though he didn't want to admit it. "Y'know, what I can't understand is, why doesn't an organization like that just use lawyers to change the things they're unhappy with. I mean, with a name like ELF, you would think they'd be willing to go to court instead of burning buildings down. When people hear the word *elf* – I think most of 'em are reminded of Santa Claus."

"Well, you would think so, wouldn't you? But as best as I can understand it, they assume the system, i.e., the court system, is rigged. Big money can hire hundreds of greedy lawyers, and a small group like ELF probably thinks the odds are stacked against them in court."

"But breaking the law . . ."

"I know. I agree. I think they go way too far. Way, way too far."

"Y'know, I'm all for saving the planet, 'cause we've obviously gotten ourselves in a pickle with climate change. I mean, since the ice caps are melting and the polar bears don't have anyplace to hunt . . . and with, y'know, global warming causing all those monster storms . . . like, it really worries me what might happen next. But a lot of people don't seem to care. They don't even think about that type of stuff. All they seem to want to do is to keep buying their gas-guzzling SUVs and keep voting for the big-business politicians who promise to cut their taxes. I mean, like, so many people are just, y'know, burying their heads in the sand. They should be ashamed of themselves. It's so heartwrenching."

Nodding his head, Mooney's mouth again opened wide; and he quickly sucked in two gulps of air, looking as if he was almost going to sneeze . . .

But he didn't. Exhaling with a sigh of relief, he lowered his handkerchief and put it back in his pocket. "Well, I'm glad you feel that way. We'd all be much better off if more people got involved and started living sustainable lives and stopped being so materialistic."

"Buy local."

"Exactly. If everyone grew their own veggies and

had chickens in their yards, that would really help cut back on the freight trucks that are hauling all of the prepackaged foods such long distances. Less diesel, less carbon dioxide. There's so much people could do that they're not doing."

"I know, and I kick myself when I think about all of the dumb things I used to do. All the dumb stuff I used to buy. I'm so glad you came along and said what you said. It really woke me up. Now I always carry a reusable shopping bag to the farmers' market, and I've also cut back on buying things at the grocery store, too. I swore to myself that I wouldn't buy anything new, besides food, if I could figure out a way to get it used. Y'know, secondhand."

"Wow. Good for you. I'm impressed."

"Hey, y'know, I try. And I've also been telling my friends they need to think more about what they're doing, what they're spending their money on. Every-one needs to bike more, ride the bus more, and stop using plastic bags."

"Well, I'm glad you feel that way. But, like you just said, a lot of people are simply going to keep sticking their heads in the sand and continue clogging their ears with static about anything and everything but the truth. And that's why some of the activists I know are saying that it's going to take a drastic rise in the ocean levels before the public actually begins to understand how much damage has already been done to the environment. Of course, by then it'll be too late."

"Oh, let's hope not. That'd be really awful. But, I

mean, now that you mention it, what you're saying does sort of remind me of a certain ex-boyfriend of mine who won't listen to what anyone else has to say about such stuff and who also continues to show up at my door . . . the last time with a box of chocolates, claiming he's changed . . . but I knew not to believe him. A zebra can't change his stripes. Some people will never stop doing what they're doing."

"I guess he told you what I said, huh?"

"Uh-huh."

"Seems I got that one wrong."

"No, it's okay. I'm sure you meant well. But Tom's one of those people who refuses to learn from his mistakes. So, like, I've been there, done that. He's not the type of guy I want to date."

"Sorry. I should've stayed out of it."

"Well, I'm sure you were simply trying to help. Tom needs to grow up. He's good at getting people to feel sorry for him. And maybe that's why I still kind of do feel sorry for him. But that doesn't mean I want to go out with him."

Coughing, Mooney pulled the handkerchief back out of his pocket and sneezed. "You don't have a cat, do you?"

"No."

"I think I'm allergic to cats."

"No cats."

Then, having spent enough time on small talk – although to her they hadn't actually been discussing inconsequential topics since she truly liked delving into the serious subjects which she wanted to understand more about – Mooney finally sucked in a deep breath, leaned forward, and said, "I guess we need to talk about why I'm here. I brought the money with me. The buyer is willing to pay you ten thousand in cash for the satchel."

"Ten thousand dollars? That's a lot of money."

"Yes, it is. And, like, it's too much money for me to be carrying around for very long, so that's why I wanted to come over and get this over with as soon as possible."

"Oh, okay. So I guess that's why you're so uptight, huh?"

"You think I'm uptight?"

"Well, maybe that's not the right word. It could be something to do with your head cold. Or maybe it's the pills you're taking."

"That's true. I guess it could be that."

"Aren't you worried someone might rob you?"

"No, I've never been robbed in my whole life. And no one knows I have that much money on me, except you."

"Oh, I see what you mean." Then, as she paused to come up with a polite way of saying what she thought needed to be said, because she wanted to pick her words carefully since she didn't want to offend him – Zetty decided that she just had to be straightforward with Mooney and hope he wouldn't think she was being too blunt. "Y'know, what I don't understand is, why would anyone want to pay me that much money for my mom's satchel? They can have one custom made for a lot less than that."

"I assume the buyer's willing to go that high because he knows it's a rare collectable. That's the only reason I can think of for him to want to pay that much for it."

"Well, I just don't get it. That's a lot of money."

"I understand. And you're right. It does seem like a lot of money to me, too."

Zetty shook her head. She suspected that there was something Mooney wasn't telling her; but she was at a loss as to how she could get him to talk about what he obviously didn't want to talk about. Also, since he hadn't said anything that was compelling enough to persuade her to part with the satchel, she thought she had no choice but to be totally frank. "No, I can't take the money. I mean, I really need the money, but I wouldn't feel good about myself if I sold it. I don't think my mom would want me to sell it. She'd want me to keep it."

"Zetty, it's ten thousand dollars."

"I know."

"Okay, so – what about fifteen thousand dollars? Cash. Right now. In your pocket."

"You just said ten."

"We're negotiating. Or, y'know, you might call it haggling."

"No, I'm not haggling. I don't know how to haggle."

"Okay, so, how much do you want for it?"

"How much do I want for it? I don't think you understand. I loved my mom more than anything, and she always told me that people shouldn't do things just for the money. She thought money caused a lot of problems in the world."

"Okay. You drive a hard bargain. I'll cut to the chase. And this is my final offer. I can't go any higher. Twenty thousand dollars."

"You're kidding me."

"No, twenty thousand."

"You can't be serious. There's no way you could possibly have twenty thousand dollars in cash on you. C'mon. You're pockets aren't big enough for that much money."

"It's in my coat. You can check if you don't believe me."

A bit shocked that he was walking around with so much money on him, Zetty was almost tempted to take him up on his offer to actually look at it. She'd never seen that much money before. But she also knew if she held all that cash in her hand, she might not be able to say "no." It was hard enough to keep a level head as it was. She didn't want to make it even harder on herself. "That's okay. I don't need to look at it. I believe you. But I can't sell my mom's satchel. I think she'd want me to keep it."

"Are you absolutely sure you're not going to change your mind?"

"Yes, I'm sure. I'm not going to change my mind."

"Okay. I understand. And to be totally honest

with you, I think your mother was right. Money isn't everything. But could you do me one small favor, if it's not too much trouble?"

"That depends on what it is."

"Would you please not walk around town carrying the satchel on your shoulder? I think it's way too valuable to take it out in public like that. Someone might see it and try to steal it from you."

"You mean, like a purse snatcher?"

"More like a crook who knows the real value of a rare collectable."

"Well, now that I know how much it's really worth, I promise you it won't be leaving my apartment. You don't have to worry about that."

Looking as if he was again fixing to sneeze, Mooney raised the handkerchief back up to his nose. But nothing happened. "Um, could I have a glass of water?"

"Oh, sure. Let me get one for you." Rising up out of the chair, Zetty walked into the kitchen. "Is tap water okay?"

"That's fine. I hope you don't buy bottled water."

"No, I can't afford it. And I also don't want to fill up the landfill with plastic bottles." At the sink Zetty filled a glass with water. She then stepped back into the living room and handed it to him.

After he took a long gulp, he blinked his eyes and looked as though he might have a slight fever. "So, have you found a job yet?"

"I wish. But there aren't any jobs. I've tried all

over town, but no one wants to hire me," she said, sitting back down in the chair.

"What do you mean, there aren't any jobs?"

"No one will hire me."

"Okay, so, what are you going to do now?"

"I don't know. I don't know what I'm going to do. I mean, I can't get unemployment 'cause I quit my job. If I'd been laid off, I'm pretty sure I would've qualified for an unemployment check."

"Have you ever thought about going back to school?"

"Yes, I've thought about it. But, like, I'm more worried about paying my half of the rent right now than getting myself deeper in debt, having to pay for tuition."

Standing up, Mooney took another sip of water and sat the glass down on the coffee table. He then walked over to the window and looked outside. Zetty noticed that his mood had suddenly changed, as had the tone of his voice. Now his words didn't have as much of an edge to them as they'd had when he was talking about the money. "Zetty, what if you had a place to stay and you didn't have to pay rent? Would that help you enough to get you through college?"

"I'm not sure what you mean. Where could I stay and not pay rent? Are you talking about a scholarship or something like that?"

Rubbing his hand across the back of his neck, Mooney turned around. The light shining in through the window behind him appeared to make him look somewhat taller than he actually was. "I used to work for a nonprofit. You'd be amazed at how many organizations have special programs to help people get through college. My sister snagged a grant that pays most of her expenses. She's studying over at the university."

"You think I could get a grant to pay my rent?"

"No, but you might could qualify for some type of financial assistance which would cover your tuition. On the rent, you could stay with us. We have a house up on the lake. You wouldn't have to pay anything toward the rent."

Flabbergasted that he was willing to help her go to college, Zetty at first didn't know what to say. She was totally surprised by his concern for her welfare. Maybe she was missing something, or maybe he did like her more than he was letting on. Being somewhat unnerved, goosebumps ran up her spine. And this time it wasn't from the chill in the apartment. No, this time the tingling emanated from a deep emotional part of her that she had only felt a few times before in her life. "You share a house with your sister?"

"Well, actually, we're just renting it, and it's not a very big place, really. But you'd have your own bedroom."

"Okay, so – why would you want to go out of your way to help someone like me like that?"

"I guess it's because . . . because I think you really do care about the environment, and I think you're deserving, and you also impressed me when you wouldn't take the money. Most people I know would've taken the money. It takes a special person to say *no* to that much money."

Pausing to think about what he'd said, Zetty could tell he was being sincere. There wasn't any hint of dishonesty in his voice. "I think you're trying to flatter me, aren't you?"

"It's not flattery if it's the truth."

"Oh, c'mon. We both know I'm not a special person. Like I said, I'm just doing what my mom would've wanted me to do, that's all."

"It sounds to me like she was a really good mother. I wish I could've met her." Turning back around, Mooney again stared out the window. "Look, you don't have to make up your mind right now. Just think about it, okay?"

"Well, I very much appreciate . . ."

"Listen, I tell you what. Why don't you come up to the house and meet my sister. Check the place out. It's really beautiful up there. Come have dinner with us before you make up your mind."

"Dinner?"

"Nothing fancy. Do you like stir-fry?"

"Uh-huh."

"What about this Saturday? Say, seven o'clock?"

"Okay. Sure. I don't think I'm doing anything this Saturday."

"Good. I'll send you an email with the directions."

And with that, Mooney stepped over to the coatrack, grabbed his coat, and put it on – then walked out the door.

It took Zetty almost an hour to get over the shock of what had happened. Once he was gone, she had sat on the sofa, dumbfounded, thinking about all of the things they'd discussed.

Had she really turned down twenty thousand dollars?

Oh, my goodness. That would've been enough money to pay my bills for a whole year.

And why had he offered to help her go to college? What was that all about? Did this mean he actually liked her?

But then again, she'd never heard of a guy doing anything like that just to get someone to go on a date with him. If he wanted to take her out, he could've simply have asked her to go to a movie. So, the more she thought about it, the more she couldn't understand why he'd said what he'd said. To make it even more confusing, he really had sounded totally genuine. She didn't think he'd lied to her. It hadn't seemed as though he'd tried to pull the wool over her head. He hadn't acted like a wolf in sheep's clothing.

Anyway, at least she had a few days to think about it. If she changed her mind, she could always just call him and say she wouldn't be able to make it. She didn't have to accept his dinner invitation if she didn't want to go, even though it would actually give her a chance to meet his sister. Zetty thought if she was able to talk to his sister, then it might help her understand what made Mooney tick. Maybe his sister would be

419

able to answer some of the nagging questions which Zetty was struggling to figure out about him.

Chapter Twenty-Nine

He never hardly ever got sick. Rarely did he even catch a cold. But some germy bug had somehow found its way into his body, and he'd been feeling miserable for several days. He didn't think it was an allergy, although he half-jokingly told himself that he might be allergic to an excessive amount of uncertainty.

So maybe scientifically it wasn't possible to be allergic to something such as stress, but his life certainly had turned topsy-turvy. For days he'd been trying to cope with all of the confusion which had been stirred up over Becky's professor being arrested. Mooney had even had a few sleepless nights worrying about what would happen if the FBI served him with a search warrant . . .

Or what might happen if Stentung Oil figured out that ArticGecko had been the disgruntled employee who'd surreptitiously infected their deepwater-drilling-rig's computer system with a wormy virus.

Yeah, and what if the guy got cold feet, spilled his guts, and fingered the underground operative who'd given him the computer mouse to do the virtuous deed with? All it would take for the bloodhounds to sniff out Mooney's whereabouts would be for a police sketch artist to draw a reasonably good likeness of his face. So it was possible that ArticGecko could've been enticed to flip per having been offered a plea deal, which meant that the guy might've then proceeded to cough up a description of the L.E.A.F. operative who'd given him the Trojan mouse in Fairhaven.

In other words, with the recent advances in facial-recognition software now being commingled and merged into the passport and driver's-license data-bases, it was conceivable that a decent drawing of Mooney's eyeball ratios to his nose and mouth might come up with an image match from the gov's vast computer system.

Hey, a guy with a sock full of money stuffed under his mattress had to think about such things.

Serving a long prison sentence wouldn't be cool.

So, in this regard, Mooney had a number of moving parts to worry about. His inner thought engine was firing on all cylinders. There were a lot of variables to keep track of.

But still, as if he didn't already have enough whirling through his mind to lose sleep over, he now found himself getting involved with an innocent civilian who'd wowed him with her selfless integrity. When Zetty had refused to take the twenty thousand dollars, Mooney immediately realized that she actually was loyal to her beliefs. She obviously had rock-solid values which she was unwilling to waver from. She was, without a doubt, her mother's daughter. The apple hadn't fallen far from the tree. And because Zetty had been too young to join L.E.A.F. back when her parents had been alive, Mooney thought that her potential to become a Flock member was now quite favorable. She'd begun languaging the right attitude. So if she needed a nudge in the right direction, he was willing to help her evolve to the next level. And this, of course, also meant that he would have to come up with yet another cover story to tell Becky. Juggling so many moving parts was never easy. Mooney had to constantly watch what he said. Letting the wrong word slip out of his mouth could be quite disastrous.

Fabricating a bold-faced lie didn't take much brainpower. But when someone then tried to massage such a blatant falsification into the complex web of everyday life and make it seamlessly fit into the verisimilitude, an inconsistency could quickly become worrisome per the possibility of a glaring mistake.

It took Mooney a couple of days to recover from his cold before he could stop taking the antihistamines. He wasn't big on popping pills.

Then . . .

Once he'd given up the chemical enhancements, his mind cleared; and his chi returned. He got back to work and banged out a winterization article, which he proceeded to post on his blog.

When it came to his new-and-improved 2.0 cover story, Mooney had been carefully biding his time. He had spent a few days fleshing it out, wanting to make sure it was airtight. Now he had a window of opportunity to see how effective it would be. It was his turn to cook dinner, and so he decided that this would be as good a time as any to float his trial balloon.

Having worked at his desk until early in the evening because he'd had a bunch of emails to answer, Mooney finally made it into the kitchen somewhat later than he'd intended. Trying to make up for lost time, he quickly prepped the vegetables and began sautéing the last handful of potatoes from their garden. He knew his immune system could use the extra carbs. He next began preparing the main dish, which was a concoction of tofu, squash, and zucchini. With the right spices, a non-foodie like him could do a fair-to-middling job with most any veggie blend. Sometimes he got lucky and was able to add just the right touch of oregano and bay leaves to get a palatable flavor; and sometimes he completely missed the mark, going overboard with too much salt or too much garlic; and his *bon appetit* attempt flunked the taste test.

Published recipes were too complicated, and they never worked anyway.

And so . . .

After a bit of simmering on the stove, dinner was only a half-hour late.

"I'm not going to get sick eating this, am I?" Becky asked, sitting across from him at the kitchen table.

424

"Too many spices?"

"No, I mean, are you sure you're over your cold?"

"Yeah, I think so. How's the chef's special?"

"Not too bad."

Picking up on her positive vibe, Mooney then ever so slyly changed the subject. "Oh, you can stop looking for a roommate. I think I found someone."

"Really? That was quick. Who?"

"A girl I met. She lost her job, and she's trying to downsize, and she needs a place she can afford."

"Moon, if she doesn't have a job . . ."

"I know, but I'm sure it'll be okay. I can cover it. I'm not worried about her paying her part of the rent."

"Wait. What are you talking about? I thought the reason we had to get a roommate in the first place was because you needed the extra money to help pay your share of the rent since you weren't making enough from the ads on your blog anymore."

"Yeah, that's true. But since Tammy paid six months in advance, we're not hurting on the rent right now. I'd forgotten about that. She had this thing about not having to write a check each month. She told me she didn't want the hassle of having to remember to pay it every month."

"Moon, you didn't tell me that."

"I forgot."

"Well, she never mentioned it to me. Seems like she would've said something about it."

"Maybe it was 'cause she didn't like talking about money."

"That's true. She didn't like talking about a lot of stuff. She had this thing about her privacy."

"Anyway, like I said, it turns out we're good for another four months on the rent. And I think the reason Tammy didn't ask for her money back was because she'd reneged on her promise to stay at least six months. She also knew I was hard up, so could be she didn't want to leave me in a lurch."

"Must be nice not having to worry about such things, huh? Wish I had a trust fund."

"She was different, that's for sure. Anyway, she also asked me to help Zetty out, too."

"Zetty?"

"She's the one who's, like, thinking about moving in with us."

"Oh, okay."

"I invited her to dinner Saturday night. I thought it'd be a good idea if you two met."

"This Saturday?"

"Uh-huh."

"But, like, Ivan's coming over. We're watching a movie."

"So? I can cook for four people."

"You're offering to cook?"

"If you don't want to, I will."

"Oh, now I get it. You're attracted to Zetty, aren't you?"

"You mean, is this going to be a date? Is that what you mean?"

"Uh-huh."

"No, I'm not trying to hook up with her. That's not why I want to help her."

"So, like, what's up? Why are you doing it?"

"I guess 'cause I feel sorry for her. She lost her parents when she was a kid, and she just quit her job 'cause I told her she shouldn't be killing flowers to make a living . . ."

"Wait. What do you mean, 'killing flowers?' "

"She was working at that flower shop where I bought the fir tree."

"Oh, that place. So how did you talk her into quitting her job?"

"I honestly don't know. It just sorta happened. I don't know exactly how it happened, but it did. We somehow got into a conversation about saving the planet . . ."

"And you made her feel guilty about what she was doing, didn't you? You're incorrigible, you know that? Maybe before you start talking to someone, you should hand out a safety flyer with a warning label so they know what they're getting themselves into." Shaking her head, his sister looked somewhat like a school-teacher who was unhappy with one of her pupils. "I mean, browbeating her into quitting her job. Moon, you should be ashamed of yourself."

"Becky, there's more to it than that. I think Zetty knew in her heart that she shouldn't be hurting plants, but she just needed someone to come along and point it out to her."

"Uh-huh. If you say so."

"It's the truth."

"I guess that also means you really are attracted to her, aren't you?"

"Becky . . ."

"I know you too well, Moon. I'm your sister, remember?"

"You always say that when you want to lecture me."

"I'm not lecturing you. Maybe you have qualms about me having a live-in boyfriend move in with us, but I'm not uptight about you having a live-in girlfriend. I mean, if you want to get romantically involved with a roommate, that's okay with me. I'm not going to get upset about something like that. I think you could actually use a steady girlfriend, if you ask me."

"Listen, that's not what this is about, alright? Honestly, it's not. I'm just trying to help her through a rough spot, that's all."

"If you say so."

And that was that.

It was what it was.

There would be no more argumentations shared at the dinner table between the two of them for the rest of the meal.

Yet still, as he'd hoped, his subterfuge had indeed worked. Becky hadn't questioned the money disconnect, and their difference of opinion had served as a good distraction. Oftentimes, since his sister was so naïve about certain things, her thinking didn't delve that deeply into the quirks and foibles of the shadowy underworld. When something dramatic would come along, such as her professor getting arrested, her initial reaction tended to involve a subjective response, which meant that she instantly would let herself get all emotional about it. Then, within a couple of days, her obsession with whatever situation would wane, and she would soon get caught up in yet another heart-thumping sequence of events about something completely different. Having so many irons in the fire as a grad student, Becky lived a hectic life. She would always have two research papers to write and a meeting to go to. His sister was a whirling dervish of constant motion, which made it easy for Mooney to slide things under her nose.

By the time Saturday had rolled around – Mooney and Becky had already gotten over their little rhubarb. They had agreed to share the cooking since neither of them wanted their dinner party to be a flop. Mooney's food-preparation skills were too precarious to depend on, and Becky wasn't about to do it all herself.

So, having smoothed over their differences, they'd both agreed that their little get-together would be a team effort. Mooney was relegated to making the salad and a side dish. Becky was tasked with preparing the stir-fry. And due to her rather rapid departure, Tammy had mistakenly left behind three authentic Indian recipes; and Becky was anxious to cook the one she'd never tasted before. The ingredients included saffron, brown rice, fresh veggies, tofu, and a dab of secret sauce. She'd been told that no one would ever complain about eating vegetarian when a steaming plate of this Delhi delight was placed in front of their hungry stomach.

A little after sunset, Ivan showed up twenty minutes early with his tablet computer, a movie DVD, and a bottle of wine. For some reason, Ivan always arrived sooner than expected for such occasions. And since Becky was quite familiar with her boyfriend's fear of being late, she would frequently factor in a twenty-minute adjustment whenever she specified an arrival time. So, even though Ivan thought he was early, he really wasn't.

Once they'd said their hellos, it didn't take long for the wine cork to be popped and for three glasses to be filled. Leaning against the side of the fridge, Ivan stayed quiet for the first ten minutes, hardly saying anything as he watched the food being prepared. For a guy who was working on his Ph.D., he wasn't much of a conversationalist, in general, until his small intestine had absorbed enough wine to loosen his tongue. Then when the alcohol short-circuited his inhibitions, he tended to become more talkative.

Yet on that particular night, for some unexplainable reason . . .

Instead of mellowing out with each sip of wine . . .

Ivan became more opinionated as the fermented

grape made its way up to his brain. He was constantly quibbling about the precise science of almost every topic that was being discussed. One of the more inane examples of this happened when Becky had said that global warming would raise the ocean levels by several feet within fifty years; and Ivan laughed and fluttered his hand back and forth in front of his face. "You know, a few academics, in the soft sciences, think that's highly probable; but I would suggest that you check the predicted climatology to make sure your timeline is completely accurate. We may see a thirty-two-inch elevation in water levels in roughly seventy-six years, give or take a few months."

Of course, Becky didn't seem to mind Ivan's eggheaded geekiness or the fact that he was shorter in height than her. At five foot six with a slim build, his physique was on the wimpy side. About the only attribute that made Ivan stand out in a crowd was his shoulder-length hair. Yet, be that as it may, Mooney knew his sister was in awe of his intelligence. Becky had this thing about Ph.D. candidates. She acted like a doctoral groupie (with a slight inferiority complex) since she was only working on her master's degree.

Anyway, nearly an hour after it had turned dark outside, Zetty finally arrived at the front door with a dinner treat in her hand. It was a blueberry pie that she'd baked herself.

Once the introductions had been made, Mooney poured another glass of wine and offered it to Zetty.

"No, thanks. I usually don't drink alcohol."

Unsure of what to say, because he didn't know if this meant that she was a teetotaler or not – Mooney raised the glass up to his nose and smelled the wine's bouquet. "It's a nice Pinot Noir. Y'know, some doctors think wine helps the digestion and is good for the heart."

Zetty shook her head. "I better not."

Then, unable to keep his mouth shut, Ivan chirped up. "I went to France one summer; and if you didn't drink wine at a French table, there was nothing else you could drink unless it came out of a plastic bottle. The tap water there tasted pretty bad."

"Well, here we have really good water, and it tastes perfectly fine right out of the faucet. And I'm not worried about my heart. I think I'm too young to have a heart attack," Zetty said.

"Statistically, you are absolutely right. Very few people have heart attacks at your age. But two years ago I read a medical study that said women needed to be more careful because they actually have as many heart attacks as men do, but they just don't have enough checkups since a lot of doctors dismiss their symptoms. Of course, since that particular study was published, there might have been some more research done, which could turn out to promote a different conclusion. So, like, don't hold me to it. I'd have to check the most recent data points before I'd advise anyone to do anything when it came to drinking alcohol."

"Ivan's working on his doctorate," Becky said as

she placed the dinner plates on the table.

Realizing where the conversation was headed and not wanting to put any peer pressure on Zetty to consume an adult beverage, Mooney turned back to the counter and sat the wineglass that he'd poured for her down next to the opened bottle.

"You're studying to be a doctor?" Zetty asked, looking over at Ivan.

"No, I'm working on a Ph.D. in environmental science."

"Oh, a Ph.D. So, like, are you saying that you don't think alcohol is bad for your liver or anything like that?"

"You mean, wine?"

"Uh-huh."

"Well, from what I've read on the subject, there seems to be a blue-ribbon consensus of sorts that a little wine with a meal is actually somewhat medicinal. Although, and don't hold me to this, there's also been some studies which have shown that strong alcohol, like hard liquor . . . might, in fact, cause cancer. Yet, as far as I know, that caveat didn't reference red wine, per se." Raising his glass, Ivan then knocked back a gulp of wine.

Shaking his head and trying not to roll his eyes, Mooney moved over to the sink and placed the washed lettuce, sprouts, and shallots into a large salad bowl. "Zetty, it's okay if you don't want to drink any wine. That just leaves more for us to quaff down."

Sighing ever so slightly and appearing to want to

fit in, Zetty ran her hand down the buttons of her blouse. "Oh, heck. I guess I could trý a little wine. If someone working on their Ph.D. recommends it – why not?"

Stepping away from the sink, Mooney smiled and handed her the glass. They then all sat down at the dinner table.

The spicy aromas smelled pretty good.

For the first few minutes, their conversation centered on comments about the food. They passed the serving dishes from right to left, moving the entrees around the table, which allowed each person to take as much or as little as they desired. "Zetty, I hope Mooney warned you. There's no meat dishes. We're doing vegan tonight."

"Well, you could've fooled me. The rice looks like it has chicken in it."

"That's tofu," Becky replied.

"Oh, tofu. So that's what this is, huh?" Zetty said, stabbing a blocky piece with her fork and nibbling on it for a few seconds before she swallowed. "I always wondered what tofu tasted like."

Becky glanced over at her. "You've never had tofu before?"

"No."

"Okay, so – what do you think?"

"Well, um . . . it's different, that's for sure."

Wiping his napkin across his lips, Ivan offered his assessment. "I read a statistical analysis a couple of weeks back; and it extrapolated out the numbers, clearly stating that if twelve-point-four percent of the world's population would stop eating red meat, then we would drastically lower the greenhouse gases in the atmosphere and probably save two hundred and twenty-six glaciers from melting all over the world."

"And everyone would live longer, too," Becky added. "A vegetarian diet increases your longevity. Red meat clogs your arteries."

Zetty then picked up her knife and used it to slide the tofu that she'd stabbed off her fork, placing it on the side of her plate. "Okay, so, what you're saying is, if there's less people eating hamburgers, then that means there'll be less cows; and if there's less cows, then there should be less greenhouse gases, right?"

"Exactly," Ivan replied.

"And that'll help save the glaciers, right?"

Becky and Ivan both nodded their heads.

Not wanting to talk with his mouth full, Mooney waited until he'd swallowed his bite of rice before he offered his opinion. "Every little bit helps, that's for sure. But a lot of people will never change their diets. Most meat eaters are not going to give up their hamburgers. So, if you ask me, I think people should just do whatever they're comfortable committing to in order to lower their carbon footprints. Some people can give up red meat; some can't . . . just as some people can get by without a car, and some can't. So, I mean, it's not like everyone has to live in tents and only eat nuts and berries, because I think that's too much to ask of most people. The way I see it, if everyone just makes a small effort and does their part, then it'll all add up and make a big difference – eventually."

Nodding in agreement, Becky finished off her glass of wine. And, as she did so, Zetty stared over at Mooney, looking somewhat like a churchgoer who was gazing up at a fire-and-brimstone preacher standing in a pulpit. "I hope no one's going to hold it against me if I don't give up meat."

"I won't," Mooney replied.

"I have a friend who won't eat mammals, but she still eats other meats like fish and chicken," Becky said. "Me, I'm a full-fledged vegan, but I know a lot of people who think it's a hard diet to follow."

"I guess your friend doesn't want to give up her protein fix, does she?" Ivan said, reaching forward and scooping a large spoonful of saffron delight onto his plate.

"Yeah, sorta. She thinks she needs the amino acids. She says she doesn't want to deplete her muscle mass. She's addicted to running."

"Yeah, we're all addicted to something, I guess."

And by that point, if her facial expression was any indication of what she was thinking, Zetty appeared to be feeling somewhat out of place. Mooney suspected that she wasn't used to this type of talk, and so maybe she didn't want to say anything that would draw too much attention to herself by inadvertently making a blunder and sounding off key. And maybe that was also why she then went into quiet mode for the rest of the meal, simply sitting there and listening to what everyone else had to say.

Later, after everyone had satisfied their appetites, they all retreated into the living room, bringing their wineglasses with them. The two grad students plopped themselves down on the floor in front of the heating vent and began looking at a slideshow of photos on Ivan's tablet computer. Mooney and Zetty sat down on the opposite ends of the sofa. He sipped his wine; and she looked at her glass, jiggling the wine around and around as though she was somewhat bemused that she was even holding it in her hand.

For the first minute or so, it stayed awkwardly quiet until Ivan finally looked up from his computer screen and glanced around the room. "So, like, what did you guys do with that little tree?"

"We released it into the wild," Becky said.

"Oh, cool. That sounds like what your favorite professor would've done. Did you hear he got bailed out?"

"Really?"

"Yep."

"Thank goodness."

Hearing them say this, Zetty stopped staring down at her wineglass. With a perplexed look on her face, she glanced around the room and quickly sat the glass down on the coffee table in front of her. "Are you guys talking about the same professor who got arrested 'cause he was in ELF?"

"ELF? No way. Billson was set up. The FBI got the wrong guy," Ivan replied as he tapped his finger on his tablet's touchscreen and pulled up an enlarged photo. "Here, check this out." Holding the computer up in his hand, Ivan showed Zetty a picture of a group of angry protestors who were waving signs at a campus rally.

"Are those his students?"

"Some of them are."

"Looks like they really got upset."

"And rightly so, too. Billson was just exercising his freedom-of-speech rights, that's all. He's not the type of guy who'd burn down a building or do something dumb like derailing a coal train."

Hearing Ivan say this, Mooney couldn't help but be surprised. As far as he knew, no one else had connected Billson to any sort of activism involving the coal trains. This was the first time anyone was talking-the-talk about derailing a freight train since Mooney had mentioned it to Darwin all those many weeks ago.

Derailing a coal train.

Those four words were hard to ignore.

So it was at that point that Mooney suddenly realized that his sister's boyfriend might actually be more of an environmental player than he appeared to be. Maybe he wasn't as geeky as he looked. It was possible that Ivan was associating with other activists and thus was keeping his activities hidden from everyone else.

As Ivan's words continued to hang in the air . . .

Mooney knocked back the last swallow of his wine and waited to see what would happen next.

"You guys aren't in ELF, are you?" Zetty asked, as if reading Mooney's mind.

Frowning, Ivan looked at Becky and shook his head.

"No, they're just opinionated grad students, that's all," Mooney said, standing up. "Who wants a piece of pie?"

"I'll pass. I'm too full," Ivan replied. He then touched his finger to his computer screen and surfed onto the Internet.

"I'll have a piece later. Let's go watch the movie," Becky said. She then rose up from the floor and picked up the DVD off the coffee table.

Following her lead, Ivan got to his feet; and they both disappeared down the hall to Becky's bedroom.

"Want a slice of pie, Zetty?"

"I didn't say anything wrong, did I?"

"No, you didn't say anything wrong. The Earth Liberation Front is just a touchy subject right now. The whole campus is in an uproar over what happened."

"Oh, I guess they would be, huh?"

"I'm going to have some pie. Want to join me?"

"Okay."

Getting up from the sofa, they both walked into the kitchen. Zetty sat down at the table and watched as Mooney cut two pieces of pie. He placed the slices on saucers and set one in front of her. "You made this yourself?"

"Uh-huh. They're easy to bake. The main thing is

to get good blueberries."

"You didn't go out and pick them, did you?"

"No, I bought them at the farmers' market. They keep pretty well in the freezer."

Smiling, Mooney sat down across from her and forked a piece into his mouth. The pie had a slightly tart flavor to it since she hadn't used too much sugar. "It's good."

"Thanks." Zetty then took a bite and nodded her head. "Not bad."

"Okay, so – now that you've had a chance to check the place out, what do you think? Want to move in?"

Pausing to think about what she should say, Zetty's eyes stayed on her slice of pie. "This is three bedrooms?"

"No, only two. Becky has one bedroom, and you'll have the other one. I'll sleep on the sofa."

"Oh."

"Our roommate moved out. You'll get the room she was in."

"You don't mind sleeping on the sofa?"

"No, I don't mind."

After Zetty took a moment to think about what he had said, she seemed somewhat hesitant to ask her next question, but then she went ahead and asked it anyway. "What do you think about tattoos?"

"Tattoos?"

"Uh-huh. Do you have a tattoo?"

Unsure of where this was going, Mooney had no idea why she was asking him about body art; but since her question was framed within the context of her decision to either move in or not move in, he could only assume that there was some reason for her to ask him his opinion about tats. "No, I don't have a tattoo. I'm not into tattoos. But if someone wants to get a tattoo, I don't have a problem with it." And, of course, he was indeed telling her the truth; yet he hadn't expanded on the "why" in regards to his decision to never get a tattoo.

Specifically, when a guy like him was working undercover, the last thing he needed was for an identifying mark of any sort to be permanently inked into his skin. That would make it way too easy for a corporate private investigator to put him in the crosshairs vis-a-vis an image search in a profiling database. And the same would also be true for the cops, too. Tats were like fingerprints, but an activist couldn't just put on a pair of gloves to cover up such indelible imprints.

Again pressing her fork down into the piecrust and appearing to be thinking about how Mooney had responded to her question, Zetty slowly shook her head. "I'm not into tattoos, either. I think they're pretty dumb." Then after she said this, she shared her thoughts as to the possibility of her moving in. "Anyway, I really appreciate the offer and everything, but I kind of like my little apartment. I can walk almost anywhere I wanna go. Up here, I'd have to take the bus or ride my bike."

"Free rent."

"Y'know, that's awful nice of you, but I wouldn't feel right about taking the other bedroom."

"We could rotate sleeping on the sofa, if you want. You could have the bedroom for, say, the first three months, and then we could switch."

"But that means I'd have to sleep on the sofa."

"Well, that's true."

"Look, I really appreciate the offer, but I'm sure I'll soon get a job. Things will work out. They always do. I'm not worried about it."

And hearing her say this, Mooney could see that she was trying her best to keep her chin up, but it looked to him as though she actually was somewhat worried about her future. "Okay, but if you change your mind, just let me know. I think you'd like living here. It's nice being so close to the park."

"If I change my mind, I'll let you know."

After they finished eating their dessert, Mooney asked her if she wanted to go outside and look at the lake. She said she did, and so they put on their coats, and he took her out the back door.

Walking into the yard, they gazed up at the moon. It was low in the sky and barely peeking over the top of the foothill that loomed up on the other side of the lake. And because there weren't many clouds floating by, an abundance of stars could be seen in the sky.

"Oh, my. It's really beautiful out tonight, isn't it?" Zetty said as they made their way over to the vegetable garden.

"Yeah, we're pretty lucky to get to live in such a

nice place as this."

"Where were you born?"

"I'm not exactly sure. As a kid I grew up in Louisiana."

"Oh, okay. So, like, I guess your parents didn't tell you where you were born 'cause you didn't grow up with them, huh?"

"We were just little kids when they put us in that orphanage."

"In Louisiana?"

"Uh-huh."

"That must've been tough on you."

"It wasn't too much fun, that's for sure. And it's really different down there, too. There aren't any mountains. So I guess that's why I appreciate a view like this. I'm guessing you grew up here, right?"

"Yes, I've lived here all my life."

"It's a special place, that's for sure."

"Well, y'know, it's really changed a lot in the last ten years. It wasn't so special when the paper mill used to stink up the air. And we also have all the rain, too. A lot of people come here and get depressed 'cause the gloomy weather hangs around for so long."

"You don't like the rain?"

"No, I'm fine with it. I'm just saying people have to have something to complain about. And when you've lived here as long as I have, none of this seems like such a big deal, actually. I guess you get use to it."

"I hope I never get that way. But maybe it helps to have lived in other places. Gives you a different perspective." Mooney then nodded his head at the light dusting of snow that was on top of the foothill. "Louisiana hardly ever gets any snow. There's not even any foothills. There's only hilly spots, but no real foothills. And the trees down there don't seem to grow as tall as they do up here. The Pacific Northwest has so many tall trees. To me, this is 'little nirvana.' I don't know why anyone would want to live anywhere else."

"Not everyone thinks like that. I know so many people who can't wait to move somewhere else, somewhere it's bright and sunny. And a lot of 'em want to move to a big city, too. They get bored here."

" 'The grass is always greener on the other side,' huh?"

"I guess."

"Do you want to move?"

"Sometimes I do. But the rain really doesn't bother me. Of course it's nice in the summer when we get a couple of months of sunshine."

"In the South it stays hot for way too long. It's not just hot in the summer. And the stupid air conditioners use a ton of electricity. People drive around in their air-conditioned cars, live in their air-conditioned homes, work in their air-conditioned offices. In the summer, most people just stay inside the whole day. They hate getting out in the heat."

"I don't know anyone who even owns an air conditioner."

"Thank goodness." Inching in closer, Mooney then slowly reached out his hand and brushed her hair away from her face. "You're so pretty. The moonlight's bouncing off your eyes."

Blinking, Zetty modestly looked down, not wanting to make eye contact.

Sucking in a deep breath, Mooney gently lifted up her chin, slowly leaned in . . .

And kissed her. He hadn't intended to give her a kiss, but a sudden urge had come over him, and he couldn't help himself. It was a quick kiss on the lips.

"I think I'm a little lightheaded. I'm not use to the wine."

"It makes your cheeks rosy."

"Are my cheeks rosy?"

"They look rosy to me."

"Well, the chill in the air can do that, too. Or maybe it's the moonlight."

"Want to go back inside?"

"Do you?"

"If you want to." He then leaned in for another kiss, but this time it was a real kiss.

As their lips touched, her hand came up to his shoulder and lightly pressed down on him, seeming to pull him in closer. He could feel her breasts against his chest. She smelled like blueberries.

Then . . .

When his lips retreated, he gently grabbed ahold of her hand, and they walked back into the house. The moment wasn't spoiled by any words. Mooney wasn't sure if he should've kissed her or not, but it had felt like the right thing to do.

Once inside, she offered to help him with the dishes, and he accepted her offer. They spent the next twenty minutes washing and putting away the dinnerware. After they had finished, Zetty looked at the clock and said she had to soon leave because she didn't want to miss the last bus back into downtown. But since it was already so late, Mooney offered to drive her home. He told her he had to go pick up some cereal for breakfast at the grocery store anyway, so dropping her off wouldn't be that far out of his way.

During their ride into town, they talked about why people always seemed to want what they didn't have, looping back to their earlier conversation as to why the grass seemed to always be greener somewhere else. Mooney told her that he thought it was simply human nature for people to think that they would somehow be happier if they could change a few of the things in their lives . . .

But then he added that it rarely ever was true. Most people, when they got up the courage to make a big move to another spot on the map . . .

Were doing nothing more than chasing an elusive windmill. He said it was sort of like a child with a new toy. No matter how great the toy turned out to be, a child would eventually get bored with it and always want yet another new toy.

Zetty agreed, but she told him that she thought people had to figure things out like that for themselves because no one would listen to such advice from someone else anyway. She also brought up the point that, in her opinion, he seemed to have found the grass to be greener in Bellingham.

And of course she was right. Yet she didn't know the whole story as to why he had ended up moving there in the first place.

And so . . .

Not wanting to get into a convoluted explanation, Mooney didn't argue with her logic. He had recently come to the conclusion that oftentimes his opinions were frequently misunderstood, being as he wasn't actually trying to tell people how to live their lives; but rather, he was instead philosophizing about social interactions that many people never took the time to think much about.

Overanalyzing could, at times, be a negative.

Parking in front of her apartment building, Mooney turned off the ignition. He had already weighed the pros and cons of what he would do if she invited him in for a cup of tea, deciding that he didn't want to come on too strong on their first date – if this was, in fact, their first date.

As they walked up the stairs to her door, he stayed noncommittal, leaving it up to her. And since Zetty didn't speak up to clarify what she wanted him to do, Mooney just gave her another quick kiss on the cheek at the top of the stairs and left it at that. He wasn't exactly sure why he was acting the way he was acting, but he thought that maybe the wine had gone to his head . . .

More so than hers.

Or, then again, maybe he just couldn't help himself. Maybe because she was such a sweet person, he had no choice but to follow his instincts. Zetty certainly had a warm personality and truly seemed to care about other people. Plus, she was seriously good looking, too. Who wouldn't be attracted to her? She didn't seem to have any pretentiousness whatsoever.

But still, in the back of his mind, because of the differences in their backgrounds, Mooney wasn't exactly sure if their personalities would be compatible. It was a conundrum he'd have to sort through before he got carried away and let the relationship go too far. He didn't want to be disingenuous, nor was he the type of guy who would simply woo a girl for a one-night stand and then up and walk away. So he knew he had to think it through and figure out if he really wanted to get seriously involved with Zetty or not.

But so far, so good.

She could cook a delicious blueberry pie, that was for sure.

Chapter Thirty

After Mooney had dropped her off, Zetty took a hot bath and went to bed. Surprisingly, she slept soundly through the whole night, not even hearing Edna-Ney when she came in from work. And because Zetty hadn't woken up in the wee hours of the morning, she wasn't sure if her roommate had invited a guy home with her or not.

But then, as it turned out, the reason Zetty hadn't heard anything to disturb her sleep was because there hadn't been anything to hear. Edna-Ney had spent the night at a friend's house. She'd accepted a sleepover invitation from a gentleman whom she'd been dating on and off for several years. The guy was a dentist, and he had a house on South Hill. Yet, needless to say, for some reason, the two of them had never gotten exceptionally serious about each other and were only cultivating what Edna-Ney referred to as a "buddy with benefits" relationship . . .

Which meant, as best as Zetty could understand it, that they both wanted to avoid any emotional attachment. In other words, their affair was just physical.

Of course, Zetty was at a loss as to why anyone would want to do something like that, but that was just the way Edna-Ney was. Her mind worked differently than Zetty's.

By the time Sunday morning had rolled around and Edna-Ney had finally made it home, looking sleepy and glum, Zetty knew not to bother her. Her roommate obviously wasn't in a talkative mood. If anything, she needed to catch up on her sleep. Their heart-to-heart would have to wait.

It was late in the afternoon before Edna-Ney got up from her nap. Zetty had just finished cooking a pot of chicken soup and was sitting in the kitchen, eating her supper when she heard the hall door swing open.

Yawning, Edna-Ney flip-flopped her way into the room and over to the refrigerator. She was wearing her pink kimono and her matching house slippers. "Hey," she said as she opened the fridge and poured herself a glass of orange juice.

"Hi. Want some soup?"

"What kind is it?"

"Chicken."

"Okay, I might have a bowl a little bit later. Thanks." Plopping herself down at the table, Edna-Ney rubbed the sleep from her eyes. "How'd your party go?"

"Fine. But it wasn't really a party. It was just the two of us and his sister and her boyfriend."

"So what happened?"

"They cooked vegetarian, and we sat around

talking. A lot of what they said was over my head, and I mostly just listened. Oh, he did say he liked my pie."

"That's it? He said he liked your pie? Nothing else happened?"

"Well, we kissed."

"Oh, he smooched you, eh? Now we're getting to the good stuff."

"Unless I dreamed it."

"Wait. So, like, did he kiss you or did you dream it? Which was it?"

"Well, I guess it was sorta both. He kissed me, and I had a dream about it, too."

"And?"

"And he's nice."

"And . . . ?"

"Well, I like him, if that's what you mean."

"Did he ask you out on another date?"

"No, but he drove me home and walked me to the door. Does that count?"

"Did he try to sweet-talk you into letting him come in?"

"Unh-uh."

"What's wrong with this guy?"

"Nothing's wrong with him."

"Yeah, right. Every man I know always comes up with some cockamamie story about wanting a nightcap or some such excuse."

"Mooney's not like that, Edna-Ney."

"If you say so."

"He's not."

"Why not?"

"I don't know. He's from Louisiana."

"Oh, he's a Southerner, huh? One of those."

"What do you mean?"

"Y'know, uptight. Conservative. Likes guns."

"No, I don't think so. I think he only grew up in Louisiana. He's not at all like those dumb yahoos you see on TV."

"Uh-huh."

"He's not. He's different. And that's what worries me."

"What do you mean?"

"Well, I'm not sure we have very much in common."

"Why do you say that?"

" 'Cause I never went to college and he did."

"So?"

"So I think he's pretty smart. He talks about things I've never heard of before."

"Look, if he's a snob, then you don't want to go out with him anyway. Case closed. Move on."

"No, he's not a snob. He's not like that. If anything, I think he's trying to help me out, for some reason."

"Why would he want to help you out?"

"Because he thinks he talked me into quitting my job."

"I told you that was a mistake. You should never have quit your job, Zetty. Selling flowers is not a crime."

"I know. But, like, doing what I was doing didn't feel right anymore. I felt sorry for the poor plants."

"Zetty, you gotta stop feeling sorry for everybody and everything that comes along. I keep telling you, life isn't a bed of roses. You just gotta learn to take care of yourself and not let people upset you."

"I know. But I think Mooney really does have good intentions. I think he honestly cares about what happens to me. And, like, if I can't find a job, then I don't know how I'm going to pay my rent. So, I mean, living up on the lake in a house with a vegetable garden is sort of tempting."

"Wait. He wants you to move in with him?"

"Uh-huh."

"Listen, no one's going to give you free rent unless there's strings attached. And, y'know, nine times out of ten, there's always strings attached. You don't see me moving in with a guy, do you?"

"But that's you. This is me. You haven't even met him, Edna-Ney."

"Look, I'm just saying, don't be naïve. Guys are guys. And it sounds to me like he's not telling you something."

"What do you mean?"

"Maybe he's not who he says he is. For all you know, he could be a bank robber."

"No way. He's not a bank robber. He has a blog. Like I said, he's very sweet."

"Well, I still say no one offers you free rent unless there's something in it for them. And when it comes to people you don't know, you have to be careful. I mean, you're the one who had that weirdo following you around, remember?"

"I know, but that was different."

Finishing her orange juice, Edna-Ney got up from the table and stepped over to the stove. She lifted the metal top off of the pot of soup, leaned down, and smelled it – then ladled herself a bowl. "Oh, I wanted to tell you . . . you know Bill, who owns the bar?"

"Uh-huh."

"He told me something you might find interesting. He said the guy who got himself killed when that big tree fell on him up in the cemetery – well, Bill was renting him a place. Like, I didn't even know it was the same guy. Anyway, I don't think I ever mentioned it to you, but Bill owns this dinky warehouse; and that guy who got killed was living there. That's where the dead guy lived."

"He lived in Bill's warehouse?"

"Yeah, that's what Bill told me." Sitting back down at the table, Edna-Ney quickly dipped a spoon into her bowl and tasted the soup. "You made this from scratch?"

"Cooked the chicken myself. Didn't use anything out of a can."

"It tastes better than canned soup, that's for sure."

"Thanks."

After eating several spoonfuls, Edna-Ney then continued with her story. "Anyway, getting back to

454

what Bill said . . . so when he heard about his renter ending up in the morgue, he decided to go to the warehouse to check things out. And get this. Bill walks in the door and sees this beautiful stone angel the guy had been working on."

"Oh, that's right. Now I remember. The paper had mentioned something about that dead guy being a stonecutter."

"Well, it seems he was a really good one, if you believe Bill. He made these beautiful statues. So anyway, Bill walks into the warehouse, and he goes over and looks at this life-size angel. And guess what?"

"What?"

"He said it looked just like you."

"Me?"

"Uh-huh. That's what Bill said. He said the angel's face looked just like yours."

"Oh, c'mon, Edna-Ney. Bill's just saying that. I didn't know that dead guy. I never met him." Zetty then paused and said, "Well, at least, I don't think I ever met him."

"Maybe you did and didn't know it. He was from around here, is what I heard. Used a nickname when he came in the bar, and that's why I didn't put two and two together. They called him 'Stoneface.' So maybe he dropped by the flower shop, and you didn't even know who he was, or maybe he saw you walking around town. Anything's possible."

Shrugging her shoulders, Zetty sighed. She honestly didn't know what to think. "I guess it's possible. Maybe you're right. But Bill's only met me a few times himself. I hardly ever go to the bar, except when you forget your keys. So, I mean, maybe Bill saw a slight resemblance, and he's just trying to make more out of it than he should."

"Could be. Bill does like to exaggerate things, that's for sure. And he likes to joke around, too."

"Okay, then maybe he was pulling your leg. I doubt the dead guy's statue looks like me. Bill probably just made that up."

"Maybe so. But then . . . and this is the God's honest truth . . . Bill tells me that the guy owed him a few months back rent, and he also said if no one shows up to pay that bill and, y'know, claim all the stuff that was left in the warehouse, then Bill's hoping he'll get to keep the angel. He said if he ends up with it, he's planning on putting it in the bar."

"In the bar? That'd be different, huh?"

"That's for sure. But, y'know, it's his bar; and I guess he can do whatever he wants to in his own bar. So, like, if it does look like you . . ."

"God, let's hope not. The last thing I need is a bunch of drunks coming up to me and telling me that I look like an angel they saw in Bill's bar."

"Zetty, if the statue looked like me – you know what I'd do?"

"What?"

"I'd lie through my teeth and tell everyone I worked as a nude model when I wasn't, like, bar-tending."

"Edna-Ney . . ."

"Hey, a girl's gotta do what a girl's gotta do. I mean, if it'd get me more tips, that's exactly what I'd say."

"Too bad the angel doesn't look like you, huh?"

"Just my luck."

Getting up from the table and putting her empty bowl in the sink, Zetty had enough to worry about as it was. The possibility that a life-size statue resembled her was the least of her concerns. She knew that Bill liked to drink too much of his own liquor to be taken seriously.

Retreating down the hall to her room, Zetty was anxious to read the Sunday paper. Earlier that afternoon, before she'd made the soup, she'd gone out and bought a copy from a vending machine, hoping she might find some newly listed jobs in the classified ads. She knew if she waited to read the paper on Monday at the library, since the city kept that government building closed on Sundays . . .

Then she wouldn't be able to circle the ads with her pen and cut them out. Also, the Sunday paper usually had the best listings, and so she rationalized spending the extra money, telling herself that if she did find an employer who was looking for someone like her – then it would be well worth it to have spent so many of her quarters on her job-hunt.

Lounging in bed, Zetty searched through the employment columns and soon came upon an ad for a floral arranger at the flower shop. Zetty was surprised that Casey still hadn't found someone to replace her, or maybe she'd already hired someone and they'd quit and now Casey needed to find someone else.

Anyway, as Zetty continued reading down that same column, she saw employment ads for a live-in maid, a midnight security guard, and a van driver.

Oh, my gosh. These absolutely weren't jobs she wanted to apply for; but now she was desperate, and so she told herself that she had to take any job she could get.

Grabbing her ink pen, she circled the jobs that she might have a remote possibility of getting an interview for, knowing she couldn't be too picky. She needed a paycheck.

Then . . .

When Monday morning rolled around . . .

Zetty got up early and hurried off to catch a bus so she could put her application in at four places near the mall . . .

Only to hear the phone ringing when she had finally made it back home and was just coming in the front door later that afternoon. Dashing inside, she didn't want to miss the call. She was worried that the caller might hang up and not call her back since the apartment didn't have an answering machine. (Incredibly, the reason it didn't have an answering machine was because Edna-Ney had tossed the last one out the window when she'd come in tipsy one night and had had to suffer through ten obscene messages from a bunch of visiting Alaskans who wanted to find out where she lived.)

And so . . .

Rushing down the hall to answer the ringing phone . . .

Zetty quickly grabbed the receiver and lifted it up to her ear. "Hello?"

It was Missy. She asked Zetty if she was still interested in working at the thrift store.

Without skipping a beat, Zetty immediately said "yes."

And right then and there, Missy hired her. Zetty had finally landed on her feet. She had a job. Things were definitely looking up. Her mother's advice had turned out to be right, yet again.

As the holidays came and went, Zetty's life soon settled into a regular routine. Working at Missy's secondhand store was more emotionally rewarding than her job had been at the flower shop. Zetty really liked helping people save money, while she was also doing her part to promote sustainability and protect the environment. And though she barely made enough money to get by, she was still quite happy doing what she was doing. She'd discovered that pinching pennies wasn't as bad as she thought it would be because she was doing something she truly enjoyed, and she wasn't homeless.

So, never one to ask for too much, Zetty knew she had a lot to be thankful for.

As for Mooney, he'd ended up calling Zetty the following week after the dinner party and had asked her if she wanted to go see a movie.

Soon, they were going out on regular dates, two or three times a week; and she really did enjoy all of the attention. The more she got to know him; the more she liked him. He was so considerate. He wasn't like anyone she'd ever dated before.

Yet ironically, what had concerned her the most when they had first started seeing each other so often — was the possible quandary that she might find herself in if she fell for him too hard. Zetty didn't want to wake up one morning and suddenly realize that Mooney was seeing someone else. In other words, because he was such a catch, she was actually preparing herself for the inevitable to happen, thinking that they might end up dating for four months or so, then he would most likely hook up with someone else, and that would be the end of it.

Yet still, Zetty was willing to take that chance. If it turned out the two of them only stayed together for a few months, then she told herself that it would have been worth it. Like Edna-Ney always said, "A girl has to try."

Chapter Thirty-One

After Tammy had up and left, Mooney moved back into the vacated bedroom. It was nice not being awakened so early each morning by the glare of the sunlight peeking through the patio curtains. He also appreciated the privacy and comfort of sleeping on a cushy mattress in a regular bed with the door closed.

Life was good.

But then, quite suddenly, as such things tended to happen, another troublesome hurdle had popped up soon after Zetty had decided not to take him up on his offer of free rent. This unexpected disruption had occurred a couple of days after their dinner party when Becky had tried to talk him into letting Ivan move in to the bungalow.

Needless to say, Mooney didn't want to live with two lovebirds, and he certainly didn't want to have to deal with the daily agony of watching his younger sister play house with her egotistical boyfriend.

No thank you.

Also, the last thing Mooney needed was for a rogue activist to be living in the same house with him.

If Ivan was somehow, even subliminally, connected to ELF or to the anarchist movement or possibly to some sort of loosely affiliated group of angry college students who were planning to inflict havoc on the coal trains – then Mooney didn't want, nor did he need, the added risk. Having to coordinate yet another tumbling bowling pin into his juggling act might cause the whole prestidigitation to fall out of sync and come crashing down on his head. And, considering the circumstances, Mooney's conscience didn't bother him at all in this regard since he knew that Ivan had a decent apartment and was also working as a TA at the university.

So Mr. Know-It-All wasn't a hardship case. Ivan wasn't struggling to make ends meet. And even though Becky had cajoled and whined, Mooney had stayed firm. He wanted to avoid the hassle of having to deal with the overly opinionated Ivan . . .

Every day.

Mooney didn't want the guy snooping around, nor did he have the temperament for such hijinks. No way. The thought of the bungalow turning into a honeymoon resort for a conceited grad student, even if the guy was well meaning, was too disturbing to even contemplate.

Consequently . . .

When Becky had finally come to the conclusion that she wasn't going to be able to talk her older brother into changing his mind, she had given up trying to argue her case, although she was obviously upset with Mooney's decision. And instead of throwing her patented little-sister tantrum (which she had, for the most part, grown out of) . . .

Becky simply sulked around the house for a few days, giving him the silent treatment by pretty much staying in her room. Yet Mooney still hadn't taken the bait. He wasn't going to cave in. He actually relished the peace and quiet. He also knew that Becky would soon get over it, and he hoped that one day she might even thank him for putting his foot down.

So, all in all, Mooney was pleased that his home-life had finally returned to a more normal routine. Such little spats with Becky were to be expected. An older brother would never fully agree with everything his younger sister wanted to do, nor would a younger sister be willing to go along with everything her older brother wanted to do, either. Most siblings had their disagreements. But luckily for both of them, their disconnects didn't last for very long. They loved each other way too much to ever let such a minor squabble over a housemate drive a wedge between them. Mooney told himself that this was nothing more than a hiccup. It certainly wasn't a worrisome biggie . . .

Whereas what he'd been losing sleep over, for way too many weeks, was of a much more serious concern. Yet that particular vexation of uncertainty was, quite thankfully, also beginning to fade. Now he wasn't waking up in the middle of the night in a cold sweat. His fear of the FBI breaking down the door and rushing in with a search warrant – had slowly begun to evaporate. He had stopped being dogged by his own free-floating paranoia soon after Professor Billson had been bailed out of jail. It was at that point that Mooney had come to the conclusion that Billson's high-profile arson case would probably drag on for years in the courts.

So, in that regard, once the initial brouhaha over the professor's arrest had ratcheted down, the incessant gossip about ELF had, more or less, subsided. And since L.E.A.F. had stayed under the radar, not making it into the news – with no investigative reports coming out of Alaska as to any claims of industrial espionage being suspected in regards to the Oceanic Venturer's malfunction – things had begun to calm down, which was the way Mooney liked it. He preferred the normality of everyday life. When there was too much tension in the air, that was when mistakes were made and people got themselves in trouble. Life in the underground moved along much easier in regular mode. A few of the higher-ups might like the news coverage that was generated by the glare of the media spotlight, but Mooney wanted to avoid the extra hassle that came with increased visibility. He didn't want to end up in jail or get another bullet in his leg. He relished his anonymity. A guy had less to worry about when he wasn't attracting any undue attention. By sticking to an average-joe, run-of-the-mill lifestyle – an activist such as himself didn't have to constantly keep his guard up. Living an uncomplicated simple life had much more going for it than most people realized.

And so . . .

Having experienced what he'd experienced, Mooney was relieved that his name hadn't been tipped to the authorities. The last thing he needed was for Zetty to read about him in the newspaper. That would've been kind of tough for him to explain, given that, right after Zetty had started her new job, Mooney had succumbed to the tug on his heart and had asked her out on a real date. He'd even let her pick the movie since there hadn't been anything at the multiplex he had wanted to see.

Having made her selection, they'd gone to the small art house theatre downtown to watch a romantic comedy, which had turned out to be quite good. Both of them had laughed at the very same spots throughout the film, and this conceivably had meant that they actually shared a similar sense of humor. In other words, despite having such diverse backgrounds, Mooney had told himself that it was possible they had more in common, psychologically, than he'd first assumed.

And because they had both enjoyed themselves so much at the movie, they then had begun going out every week. Mooney couldn't resist Zetty's warm-hearted charm. She was so sincere. And she truly was serious about learning as much as she could about helping the environment. She had, in fact, surprised him when she'd told him that she had just finished reading two books on ecology and was already several pages into her third. On their second date, she'd even asked him about an innovative sustainability program, which he hadn't, up until that point, heard anything about.

So for him, that had been a eureka moment. It was obvious that Zetty had an inquisitive mind. She certainly had a lot more going for her than simply having a pretty face. Her positive attitude and enthusiasm to learn had really begun to impress him.

As for L.E.A.F., the fluctuating situation had suddenly taken a drastic turn when, right before Christmas, Mooney had pedaled into town in order to do a visual pass-by on his subcommander's location (just to make sure nothing was wrong) . . .

But then he'd been shocked to see that Darwin's RV spot was empty and his travel trailer was gone. His Flock contact had flown the coop, and he hadn't even told Mooney that he was leaving.

Yet still, this had been as it should be. By not giving any notice he'd be departing that location, Darwin had kept the safety of the remaining underground cell better protected. The first priority was to insulate the organizational integrity and limit any leaks. If no one knew that an operative was leaving town, then the chances were minimized that he or she would be followed to their new assignment. So without any prior knowledge of a departure, a tipster working with the authorities had less of a chance of knowing ahead of time what was about to go down.

Thereupon, once Darwin had hitched up his trailer and skedaddled out of Bellingham, Mooney was relegated to a lengthy stint in hibernation mode. It seemed that the ELF scare had spooked the Flock in the same way it had unnerved Mooney. When a subcommander invoked the "cut-and-run" protocol, this meant that the remaining cell members were to immediately cut off contact with all of the other members. Per the dictates of the training manual, no one was supposed to communicate with anyone else until they had received further instructions at some point in the future.

And naturally, such occurrences had happened numerous times before. Every two or three years a mass uneasiness would sweep through L.E.A.F., and there'd be a spike in fretful worry. This usually happened when a Flock member was arrested or when the higher-ups thought that a cell had been breached.

Then, as if struck by a bolt of lightning from on high, the jungle drums would abruptly stop, and all the scheduled activities would cease. The Flock would go into hibernation. It then became a silent waiting game, with the members biding their time until the channels of communication were slowly reestablished.

If Mooney had his druthers, he'd opt to stay active in regular mode. But considering the risk involved, there was nothing he could do except wait to be contacted. The protocol was clear, and he did as he had been trained to do. He followed instructions.

So, because he now had more time on his hands, this meant that he could repair some of the holes in his personal life. The lull in his L.E.A.F. activities gave him a chance to get to know Zetty a good deal better since he wasn't having to constantly tell her white lies in order to explain the things that he couldn't otherwise explain. In short, hibernation mode was much easier on him. He could be more truthful.

As the months progressed, Mooney's routine of seeing Zetty several times a week continued. And it didn't take him long to realize that their emotional connection was, in fact, beginning to get serious. He'd even begun to wonder what the future might bring . . .

Because he honestly didn't have a clue as to how it all would work out — although, early on, he had concluded that Zetty truly did have L.E.A.F. potential.

But still, Mooney knew that he had to be exceptionally careful. Recruiting her into the Flock required upper-level approval, and since he was now stuck under the restrictions of the "cut-and-run" protocol, he had no choice but to wait until his local cell came out of hibernation in order for him to broach the subject with his superiors.

Again, the protocol was quite clear. All new inductees had to first be vetted by a background check vis-a-vis the membership committee, and the higher-ups were extremely cautious about whom they let join the Flock.

Therein, having no other option, Mooney had decided to just take it one day at a time, one week at a time, one month at a time — and not think too much about what the eventual outcome would be.

But then . . .

His perspective abruptly changed when he was blindsided by an unexpected revelation. This occurred when Zetty had taken him to see her foster mom at the nursing home. An artic cold front was barreling down from the Fraser Valley in British Columbia, and the weatherman was predicting that Bellingham would be covered in almost a foot of snow by the next morning. Thinking ahead in regards to being stuck at home per the icy streets, Zetty had wanted to go see Miss Pineford before the town was snowed in.

It was a small favor to ask, and Zetty hardly ever asked him to do something such as that.

As they walked down the sidewalk from the bus stop toward the nursing home, Mooney reached over and gently took Zetty's hand. This was the first time he'd be meeting her foster mom, and he wasn't exactly sure what to expect. "Her memory still comes and goes?"

Zetty nodded her head. "But she's doing better than she was. For a while she couldn't remember what happened to her the day before. Then they put her on some new medicine. Now she doesn't forget as much as she did. What's hard to understand is, she doesn't seem to have a problem remembering what happened to her fifty years ago."

"Short-term memory loss."

"Uh-huh. So she has her good days and her bad days. Maybe she'll keep improving on this new medicine."

Listening to Zetty share her concerns about Miss Pineford, Mooney couldn't help but think about his own mother. He still had vague memories of her that he never talked about. It was too painful for him to tell anyone what he remembered about why his mother had done what she'd done. Going through the trauma he had experienced as a six-year-old, he sometimes wished those early memories hadn't been seared so deeply into his mind as they obviously had. And even though Alzheimer's was a terrible disease, Mooney also understood how forgetting certain things might actually be beneficial to a person's wellbeing.

Walking through the care-facility's front door, they strode by the nursing station; and Zetty waved at an attendant, who was sitting at a desk reading a magazine. Not looking up, the attendant smiled and nodded his head.

They then made their way down a long hallway. At the very end, the door to Miss Pineford's room was slightly ajar.

Quietly easing it open, Zetty first peeked her head in to make sure it wasn't an inopportune moment. "Is she awake?" Mooney asked.

"Looks like it." Zetty then entered the room, and Mooney followed her inside. "Hi, Miss Pineford. I brought someone to see you."

"Oh, hello," her foster mom softly replied, looking over at Zetty. Miss Pineford was propped up in bed with several pillows behind her head and back. That end of her hospital bed had also been titled upward, which allowed her to sit upright.

"This is Mooney."

"Hey, Miss Pineford. Nice to meet you," he said, inching in closer to her bed.

"You're not a doctor, are you?"

"No, ma'am."

"He's a friend of mine, Miss Pineford."

"Oh, he's your boyfriend. I see. Nice looking young man." Miss Pineford then turned and stared out the window. "I was just sitting here, looking out at those dark clouds. I think it's going to snow."

Across the room, the curtains on her window were open, and an ominous band of clouds could be seen off in the distance. Swaying in the wind, the maple tree that was growing a couple yards in front of the window was completely devoid of leaves; yet the texture of its bark made it easy for Mooney to identify what type of tree it was since he had seen so many similar maples in the park.

"I think you're right, Miss Pineford. On the radio they said we might get a foot of snow by this time tomorrow."

"Good. I like it when it snows. It reminds me of home."

"How are you feeling today?"

"Well, I've had some pain in my legs, but they gave me a little blue pill, and the pain went away."

"You've had that pain before, haven't you?"

"I don't know. Have I?"

"Remember, a few months back?"

"I don't remember, sweetheart. They give me so many pills, it's hard for me to remember." Miss Pineford then turned her eyes back to the window and pointed at the maple tree. "Look how tall it is. It really has grown, hasn't it?"

Nodding her head, Zetty looked over at Mooney. Her eyes were tearing up, so he decided to answer the question for her. "Yes, ma'am. That's a healthy-looking tree, that's for sure. Is that a bigleaf maple?"

"Yes, that's right. In a few years its leaves will be as wide as two of my hands." Miss Pineford then held up both of her hands and pressed them together side-by-side. "See, this big."

"Yes, ma'am. That's a really big leaf. It's a beautiful tree."

"Zetty, is this the young man you told me about? Is he the one who was interested in your mother's blue satchel?"

"Uh-huh, but how did you know that?"

"I didn't until you just told me." Miss Pineford then turned and looked at Mooney, giving him an inquisitive stare. "Do you know where her mother got that satchel from?"

"No, ma'am."

"I do, but I'm not telling anyone. I'll go to my grave and never tell. No one will ever hear me talking about it."

"Miss Pineford, like I told you months back, I'm keeping the satchel. It meant too much to my mom. I can't part with it. And Mooney understands. He's not trying to talk me into selling it."

With her eyes slowly glancing back and forth between Zetty and Mooney, Miss Pineford smiled. "Good for you. I know that's what your mother would've wanted. When I die, and they bury me under my tree up in the cemetery, I'll rest easy knowing you followed her wishes."

"Oh, you're not going to die anytime soon, Miss Pineford."

"Sweetheart, I'm not scared of dying. It happens to all of us sooner or later. I just hope I did my part to make the world a better place to live in, that's all. It breaks my heart to hear about so many people hurting others for no reason these days. Violence never does anyone any good." She then turned her gaze back toward the window. " 'May the trees grow as tall as they can, and may their green leaves always bless us with their wonderful beauty.' "

And when Mooney heard her recite those words, he knew he was in the presence of a founding member of the Flock. Miss Pineford was quoting verbatim from L.E.A.F.'s secret oath. It was an oath that had never been written down, as far as he knew. Flock members were required to memorize several such paragraphs once they had attained their so-called feathery wings. Their acceptance into the group only occurred after they had successfully fulfilled three assignments and thus were granted their wings to fly. So to him, it sounded as though Miss Pineford must have soared into the sky a long time ago. She was, indeed, a very rare bird.

Being overwhelmed by this sudden insight, Mooney felt goosebumps run down his spine. His eyes began to mist up. He was at a loss for words. Not wanting to show his emotion, he turned away from the bed, stepped over to the window, and stared out at the maple tree.

Seeing his reaction, Zetty obviously sensed something was wrong; and so she reached out and patted her foster mom's hand and continued the conversation by talking about all of the trees the two of them had planted in Miss Pineford's yard over the years.

Standing at the window with his back to them, Mooney quietly wiped the tears from his eyes. He never thought he would actually get the chance to meet one of the founding members. But after so many years, it finally had happened. Yet regrettably, he couldn't thank her for all she'd done to help the Flock. His oath of silence prevented him from saying anything to her about their shared activism. And though he wanted to tell her how proud he was to carry on her work, he wasn't able to discuss it with her, nor could he let her know how much it meant to him to have met her. So it was hard for him to stand there and not say anything; but that's what he had to do. He kept his face turned toward the window until he was able to regain his composure.

"May the trees grow as tall as they can, and may

their green leaves always bless us with their wonderful beauty."

Seeing that the weather was continuing to worsen outside, their visit to the nursing home had to be cut short. Also, Miss Pineford had begun to tire easily; and so when she began drifting off into a nap, they'd said their goodbyes and left her bedside.

Walking out into the cold air, neither of them flinched as a gust of frigid wind hit them in the face. Mooney put his arm around Zetty and pulled her closer. Smiling, she leaned up and kissed him on the cheek.

When they stepped off the walkway and moved across the front lawn, a few snowflakes began fluttering down in front of them. There wasn't a lot of the white stuff falling from the sky, but there was just enough to catch the eye.

They then stopped at the maple tree that was growing in front of Miss Pineford's window; and Mooney reached out his hand and patted its trunk. He wanted to thank the bigleaf for watching over a Flock member. He was heartsick that he couldn't do more for Miss Pineford, but he knew that there wasn't much that could be done other than what was already being done. It truly was sad to see her slowly slipping away as she was. "She doesn't know about the cherry tree dying up in the cemetery, does she?"

"No, I didn't tell her. I couldn't. She thinks she's going to be buried under that tree. I thought it was best if she didn't know it had died."

Standing there with the snowflakes falling down around them, Mooney looked up into the bare branches of the little maple. "Well, at least she has this one growing outside her window."

As they turned to go, Mooney could see Miss Pineford sleeping inside her room. The irony of who she was wasn't lost on him, yet he understood why she'd kept Zetty in the dark in regards to what her parents' role in the Flock had been all those many years ago. Miss Pineford obviously hadn't wanted to put her foster child at risk by telling her things that she was better off not knowing. After what had happened to Zetty's parents, Miss Pineford had probably just wanted to protect Zetty as best she could, while not giving away any of the Flock's secrets.

". . . and may their green leaves always bless us with their wonderful beauty."

Now that Mooney had had the chance to talk to a founding member and had seen how she was still keeping mum about her activities, not even telling her own foster child – Mooney thought he better understood how the originating group's core philosophy had been shaped from the very beginning. It was obvious to him that the founders of the Lifesaving Eco Activist Flock had never intended for "the ends to justify the means." The nonviolent methods that the early members had used to get things done had, indeed, been as important as the environmental goals that they had worked so tirelessly to achieve. Miss Pineford had said as much when she'd talked about violence never doing

476

anyone any good.

So, having heard her express her thoughts on the subject, Mooney now knew that it seemed as though at least one of the original members of L.E.A.F. was firmly against the use of violence, thinking that it was wrong. The eco struggle wasn't about activism for activism's sake. Instead, it was about helping passionate people do good deeds to help the planet without harming anyone else along the way.

Aubrey M. Horton

Aubrey M. Horton (MFA, UCLA) has consulted on projects for Warner Brothers, Paramount, & HBO. *Creative Screenwriting* magazine rated him as a "highly recommended" script doctor. For the Directors Guild of America, Horton edited five books on Hollywood's Golden Age. In 1987, the Colorado Council on the Arts and Humanities awarded him a prestigious writing fellowship.

to purchase this book, go to:

www.createspace.com/5491258

Made in the USA
Columbia, SC
17 October 2018